ALSO BY SALLY KOSLOW

Little Pink Slips
The Late, Lamented Molly Marx

WITH FRIENDS LIKE THESE

WITH FRIENDS LIKE THESE

a novel

Sally Koslow

BALLANTINE BOOKS NEW YORK

Copyright © 2010 by Sally Koslow

Published in the United States by Ballantine Books, an imprint of The Random House Publishing Group, a division of Random House, Inc., New York.

Ballantine and colophon are registered trademarks of Random House, Inc.

Library of Congress Cataloging-in-Publication Data

Koslow, Sally.
With friends like these : a novel / Sally Koslow.
p. cm.
ISBN 978-0-345-50622-1
1. Female friendship—Fiction. 2. New York (N.Y.)—Fiction. I. Title.
PS3611 O74919W58 2010
813'.6—dc22
2010014957

Printed in the United States of America on acid-free paper

www.ballantinebooks.com

2 4 6 8 9 7 5 3 1

First Edition

Book design by Diane Hobbing

Robert, Jed, and Rory, you are my home page, always.

I no doubt deserved my enemies, but I don't believe I deserved my friends.

— WALT WHITMAN

WITH FRIENDS LIKE THESE

Chloe m Xander stock/Dash
Talia m Tom/the teacher Henry
Quincy m ʃ lawyer
Jules m Arthur

Then

Before husbands, before babies, before life claimed other loyalties, it started with a wish. Each of them wanted a place to return to that they could call home, a nest where they could hatch and polish their dreams.

They didn't say it even to themselves—they might not even have realized it—but most of all they wanted friends.

. . .

Chloe refolded her paper napkin, propped her knife and fork at five o'clock, and reread the ad she'd circled. Across the table Talia sucked a drag from what was now a cigarette stub. Chloe couldn't understand why anyone as clever as Talia would smoke, but the virtues she'd attributed to her—intelligence, passion, kindness—outranked this detail. Talia surfed the inhospitable sea of Manhattan as if she'd lived there all her life, while Chloe, who'd grown up an hour north of the city, found it as foreign as Marrakech, not that she'd visited Marrakech or, for that matter, Miami.

"Four real bedrooms," Chloe said.

Talia leaned back in the booth and crushed her cigarette in the metal ashtray. Her eyes were too dark for Chloe to make out the pupils. "One 'bedroom' is going to be the foyer, which will have no window," Talia said. "The second is the dining room—it will face an air shaft—and the third and fourth will be a living room sliced down the middle."

"The open house starts at two," Chloe said. "It's a man who's looking for a roommate, and I don't want to"—*can't*—"walk in there alone." She and Talia had during the course of the last six weeks vetoed fourteen possibilities, each wrong in its own dreary way. Today's apartment was ten blocks north of the boundary Chloe considered a secure border for her first adult home. She was trying to be flexible. Talia flagged the waiter, placed two bills on the tabletop shiny with grease, and reached for her coat. She started laughing. The sound reminded Chloe of her mother, whom she was surprised that she missed, because half the point of moving had been to escape her unremitting perfection. "Thanks, but we can split it," Chloe said. Talia was as strapped for cash as she was. While stalking jobs of the sort liberal arts grads dream of, they'd registered as temps, whose sporadic assignments—receptionist for a chiropractor, assistant to a head of circulation—had been notches below interesting.

Talia thrust her arms into her newly acquired winter coat, red bouclé wool with a black Persian lamb collar—a Saks pedigree found at a thrift shop for ten dollars, a dollar more than lunch. "You'll get the next one," she said, and pulled a beret over her curls. She was proud of her hair—nearly black, though by the time she was thirty she'd be plucking gray strands, and by thirty-five coloring it sable brown. "I know where to find you." They were living in a starchy women-only hotel, their rooms identically overheated and overpriced.

"Okay," Talia said. "Let's do the open house."

Outside the diner, she and Chloe threaded their way up Broadway, kicking aside litter. Chloe counted the storefronts: four Irish bars, three Chinese laundries, and two check cashers happy to wire money to Puerto Rico. Outside an OTB parlor, a patron shouted, *"Hola, mami,"* then whistled.

Chloe picked up the pace. "Big mistake," she whispered.

"*En sus sueños,*" Talia yelled back. "Relax, it's the quiet guys you worry about," she added as they turned west on Ninety-second, a street with leafless trees and the odd bicycle held hostage to a lamppost. "And I like the look of this neighborhood. I believe Edith Wharton just stepped out of that brownstone." Talia pictured Edith as tall and handsome, though photographs she'd check later would suggest otherwise. In the absence of a social life—Talia's boyfriend, Tom, was studying at Oxford—she'd been exercising her English major. She'd tried to sell Chloe on *The Age of Innocence,* but Chloe's loyalty remained with Mary Higgins Clark.

The women paused at the corner of West End. Despite her headband, a gust carrying the November damp of the Hudson tangled Chloe's fine blond hair. She pointed across the street. "That one," she said. The building's foundation and first five stories were limestone covered by soot, the upper portion red brick enhanced by gargoyles, whose scowl Chloe returned. The women walked toward the entrance and pushed open a heavy wooden door. Across a terrazzo floor dulled to the color of dirty rainwater, grocery store flyers sat on a table where a uniformed man was resting his well-lubricated hair. The air smelled of yesterday's cigars and today's salami.

"A *doorman* building," Talia said.

Chloe stepped forward and cleared her throat. A deep snore answered her.

"Let's go up," Talia mouthed, cocking her head toward the elevator. She pressed the button. Minutes passed before the door swung open. When they reached the tenth floor, Chloe rang the appropriate doorbell. She buzzed twice more, knocked loudly, then shrugged as she felt her face redden. "I should have called to confirm. It's probably rented." She bit her lip. "I'm sorry."

"We schlepped uptown," Talia said. "Let's call him."

Chloe followed Talia's suggestion, as she often would during the years to come. They retraced their way out to the avenue.

As they approached a pay phone on the corner, a tall woman, her sandy hair cropped, took note of *The New York Times* real estate section in Chloe's hand and stopped her. "Excuse me," she said. "Are you here for 10-B?"

"Do you know the owner?" Chloe asked, thinking that Quincy Peterson, Columbia grad, was fortunate to have not only a large apartment but a girlfriend with no hips and cheekbones like jutting parentheses, the type of bones Chloe had always wished were the scaffolding of her soft, round face.

"I'm Quincy. I don't own the place, but I did just sign a three-year lease." She held up an orange and white bag. "Snacks," she said as she smiled to reveal a slight gap between her front teeth.

"We like you already." Talia grinned, extending her hand.

Quincy took in the elbow-length gloves. Actress/waitress? She hoped not.

"Talia Fisher."

"Chloe McKenzie." Her cheeks were nearly as pink as her turtleneck, her voice high.

Quincy shifted the bag to the other hand. "You two are my first customers this weekend." They reentered the building. "*Buenos tardes*, Jorge."

"Help with your package, Missus Quincy?" The doorman stood to his full five-five.

"I'm fine, *gracias*." The elevator arrived as if it were expecting her. At the tenth floor, she opened three locks and the women were met by sunlight that blasted the vast, vacant foyer. Quincy placed the bag on the scuffed parquet floor. "Take your coats," she said. It wasn't a question.

Talia and Chloe followed her past a shiny brass chandelier as big as the scratched oak table beneath it. "Dining room," Quincy announced as she continued toward four naked casement windows that faced west. Between two buildings, a sliver of river was visible a block away. Quincy cracked one window a few inches, letting in the cold. "Sorry—it's an oven in here." And none too quiet—a small orchestra's percussion section rumbled from the radiators. "Why don't you look around?" With that, she disappeared.

Chloe grabbed Talia's hand and squeezed it tightly. "The place could use some work—"

"But we haven't seen the rest."

The first door off a hall opened to a bedroom, empty but for a rocking chair. On peeling wallpaper, purple irises clung to a background of green. The next door led to a bathroom. "Clawfoot tub," Chloe announced. It was ancient, spotless, deep. She pictured herself soaking in froth and allowed a few bubbles of optimism to float to the surface of her big-city dream. She and Talia returned to the corridor. Behind the next two doors were bedrooms, each with a closet the size of a cupboard; the last opened into a larger room whose iron bed was crisply made with white linen. From a window, the Hudson shouted for attention. Chloe squinted into the sun, turned to Talia, and for the first time that afternoon noticed that she no longer felt a yoke of tension harnessing her narrow shoulder blades.

"Hold on," Talia said. "We're probably numbers fifty and fifty-one on the wait list." The sound of a trumpet drifted toward them. Wynton Marsalis? Miles Davis? Only since she'd moved to Manhattan two months ago had Talia discovered jazz; although she knew she should be saving every nickel, she bought a CD each time she deposited a check.

She and Chloe returned to the living room, where Quincy had arranged a wedge of pale cheddar, sliced apples, water crackers, and a fourth food—small, circular, and brownish—on a wooden tray. There were tall glasses filled with ice and sparkling water. "Want to see the kitchen?" Quincy asked, and led her guests through a portholed door. "You cook?" she asked.

"Learning, and so is Chloe," Talia answered, addressing Quincy's back. She would keep to herself that, inspired by a copy of *The Moosewood Cookbook* unearthed at the Strand, she was on the cusp of turning vegetarian and that Chloe rejected every vegetable except corn on the cob. "You?"

Quincy smiled, barely. Talia decided that the gap in her teeth was, on second look, an asset. "My boyfriend did the cooking, but he's history."

Please, God, Talia prayed, *don't let this be Heartbreak Hotel,* because she liked Quincy Peterson, and she liked the apartment even more. "My condolences," she offered.

Quincy waved her hand as if to brush away an insignificant memory. "When he let me keep an eight-room, rent-controlled apartment I knew for sure he cheated. Guilt's the ultimate motivator, don't you think?"

In years to come, both women would reconsider this question, but for now it was all about the apartment. The kitchen was roomy and plain, with an avocado green refrigerator and glass-fronted cabinets that reached the ceiling. Chloe slid into a nook fitted with pine benches. "I've wanted a kitchen like this since I read *The Three Bears*," she said, her tone now as cheery as a daisy.

Jeez, is this cocker spaniel of a girl for real? Quincy wondered. She shepherded the pair to the living room and gestured for them to sit on the couch. Quincy was looking for three independent roommates, not a matched set. What if Salt and Pepper did everything in tandem? On the other hand, these women seemed more approachable than any of the unfortunates she'd welcomed at last weekend's open house—when it was over, she'd tossed every phone number, including the Iowa cellist's. "Here's the deal." She chose her words with reserve, a trait despised by the man who'd moved out, who'd accused Quincy of not having displayed an act of spontaneity since they'd met. "My room is the big one at the end, with its own bathroom. To make things fair, I expect to pay more than the other three renters."

"Fair enough," Talia said. The rent was forty dollars less than anything else she and Chloe had seen. In order not to grin, she popped one of the small brown nibbles into her mouth. Talia had never tasted an oyster, smoked or otherwise. She liked it.

"I'll be honest: when I'm here, I need quiet because"—Quincy weighed how she would be perceived—"I'm trying to write a book." Definitely haughty, she decided. "Don't worry. It's not even *Men Are from Mars, Women Are from Venus.* I'm an assistant at *People,*" she added, as if that explained everything. "Most nights I don't get home until ten. By ten-thirty, I'm dead." The apartment hunters stared at her, unreadable. "I'm also universally described as a neat freak."

Talia was stuck on considering how it would feel to have a job where you were important enough to be required to work well into the evening. She'd have liked to know that feeling, but what she said was, "Define 'neat freak,' please."

"I promise I won't wax a floor or wash a window more than every few months, but I cannot live with food rotting in the fridge or the drain." Quincy had narrow fingers with short, square nails, which she tapped on the table as she spoke. "I especially hate rugs that get crunchy." Talia stared at the bare wood floors. "There used to be rugs. He took them."

"My parents promised me some old Orientals," Chloe said. "My dad could drive them down from New Canaan."

Quincy wondered if she had misjudged the blonde, about whom there was a sweet eagerness. Quincy was twenty-five. Chloe, she thought, must be younger. "I also can't live with drinkers."

"We're definitely not that," Chloe laughed. She'd worked up to a sociable Chardonnay; for Talia, it was a weekend beer, two at the most.

"And while I don't mind a joint at a party, I can't abide cigarettes. Neither of you smokes, do you?"

"Absolutely not," Talia said, feeling Chloe's eyes. She knew she could quit. Tom hated her habit as much as Chloe did.

The three waited for someone to speak. "I assume you'd know better than to let boyfriends hang around in boxers." Quincy stopped and— what the hell—declared her fantasy. "But one thing I do care about is having dinner with my roommates, at least every Sunday. Not that it's a deal breaker."

Chloe jumped in, although she would later wonder how she'd found it in her to be so bold. "We're hoping to find a house share where we could all be friends." Quincy might be another Talia, a woman who could help unlock the city.

Quincy wondered the same. Could she be friends with these women? She'd never had female confidantes, never wanted to be part of a sorority,

Greek-lettered or otherwise. By the time she decided she liked another woman enough to hope to befriend her, that person had generally dismissed her as too midwestern, too anal-retentive—two *too*'s her boyfriend had liked to list. "Okay, I'm prattling," she said. "Your turn."

"I graduated from Trinity last spring, majored in art history," Chloe began. They heard a buzzer.

Quincy walked to the intercom. "Sure, send her right up." She returned. "You were saying?"

Chloe did a quick climb through her family tree. Her father was a pediatrician; her mother grew orchids; her only sibling, Jack junior (she chose not to refer to him as Jack Off, the nickname of which he was proud), played lacrosse. Chloe moved on to her love of tennis and museums and skipped her college boyfriend. A woman fresh from a breakup didn't need to hear about Xander.

The foyer door opened. A woman strolled toward them as if she were taking center stage at the Metropolitan Opera. The first thing Chloe noticed were her fingernails—impossibly long, in a shade of orange that matched Quincy's Zabar's bag. The first thing Talia noticed was the woman's hair, as curly as hers. The first thing Quincy noticed was the lavender roses, which convinced Quincy that her prospective tenant must be in sales. All three women stood to meet her.

"I'm Julia de Marco." She presented the bouquet.

"Quincy Peterson, and this is"—she considered it promising that she was able to remember the other names—"Chloe and Talia." They smiled at the woman, all of their eyes widening that on a Sunday afternoon she was wearing an ankle-length black velvet skirt.

"Call me Jules." Her voice was sultry, musical.

Quincy nodded. "You talk while I find a vase."

Jules sat heavily in the armchair. She was not a small woman. "Do you two know each other?" she asked.

"Barbizon Hotel escapees," Talia explained.

"Is it true that Grace Kelly's ghost waltzes down the hall wearing a white negligee?"

"That was Chloe."

Talia swept her hand toward Chloe in thanks. Jules laughed and picked up a glossy magazine on the coffee table, opened to a butter churn photographed with the reverence usually given to a Louise Nevelson sculpture, and examined the cover. "Who's Martha Stewart?" The women facing her only shrugged. She stopped turning pages and looked up. "This neighborhood—junkies, no?"

"Junkies?" Chloe said, as if a rat had leaped from Jules de Marco's bulging purple suede tote. "We'd better ask about that." When Quincy returned, she did.

"The simple answer is I wouldn't linger in the park after dark, but as long as you stick to the promenade during the day, near the dog walkers, it's safe." Years later, when the neighborhood had become studded with sidewalk cafés selling pomegranate martinis, this building would be converted into condos—wine refrigerators! six-burner stoves!—and every one of the women except Chloe would wish she still lived there. Quincy, especially, would regret that she failed to keep her name on the lease and receive a vastly discounted insider's price when the apartment was presented for sale. When this happened, she would know she had become an official Manhattan cliché.

"Mind if I snoop?" Before Jules got an answer, she'd abandoned Martha's magazine and shot down the hall. "Well, aren't you coming?" The others fell into step.

"Are you from around here?" Quincy asked Jules.

Isn't that obvious? Talia thought. She knew the accent was indigenous; eventually she would take pride in being able to tell Jersey from Brooklyn, though she would never be able to distinguish Brooklyn from the Bronx.

"Staten Island," Jules answered. They wandered through every room; when they entered the dining room she stopped and put her hand over her heart. "Holy crap. My ma's whole fucking house could fit into this corner. But when was it painted, 1975?"

"The landlord won't discuss it—not at this rent." Again, Quincy quoted the number.

Jules whistled. "Good thing I know a contractor who could do the job in a weekend, no sweat. And you're also obviously hurting for furniture, but I've broken up with my scumbag boyfriend and I've got a shitload because I sell antiques on the side."

On the side of what? came to the others' minds. "You're coming off a breakup?" Quincy asked.

"Big drunk, which I failed to notice on account of his big you-know-what. But I'm over him. How about you?" Before Quincy could answer, Jules continued. "Not a bad kitchen," she said, circling the room, opening cupboards and letting her fingers caress the stove. "My nonna taught me everything on a Royal Rose like this."

"You cook?" Quincy asked.

"Does the Pope wear a party hat?"

"I believe it's called a miter," Chloe offered, which, out of politeness, the others ignored. From the foyer, the intercom rang—once, twice, three times. Quincy walked toward it, reaching a finger toward the answer button. Jules followed and topped Quincy's hand with her own. "Hey, Quincy Peterson, what do you say you tell whoever's coming up that this place is rented?"

Isn't this my decision? Quincy thought. But Jules de Marco wasn't finished. "I have a feeling about us." She stepped back and drew all three women toward her, half huddle, half hug. It made Talia laugh, Quincy stiffen, and Chloe blush. "Something," Jules declared, "tells me we're all going to be great friends."

For ten years, they were.

CHAPTER 1

Quincy

"A fax hit my desk for an apartment that isn't officially listed yet—you must see it immediately." Horton's voice was broadcasting an urgency reserved for hurricane evacuation. But in 2007, anyone who'd ever beaten the real estate bushes would be suspicious of a broker displaying even an atom of passivity. Shoppers of condos and co-ops in Manhattan and the leafier regions of Brooklyn knew they had to learn the art of the pounce: see, gulp, bid. Save the pros and cons for picking a couch.

Several times a week Horton e-mailed me listings, but rarely did he call. This had to be big. "Where is it?" I asked while I finished my lukewarm coffee.

"Central Park West." Horton identified a stone pile known by its name, the Eldorado, referring to a mythical kingdom where the tribal chief had the habit of dusting himself with gold, a commodity familiar to most of the apartment building's inhabitants—marquee actors, eminent psychotherapists, and large numbers of frumps who were simply lucky. With twin towers topped by Flash Gordon finials, the edifice lorded it over a gray-blue reservoir, the park's largest body of water, and cast a gimlet eye toward Fifth Avenue.

"I couldn't afford that building," I said. If Horton was trying to game me into spending more than our budget allowed, he'd fail. While the amount of money Jake and I had scraped together for a new home seemed huge to us—representing the sale of our one-bedroom in Park Slope, an inheritance from my mom, and the proceeds from seeing one of my books linger on the bestseller list—other brokers had none too politely terminated the conversation as soon as I quoted our allotted sum. What I liked about Horton was that he was dogged, he was hungry, and he was the only real estate agent returning my calls.

"That's the beauty part," he said, practically singing. "You, Quincy Blue, can afford this apartment." He named a figure.

We could, just. "What's the catch?" In my experience, deals that sounded too good to be true were—like the brownstone I'd seen last week that lacked not only architectural integrity but functional plumbing.

"It's a fixer-upper," Horton admitted. "Listen, I can go to the second name on my list."

"I'll see you in twenty minutes," I said, hitting "save" on my manuscript. I was currently the ghostwriter for Maizie May, one of Hollywood's interchangeable blow-dried blondes with breasts larger than their brain. While she happened to be inconveniently incarcerated in Idaho rehab, allowed only one sound bite of conversation with me per week, my publisher's deadline, three months away, continued to growl. I hid my hair under a baseball cap and laced my sneakers. Had Jake seen me, he would have observed that I looked very West Side; my husband was fond of pointing out our neighborhood's inverse relationship between apartment price and snappy dress. As I walked east I called him, but his cell phone was off. Jake's flight to Chicago must be late.

Racing down Broadway, I allowed myself a discreet ripple of anticipation. Forget the Yankees. Real estate would always be New York City's truest spectator sport, and I was no longer content to cheer from the bleachers. Two years ago, my nesting hormones had kicked in and begun to fiercely multiply, with me along for the ride. We were eager to escape from our current sublet near Columbia University. I longed to be dithering over paint colors—Yellow Lotus or Pale Straw; flat, satin, or eggshell—and awash in fabric swatches. I coveted an office that was bigger than a coffee table book and a dining table that could accommodate all ten settings of my wedding china. I wanted a real home. I'd know it when I saw it.

Horton, green-eyed, cleft-chinned—handsome if you could overlook his devotion to argyle—stood inside the building's revolving door. "The listing broker isn't here yet," he said, "but you can get a sense of the lobby." A doorman tipped his capped head and motioned us toward armchairs upholstered in a tapestry of tasteful, earthy tones. Horton unfurled a floor plan.

I'd become a quick study of such documents. "It's only a two-bedroom," I said, feeling the familiar disappointment that had doused the glow of previous apartment visits. Was the fantasy of three bedrooms asking too much for a pair of industrious adults more than twelve years past grad school? Jake was a lawyer. I had a master's in English literature. Yet after we'd been outbid nine times, Jake and I had accepted the fact that in this part of town, two bedrooms might be as good as it would get.

"This isn't *any* two-bedroom," Horton insisted. "Look how grand the living room and dining room are." Big enough for a party where Jake and I could reciprocate every invitation we'd received since getting married five years ago. "See?" he said, pulling out a hasty sketch and pointing. "Put a wall up to divide the dining room, which has windows on both sides, and create an entrance here. Third bedroom." He was getting to how cheap the renovation would be when a tall wand of a woman tapped him on the shoulder.

"Fran!" Horton said as warmly as if she were his favorite grandmother, which she was old enough to be. "You're looking well."

The woman smiled and a feathering of wrinkles fanned her large blue eyes. The effect made me think that a face without this pattern was too dull. "Did you explain?" she said. Her voice was reedy, a piccolo that saw little use. She'd pulled her silver hair into a chignon and was enveloped in winter white, from a cape covering a high turtleneck to slim trousers that managed to be spotless, although they nearly covered her toes.

"We were getting to that, but first, please meet my client, Quincy Blue. Quincy, Frances Shelbourne of Shelbourne and Stone."

I knew the firm. Frances and her sister Rose had tied up all the best West Side listings. I shook Fran Shelbourne's hand, which felt not just creamy but delicately boned. She stared at my sneakers and jeans long enough for me to regret them, then turned her back and padded so soundlessly that I checked to see if she might be wearing slippers. No, ballerina flats. Across the lobby, elaborately filigreed elevator doors opened. Fran turned toward Horton and me and with the briefest arch of one perfectly plucked eyebrow implored us to hurry. When the doors shut, she spoke softly, although we were alone. "The owner's a dear friend," she said. "Eloise Walter, the anthropologist." She waited for me to respond. "From the Museum of Natural History?"

I wondered if I was supposed to know the woman's body of work and bemoaned the deficiency of my Big Ten education.

"Dr. Walter is in failing health," she continued, shaking her head. "This is why we won't schedule an open house."

Every Sunday from September through May, hopeful buyers, like well-trained infantry, traveled the open-house circuit. Jake and I had done our sweaty time, scurrying downtown, uptown, across, and down again, with as many as a dozen visits in a day. Soon enough, we began seeing the same hopeful buyers—the Filipino couple, the three-hundred-pound guy who had the face of a baby, a pair of six-foot-tall redheaded teenage twins who spoke a middle-European tongue. By my fifth Sunday, in minutes I could privately scoff at telltale evidence of dry rot. Silk curtains draped as cunningly as a sari could not distract me from a sunless air shaft a few feet away, nor could lights of megawatt intensity seduce me into forgetting that in most of these apartments I would instantly suffer from seasonal affective disorder.

"You'll be the first person to see this one," Horton added by way of a bonus. I could feel the checkbook in my bag coming alive like Mickey's broom in *Fantasia*.

When we stepped out of the elevator on the fourteenth floor, Mrs. Shelbourne gently knocked on a metal door that would look at home in any financial institution. From the other side, a floor creaked. A nurse in thick-soled shoes answered and raised an index finger to her lips, casting her eyes toward a shadowy room beyond. The scent of urine—human, feline, or both—crept into my nostrils, followed by a top note of mango air freshener. "Doctor's sleeping."

My eyes strained to scan a wide room where old-fashioned blinds were drawn against the noon sun. An elderly woman, her hair scant and tufted, was folded into a wheelchair like a rag doll, despite pillows bolstering her skeletal frame. Dr. Walter looked barely alive. Mrs. Shelbourne placed her hand on my arm. "We shouldn't stay long in this room. I'm sure you understand. Alzheimer's."

"I do—too well," I said, rapidly beholding the high ceiling and dentil moldings, while memories of my mother, scrupulously archived yet too fresh to examine, begged for consideration. I pushed them away even as my mind catalogued herringbone floors with an intricate walnut border and the merest wink of a crystal chandelier. Mrs. Shelbourne grasped my arm and we hurried into a small, dark kitchen with wallpaper on which hummingbirds had enjoyed a sixty-year siesta. In front of the sink, which faced a covered window, linoleum had worn bare. There were scratched metal cabinets and no dishwasher, and I suspected the stove's birth date preceded my own. I thought of my unfinished chapter, and cursed my wasted time.

Halfheartedly I lifted a tattered shade. "Holy cow," I said, though only to myself. Sun reflected off the park's vast reservoir, which appeared so close I thought I could stand on the ledge and swan-dive into its depth. Far below, I could see treetops, lush as giant broccoli. The traffic was a distant buzz. I felt a tremor. The subway, stories below? No, my heart.

Picking up my pace, I followed the brokers through the spacious dining room and down a hall where I counted off six closets. I peeked into a bathroom tiled in a vintage mosaic of the sort decorators encourage clients to re-create at vast expense. We passed through a starlet-worthy dressing room and entered a bedroom into which I could easily tuck my current, rented apartment, with enough space to spare for a study. As Mrs. Shelbourne pulled the hardware on draperies bleached of color, I could swear that a strobe had begun to pulse. From the corner of my eye I saw a black cat slink away while Horton kicked a dust bunny under the bed, but I took little note of either. As I stood by the window, I was gooey with the feeling I'd experienced when I first laid eyes on the Grand Canyon.

The silvery vista spread casually before me might be the most enchanted in the entire city. I closed my eyes, traveling through time. Women were skating figure eights in red velvet cloaks, their hands warmed by ermine muffs. Bells jingled in the evergreen-scented air as horses waited patiently by sleighs. I blinked again and the maidens wore organdy, their porcelain skin dewy under the parasols shielding their intricate curls. I fast-forwarded to my girlhood and could imagine the large, glassy pond below was the crystal stream beside my grandparents' log-hewn cabin in Wisconsin's northern woods, the bone-chilling waters of Scout camp, perhaps Lake Como of my honeymoon scrapbook.

Beside this champagne view, the fifty-four other apartments I'd considered seemed like cheap house wine, including the possibilities that cost far more—almost every one. I pulled myself away from the window and looked back. Walls were no longer hung with faded diplomas, nor was the carpet worn thin. Mirroring the reservoir, the room had turned gray-blue. I saw myself writing at a desk by the window, lit by sunbeams, words spilling out so fast my fingers danced on the keyboard like Rockettes. This time my manuscript wasn't a twenty-year-old singer-actress' whiny rant. It was a novel, lauded by the critics and Costco customers alike.

I could see myself in this room. My face wore deep contentment. The bed was luxuriously rumpled, since a half hour earlier Jake and I had made love, and now he was brewing coffee in our brand-new kitchen, as sleekly designed as a sperm. Perhaps he'd already gone out to bike around the park or was walking our shelter-rescued puppy. Tallulah, the little rascal, loved to chase her ball down our twenty-foot hall.

In every way, I was home.

Then I snapped out of it. I was wearing my real estate heart on my sleeve, all but drooling. *Quincy Blue, you dumb cluck.* I sensed Horton looking at me as if he were a cannibal in need of protein, and checked to see if he and Fran had excused themselves to decide whether they should triple the apartment's price or merely double it. We walked past another bathroom, this one housing a tub as long as a rowboat, ambled back through the dim hallway, and ended in the living room.

"The view's even better from here—a pity we can't pull up the shades," Mrs. Shelbourne whispered as she walked toward the statue slumping in the wheelchair and greeted her. "Hello, Eloise dear." She took the woman's listless hand. "It's Frances. I wish you could sit at that piano"— she pointed to a piece of shrouded furniture—"and play me Chopin."

The woman emitted a dry rattle, craned her neck toward Mrs. Shelbourne, and smiled. She was missing several teeth.

"If you wish," she said clearly. Suddenly Dr. Walter tried to raise herself in the wheelchair. "If you would be so kind as to assist me." The nurse lumbered to her side. On her aide's sturdy arm, Dr. Walter walked toward the piano, her posture better than my own. She settled on the cracked black leather stool and stretched her knobby fingers. I covered my mouth with my hands, afraid I might gasp. Her hands fondled the ivories and began to play an unmistakable Chopin mazurka. The Steinway was out of tune and the pianist wore a faded housecoat, but Dr. Walter's rendition pleased her audience to the point that even Horton was wiping away tears. The concert continued for almost twenty minutes and then, as if someone had pulled a plug, the pianist's hands froze. Like a small child, she looked around the room, confused. I was afraid she, too, might cry.

We clapped. "That was exquisite," Mrs. Shelbourne said hoarsely as the nurse helped her patient back to the wheelchair. "Simply exquisite."

Dr. Walter closed her eyes and in less than a minute was sleeping. Mrs. Shelbourne thanked the nurse and hurried Horton and me to the elevator. I waited for his chatter, but it was she who spoke. "Tell me your story. I can see from your face that you have one." She looked at me as if she were the dean of women.

I found myself speaking. "It's my mother," I said. "The owner—Dr. Walter, is it?—she's a good bit older than my mom, but that's exactly how she looked." I thought of our final visit, two years ago. My mother had been only sixty-six, but dementia had been strangling her for almost a decade. "When I see anyone like that..." My voice trailed off. "Mom had been a history teacher—smart and funny, a great dancer, a swimming champ—and at the end, she was..." I searched for words. "Like a chair." I winced. "That came out wrong. I should be able to do better than that— I'm a writer."

"I'm deeply sorry," Mrs. Shelbourne said, and took my hand as she had Dr. Walter's. "It's the most devastating way to go. Did you and your father help each other get through it?"

"He passed away when I was a kid," I said, aware of how pitiful it sounded when I played the orphan card.

She continued to clutch my hand. "If you could have seen Eloise years ago, holding court the first Sunday of every month at a musicale. The most glittering minds, razor-edged wit." *This explains why she was too busy to have the place painted*, a small, nasty part of me thought. "Now she's alone, in every way."

"No family?" I asked. Horton, I noticed, stood back from the conversation.

"Her closest tie's her banker, her legal guardian, who's put the apartment on the market. As soon as it's sold, he'll move Eloise to a nursing home."

We followed Mrs. Shelbourne down to the lobby, where she returned the key to the doorman. The three of us stood awkwardly in front of the entrance. It had started to drizzle, and we crowded under her large umbrella.

"What did you think?" Horton asked. I sensed that he'd been working to contain himself.

"The apartment's very . . . unusual."

Mrs. Shelbourne corrected me. "It's extraordinary. Frankly, the price should be thirty percent higher, but her banker wants a quick sale with minimal fuss. I can't show this apartment aggressively, you see," Mrs. Shelbourne added. "Hordes traipsing through—I'd never trample on Eloise's dignity that way."

She pinned me in her gaze. I got the point and stammered, "I—I love the apartment, but my husband needs to see it, too."

"When?" Horton asked.

"Saturday?" Today was Thursday. The brokers' eyes spoke in code I could not decipher.

"I'm showing the apartment again tomorrow at five, and then I'm off to the country and won't be back till Monday. That's when the listing will circulate within the larger real estate community. I'd expect the apartment to be gone by the day's end."

"Could you bid without Jake?" Horton asked.

For the biggest purchase we might ever make as a couple? "I'll see what I can do," I said.

• • •

As I walked home, Jake returned my call. "What's wrong?" I could feel his worry from seven hundred miles away.

"Not wrong, right." I was afraid I squealed. "I've found it. The apartment." I offered succulent details—the view, the dimensions, the price, the lofty ceilings, the view, the fireplace, the moldings, the price, the view. I repeated the building's name.

"Isn't that where Jules' new boyfriend bragged about living?"

"I don't know—you were the one talking to him." Since Jules de Marco's breakup she'd introduced us to so many men I'd learned not to overinvest in any of them, but I remembered now that the bald guy who boasted about his derring-do in advertising had said he lived there. The coincidence could be fortunate. We'd need to pass the review of a co-op admission board. Maybe he could write us a reference letter, skilled copy-writer that he claimed to be.

"If you like this place so much," Jake said, "we'll see it next week. I'll check my schedule." The seconds moved slowly. "Monday and Tuesday are going to be hell," he said, "but Wednesday after work... Tell your pal Holden I'll see it then."

"Wednesday?" I shouted "This place's going to be snatched up by then. And it's Horton." The silence sliced down between Chicago and New York.

"Spit it out, Q," Jake said. "What do you want from me?"

"Get on a plane after your morning meeting so we can see it tomorrow. The other broker's showing the apartment at five and I don't want to be outbid." I followed with a sigh. "Again." I reminded Jake about the river-view condo that we'd lost because of shamefully civilized behavior.

Jake started to hum. A good sign. "Okay, make an appointment for four tomorrow."

"I love you, Jake," I said. "Thank you, honey."

"You're breaking up, Q. Did you just say you were giving me the best blow job of my life?"

"I did, Jake. That's exactly what I said."

I reached Horton. "Jake and I can see the apartment tomorrow after-noon," I said. "Could you make an appointment for four?"

"That late?"

"He's cutting a business trip short."

"I'll try to work it out," he said. "You never know with Fran, but confi-dentially, I think you made a good impression—and she's the intuition witch."

"Let's hope," I said as my phone indicated a second call. "Sorry. Will you please call me back the very second the appointment is confirmed? I've got to take this." I clicked to the waiting call.

"Where are you?" Jules asked, annoyed.

"Oh, God, I'm so sorry."

"Yeah, well, I'm waiting fifteen minutes already—are you showing or what?"

I had a lunch date downtown—I'd completely forgotten—and Jules was not a friend to be kept waiting. To get to Soho by subway would take a half hour at minimum. While I was cursing my behavior—self-absorbed, thoughtless—a taxi stopped at my feet to discharge a passenger. I silenced the frugal Minneapolis girl within me and opened the door. "See you in twenty minutes," I said to Jules as I sped away.

Later, I wondered why I hadn't identified that taxi as an e-ticket to hell.

CHAPTER 2

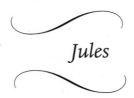

Jules

I was parked on a crimson banquette, sipping wine, trying to talk myself
out of ordering *frites*. The longer I waited, and the more I smelled the over-
flowing paper cones being delivered to every other table, the more I wanted
what was in them—salty and crisp on the outside, tender and mushy inside. Which was exactly how I'd described myself the year before in a personal ad that attracted no one I'd want to lie next to, even on a gurney.

Finally Quincy showed. "Jules, I'm so sorry," she said, bending to kiss
me on the cheek, the rim of her cap bumping my face.

That she was wearing faded Levi's I could overlook, but sneakers? Not
that a leggy, 118-pound woman can't get by with minimal effort. "You're
forgiven," I said, because that's what I do, forgive people, providing they
aren't my blood family. "But this isn't the first time, you know." Ever since
Quincy Blue and I'd shared an apartment she'd run behind schedule by
the same forty minutes. I waved over the waiter. "Drink?"

Quincy cast a dubious eye on my wine's salmon tint. I suppressed an
urge to lecture her on the current cool quotient of rosé. "Sauvignon
blanc, please," she said.

"We should order. I've got a lot going on today." Officially I might have forgiven her, but I felt cranky nonetheless.

"In the time it takes me to make a list, you've knocked five items off yours."

"Why, thank you," I said. It's true that I am efficient, a woman who's learned to power her life by insomnia, a woman with a lot of balls in the air—though as far as that kind goes, only one set at the moment. Whenever I need to complete a form identifying occupation, I'm never sure what to write. Personal shopper/actress/hand model?

This afternoon Quincy and I were celebrating that I'd gotten my first residual for a commercial I'd filmed six months ago. I'd played a bride ecstatic about drain cleaner, and the irony wasn't lost on me, since on the day we wrapped, Ted moved out, disengaging at the moment when I was sure he was going to ask me to become attached forever. I might be smart, but not about men. Thirty-four sessions of couples counseling had convinced Ted to quit law school. Now he was in Hawaii, finding himself in the surf, and I was dating Arthur Weiner.

"What's going on?" Quincy asked as we waited for a two-tiered seafood platter accompanied by, yes, a double side of *frites*.

"I have an audition at three, a client at five, and dinner with Arthur."

"How's it going with him?"

I searched her words for an edge of condescension. A few weeks ago, when I'd introduced Arthur to Quincy and Jake, I'd caught a judgy whiff. I'd been seeing Arthur for two months. He is older, shorter, and balder than Ted—shorter and balder than most men. The mastermind behind our relationship was our fourth former roommate, Chloe—Arthur used to be her boss at an ad agency—and despite his high negatives, it was she who'd badgered me into giving him a shot. Now, on a daily basis, I allow Arthur to tell me that I'm the best thing to happen to him since puberty. On his arm, I see myself as he sees me—as a girly brunette goddess, not a candidate for a weight-loss scam.

"I like Arthur," I said. "He's talented, he's smart, he worships me. He might be a keeper."

Quincy laughed. "Still so cheap?"

The trouble with confiding in friends—Chloe excepted—is that they tend to discount the good and fixate on the bad. It's true that when my birthday rolled around last month, Arthur wasn't playing at four-star level. Not that a woman doesn't appreciate an inflatable travel pillow, but she'd also like the trip to go with it.

"I'm working on it," I said as our food arrived. Quincy liberated two fries, then three more. Forget married; I'd settle for her metabolism. "Arthur strikes me as the type who'll learn to respond to my powers of persuasion."

I have my own set of rules to follow—Jules' Rules. I recognize what I want—which may explain why I'm self-employed and live alone—and recognize when I'm right, which occurs on an uncannily regular basis.

"If you like Arthur, I like Arthur. You know I wish you only the best." Quincy has proven this. When Ted dumped me, it was she who'd dragged me out of bed and listened day and night, in person, by phone, by text, and by e-mail, as I deconstructed where he and I had gone astray and figured out how I could reconstitute my granulated self-esteem. We have our differences, blah, blah, blah, but Quincy, Chloe, and Talia are true friends.

"How's the book?" I asked.

"*Crazy Maizie?*" she said, stuffing more *frites* in her pretty little mouth. "Forget the book. Something much bigger and better's happening."

"Oh, my God," I said. She was pregnant. Quincy and Jake had been trying for several years. She'd had two miscarriages, and after each she'd retreated into a private funk. "Tell me all about it," I said as I swiped a glance at her stomach. It looked as concave as ever.

While it isn't on my own to-do list, motherhood consumes Chloe and Talia. Quincy wanted to join their tribe, trading belly-button-baring maternity clothes and pontificating about kiddy joggers and organic teething biscuits. I've never been able to understand the gravitational pull most women feel toward wanting to reproduce—people say *I'm* narcissistic?—

but I've learned the hard way to keep my big mouth shut. "Tell me every-thing," I said.

"It needs a complete gut job and isn't huge, but the minute I looked outside I had that *Time and Again* sensation, like this was my destiny, as if I'd lived there in an earlier life. That's how much I love it."

It took a few seconds for my wires to connect. "An apartment," I said, like a cretin. I might have guessed. During the past year Quincy had Monday-morning-quarterbacked countless open houses whose apart-ments she blew off as either too dark, too small, or too graceless. This was when she wasn't being outbid, which had happened to her every time she tried to buy something.

"Not just *an* apartment," Quincy mimicked. "*The* apartment."

"Which building?"

Quincy had a look on her face that I could imagine on mine only if someone was begging for my hand in marriage. "Arthur's," she said, "and the apartment has a view of the reservoir." Which Arthur's does not.

Everyone wishes they lived in a building like Arthur's, collecting their mail alongside boldface names as well as those simply stinking rich. I'd stopped counting the times he'd retold the story of how perspicacious he was to buy his apartment two decades ago, because now its price tag was in the ozone. He'd rattle on. If he sold, he could make a killing, the num-ber growing with each telling of the tale. The vexing question was, where would he move? Arthur had arrived in his neighborhood when it was a dump, but now he couldn't bear the thought of migrating to a lesser ad-dress. He was trapped by entitlement.

But I was confused. "Isn't that building pricey?" Yes, I was indelicate, but Quincy is an old friend, and unless something had recently changed in her fiscal spreadsheet, Arthur's building was out of her league.

"That's the other half of the miracle—we can afford this particular place."

Had Jake's year-end bonus arrived with zeroes she'd forgotten to men-tion? Had another relative died who'd left her a pile of dough? I gave her a dubious look.

"Don't ask," she said.

My brain was working fast now. "I'd love to see it—you know how much I like looking at apartments." Not that I'd ever gone with Quincy to scrutinize any of the others. I myself am happily nested in a sweet suburban townhouse.

She paused. "I don't know," she said, offering me the last *frite*. "Jake hasn't been there yet. He's coming home early from Chicago. We have an appointment tomorrow."

"When?"

"Late afternoon."

"I'll join you."

You'd have thought I'd suggested sex with a goat. Finally, she talked. "The woman who lives there is old and sick and the brokers don't want a lot of people around."

"Brokers, plural? I thought you were just working with that guy. Who's the other broker?"

I waited for Quincy to drop the name or change her mind about having me accompany her. All she did was finish her wine and say, rather primly, considering that I'm a friend who's held her head when she was puking, "If Jake and I go ahead with this, I'll be thrilled to get you in to see it, but not now."

"Right." We began discussing my latest shopping client, a television producer who wanted a wardrobe worthy of her face-lift. We moved on to Quincy's tribulations with Maizie May, the ninety-five-pound drama queen whose book she was ghostwriting. Soon enough the subject came up of where we should all go on our next girls' getaway. Inexplicably, Chloe was lobbying for Las Vegas; I suppose she'd heard about the excellent stores there. Talia wanted to drive up to that rubbish heap her husband's family owns in Maine. I'd proposed a quick hop to Heaven, Italy—that would be Rome. Quincy wanted Graceland.

The check arrived. She grabbed it. "This one's on me."

"Hey, I'm the one with the big payday."

"I forgot to even ask about that!" Quincy said.

"True."

"All the more reason for me to take this," she said. "Besides, I'm feeling lucky."

I thanked her and we said goodbye in a snowstorm of cheek kisses. For the next two hours I wandered in and out of shops in Soho, but I kept tripping over the four-leaf clover on steroids that Quincy had found that now gave her the chance to buy what must be an extraordinary bit of real estate.

I realized I wanted to tell Arthur the whole implausible, inequitable story. Was that wrong? It wasn't illegal, and all I was going to do was share the information—and maybe, for kicks, take a peek at the place.

I began to feel like a child waiting for her birthday party, and soon enough my need became an itch I couldn't ignore. "Hi there," I said, catching Arthur on the first ring. We were still in that primitive state of romantic thrall when he wouldn't have the balls to tell me I'd interrupted him at work, which I probably had. "You're not going to believe this," I began, using my most seductive voice, "but guess who may become your neighbor?" I retold the saga, possibly mentioning—I recall—that Quincy insinuated the apartment was a steal. But who was I kidding? The real point was that, given Quincy's lousy track record on having bids accepted, she'd eventually lose out on this apartment and a stranger would land this deal. I couldn't let that happen.

"Which floor's it on?" he asked.

"She didn't say."

"If it has a reservoir view, that narrows it down."

I detected excitement.

"Who's the broker?"

"Howard something."

"Is that his first name? What company is he with?"

I could see where this was going and felt a spasm of guilt on Quincy's behalf. On the other hand, she was the same friend who'd forgotten to congratulate me on my starring role in a major commercial, the friend who didn't want me to see the apartment with her. Also—and this seemed far more compelling—I kept returning to the point that Quincy would eventually get outbid on this apartment, and this place sounded too good to let float away when Arthur was a resident in that very building, as well as maybe my future. If that apartment had anyone's name on it, it was Arthur's.

"I've got to see this place," he said. "If I could sell my apartment for a bundle and stay in my building but get a place with a million-dollar view, well, all around, that'd be a pretty fair trade. My apartment has no view, but it's huge. I'd definitely come out ahead."

And with my subtle guidance, I thought, he'd invest that profit in me—travel, jewelry, a rental in the Hamptons, or a house in, say, Dutchess County? I briefly pictured myself riding to hounds, and then shook away the fantasy. De Marcos bet on horses; we don't ride them.

"Aren't you getting a little ahead of yourself here?" I asked him, as I thought the same thing of myself. But perhaps not. I'm past forty. Arthur is fifty. Sometimes in life you have to stop overthinking and just haul ass.

He laughed. "Hang tight, kid. I'll see you at dinner."

Four hours later I walked into the bistro I'd suggested on Columbus Avenue. Arthur was waiting, along with two chilled glasses of champagne, a most un-Weiner-like flourish. "What's going on?" I asked.

"Do we require a special occasion to toast ourselves?" He stopped slightly short of a smirk. *Oh, my God, what if this man is asking me to marry him?* My mind instantly inventoried his less attractive qualities, beginning with his braying laugh. But there wasn't a diamond twinkling in the bottom of my flute, nor did the waiter deliver even an opal hidden in an escargot. "Julia de Marco, I like the way you think," Arthur said, raising his glass. "Thank you for being in my life."

We drained the champagne, and the waiter asked us if we'd like a refill. Arthur answered immediately. "No, we're ready to order. We'll start by sharing the mussels." Cheapest thing on the menu.

CHAPTER 3

Talia

"Henry needs new sneakers. Don't forget to take him to the shoe store," I said to Tom.

"Since when do I ever forget?" he answered, kissing me goodbye.

Since never. "Don't let that son of ours talk you into the kind that light up."

"Do I look like the kind of dad who can be easily coerced?"

You do. I am definitely Bad Cop, though, as my *bubbe* would point out, Tom's the parent who resembles a Cossack. "Should I stop at the supermarket on the way home?" Our cupboards were sadly bare.

"Don't bother. We'll figure dinner out later." Tom beamed. My husband, like a trick candle that burns bright no matter what. "You'll be late. Just go."

I let two trains go by my stop in Brooklyn before I wedged myself into a third, where I stood for forty-five minutes between a tourist's backpack and a hugely pregnant woman whom people fortunate enough to have seats were actively ignoring, then got off at Manhattan's Union Square and walked seven blocks to my office, arriving barely in time for a staff meeting. While our team crafted what we were sure our clients would agree was a stellar pitch for roach motels, I used every trick I knew to stay awake. Three hours passed before I got to return to my desk and sort through the pile of paper our intern handed me.

That's when I saw it. The message was from the much-touted June Rittenhouse, whom I knew by reputation as my field's top-gun head-hunter, a woman who handles positions in companies known to pay exceedingly well, a list that does not include the ad agency where I work. "*Urgent,*" the acid-green note shouted. It was addressed to Chloe Keaton.

I reached for the phone to dial her number. Chloe and I aren't just close friends. We go back to Dartmouth, where we briefly met when we were both visiting our boyfriends for homecoming. After graduation, we recognized each other at a prissy women's hotel. Now we share a copy-writing job and are in almost constant communication. Chloe's cell phone had rung twice when an evil voice in my head began to speak. I call her Mean Maxine.

Why should Chloe get all the breaks? Maybe June Rittenhouse is cold-calling and simply works in alphabetical order. You, Talia Fisher-Wells, are equally talented—maybe more talented—and need a better job ten times as much as Chloe does. Or the headhunter might be mining candidates for a position neither Chloe nor you would ever want, in a suburb of, say, Bismarck.

Mean Maxine snarked away until, unconvinced and disgusted, I shut her down and got on with my work, even taking several calls from Chloe. She asked for her messages. I gave them to her, all but one.

On the ride home, from within my bag the green stickie continued to shriek, *I belong to Chloe.* Mean Maxine hooted back, *No way. Talia, don't be a fool.* The debate segued into one of my least favorite quotidian themes, life's mysterious, unjust collision between money and luck. By the time I walked into our apartment in Park Slope, I'd worked myself into a lather. This never bodes well for Tom. I sat at our kitchen table and opened mail, which today contained not only bills but an article featuring restaurants in Rome. *Think about it, my lovelies,* Jules had scrawled on the top in her back-slanted handwriting. *Diet* domani. Jules, Chloe, Quincy, and I were planning to get together to hash out plans for our annual trip, and as if it were a presidential primary, Jules had been campaigning. She is nothing if not strategic.

I kvetched aloud. "Why am I the only person who ever has to think about money?"

Tom groaned, folding his arms over his broad chest. "Is this a question I'm expected to answer?" He hates when I bitch, as much as I resent the lectures he can't resist giving about how I notice only the world's haves. On this subject, we hit an impasse fast, because I like to point out that if he applied for membership to the have-not club, they'd reject him based on genealogy. What's more, innuendoes suggesting that my value system is out of whack strike me as cheap shots because I think Tom and I agree that I, Talia Fisher-Wells, qualify as one of the good guys. I keep my carbon footprint dainty, and I'd compost if our backyard were bigger. Each month, I find four hours to donate to a food co-op in exchange for a deep discount on rutabagas and twenty kinds of beans. On a scale of 1 to 10, my materialism barely scratches 5. If I belonged to their tribe, the Catholics might canonize me.

"Forget I broached the subject," I said. "In fact, why don't you go for a bike ride?" With that, Tom did, but I continued to ruminate, *farklempt*, even after I parked Henry at the kitchen table and watched him scribble with his fat crayons. Shouldn't Tom be able to comprehend how frustrating it is that my three friends on speed dial happen to be preeminent haves? These perfectly agreeable people never blink before buying another pair of shoes they want, a verb they confuse with *need*. When their roots grow in, they make an appointment, not a purchase from the drug aisle. They use their airline miles to upgrade, since they don't have to hoard them for a ticket, which in my case is for my twice-yearly visit to my parents in Santa Monica.

Am I envious? Yes. And I think of this defect as more pathetic than my inability to calculate a percentage. I recognize that I lead a blessed life, and I am not a woman who flings around that adjective casually. I am healthy, with a husband, and not just any husband, but Tom Wells, a loving mensch, smart and funny. I have Henry, our delicious little boy. I have a job that engages my brain and student loans that are 75 percent paid off. Yet despite how often I remind myself of my considerable privileges, Mean Maxine points out the economic chasm between my life and my friends' lives, which every year yawns more profoundly. Next to any one of them, I, Talia Fisher-Wells, am a third-world country. What I need—no, want—from my husband isn't judgment. It's sympathy. And I wouldn't mind if he produced a bigger income.

"That Maine is cheap isn't even the point," I complained to Tom, who soon enough returned and was unloading locally grown vegetables from canvas bags we carry to the food co-op in our bikes' baskets. "I've got it worked out. We'll stay at your family's camp. In September the ocean's practically a swimming pool. We'll hang around the lake, hike and bike, and go to lobster pounds every night."

"Preaching to the choir, babe," Tom said as he began to rinse a head of buttery green lettuce while he entertained Henry with silly faces. "I've gone to that dump every year of my life."

"It's authentic." Last year, when Chloe and Xander moved into their brownstone, her decorator talked her into buying moose antlers to hang over her fireplace. I'm fairly certain that beast's ancestor hangs in Tom's family's living room, shot by Grandfather Wells. "Chloe just spent a thousand bucks on two new Hudson Bay blankets."

"Dammit, no one can accuse my family's blankets of being new." Tom pounded his fist in mock indignation, which made Henry wave his pudgy hands. A crayon bonked Pontoon, our dog of indeterminate parentage and large appetite, who was snoozing under the kitchen table. The animal shook his hairy snout, and Henry started giggling so hard I couldn't get him to look in my direction, even when I called "Henry Thomas" three times.

"Where does Mrs. Keaton want to go?" He never fails to be amused by the fact that Chloe's husband, Alexander Keaton, has evolved from being someone who used to intern for Al Gore into a guy who quotes *Wall Street Journal* editorials. Does Tom expect that because Xander was raised in

Tennessee he should sing songs with lyrics like *the squirrel ate the cat and the cat ate the dog and they all danced a jig on the leg of a hog?* Since college he and Xander have both grown, in opposite directions.

"Chloe wants Vegas."

"Does she like the slots or the craps table?"

"She likes to flip a coin between Fendi and Gucci."

"Remind me why you're friendly with her."

"Because she's the best present you ever gave me." Tom and Xander, who were in the same fraternity, had been pleased when their girlfriends formed a mutual admiration society, one that in recent years has been more enthusiastic than their own. It's also not a small thing that Chloe regards me as the ultimate source of motherly wisdom, although Henry's only four months older than Dash.

"If you'd admit you can't afford these trips, they'd work around it," Tom said. "These women are your friends. Trust them. They deserve some credit."

There he went, being reasonable. How did I wind up married to an emotional mutant, a man envious less often than I vote? Tom takes far too much devilish delight in the fact that his family's quaintly rotting vacation home was shabby before the term got affixed to chic. He would walk two miles out of his way to resole his boat shoes rather than buy a new pair on sale.

"I hate to plead poverty." What I wouldn't say was that the disparity in our personal economics came from our husbands. Chloe and I earn an identical salary, down to the decimal point. Xander runs a hedge fund, for which he is rewarded in capital-*C* compensation. Tom teaches high school English and gets rewarded hardly at all, but as I remind myself often, Mr. Wells is everyone's favorite teacher, and thanks to his schedule, on the days when I'm in the office Henry only has to stay with our sitter—Agnes from downstairs—until three-thirty, which is when Tom usually arrives home. This gives father and son plenty of guy time and me peace of mind. Another fact I refrain from pointing out, at least to Chloe, is that Xander goes for days without seeing Dashiel awake.

"How about if I cook tonight?" Tom scooped up Henry and brought him to the sink. "I'm thinking fusilli with sun-dried tomatoes and fresh mozzarella." He rinsed Henry's sticky fingers as quickly as if they were ten baby carrots.

"You cooked last night."

"That's your problem," Tom said with a grin. "You keep score. I swear you have a spreadsheet hidden somewhere."

I walked over to my lanky husband, pushed back his reddish hair, badly in need of one of his fifteen-dollar haircuts, and thought, *You I will always love, always trust, and always respect, and every one of those things is more important than money.* "Talked me into it," I said. "I'll do Henry's bath," I called out as I walked to our small bedroom in the back of the apartment.

An extra half hour alone was like a slice of cheesecake with none of the calories. I could swallow it in one immense gobble by napping, or I could savor it in multitasking nibbles as I read a few pages in the book I'd started reading last month—no, last fall—and called my mother or watched TV. While I was savoring my options, the phone rang.

"Hi there." Chloe sounded even more chirpy than usual. "Jamyang said yes."

"Going to give her a day off for the Dalai Lama's birthday?" Mean Maxine inquired. Xander had lobbied for a Chinese nanny so that Dash could learn Mandarin, but Chloe thought a Tibetan child care worker would bring serenity to Brooklyn Heights.

"My only concern is she's seriously gorgeous," she said. "Jamyang is this exquisite creature with long, silky hair." Not unlike Chloe, I thought, who's gone through life being compared to a doll, while I—taller, with sharp angles everywhere—live in fear that someone might notice my uncanny resemblance to Abraham Lincoln. "She's starting Monday, so I'll be back at work next week." Finally. For the last month, with Chloe between nannies, I'd been handling our job solo. Then again, Chloe had filled in for me when I visited my parents last winter. Such was our deal.

Chloe and I had started to brainstorm for a sales pitch when Tom stepped into the bedroom, holding Henry's hand. "Dinner in five," he said. "Pasta awaits."

"Tom's cooking again?" Chloe asked. "No take-out over there in the Slope?"

As if the Fisher-Wells family would ever splurge on ordering in. "You know our dirty little secret. Tom loves to cook, and don't get him going on stain removal or he'll whip up a poultice so fast your marble won't know what hit it." Tom had acquired his domestic engineering technique courtesy of his parents' housekeeper. "Got to go," I said, "but I'll think in my sleep and e-mail you in the morning."

After taking Pontoon for a walk, Tom topped off dinner with peach cobbler as we did a rundown of Henry's latest, most winning accomplishments. That's when Tom asked the question I was expecting. "Have you made up your mind?"

"As a matter of fact, I have," I answered calmly, although my insides were swing-dancing.

He pushed up the bridge of his wire-rimmed glasses, an anxiety indicator as reliable as another man's grinding teeth, and gave his fork the kind of attention due a fossil as I said, "Not even a choice, really."

For so many summers I'd stopped counting, Tom had worked at Camp Becket in the Berkshires, where I'd join him most weekends—for the last three with Henry in tow. The unspoiled lake and equally unspoiled boys who benefited from his patient attention as athletic director; the accommodations in the stone lodge bearing the name of the original Henry Thomas Wells, Tom's grandfather—it was a needlepoint throwback to an era before stress became a verb. Everything said 1960, including Tom's salary. His camp contract was on the desk, as was the contract for option B, a grown-up summer job: doing research at Xander's firm. When Xander had offered the position, my first thought was that pity might be the catalyst. My second was that if this was what Tom could earn for twelve weeks of slave labor, the Keatons were even wealthier than I'd guessed.

Tom had said that if I wanted him to work at Xander's company, I'd only have to shout *go* and he'd suit up for Wall Street. I felt he was a wimp for not making the decision himself, and said as much. Taking Xander's job was what I wanted, but I wanted him to want it, too. "I can live without the suspense," he said.

"Okay," I said, drawing out the word. "I'm going with"—I looked at my plate—"option C." For Tom to try to finish his dissertation.

Tom's relief was almost visible. "You're really on board with this?"

"Yes," I said. *No,* I thought.

Not for the first time, I'd voted my heart instead of my head. Since Tom's academic effort would contribute a grand total of nothing to the family coffers, it would mean us doing without. What we'd be sacrificing, specifically, I wasn't sure. Tom and I didn't operate within a budget; we simply tried to economize with' panache. Cabs and Broadway shows? Never. Metrocards and free nights at the Brooklyn Museum? Now you're talking. Let me loose in a thrift shop and I can dress myself with such *je ne sais quoi* that I get assaulted by rogue fashion stylists who want to know where I found my *shmattes*, my rags. Dinners out? We invite friends over instead: ten times the work, one-fifth the cost. Stoop sales? The Fisher-Wells Olympics.

Tom had been finishing his thesis for years, but since we'd become parents, his work had slowed, with those hours previously dedicated to research funneled into Henry. Our child was our own blue chip, but one who'd made our expenses soar. The logistics of family life make my head ache. If I weren't working, Tom would have plenty of time to write, but we require my paycheck, the heftier one in the family, even though my job is part-time.

Henry Thomas Wells Ph.D., would be able to teach college. "The degree is an investment," he often says. Not exactly like buying Google in 2004, but the ticket to the kind of position Tom wants and deserves. He got up from his chair, pulled me toward him, and said thank you with his well-educated lips.

Kissing led to more-than-kissing, and this accounted for why I slept only five hours that night. I got up in the morning, took one look at Tom, and wished I'd had the nerve to say, *Stop chasing the degree. Grab the money job. It won't kill you to work as hard as all the other guys on the Street and take the burden off your poor wife, who—if you haven't noticed—feels as if she's single-handedly tugging a barge upstream.* But I am bred to try to do the right thing; I said none of this.

A day went by, then another. Tom and I put ourselves through the monthly ritual of trying to decide which bills to pay in full and which to let slide. Agnes raised her rate. Our washing machine went on the fritz, forcing me to drag our clothes to the launderette blocks away. An old friend from college sent one of those *listen up—life is not a dress rehearsal* chain e-mails to pass on or risk dire consequences. It was falsely attributed to Maya Angelou, but creepily resonant just the same. I found more gray hairs.

Meanwhile, the stickie scoffed at me every time I opened my tote, where it was hidden. I had almost managed to convince myself that June Rittenhouse had never called, except that as I was leaving the office one night, I picked up the phone. Again, she was asking for Chloe.

"Oh, I'm so sorry, but Ms. Keaton's taking personal leave," I said. "When will she return? I honestly don't know—she's away because of a . . . family emergency." I took a deep breath, then another. Mean Maxine growled. *Say it.* "This is Talia Fisher-Wells—the two of us share our job. May I help you?"

June Rittenhouse gave me an appointment.

CHAPTER 4

Chloe

"When you wash the baby's laundry, please use this." Jamyang said nothing as I raised the barbell-weight container from the shelf. "It's fragrance and dye free." I moved on to nontoxic, hypoallergenic, and biodegradable. Jamyang offered a nod, which made her hair sway, its shine catching the light filtering through the window. "Have you ever used one of these?" I pointed to the washing machine, whose porthole appeared to have escaped from an ocean liner.

"Yes, ma'am." Her voice was faint, her expression inscrutable. I hoped she meant what she said, because I wouldn't have known how to operate that particular appliance, not to mention four out of five cycles in the top-of-the-line German dishwasher or the rotisserie in our restaurant-worthy oven. Why I'd once thought we needed it was its own mystery, since I can't see myself roasting a lamb on a spit anytime soon. I prefer to admire our home technology from a safe distance. Two of my worst days of the year are when our eleven digital clocks need to be reset.

"The floors are bamboo." Did they even grow bamboo in Tibet? Where was her native land, exactly—near China? No, India. No, China. Should I have hired the Irish girl who jabbered during the interview, wee lass this, wee lass that? "I think we're finished here," I announced. Jamyang had already seen and seemed to approve of her room. Decorated with chintz, a small flat-screen TV, and walls painted apple green, it was located on the semisubterranean floor that the previous owner had proudly called an English basement. "Let's see if Dash's awake."

We took the back staircase, bypassing the parlor floor with its formidable living room and dining room, and peeked in on Dash, whose tiny chest was rising and falling as if set to a metronome. I brushed away a strand of blond hair, but he didn't stir. I'd kept him up late with the hope that his father might arrive in time to see him. Last night Xander had missed him by twenty minutes.

"Pity baby," Jamyang said. "Very pity."

"Pretty," I said, softly rolling the *r*. "Thank you very much."

"Yes, ma'am," Jamyang said. "Pity."

We tiptoed into Dash's bathroom, where Jamyang scrutinized the flotilla of rubber ducklings and stacks of monogrammed towels—*DMcK* for Dashiel McKenzie Keaton—walked through the playroom, and U-turned into a corridor that led to Xander's literary Fort Knox. I hesitated before I opened one of its double doors. How should I explain that my husband could detect at twenty paces if a visitor had misshelved *Tender Is the Night* with the Henry James collection? Then again, what were the chances that Jamyang would want to cozy up with an early-twentieth-century first edition? "This is the library," I said as we entered the mahogany-paneled room and spread my arms wide. "Many, many books!" Jamyang pinched her nose. "Sorry, Mr. Keaton smokes cigars."

"Febreze," she announced, in our most promising exchange of the day.

I walked across the room to open a window. When I turned around, Jamyang had bent down to trace the intricate leaf pattern of the rug's rich ochre weave. "Pity," she said.

"From your country." I seriously hoped that we hadn't flung a sanctified prayer rug across the lesser nirvana of our Brooklyn Heights floor, where Xander would occasionally flick cigar ashes and spill single-malt Scotch. Jamyang responded with a spatter of words. I smiled, vacantly, I'm sure. She arched her eyebrows in a grimace and resumed a placid expression as she got up to review the rows of leather-bound books.

This was going to be the first of what I had just realized would be at least several endless days. "Excuse me," I said, pointing to my watch, and bolted to the master bedroom suite on the top floor. My desk and computer were tucked into a dormer window across from our dressing room. "I may have made a huge mistake," I whispered when Talia answered her phone. "I forgot to hire a translator."

"Sure she's not just shy?"

You'd think one shy person would have radar for another. I'd lived through a whole childhood of being ordered to smile. Usually I was terrified, not least by Mother. If she hadn't drummed into me that rule number one of proper manners is showing an interest in others, I wouldn't have a friend in the world. Jamyang might be shy—or judging me. "All I know is I can't leave Dash with her quite yet. I'm so sorry I'm hanging you up."

"You mean 'hanging me up longer'?" Talia asked, though she sounded more amused than angry, one of many reasons why I love her, my most instinctively thoughtful friend.

"You're amazing," I told her. "I'll make it up to you."

One peace offering was waiting, gift-wrapped. The sweater I'd chosen—sumptuous, ruby red three-ply cashmere—was don't-ask-don't-tell expensive, nothing Talia would buy for herself, but shopping for friends gives me infinite pleasure. I had something for the others, too. When we got together for dinner the next week, Jules would receive a novel set in Rome—if we didn't visit, she could at least read about it—and for Quincy I'd found a vintage photograph of Central Park, because she'd seen an apartment near there that she'd loved.

"Just get your tush back as soon as you can," Talia said.

"Messages?" I asked, since we function as each other's answering service.

I heard her rustling around on her desk. "Not much," she said. I jotted down information on two calls—one about the meeting of a women's shelter where I sit on the board, and the other from a consultant who guided parents through the lunacy of school applications. Xander had gone to prep school and college on scholarship, and the position for which that education had prepared him now allowed him to provide a private-school education for Dash. He wanted us to pick the best school, a topic he'd been raising every day.

"Should I get you up to speed about this morning's meeting?" As Talia started a play-by-play, I thought about how little such details interested me. I was surprised no one else had commented on my lack of enthusiasm, no one but Xander. He, for whom it took a month to register that I'd chopped off six inches from my hair and gone two shades blonder, had said, more than once, "You're bored with that job—why stay there? We don't need your salary." He stopped just short of modifying *salary* with *measly*. By week three of my recent frenzied nanny search, he'd started saying, "This is ridiculous. Quit working." But if I didn't work, I'd expect myself to be permanently attached to Dash, poor child. Soon he'd require daily psychoanalysis, not preschool.

"If I quit," I asked Xander, "what do you suggest I do, be some sort of dilettante?" We refer to his boss's wife as Charlene the Chatelaine, tied down as she is with dressage, the Met's Costume Institute gala committee, and controlling the purse strings at her husband's charitable foundation.

"How about more volunteering? We're writing checks to enough organizations."

"Maybe you'd like me to find an internship in Zimbabwe?"

"Sarcasm doesn't become you, Chloe. I'd back you in either a foundation or a business. You know, like that lady who started eBay."

That was when I suspected that what my short, towheaded husband— my twin, some people have thought—wanted was bragging rights. If I were to go on a steady diet of philanthropy, he wouldn't be satisfied until I became a benefit chair. If I started a business—baking blueberry muffins, let's say—in five years he'd expect me to take those muffins public. Xander is a smart guy, but he overlooks a key fact: I am not a leader. I'm not even a woman who would skim a self-help book on leadership.

I like my job's predictable grid of assignments and deadlines and—in small doses—its conversation, which doesn't revolve, like a never-stopping carousel, around children. I also appreciate the part-time schedule, which is ideal and uncommon. My arrangement with the agency and Talia would be hard to duplicate, not that I've searched for alternatives. Simply keeping track of Dash's schedule—swimming! music! numbers classes!—exhausts my organizational skills.

As Talia continued, I added the appropriate "Really?" but when the intercom came alive, I was grateful. Dash was awake, and he wanted the whole house to know. "Can you hear that shout for Mommy?" I said abruptly. "I'll have to call you later." I walked downstairs. With blue eyes open wide, my son was sizing up Jamyang, who was hovering in the doorway.

"Pity boy awake," Jamyang said, cooing in a language I couldn't understand: our comprehensive library could use a copy of *Tibetan for Dummies.* "Dashiel," I sang out, "did you have a wonderful nap? This is Jamyang. She's going to be taking care of you."

For the first time, Jamyang smiled broadly, displaying tiny, straight teeth. She turned to my son and said, "Does Dashiel want to play?" He answered with a giggle and handed her a stuffed cow.

Everything's going to be all right, I realized. I sighed so loudly Jamyang turned around. "Why don't I leave you two to get to know each other? Bye-bye, sweet prince." I kissed my son's rosy cheek. "I'll see you in ten minutes." I spoke then to Jamyang. "After you two get acquainted, meet me in the kitchen, please, and I'll show you what Dash likes to eat." Then we'd circle through the neighborhood and onto the Promenade.

I walked upstairs, found the number for the school consultant, and dialed. "Hannah McCoy's office," a crisp voice announced before it buried me on hold. "Mrs. Keaton," Hannah McCoy said finally. "I'm sorry to keep you waiting, but the phone's been ringing off the hook."

"I'm sure I'm calling way too early." I said, embarrassed, "but I wondered if I could make an appointment to meet about my son for school next fall."

"You're not calling a bit early," Hannah McCoy answered, chomping on *bit*. "I'm well along with meetings for your child's peers."

Dash still went to bed at night in UnderJams, but apparently he already had peers, eager toddlers whose mothers were more plugged in than I. "Better make an appointment to meet soon, then. What do you have available, please?"

"Let me look—so sorry, have to take this call. May I put you on hold for a moment?" Six minutes later she returned. "It's your day, Mrs. Keaton—I had a cancellation for Monday."

Monday was when I would be returning to the office. "How about later in the week?"

"I'm booked solid for the next month." She paused. "July sixth?"

Xander and I had rented a house in Nantucket and were planning to take off the entire holiday week. "Sorry, that's not possible. What do you have the following week?"

After a long pause, she spoke. "One opening—on Wednesday, at eleven."

"Great," I said. "I'll take it. It's Keaton, Chloe Keaton, K-E-A-T..." I continued with my vital statistics, including an AmEx number for the sizable deposit. "Is there anything else I should know?" I wanted to learn, fast.

"Only this—pardon me for asking, but are you single?" Hannah McCoy's tone had turned cloying.

"No. Why do you ask?"

"You said 'I.' Traditionally, both parents attend the appointments."

Why hadn't I figured this out? "In that case, eleven isn't going to work, either." After two more sessions on hold, Hannah McCoy suggested an appointment for a full six weeks from now. By then all of Dash's peers probably would have learned to conjugate French verbs. "You know what?" I said. "I've changed my mind. I'm going to grab the slot on Monday." Talia would have to work one more day, and Xander, whether he liked it or not, would have to get with this program.

CHAPTER 5

Quincy

Jake and I woke early, despite three celebratory romps in bed last night. He ran his warm palm from the curve of my shoulder down to the small of my back, over my behind, and along my leg, which was almost the length of his. "What do you say we hit the road, Q?" he asked. It was Saturday, and the two of us always loved an uncharted trip, whether we splurged on a four-star hotel or pitched a tent. Within an hour, we'd packed a bag and rented a car.

I can sniff out an antiques store miles away, but today, as Jake and I drove north on back roads, I barely took note of the dusty shops, the delicate church spires, or the farm stands selling the season's first pumpkins. All I could think and chatter about was the apartment, which we'd bid on before we'd even ridden down the building's elevator.

Jake had followed through on the plan we'd rehearsed, should he decide that he liked the co-op as well as I did. "We'll bid five percent above asking price," he told Horton as I felt liftoff in my heart, speaking these words with the same bravado that had convinced the silvery sages head-ing his law firm to make Jacob Benjamin Blue a junior partner before he turned thirty-three.

If we canceled our trip to Costa Rica and liquidated 75 percent of our savings, we could manage the purchase. If we ever required a third bedroom, Horton was right, we could eke out a good-sized space from the enormous, sunny dining room. When I imagined Jake and me in what I was beginning to think of as our home, I saw us happy, with child or without. We were our own family.

By eleven we spotted an inn fronted by weeping willows. "What do you think?" I said, pointing to the vacancy sign. As we pulled into the cobble-stone driveway, my cell phone rang. It was Horton, crowing. "Fran's delighted with your bid and has submitted it to Dr. Walter's legal guardian." I felt a beat of pleasure. Mrs. Shelbourne was a woman I wanted to please, a woman who made me want to stand up straight. My hand shot up in a victory salute Jake returned as I said, "Excellent. Anything else we need to do now?"

"Not yet," Horton answered. "I'll keep you in the loop, but don't expect to hear from me until Tuesday. Congratulations—you're on your way to owning a very special piece of property. Now enjoy your weekend."

That we intended to do. As soon as I pushed open the inn's screen door, I liked the parlor, which hadn't an inspirational plaque in sight. A pile of art books stood on a trestle table next to a bowl of plums. When I pressed the bell for service, a curly-haired man walked through a hallway wiping his hands on a snowy apron. "Welcome to the Black Cat," he said, smiling. "May I help you folks?"

"I hope so," Jake said. "Could you show us some rooms, please?"

"Certainly, but there are only two left."

The first room had a pencil-post bed layered with what appeared to be a faded bridal trousseau, but from the window seat of the second choice I saw a stone patio with wicker chairs and broad white market umbrellas. The room was larger and lighter, with a bath whose centerpiece was a deep claw-foot tub that reminded me of my first apartment. Jake took my hand and squeezed twice, our standard signal of agreement, the one we'd used to indicate approval on the apartment. I squeezed back. "We'll take it," he said.

"I wish we were staying longer than one night," I whispered as we walked downstairs.

"I don't see why I can't be late on Monday." He raised his eyebrows in his most lascivious Groucho glare. "I'll book it for Sunday, too."

I couldn't recall one occasion when Attorney Blue had taken a sick day, not even when he broke his femur on a ski slope. It was at moments like this when I truly believed that even if I never had a child, my life was nevertheless going to be much more than fine. Jake is everything I want in a husband, and while putting up with my quiet spells heads the list, the unquenchable attraction I feel for him is not far behind. When I returned downstairs, he'd already arranged for a picnic to eat after a hike to the area's main draw, a covered bridge. Arms around each other's waist, my straw hat tickling his ear, we wandered down the inn's driveway.

We hadn't gotten fifty feet past the gate when the trill of my phone competed with a moo. "What's up, Horton?" I said.

"Dr. Walter's adviser thanks you for your offer but wonders if you'd be willing to increase it."

"Uh-huh," I said feeling a familiar disappointment snake up from the pit of my stomach, grip my insides, and give them a good yank. Every other apartment bid had run along these lines. "We'll discuss it and I'll call you in a bit." I clicked off and explained.

"What it comes down to, is, do you really want this place?" Jake asked reasonably.

I thought of all my addresses in thirty-some years—the solid, three-story house in the Minneapolis of my childhood; the rambling Manhattan apartment I'd shared with a boyfriend, and then with Jules, Talia, and Chloe; Jake's cozy hovel, which I moved into when we became engaged; our current rental in a building that looked like a stack of ice cubes, its balcony the size of a coffin. In the Central Park West apartment, I felt as embraced as if I'd lived there in a previous life of extraordinary contentment.

"My gut says go," I admitted, "but maybe I'm getting carried away. I need a reality check."

We walked in silence until Jake sat down by a stream we'd been following. He began picking up pebbles and idly throwing them into the rushing water. A dozen pebbles later, he spoke. "Q, you're not crazy. It's a terrific apartment, and probably a pretty sure investment if we decide to move somewhere like this for good." Whenever we got fifty miles outside of Manhattan, he invariably launched a Norman Rockwell fantasy, forgetting that he was well on his way to a prosperous career representing white-collar crooks, a species he'd find in short supply here in the land of the rake and the rooster. "If you want it, I want it. We can up the offer five percent, but that's the limit. I draw the line at food stamps."

I hugged him as he left a message for Horton. Then Jake and I trundled off to the bridge, spread a quilt nearby, and feasted on sandwiches thick with turkey and Brie, washed down with sparkling lemonade. Stuffed, the two of us lay back hand in hand and counted clouds floating in the sort of pool party sky you never see in a city. Soon I began to doze. I dreamt of us unpacking boxes in our new apartment. Inexplicably, I was playing the cello, accompanied by Eloise Walter. After a bravura performance I retreated to a bedroom, where I discovered a door that Horton hadn't shown us. It was locked. I didn't have the key. I banged, again and again.

I woke to Jake shaking my shoulder. "Q—you're moaning."

"What did I say?" I asked, blinking in the light. I've been known to dream in convoluted, Spielberg-worthy plots, which I try to recount for Jake, who finds them considerably less captivating than I do.

"I have no idea, except that you scared the nuts off me." He stood and extended a hand. "C'mon, we have plans."

During my nap, Jake had read a borrowed guidebook and made a reservation at a nearby restaurant. Our dinner lived up to its billing—red snapper for him, duck breast for me—as did the brandy we sipped later in front of the inn's hearth. It was nearly midnight when we tiptoed up the Black Cat's stairs.

On Sunday, the aroma of sizzling bacon woke us and we stumbled down to breakfast. I was at risk of taking a third helping of waffles, using up the owner's entire winter store of maple syrup, when he said, "Do you two enjoy auctions?" That was like asking me if I, as a human being, enjoyed oxygen. In twenty minutes, Jake and I were in the back row of a crowded barn, listening to an auctioneer sell off the possessions of a local gent enamored of guns and bugles repurposed into lamps. We were ready to bail when the auctioneer announced the final lot, items from the home of the family for whom the town was named.

"This sounds promising," I whispered. "Can you stand ten more minutes?"

"Stay as long as you want," Jake said. "I'll go outside and make some calls."

First up was a spinning wheel, too Colonial Williamsburg for my taste. Ditto for a mallard posing as a door knocker. I was ready to join Jake in the parking lot when the auctioneer lifted a small pine cradle. "Looky here, folks," he said as he turned it from side to side. "This treasure's from the sixties. That's eighteen-sixties, handed down in the seller's family. Every baby started his life in this little bed, and damned if they didn't all live to be centenarians, legends in these parts."

As I walked forward, the auctioneer told tales of the cradle's distinguished occupants: Great-Granny Mabel, the suffragette; Uncle Buster, who ditched the booze and became a circuit court judge; and Grandpa Al, that prankster, who almost incinerated the one-room schoolhouse. I got within a foot of the cradle, which showed only the tenderest wear. It was painted blue.

"We'll start at forty," the auctioneer said.

"Forty," I shouted back.

"I hear forty—do I hear fifty?" He did, and in rapid succession.

"I bid a hundred," I said, shaking my paddle like a maraca. Across the room, a spirited competitor—or a shill—shook hers, too, and went to $125. From another corner, someone bid $150.

"Do I hear one seventy-five for this hand-crafted heirloom?" the auctioneer asked, pronouncing the *h* in *heirloom*. In a sweet tenor, he began to croon. "Hush, little baby, don't say a word. Papa's gonna buy you a mockingbird." He laughed. "Maybe not a mockingbird, but damn if this ain't special."

Heck, damn if it ain't. Mama Blue went to $175.

The auctioneer sang, "Sleep, baby, sleep. Your father tends the sheep." The auctioneer heard $200 and switched his tune. From the front of the room he belted out, "Little boy blue, come blow your horn. The sheep's in the meadow, the cow's in the corn."

"Two hundred twenty," I screeched. "Two hundred twenty."

"I hear two-twenty," the auctioneer boomed. "Do I hear two-thirty?" The room fell silent. "Do I hear two-thirty?" He did not. "Going once, going twice. Sold to the tall lady in the straw hat for two hundred and twenty dollars!"

I caught my breath and raced outside to find Jake. "Ready to leave?" he said, snapping shut his BlackBerry.

"As soon as I pick up my purchase." He gave me a look of feigned surprise.

"Why don't you go to the car and pop the trunk?" I went inside, counted out my cash, lifted the cradle in my arms, and hauled it to the car.

"What's this for?" Jake said gently. I couldn't identify his expression. "Q, what are you trying to say?"

He'd taken the sorrow of the miscarriages every bit as hard as I had, but the tragedies were no longer discussed, filed away like failed exams. My eyes went from the cradle to my husband's face. *Honey, I wish I did have something to tell you,* I thought, but all I could offer was a mental telegram of optimism whose source I could attribute only to the good fortune of finding the Central Park West apartment. "No, sweetheart, no news," I said, and tried to sound, if not breezy, at least neutral. But the mood had shifted as surely as if a thunderstorm were blowing into town. I refused to see the cradle as he must, a receptacle for lost hopes. "I was thinking of it for magazines," I said, offering up the first thing that came to mind. "You know how they multiply on my side of the bed."

He lifted the cradle into the trunk and got behind the wheel, the look on his face the one he usually saves for cross-examinations, enigmatic beyond my understanding

"Did you let the firm know you'll be late tomorrow?" I asked as we drove to the inn.

"About that." I could hear him thinking. "Turns out I shouldn't take off. In fact, we'd better leave."

I knew the finality in his voice, a tone as specific as an exclamation mark. To return to the city we took the parkway instead of back roads. About an hour outside of New York my phone rang. "Is anything wrong?" I said as soon as I heard Horton's voice.

"Not necessarily, but it's gotten complicated." He paused. "There's a second bidder."

"So our bid wasn't accepted," I added, confused.

"This can happen with a red-hot property. I'm sorry."

"Is it those people we saw?" Another couple had been waiting to see the apartment with Mrs. Shelbourne after she gave Jake and me our joint tour.

"They found it way too small...." Horton's voice trailed off.

"What's going on? What aren't you saying?"

"Full disclosure—the other bidder's an insider."

"Define insider."

"A resident. In the building."

"Is there a posting or something that tells which apartments are for sale?" I pictured a memo slid into every mailbox.

Horton snorted. "If that were the system, how would working stiffs like me make a dime? The information brokers have is *privileged*." He spoke the word as if it were his bank account's PIN number. "In fact, as a result of your offer, Fran had decided not to do her usual all-points listing to alert other brokers. She wanted a fast deal, remember? She thought you and your husband were ideal."

I sensed that Jake wanted to rip the phone out of my hand and talk directly to Horton, but I asked with considerable patience, "What happened, then?"

Horton picked up his pace. "What happened is that some guy who lives in the building harassed the doorman into telling him which apartment with a reservoir view was up for sale. This gentleman buttonholed Fran in the lobby and practically wrestled the poor thing to the ground till she gave him a walk-through." Horton stopped to breathe. "He was accompanied by a wife or girlfriend—Fran wasn't sure which, except that they were both too loud for her taste. Fran only let them stay a few minutes, but it was long enough for the pair to agitate Dr. Walter." Everything that had felt right was going wrong. "The bottom line is that you and Jake need to think fast about whether you want to top the other bid." He floated the number we'd need to surpass.

I gulped. "Okay," I said. "We'll call you tomorrow."

I waited for Horton's goodbye, but what he said was, "Quincy, there's one last thing." I could hear him breathing. "When you saw the apartment the first time, you mentioned you knew someone in the building."

"Yes." My stomach lurched. "My friend's boyfriend, Arthur somebody."

"Did you tell him you were bidding on an apartment?" Horton asked. "Because Arthur Weiner is your competition."

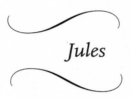

CHAPTER 6

Jules

When Talia invites you to dinner, she'll *shtup* you with an enigmatic vegan casserole. Chloe will serve exquisite morsels catered by whatever venue the privileged class has most recently anointed as noteworthy—last time, the entire menu was raw, for that special moment when you crave arctic char marinated in watermelon juice. Quincy's cuisine, along with her creativity, fluctuates: depending on the time of the month, your meal could range from shrimp luxuriating in a sublime ricotta fondue to her mother's hamburger hotdish. Not that I'd refuse, either, but when friends visit my home, nobody leaves hungry or with a prickle of cactus pear stuck between her molars. For tonight I'd whipped up pasta with lemon and pistachios, a Jules de Marco trademark with Marcella Hazan in a supporting role. We'd finish with olive oil cake, which tasted far better than it sounded. I might as well have put up a billboard saying that Rome should be our next destination, because planning a September getaway was the special entrée on the night's menu.

As I was frizzling artichokes, the phone rang. "Need any wine?" Talia said, calling from Chloe's car. "Last chance to hit that liquor store in the Village."

"Thanks, but I'm good." Decanted Chianti sat on my walnut sideboard, reflecting the setting sun. Two more bottles waited, with prosecco in reserve for toasting should Rome win the bake-off.

"In that case, you'll see us in ten minutes," Talia said, adding, "If we don't wind up in New Haven." She let loose with her gravelly laugh, a sound that I imagined had, pre-Tom, hijacked many a man-child lost in a fog of lust.

"Not fair—this time I know where to go," Chloe shouted over a robotic voice politely urging a right turn.

"How late are we?" Talia asked. "Is Quincy there yet?"

"No sign of her," I said as I hung up.

Quincy had been incommunicado all week, though I'd e-mailed her. Twice. I was hoping she wouldn't roll in an hour late claiming she'd been shanghaied by that holy state she'd spoken of when authors blast through their writer's block and compose like hellhounds. Quincy could go wherever her effing flow took her as long as she didn't forget about our dinner, which would mean postponing our decision about this vacation that had all four of us politely posturing.

Blowsy roses cut from my garden faintly perfumed the screened porch where we'd be eating. I considered playing some opera—*nah, overkill*—and popped in Sinatra. As I walked back to the kitchen, my phone rang again. "Hi, doll," Arthur said. "Am I interrupting you and the ladies?"

"No, but I can't talk." I ground more pepper into the sauce. "Good real estate karma?"

"Fuck no," Arthur grumbled.

When I'd mentioned the apartment in his building, within the hour Arthur had conned the doorman into telling him which unit was for sale, then insisted that I rush over to meet him in the lobby. The two of us sat like fools, feigning animated conversation, for almost an hour until the broker glided in, the kind of bitch who'd wait on you at Bloomingdale's while she broadcast the not-so-subliminal message that you'd best stick to the plus-size department in the store's bowels. I detested her on sight, and didn't care if the feeling was mutual. It only juiced my competitive streak and made me salute Arthur's ingenuity—not that I didn't want to piss in my pants as I crossed the threshold of a find that Quincy had laid claim to as if it wore a plaque with her name on it. I had to remind myself that there was no way she was going to get that apartment. If anyone deserved it, it was a person from the building. Let's call that person Arthur.

"No luck? Well, that's a bitch," I said to him. The loyal girlfriend-me was galled, the friend part relieved. "What did the hag broker say?"

"She won't return my calls."

"Sorry." I couldn't cough up a *darling* or a *sweetie*, and wanted to ditch this topic. "What else's going on?"

"Which movie should I rent for Friday?" So we weren't going to a Broadway show. One thing about Arthur: with respect to being stingy, he was consistent. "I'm thinking that Jesse James flick."

Pretentious, too. Nonetheless, I was about to wolf-whistle on the leading star's behalf when the doorbell chimed. "You hear that? I'll call you when they leave."

Although my townhouse isn't large or even detached, my end unit's leafy backyard gives me the illusion of privacy. And it's mine, all mine and the bank's, from its Dutch door overlooking steps bordered with purple petunias to a fieldstone fireplace that climbs to the second floor. Two extra bedrooms are tucked into the eaves. I don't invite tall guests.

Talia thrust a bouquet of daisies in my arms as we greeted each other with the usual kiss parade. "Love the sundress," I said as she twirled, her white skirt billowing around long, slim legs I've been envying for years. "Very Marilyn."

"Twenty bucks at a consignment shop."

Like there would ever be anything for me at such a shop that didn't look as if it belonged on my aunt Magdalena.

When Talia stopped spinning, her eyes surveyed the room. She missed nothing. "I love those pillows," she said. "New?"

"If they're purple, they follow me home."

"For you." Chloe stepped forward. She offered a gift that appeared to have been wrapped in origami and tied with a chiffon bow. "Where can I park these?"

"Hand them over, dollface," I said, and put her present and travel brochures next to a platter of antipasto. "Help yourselves." I pointed to the wine as I walked back to the kitchen, adding, "Quincy does remember we're on, right?"

"Definitely," Talia said. "I spoke to her this morning."

"I offered her a ride," Chloe shouted, "but she rented a Zipcar."

Oh, holy Jesus, everyone had spoken to that woman but me. I walked out with a bowl of olives. "How are the kiddies?" I asked.

"Dash's taking to Jamyang," Chloe said, "who I suspect knows more English than she lets on."

"Yesterday I noticed it was way too quiet. Henry had climbed into the bathroom sink, opened the medicine chest, and was about to try out Tom's razor. The books don't tell you to childproof cabinets five feet off the ground."

When Chloe moved on to advanced potty training, she must have noticed me squirm. "How's it going with Arthur?" she asked. Chloe, my matchmaker, possessed an owner's curiosity about the relationship.

"He gives good phone."

"The hands?" Talia asked. I'd drilled it into all of them that one of Jules' Rules is that hands are second only to tongue.

"Hands good." But I didn't want to discuss Arthur. I was about to ask whether either of them knew what was going on with Quincy's apartment search when she pushed open the bottom half of the door.

"Anybody home?" she sang out. She met me with chocolates from Manhattan's latest Willy Wonka. I peeked in the box. Each candy was so delicately designed I wished I could tile my bathroom with them. Quincy almost gave me a kiss, leaving more than the normal amount of air between her pouty lips and my cheek, then greeted Chloe and Talia with the sort of full-tilt enthusiasm I usually receive. I doubted that Talia and Chloe would notice. It was all in the fine print: Quincy Blue, ticked off.

This struck me as an opportune time to bring on the home cooking. "It's getting late," I said. "Ladies, the porch."

"Your meals are worth starving for," Chloe said. "Which I've done, all day." She meant well but delivered the line in the spirit of a woman who's never said a Hail Mary before looking at a scale. Chloe had gained fifty pounds when she was pregnant, and for six months she'd looked like a teakettle, but now she was down to her prepregnancy weight plus, she said, a mere seven pounds.

As women do in the privacy of their gender, the four of us wolfed down our food, which did not disappoint. I batted away compliments. Not that I live for the praise—feeding people is how I care, which I admit without a teaspoon of my standard cynicism.

"Time to talk turkey," I said after I nibbled crumbs from all four cake plates and served cappuccino. "And since it's my house, I go first. Rome," I began, "is the city of love."

"Since when?" Quincy broke in. "Paris is the city of love."

"Isn't Paris the city of light?" Talia asked.

I ignored them both and proceeded to practically warble an aria to Italian men, Michelangelo in particular, the balmy climate, the Villa Borghese, soccer—or "football," thank you, Quincy—the colosseum, the Spanish Steps, hazelnut gelato, and all the priceless art of Vatican City, along with the thousands of seven-foot-tall Senegalese guys who hawk wholly credible knockoffs on the bridge leading to it.

"I have to admit it's sounding pretty sweet," Chloe said. "The Italian part of *Eat, Pray, Love* was my favorite!"

"That's everyone's favorite," Talia sniffed. "Strangle me with my prayer beads if I ever agree to stay even one night at an ashram."

"Didn't you love that because the author was such a squawk box the monks turned her into the ashram's hostess?" Quincy asked.

"On point, gang," I said shrilly, while I considered that if I were to visit

an ashram—an event as likely as me moving home to Staten Island—
that's the job the brothers would assign to me. "We're still talking Rome.
You know, the Eternal City."

"We could be like Audrey Hepburn in *Roman Holiday*," Chloe said.

Chloe and I share the belief that romantic movies peaked before we
were born. "Or the women in *Three Coins in the Fountain*," I added.

"There were three friends in that story," Quincy said. "Who stays
home?" This time no one could miss her blistering tone.

"What's your problem?" Talia asked, turning.

"Actually, now that you mention it, the euro," Quincy said, and but-
toned up her face. Even in the flattering amber of my living room light, I
saw a crease on her forehead that I'd never before noticed.

"You're right," Talia said without skipping a beat. "What are we thinking? Italy would be *molto costoso*."

"Who said anything about fancy?" I said, failing to suppress my
annoyance. "I know any number of reasonably priced hotels and restaurants."

But Chloe was talking over me. "I got bedbugs once at a four-star hotel
in Venice. Red tracks running up my arms like some sort of addict. I was
mortified to show them to a doctor." The other two seemed riveted by her
account of dermatological distress. "I doubt we'll get bedbug bites in
Vegas."

"I see," I said. "You'd rather go to the ersatz Italy, the one in Nevada?"

"The fountains at the Bellagio are choreographed to opera," Chloe said.

As if that were a selling point. "Go on," I drawled.

"You can ride in a gondola at the Venetian," she added.

"The gondolier will have a ya-you-betcha accent," I countered. William
Macy in *Fargo* had wormed his way into my brain in my attempt to see
Arthur's features as quirky rather than porcine; I'd been thinking about
an article I'd read on sexual attraction that insisted that only unimaginative women require handsome men.

"I've read about great deals to Vegas," Talia said. "You can stay at
Caesars Palace for about a hundred bucks a night."

Quincy cut in. "But isn't it a dump?"

Chloe looked hurt. "Midweek every hotel's a bargain in Las Vegas, even the Wynn."

"Midweek won't work," I said, "at least not for me. We blocked out a long weekend months ago. I can't change my schedule." *I'm not like the rest of you, whose lives come with male safety nets.*

Chloe had retreat written all over her face. "Of course we'll stick with those dates. But think of all the shows."

I was trying not to.

"What about you two?" Chloe turned to Quincy and Talia.

"Vegas is depressing," Quincy said. "People gambling away rent money and chasing ninety-nine-cent shrimp cocktails." I tried to catch her eye, to show that I agreed. She looked through me. "Graceland. That's America." She got up, hummed a few bars of "Don't Be Cruel," and announced, "I'm already holding the Gold and Platinum Suite."

And they thought *I* was pushy?

"The hotel plays Elvis movies on a constant loop." I saw Quincy's mouth continue to move and Chloe and Talia respond. Had I really screwed Quincy? Absolutely not, since under no circumstances would she and Jake wind up with that Eldorado apartment. In that case, shouldn't Arthur have a crack at it? He'd already lived for years in that pile of choice bricks. Bottom line, it had nothing to do with me. He and the young Blues could slug it out.

When I woke from my coma, Talia had transported us to Maine, with all its bushy-tailed wholesomeness. "We'll burn calories every morning hiking or sailing or riding bikes," her California voice-over was saying, "hang around the lake, go antiquing, and finish each day with lobster everything and corn on the cob, washed down with local wine."

"Do we buy it at L.L. Bean?" I asked. "Does it come in a box? With a screw top?"

"Or we'll drink beer and after dinner light a fire, make s'mores, read big beach books, and sleep like the dead."

"What if it rains?" Quincy asked.

"Factory outlets."

"I've never been to one," Chloe said.

I had, and would pass on the chance to shop for seasons-ago five-inch Swarovski-crystal-encrusted Lucite heels that "may" be Christian Louboutin. "Hear, hear," I said. "I call for a vote." I sensed that Rome had not caught fire but, since we weren't gamblers, Vegas was no better than going to Madison Avenue. Graceland appealed to me far more than Maine, no matter how many blueberry pancakes I could eat, but why should Quincy get her way? She'd had a loose hair up her ass all night.

We cast our secret ballots. Chloe, the evening's designated Pricewater-houseCoopers tabulator, made a show of counting the votes. "We have a clear favorite," she announced. "The winner is . . . the magnificent state of Maine."

Talia bowed to our applause. "Don't worry," she said. "The indoor plumbing will be installed any day now."

I was ready for every guest to leave so I could get to part two of the evening, since I wouldn't exhale until every leftover had been plastic-wrapped and each pot all but sterilized, but I spotted the gift from Chloe. You could set your watch by that woman's kindness. I opened the wrappings and found a bestseller. While I hugged her, I yawned. Chloe and Talia took the hint and said their goodbyes.

I hoped Quincy would join them. If she was ready to stick me in front of a firing squad over the fucking apartment, I'd defend myself, but what I really wanted was for her to go home. She'd disappeared into the bathroom and now walked back to the foyer, where I pretended to sort my mail while I felt her stare.

"Is there something you want to tell me?" she asked. There wasn't an edge to her voice, which made me more uneasy than if she'd bombed me with four-letter words. "I've waited all week."

I do outrage rather well myself. "Excuse me? If anyone should be pissed, it's me. You ignored my e-mails."

"How could you?" she said.

"Help me out here."

"When were you going to tell me you looked at the apartment Jake and I hope to buy? That you told your boyfriend and he went after it?" The stiffness in her voice was freezing into anger.

"Oh, that." I shrugged. "Good Lord, it's no major Machiavellian plot. Arthur thought the apartment might work for him. He's thinking of downsizing." She continued to glare. "The doorman told him about it." Technically, it was true.

"How did he hear about it?" Quincy's face was getting red. "It had to be from you, my friend who hurried over to see my dream apartment the first chance she got."

I folded my arms under my breasts and remained composed. Thank you, twenty-five years of acting classes.

"Did you think I wouldn't find out?" Quincy said when I wouldn't react.

"Arthur had every right to look at the apartment." Was my manner a tad imperious? Perhaps.

"You seem to be missing the point." Quincy had balled up her hands as if she was going to throw a punch. "Maybe I need to put this in terms you can understand. If we were shopping at the Barney's warehouse sale," she began, dripping condescension, "and I spotted a pair of pants and took them to the try-on area, when I turn my back you don't get to grab them."

As if we'd ever wear the same size. This was an insult on so many levels. "Maybe I need to put this in terms you can understand," I countered. "Arthur is entitled to go after the apartment—he already lives in the building." That had to count for something.

"But you gave him information you stole." Her voice was low and slow. "Don't you know it's wrong to misappropriate intellectual property?"

I wasn't about to admit any such thing, and I doubted if Mrs. Lawyer was even using that term correctly. *Was* I wrong? Wasn't real estate an open market, like love, war, and corporate expense accounts, where she who's most clever wins? I pinned Quincy with my eyes and low-and-slowed her back. "I'm sorry you're upset." It was the kind of bogus apology designed to drive people nuts.

She did an eye roll. "You! Who claim to be my friend." With that, Quincy walked out the door.

I stood in my foyer for a good five minutes before I popped open the prosecco, filled a tall tumbler, drank it down, and dialed Arthur.

CHAPTER 7

Quincy

I roared out of Jules' driveway and started composing what I'd scribble into my journal later tonight.

If I didn't love Jules, her betrayal would be easier, I started. *I'd turn my back and never look at that woman again. Except we have too much history and I always thought she was the one who really got me. I haven't told either Chloe or Talia about what's going on because . . . do they pity Jake and me? Try to take the shine off their mommy gloss when I walk into the room? Or is it that their kids have brought into focus what I should have noticed years ago: Talia's a tough nut no one's ever going to crack—maybe not even Tom—and Chloe will forever float in insecurity, despite having the baby, the beauty, the luxuries, the love?*

I turned onto the highway and pushed the gas pedal. I'd forgotten about the pure exhilaration of driving, every Minnesota girl's preferred escape.

Jules has always been different. I've lived off her fumes, ignoring that they were toxic. I've seen her be stubborn and irrational, but until now it's amused and even amazed me. If Jules had the faintest interest in politics, she'd clean things up in the Middle East before she cooked the troops dinner.

I passed one car. Then another.

But this time she's really done it.

I passed a third car, cutting in close. The driver gave me the finger. I gave it back. *Ja, I'm talking to you, Herr Doktor in the black Mercedes. Achtung.*

Where does Jules get her shameless-girl guts? Not from her pop, who left for the track, permanently, or that mother who likes gin better than Jules. Definitely not from the older sister Jules idolizes, the one who was forced to give up a baby and got back at her parents by going AWOL, leaving Jules waiting for visits. But Jules would never feel sorry for herself this way, as I would. She moves ahead with no apparent regret, no wallowing.

I glanced at the speedometer. Eighty mph. My fury was powering the car. Except that it wasn't. I needed gas, and probably a good Tasering from a state trooper. I spotted a gas station and pulled in. With any luck, it would sell over-the-counter Xanax.

I filled my tank and called Jake. "You need to talk me down from the ledge," I said. "The one I want to push that selfish pig Jules off."

"Ah, and what did you all eat for dinner?" Jake followed with the sort of laugh you have to call a chuckle. When he tries to calm me I usually melt into a puddle of butter, but not tonight.

"Jules thinks she's actually in the right!" I screamed. This took a certain talent while crying. "Or at least not wrong." In the moment I gave myself to decide if there was a difference, a ten-foot-tall guy beelined to my car.

"Everything okay here, ma'am?" he asked in a chewing-tobacco accent, tipping his cowboy hat. Had he wandered out of a country-and-western ballad or was he simply a serial killer dressed for a rodeo?

"I'm fine," I lied. I didn't care who heard and saw me, not even with snot dripping onto my hand, which I wiped on my jeans before I waved him away. "Just fine." The Marlboro Man returned to his pickup but gave me a sideways look.

"Q, who the hell was that?"

"No one," I said, and wailed, "It's not fair. But it's not the apartment, it's the hubris." I reconsidered. "No, it *is* the apartment. I found it. I want it for us. Heck!"

Jake and I had talked about walking away and letting Arthur buy the apartment, where I pictured him living unhappily ever after. We would continue in our quest for a home. But Horton had had another opinion. "Are you out of your mind?" he'd bellowed when I ran the idea past him. "Listings like this are comets that fly by every fifty years. You're not going to get another chance. If you buy this place, you could live there for the rest of your life—Central Park isn't going anywhere, kiddo. And if you want to resell later, at this price you'd make a killing. Besides, I thought you and Jake loved it."

"We do." In my mind I'd seen walls with the faintest blush; bare ebony-stained floors, squishy white couches, a long buttery gray suede chaise, and bouquets of peonies in tall clear glass cylinders. The windows would be free of curtains to welcome the view. My home would be airy, filled with light. A happy but subtle sound track would always play.

Horton had continued. "I say this now as a person who's looking out for you: finders keepers. Don't let that snitch friend of yours and her— you should excuse my French—A-hole, rat-bastard douche of a boyfriend walk off with a property you deserve. And by the way, Fran wants you to have it." I could hear Horton hyperventilating. "I can recommend an attorney today and she can draw up the contract. What do you say?"

I'd said yes. Later in the week Jake and I met with Horton's lawyer lady and soon we were shifting around money and writing checks, one with a stuttering echo of zeroes. Ten percent of the apartment's price went into escrow; another chunk was set aside for attorney's services.

The next day I looked at our accounts and broke out in buyer's remorse. Not that we were necessarily buyers. We had weeks of drudgery ahead to complete a meandering paper trail so that Horton could present a thorough invasion of monetary privacy to the building's admission board. These strangers would learn details about us that we wouldn't even tell my parents if they were still alive. Only after the board received our set of Peeping Tom documents would they consider scheduling an interview. His point was that I should prepare to be patient, extremely patient.

"What have we done?" I'd asked Jake the week before. "Did we rush into this?"

"I hate when you second-guess," he said, which I do, regularly. To me, a decision is a suggestion with a short-term expiration date. "We've settled this—we're getting into a damn good deal and we're both sick of looking. Besides," he predicted, "that Arthur guy will go away as soon as he knows we have a contract."

Except he didn't. According to Horton, who heard it from Fran, Arthur Weiner did everything short of holding a public symposium in the Sheep Meadow on why he, Mr. I-Bought-in-1989, deserved the apartment. I pictured him assaulting his neighbors until he filled a petition to have our contract tossed into the Bethesda Fountain.

"Don't you want the apartment?" Jake repeated as I stood at the gas station. I looked at my watch. Ten-thirty, my witching hour.

"Very much."

"Fine. Settled. Now get yourself home. I'll make it worth your while."

He did. Jake had set the table with the good stuff. "I took one look at your ribs this morning and decided you needed fattening up," he said. "Sit down." After he popped the cork and filled two flutes with champagne, he returned to our molecule-sized kitchen and emerged with a soufflé, sagging dramatically, but a love offering just the same. "My mother's recipe," he announced as he smothered the chocolate fluff with whipped cream.

I realized I was hungry, in every way. Dessert led to kissing and kissing led to bed, which led my fingers to the drawer where we kept the condoms. I was reaching for a foil packet when Jake stopped me. "Listen, Q, I'm thinking..." He hesitated. "I know I've been a prick since that business with the cradle, but maybe we should try again."

Could I take myself to the baby altar one more time and call on a God whom I'd abandoned when I felt He abandoned me? Was I the definition of crazy, repeating the same mistake, hoping for a different outcome? Jake held me tightly, murmuring, "Baby, baby, baby." I didn't know if it was a term of endearment or a prayer.

"Honey, I'm afraid," I said, talking to his chest. "I can't handle another—"

He put his fingers on my mouth and tenderly traced the outline of my lips, then slowly caressed my neck, my breasts, and the pathway between them that led to even greater pleasure. My hands repeated the pattern in reverse.

"Do I have to make every decision?" he said. When Jake left the condom in the drawer and entered me, he had a smile on his face, which I always find most handsome when it is millimeters away from my own.

"Do I have to tell you how much I love you?"

"You do, Mrs. Blue," Jake answered. "You do."

"The verdict is in, Attorney Blue. I love you, love you, love you," I said, timing my words to his thrusts, raising my face to find his fine gray eyes. They were closed.

"Keep talking, Q baby," Jake said. "Keep doing what you're doing and keep talking, baby."

"I love you," I yelled as he came and I came, almost together. I closed my eyes and let my mind go blank as it took me to a place tinted by the flush of hope. I reached for his hand in the darkness, holding it tightly.

CHAPTER 8

Talia

"What was going on back there?" Chloe asked as she backed out of Jules' driveway. "It wasn't just Jules being Jules, stamping her feet and wanting her own way. There's got to be more to it. She and Quincy are furious at each other about something."

"No one's unloaded a thing on me."

I tried, but failed, to imagine Chloe angry enough to ice me with a glance. At least four times every day, I'd think about how she'd feel if she found out that I was all over a job possibility meant for her. Would she say, *No big deal, go for it—the position doesn't interest me in the least?* Perhaps, but more likely she'd be shocked and hurt. No Mean Maxine controlled her like an evil cyborg. This is a woman who changes the toilet paper roll in public restrooms.

"Quincy was a little cold," Chloe said with uncharacteristic certainty. "Jules had gone to all that trouble to make dinner."

"Come on. That show was pure calculation. I was waiting for Placido Domingo to serve the pasta. Jules guilts you into letting her have her way. Maybe Quincy's sick of it."

"What went on back there wasn't about where we'd go on vacation. I can't imagine Quincy cares that much. I don't."

I did. "You're not annoyed we didn't pick Vegas?"

She turned toward me. "Of course not," she said. "I can go there some other time, with Xander.... Are you happy we picked Maine?" she asked after a few miles of companionable silence. I could hear her smile.

"Of course," I said. Still, Maine meant another mountain of work. Tom and I hadn't visited since the previous summer, and it was entirely possible that the locals might have appropriated the place for firewood. I'd need to drag my tush up there at least three days before my gang arrived. That would mean renting a car, driving nine hours, cleaning like a one-woman sanitation crew, stocking the cupboards beyond my in-laws' cocktail olives and soggy Ritz crackers, and shopping for extra towels, sheets, and blankets. Mousetraps, too. Chloe was thousand-thread-count royalty. Jules and Quincy liked their creature comforts, too, though not the small, furry ones, which last year had invaded the linen closet, partied, and multiplied.

"The weekend when we're gone Tom and Henry could do the natural history museum with Xander and Dash," I added. "All four boys together. How cute is that?"

"Maybe Sunday. Jamyang would appreciate the break."

"Isn't she always off for the weekend?"

"You know Xander—all work, all the time—so I hired her for the days I'm gone. We offered double salary."

What would Tom say about that? Nothing as nasty as what Mean Maxine was thinking. We'd be better off talking about work.

"You did an incredible job on the storyboards for the cream cheese account." Chloe's pitch was so smooth that after seeing it, you'd never again dream of reaching for mascarpone. I was able to keep a conversation going about the campaign until we reached the Brooklyn Bridge, surprising myself with my knowledge of butterfat and lactic acid bacteria— because the other major topic I hoped to steer away from was school.

When Tom had started in about wanting to see Jackson Collegiate, I was dumbstruck. "One thing I felt we were hard-wired for was going public," I said the day he sprang the tour on me. "I've barely set foot in a private school." I'm a proud graduate of the Santa Monica–Malibu Unified School District. I still know the words to "Dear old SaMoHi," which I warbled. For an encore, I waxed eloquently about my two years at UCLA—no regrets at all, except the bite Astronomy 101 took out of my grade-point average. How did I know I'd be expected to distinguish Andromeda from Cassiopeia? I'm from southern California. I thought it would be like reading tarot cards.

I rattled on about public schools' indisputable superiority until Tom got us back to Jackson. "It's an exceptional school and Betsy O'Neal is an extraordinary educator."

Still, I persisted. "Brooklyn's public schools are why people who could live in Manhattan buy here. You teach in a public school. This decision should be simple." I was exasperated by Tom's seemingly deviant behavior—and suspicious. With a fancy WASP background like his, did a latent private school gene eventually kick in, an academic equivalent of adult-onset diabetes? Before he topped things off with an Ivy League diploma, he'd attended the same boarding school where two previous generations of Wells men had followed the family tradition of playing rugby until they tore every ligament and needed knee replacements by the time they were sixty.

"Sometimes you're rigid to the point of ridiculousness," he said. "All I'm asking you to do is have a look-see."

That's when I decided to play the money card. "How would we ever pay tuition when we're having a hard enough time with rent and the occasional bottle of shiraz?"

"Have you never heard of a scholarship?" His voice was calm, worse than yelling.

I wondered what kind of conversation Chloe might be having at that moment with her husband. Deciding how huge a trust fund to establish for Dash, perhaps.

Who says he doesn't already have one? Mean Maxine asked. *You'd better go after that job, missy.*

CHAPTER 9

Chloe

"When you take Dash to music class, don't forget his Goldfish, please." I went into our fully stocked pantry and pointed to several packages.

"Yes, Mrs. Keaton." Jamyang nodded politely

"And a change of clothes," I added. "And please don't forget his jacket."

"Yes, yes." In the three weeks Jamyang had been looking after Dash, not only had she captured my son's devotion, she'd displayed the managerial capability required to run a chain of day care centers. Still, I couldn't resist reviewing the basics. I knew I was being annoying.

In less than an hour Xander and I would be touring yet another nursery school, the last of seven visits set up by Hannah McCoy. By next week, she'd want us to start filing applications. The pressure was mounting, and Xander wasn't helping. At the end of each tour, he bombarded the director with questions. *How does the education here foster intellectual independence? What do you do to stimulate a child's imagination—examples, please? Could you explain why your theories are considered to be progressive? Or not.* We'd started to have a nodding acquaintance with parents on the circuit, and I cringed to think that they'd pegged my husband as a fast talker in a well-cut suit. They didn't know the man I did, a hardworking perfectionist who only wanted the best for our son.

I, on the other hand, rarely peeped, except to praise the tidiness of a block corner or to ask if the children were supervised on the swings. We'd sat through Mrs. McCoy's tutorial on how to handle a tour—ask questions without speaking too loudly, she advised, which apparently some parents needed to be told. Every pre-K classroom looked like the one I remember from my own childhood, with a bored bunny twitching in a cage, dress-up clothes, and a bathroom whose toilet barely clears an adult's ankles. The only substantial change since my day was the names. Theo, Ariel, Dylan, Aspen, Charlie, Brett, Alex, and Morgan—were they boys or girls?

Every director made sweeping statements. "Here at the Whatever School we help our students grow within an atmosphere of civility.... We embrace both an ethical and developmental perspective.... It's our rich heritage that encourages well-rounded individuals.... The depth and breath of our program nurtures a student's desire to make connections between the classroom and the larger world." Whenever these declarations began, my mind would meander. Other parents might nod knowingly, but I was tempted to say, *Huh? English, people.*

No tour guide addressed what I was afraid to ask: Would this be a school where boo-boo kissing was practiced or forbidden? How would a teacher treat Dash if he couldn't tie his shoes properly? Was the school going to help him become a nice person or was "nice" obsolete, like—I speak from the humiliation of personal experience—innocently referring to your Chinese college roommate as Oriental? I was already worrying that Dash was at the beginning of a long life on the slow track, that lonely line that crawls below the spiking EEGs of brighter, more aggressive little boys, boys like Henry Fisher-Wells, who was only four months older but did everything ahead of schedule. Henry could already recite the alphabet. Every letter!

"You go now," Jamyang urged. Apparently I'd been frozen in place. "Dash and I fine."

I knew I shouldn't be imposing my insecurities on my nanny, and especially not on my child, who'd hit every mark—sitting up, walking, holding a sippy cup—exactly on schedule. "Thank you," I said, and turned from her to Dash. "Give Mommy a kiss, sweet prince."

He giggled, touched his lips, and danced his fingers, miniatures of Xander's, in my direction. I quickly pressed my mouth to his rounded cheek and forced myself to walk out the front door, moving briskly in my flats. I wanted to present myself as a respectable young matron, an image I hoped was amplified by my yellow cardigan and pearls.

Jackson Collegiate School, five blocks from our home, was near the wide cobblestone promenade that overlooks the East River. For more than a hundred years, Brooklyn's finest, along with children who lived across the river in the Village, had begun their education here. The school, originally girls only, took up a row of six tall, matching brownstones connected like a chorus line of dignified spinsters.

I pushed open a heavy wrought-iron door and entered a wood-paneled hall heavily scented with lemon oil. The walls were hung with many portraits, mostly of tightly cinched, high-breasted women in buns and starched white collars. These ladies had been dead a hundred years, yet I could feel their narrowed eyes judge me as I walked toward a young redheaded man seated at the corridor's end. "Here for the open house?" he asked.

"Chloe Keaton. Please tell me it hasn't already started?"

He checked off my name on a list. "We're still waiting for all the parents," he said, and gestured. "Right this way."

I entered a room with a wide view of the Brooklyn Bridge, which stood like heavy black lace against the sky. As many as forty other parents—mommies and daddies, daddies and daddies, mommies and mommies—filled rows of straight-backed chairs. Xander had five minutes in which to arrive. While I looked for a seat toward the back, I heard a familiar voice stage-whisper from several rows in front of me.

"Chloe!" Talia was waving her hand like a traffic cop, forming the words "sit here" and leaning over Tom to tap an empty chair.

What was Talia doing here? She was supposed to be at our office today. I walked over to see my friends and showed them a smile as big as a poodle.

"Sit down," Talia said after the three of us kissed hello.

"I'm waiting for Xander," I said, seeing only one empty chair next to them. "I'll look for you during the tour." I couldn't bring myself to ask Talia why she hadn't mentioned that she'd be here. Preschool was a subject we'd been discussing since our breast-feeding days, but our conversations politely sashayed around specifics. I hadn't planned to admit—ever—that I'd hired a professional to guide me through the school application process. That was like confessing I needed to pay a personal shopper—Jules, for instance—to pick out my clothes. But there was more. I'd gotten the impression that Talia and Tom wanted to wait another year before enrolling Henry anywhere. "Does a four-year-old really need school?" had been her exact words just last week, which had shut me up fast. What surprised me more was, why Jackson Collegiate? Hadn't Tom and Talia made a commitment to public school, on account of Tom working, as he likes to say, "in the public sector"?

I didn't have to speak. Talia read my mind. "Tom's adviser at Columbia is married to the head of the lower school," she offered. "Her name's—"

"Betsy O'Neal," Tom said. "Her husband's my thesis adviser."

I kept my smile going while a thought snuck up like a burp. Was that the thesis Tom Wells had never finished, the one Talia complained about with regularity?

"Betsy nagged us to check out the school...," Talia said, and lifted her eyebrows ever so slightly to telegraph to me that she was a skeptic.

"Jackson's got a great reputation," I said. It was the most sought-after private school in Brooklyn, I'd learned from Hannah McCoy, and enrolled students from as far away as Gramercy Park and Chelsea.

"We'll be the judge of that." Talia laughed. "Let's see how they deliver the goods."

I wasn't used to feeling flummoxed around my best friend. Fortunately, I spotted Xander walking through the door. "Do you want to have coffee later?" I asked Talia.

"I have to get back to the office," she said. "There's a limit to how long a faked eye doctor appointment lasts."

"Then let's talk tonight," I said, and walked to the back of the room, where Xander had carefully folded his black overcoat over his arm as he found two chairs.

"What kept you?" I whispered when we were seated.

"I'm lucky I got here." He was slightly out of breath. "I have to leave in exactly an hour."

That hour fled. Dr. O'Neal introduced department heads and specialists—every witty one of them had spent summers running programs for children in third-world countries. Following the faculty rundown, we were treated to an a cappella choir singing Native American folk songs, a Dixieland band, and an abbreviated performance from *Swan Lake*, accompanied by a four-foot-tall string quartet playing Tchaikovsky. Only after Odette and Odile took their bows and the director introduced the mathletes did Dr. O'Neal lead the parent group—we must have totaled close to one hundred—around the school like a trail of tall, gawking geese.

I counted no more than sixteen children in each class, and faces of every hue, all sunny side up. Not one teacher appeared scary, burned out, or in need of immediate dental attention, and every classroom seemed to pulse with laughter and good health. I couldn't imagine a child here getting lice or, God forbid, fat.

"At Jackson Collegiate we have a historical emphasis on the arts," Dr. O'Neal said as we stepped inside a room filled with first graders painting at individual easels, "but we value all the disciplines—science, the humanities, and physical education, too."

"What sets Jackson apart?" Xander asked as we caught up to her. Talia wasn't far behind.

"What's most important here is building character," Dr. O'Neal said. "We try our best to cultivate authentic respect for one another."

I'd heard more or less the same speech from every director, but this was the first school where I felt that it might be true. Maybe here "nice" wasn't a dirty word left in the dust of "hi-ho, Harvard." This might be a school where Xander, Dash, and I would all fit in and make friends. I stayed close to him as we migrated back to the hall. "What do you think?" I whispered into his ear.

"I like it," he said. "I think I like it the best yet."

"Me too," I answered. As I gave his arm a squeeze I felt a tap on my shoulder.

"Wouldn't you have killed to have gone to a school like this?" Talia said, grinning. "Poetry on the walls, for God's sake."

"What about the science labs?" Xander said. "A sixth grader could cure cancer in there."

"And the library?" she said. "That's where I'd like to spend the whole afternoon."

Tom caught up to us. "Now do you see why Betsy's my idea of an educator?"

"It would be great if Henry and Dash could be in the same class," I gushed, and then felt embarrassed. Dr. O'Neal hadn't mentioned money—nobody did on these tours—but I'd read the fact sheet, and tuition was higher than at any other school we'd seen. What if Tom and Talia couldn't afford this school, which cost an arm and a leg and maybe a spleen? The four of us took seats, and Dr. O'Neal began to field questions.

"Do you give preference to brothers and sisters of current students?" the woman to the left of me asked.

"We believe in family traditions and give siblings every consideration," she said. "But unfortunately, we can't offer guarantees."

"Last year eighty percent of the class was siblings," a woman in back of me carped to no one in particular. "In vitro run amok—too many frigging twins."

"When do you introduce foreign languages?" asked a man in a white turban.

"Second grade," Dr. O'Neal said. "Spanish, French, Chinese, Japanese, Punjabi, Arabic, Hebrew, and Italian." Sports facilities, trips to museums, and religious education—there was none, unless you counted the history of Eastern spirituality—had all been covered by the time Tom asked, "What's your policy on scholarships?"

"We handle them case by case," Dr. O'Neal said, "but yes, we have resources for especially deserving students." Tom glanced at Talia. I couldn't see her face.

Finally the director called on Xander. "How many applications do you expect to receive this year?" he asked.

I couldn't miss her pride. "If last year is any indication, I'd say at least a thousand."

"How many spots are there?"

"In preschool, thirty-two."

These numbers could mean only one thing. If Dashiel McKenzie Keaton was to get into this school, his parents would have to play the game. The question was, how?

CHAPTER 10

Talia

Though I'd spent forty minutes wielding a blow dryer and a round brush, I was crowned with a halo of frizz: I looked like the love child of Botticelli's Venus and Tom Wolfe. The morning was, as my father might say, as hot as a Hasid in Haifa. My white linen suit was losing starch with each limping step.

In June Rittenhouse's waiting area, every chair was slick and uncomfortable; even the tall French tulips on the desk wore wires up their ass. Almost half an hour ticked away before I was ushered into a conference room fitted with a black marble table and two glass bottles of Evian. *Let the inquisition begin. I'm guilty, Detective. I confess to being here under false pretenses.*

Yet when the headhunter entered the room, she was apologetic for the delay as well as refreshingly wrinkled. With more sense than I had, June Rittenhouse had pulled her hair into a chignon, although I could see the real deal was as kinked as my own. This made me like her. "Happy to meet you, Ms. Fisher-Wells," she said, shaking my hand. "Have a chair. I've looked over your résumé, and you've accomplished quite a lot."

I wondered if at this point I was expected to display humble gratitude for a compliment or was supposed to brag about my incomparable qualifications. I stuck with "Thank you."

"All right, let's start. What do you consider your greatest accomplishment?" She stared into my eyes so intently I would have backed away if it wouldn't have suggested that her breath might be less than minty fresh. Faking sanity at work when Henry hadn't slept through the previous night? Getting my mother-in-law, Abigail Wells, the great-great-great-granddaughter of austere New England preachers, to tolerate me? Those were accomplishments. But what I said was, "It had to be the time we had only twenty-four hours to pitch Odor-Eaters and my approach nailed a multimillion-dollar account." I narrated my story with beguiling anecdotes augmented with numerical flourishes, and watched the woman take notes as I silently lamented that my life's work had been dedicated to training people to be spendthrifts.

"Do you prefer to work alone or as part of a team?"

Tricky. Was the job in question—if there was a real job at stake—for freelance consulting ("I work best independently, preferably on the tundra for months on end") or a traditional inside position ("I'm a team player and love to brainstorm endlessly with witless morons who grab credit for my ideas")? "Actually, I'm one of those people who swings both ways," I said, and gave examples of star performances on both the autonomous and Ms. Congeniality fronts.

She offered a cryptic "Aha," asked a few more easy questions, and then said, "For the right position, Ms. Fisher-Wells—"

"Talia."

"Talia, would you relocate?"

"I wish I could tell you the answer is yes," I admitted, "but my husband's a teacher and we're committed to staying here because of his job, although I could imagine a position in, say, New Jersey or Westchester."

"Where does your husband teach?"

"James Madison in Brooklyn."

"No!" She beamed. "I can't believe it. My housekeeper's son is a student there. What's your husband's name?"

"Thomas Wells."

"You're Mr. *Wells*' wife?" she said, as awed as if I'd just revealed that Tom was in line for the English throne.

"That would be me."

"I can't begin to tell you what a godsend Mr. Wells is, the way he's been tutoring José for the SATs and how he started that basketball team. He's all I heard about last year."

Me too.

"It would be a crime if your family left Brooklyn," she said, and once again beamed her freakish astral stare in my direction. *This interview is over,* I thought, but she seemed to be revved up for more. "I wanted to see you about two different positions. Obviously, the Cincinnati job isn't right for you, but there's this small agency in Tribeca. My client needs someone with particular flair in fashion and home decorating, and he hopes to branch out into travel and wine and spirits."

No personal hygiene sprays? No anticoagulants for tragically clogged pipes?

"Does this interest you, given your strong background in packaged goods?"

Well married as I might be, I had no background in any of the glittering specialties she'd mentioned. Chloe did, I couldn't help thinking, which was why someone had recommended her for the spot. Still, I had the temerity to say, "I'd be very interested. I've reached the stage where I need a different challenge and the idea of a new company sounds..." I searched for a fashion-forward adjective. All I could come up with was *dynamic*, a word that was anything but that.

"Fair enough. The next step is for you to prepare a sample account pitch. Everything you need to know is here." She handed me a computer disc. "Would a week be enough time?"

"I have a big assignment due in three weeks at work," I lied. "Could we stretch it a bit?"

Her unblinking stare reappeared. "Two weeks from today, then," she said in the spirit of a woman not used to negotiating, and stood up, ready to shake hands as my cell phone rang.

"I'm so sorry," I said. "I forgot to turn this off."

She chuckled. "You'd better take the call—maybe it's your husband."

The saint? "Oh, it's not important," I said. I recognized the Norah Jones ring tone and snapped off the phone. It was Chloe.

. . .

The next morning, the phone rang about ten o'clock. "Did I vake you, sveetheart?" Since she'd moved to this country at fifteen, Mira Fisher had lived four blocks from the Pacific Ocean, yet her Zsa Zsa accent clung like glaze on Sacher torte.

"No, Mommy. Henry and I have been up for hours," I said.

"How's that grandson of mine?"

As I recited Henry's CV—his exploding vocabulary, the way he fearlessly climbed the Everest of a playground slide, and how he willingly ate jicama—the longing for my mother became so great I felt she was almost in the room, her hazel eyes twinkling unconditional approval. Tom may be the world's best husband, but no one on earth will ever love me as fiercely as my mother. It's what females in our family do. Bubbe, who lives with my parents, is no different. Lioness ladies, Tom calls them.

"Has Chloe come back to vork? Have you gotten a break? I vorry about you."

I cautiously considered my next few words. "Everything's good, Mommy. I just might have another opportunity—a very good one."

"Shhahh," she said, and puh-puh-puh'd as if an incantation could blow away the evil eye. For women in our family superstition is the true religion, to which we adhere far more than any everyday practice of Judaism. The way we throw salt over our left shoulder, you'd think the three of us were living on a dirt road near Anatevka, peeing in a pot and plucking chickens. Even Tom, as High Church as they come, has learned to say *kinehora*, a reverse curse I taught him to spit out whenever someone speaks of the auspicious. If you don't say it, then *ukh un vey*—tough tooties. Your good luck just got deported to Siberia.

"If there's good news, you'll be the first to know, believe me," I said.

The bond between my mother and me is nothing less than symbiotic. We dwell in each other's heart like pacemakers that activate hope and optimism. I know Quincy grieves for her own mom, who died of Alzheimer's. Chloe seems terrified by her swizzle stick of a mother up in Connecticut, and Jules bitches about her ma, who, when she's not plastered, has her hand out for money. Neither of these last two women is a perfect maternal specimen, yet why can't my friends fix whatever was wrong? These are their *mothers*. I am completely intolerant.

When I graduated from Wesleyan—Xander wasn't the only scholarship kid—I decided to try New York. I predicted that when I told them, my parents might impale themselves with grief. But Mira and Sam Fisher's strategy was to give me time to come to my senses, assuming that after a season or two of gray skies and maxed-out subways, I'd miss the beach and, yes, our *ganze mishpacha*, our whole family.

What they hadn't counted on was my goy boy. No Fisher could believe that Tom and I would last. But since the morning after the first time we slept together I would never look at another man. My family also hadn't expected me to ditch marine biology and announce that I absolutely had to move to Manhattan, not only because Tom planned to land there after a year in England but because that was where you went to be a book editor, which I'd suddenly decided I wanted to become.

That I fell into advertising instead is a short story. The first interview I went on was at a magazine's promotion department, as close to book publishing as I could get. Where most of my friends had to sweat landing a job, I was hired on the spot and moved up the ladder with such shameful constancy that I lost my incentive to become the next Max Perkins holding the hand of my generation's F. Scott Fitzgerald. Copywriting was too easy—yak, yak, yak, talking on paper. From magazine copywriting I switched to advertising.

"Tell me about the job as soon as you know something, promise, *bubbele?*" my mother was saying, pulling me back to now.

"I promise. Now can I say hi to Daddy?"

"He's at *shul.*"

Of course. He'd be at the morning *minyan* in a boardwalk synagogue ten steps away from the tattoo parlors supported by Valley teenagers. "Give him a kiss for me. Tell him Henry adores the book you sent."

"That's all you vanted to do as a girl, you vith your nose in a book. Ve knew you'd be a writer."

I'm horrified to think that my mother considers me Joan Didion, but I've given up on correcting her. "Bye, Mommy. I love you."

"I love you, too, my darlink." She hung up, and I closed my eyes as I ticked off the months—too many—before my parents' next visit. I've stopped suggesting that they move to the East Coast, because for all their Old World habits, they're Angelenos hooked on a balmy climate. And Tom would sooner relocate to Tanzania than spend more than one week per year in southern California, where he's convinced that topic A is invariably how long it takes to drive from B to C and why that time has, year by year, increased exponentially.

I returned to my laptop to punch up verbs on the two paragraphs I'd written on June Rittenhouse's pitch.

"What are you doing?" Tom said as he wandered into the bedroom. He was, according to my preferences, in sex symbol mode, wearing a clean white T-shirt and faded jeans. I considered stopping my work—then reconsidered. Henry's naps had become abbreviated, and by tonight I'd be brain-dead from how that child answered every conversational bounce with another question.

"Sorry," I said, returning my eyes to the screen. "I'm working."

"On what?"

"No big deal. I had an appointment with a headhunter and she gave me an assignment," I tossed off, although it did feel like a big deal. I hate to lose—arguments, poker, face.

"A headhunter called you out of the blue?" We both knew the

subtext—*as if that would ever happen to me.* The likelihood of Tom's being solicited for a better position was, on a scale of 1 to 10, maybe a 2, largely because he'd never look for his luck. If only I could amputate half of my competitive edge and donate it to him like a kidney.

"The headhunter called the office," I said, skipping over the fact that she'd asked for Chloe. I tried not to think about that part, though this time Mean Maxine and I agreed. We knew we were wrong.

I also realized the reason I hadn't told my mother about the head-hunter meeting was because she'd have said, *You stole an opportunity from your best friend? I didn't raise a daughter to be a goniff,* followed by an icy coast-to-coast pause. I couldn't reveal that I felt my possible stroke of professional and thus financial good fortune was *beshert*—fated—and that I needed to stalk it to help my family. This would have led to a diatribe on why I wanted *more* when I should be satisfied with *enough.* My mother would never believe that even if my salary tripled, our Fisher-Wells ways would still be far from extravagant by the standards of this city, where—despite rumblings about a recession—cramped apartments with papery walls sold for enormous sums and yearly tuition for private preschool cost 30 percent more than my parents' Prius. I'd have a hard time defending myself without diminishing Tom, and explaining the whole June Rittenhouse thing to him would be worse. I wanted to stay ethically chaste in my husband's eyes, which missed nothing.

"What's going on with you?" he said. "You look tense."

"I'm trying to concentrate on this before Henry gives up on his nap." I knew I sounded snappish.

"In that case, I'll hunker down with my concubine, *The New York Times Book Review.* Anything you need?"

Need? No. Want? Lots.

CHAPTER 11

Chloe

"Cookie!"

The name took me back to when I was fourteen, with a concave chest and an acute case of perm.

"Arthur!" I said, tucking the phone under my chin and continuing to pack. The trip to Maine was a week away, but I've always liked to be prepared. Would I need thermals? A flannel nightgown? I'd already laid in a substantial supply of insect repellant, with and without DEET. Lyme disease is everywhere.

"I've been meaning to call," he said. Arthur Weiner always speaks at fortissimo. I put down the piles of clothes and moved the receiver away from my ear. "For two reasons—but first, how's the captain of industry?"

"Xander's fine, thanks."

"And how are you, Cookie?"

"Remember? I'm Chloe now." I sounded sharper than I intended. "Please." I walked to my closet. Hiking boots? One of those shiny yellow sou'westers that ties under the chin? I could speed-order one.

"Giving a lot of tea parties, are we? Are you old enough to be a Chloe?"

Before I had a chance to earnestly report my age he said, "Shit, do younger people have birthdays, too? What does that make me? Anyway, I've been meaning to say thanks for setting me up with your friend. What a broad."

"Jules mentioned you'd hit it off." *Even though you call her a broad.*

"Smart as Oprah. A lady in the living room, a whatever in the bedroom. Always a step ahead, if you get my drift."

Unfortunately, I did.

"Yeah, we're totally on the same wavelength. You did good, kid."

Right out of college, after I stopped temping, Arthur Weiner had been my first boss. If it weren't for him, I wouldn't be in advertising—he's excellent at what he does, including teaching me how to write decent copy. I'd hesitated before introducing him to Jules, though—my idea of attractive is not a man unaware of his own nose hair. But last December during our annual holiday lunch at a coffee shop near our old office, Arthur had started to get personal. Not coming-on personal, though I'm not sure I could tell; Talia regularly informs me that men are flirting when I take hello for strictly hello. Over grilled cheese sandwiches, he'd started describing how a woman he was living with had broken up with him and moved out. At first I got the feeling that he was in mourning for the premium cable channels she'd paid for that he'd watched on her fifty-two-inch HDTV. Then he said, almost as if he were talking to himself, "I don't know why I always wind up alone. I know how to treat a lady. I don't want to be fifty and every night opening up cans, eating dinner in my underwear." After I shook away that image, I realized I was touched. Arthur was lonesome, though if I was doing the math right, he was already fifty.

This happened not long after Ted, who was eight years younger than Jules, had left for Maui with a suitcase full of aloha shirts. Even though I wouldn't have called Jules lonely—her calendar has always been so jammed I imagine her penciling in time to pee—why should she be alone? Impulsively, I gave Arthur her number. I wasn't sure if he'd call, if she'd agree to have even a glass of wine with him, or if she'd be angry after she did. But I've never gotten chemistry. What made me go for Xander? I'll save that one for a therapist, should I ever decide to see one.

"You're absolutely welcome. I'm glad you two . . ." Hooked up? That's for teenagers. "Clicked. I hope you're having fun."

"Fun? She's a one-woman Mardi Gras, that Jules. Comes up with out-of-the-way restaurants."

Even I knew that, when applied to New York City, *out-of-the-way* translates to *cheap*, and I started to remember Arthur's legendary stinginess. My going-away present from him had been an ashtray engraved with the logo of the Ritz-Carlton at Half Moon Bay, and the last Christmas gift he'd given me had been a coffee mug courtesy of the Diorissimo account. When Dash was born, Arthur sent him a onesie with a Coppertone illustration, still in the press kit.

I pressed the phone to my ear again and threw in beach shoes. I wanted to get my clothes together before Dash and Jamyang returned, so we could all eat lunch. I needed alone time with Dash and planned to show him the hand puppets I'd bought—the surgeon was my favorite. I should have told Arthur I'd call him back, but he kept jabbering.

"Did you hear the coup de grâce?" he whooped.

Coop de what? "I don't think so."

"Jules found a drop-dead-gorgeous apartment for me. Pulled it right out of her ass."

"Where is it?" I said absentmindedly. The red bathing suit was there, as was the one with pink polka dots, but the blue one that made me look as if I had curves in the right places? Nowhere. "Tell me about the apartment," I said, half listening. Was I coming off as disinterested as I felt, I who almost fell asleep when Xander tried to explain a two-tiered stock structure?

"Ask your friend to tell you. All I'll say is, the co-op's under my nose, so to speak."

I spotted my blue swimsuit, tangled in a pile of sarongs. *Should I bring a few of those, or would sweatshirts be better?* "Didn't you tell me you were calling for two reasons?"

"Of course," he said. "Almost forgot. Getting old, Chloe." He dragged out my name as if he were a French professor introducing a new word. "What I wondered was, have you heard from a headhunter, my friend June Rittenhouse?"

"No, it doesn't sound familiar."

"That's strange. I gave her the lead weeks ago, but I've been dealing with this apartment crap. Slipped my mind to tell you."

Arthur, always a scorekeeper, wanted credit for the good deed, I realized. "I've been busy, too," I said, "hiring and training a new nanny." I waited for him to run with that subject. He didn't.

"The position's a plum. Brand-new agency with accounts up your alley—fashion, fragrance, decorating, restaurants. You could write their copy in your sleep, and like I always say, one good deed begets another," he said. "Besides, there's something in it for me if you get placed."

I heard Jamyang's keys in the front door. "Got to go—I'll let you know if I hear from that headhunter. Thanks again, and good luck with Jules. I'm happy for both of you!"

"Get yourself hired, Cookie, and we'll be even." With that, finally, he hung up.

Maybe I should *try to switch jobs, to get Xander off my back,* I thought. When I spoke to Talia, I'd ask her about the call. That is, if the woman had indeed called. It was entirely possible that she'd yessed Arthur simply to get him off her back and had never even written down my name.

Just then a small voice drifted upstairs. "Mommy!" Dash shouted. "Mommy!"

Arthur was right. I did want a tea party. I wanted it all!

CHAPTER 12

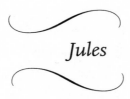

Jules

I was finishing my manicure. The polish was new, the screaming coral of a lobster—ideal for Maine. *He loves me,* I thought as I layered on a final stroke. *He loves me not. And does it matter when we're having sex?* It has become a feminine truth, all but universally acknowledged, that it does, but a long time ago I decided it didn't. My ma lusted after the scumbag who was my pop, and where had it gotten her? Broke, mean, bitter,

Arthur strutted out of my bedroom on his sturdy, slightly bowed legs. Was he good in bed? Good enough. I've discovered that when I'm with a man, I have to be the belle of my own ball, which is one of Jules' Rules every woman should follow way before she's my age: pushing forty. Well, forty-two. Okay, closer to forty-three, which no one knows and no one will. It's not as if I have to worry about ma revealing my true date of birth, which I suspect she's forgotten, and since I didn't graduate from college, I'm at no risk of being outed by some casting director's dogged cyber-search.

"Doll," Arthur said, "what do you say to another bouncy-bouncy?"

Arthur, who should know better than to keep his driver's license in plain view—in his wallet, if we're getting technical—is also older than he claims, which is perhaps why he takes such pride in being endowed with an extraordinary supply of self-generated Cialis. Generally, I applaud a partner who can give it three times in a go. Just not today.

"No can do," I informed Arthur. "I have an audition." *At four-thirty, hours from now.*

A friend who teaches early childhood development once informed me that a human being's core personality changes only slightly past the age of four. I see the same thing in relationships, counted by weeks. By the end of one month as a couple, patterns become etched as deeply as, in my case, the crevices bracketing my mouth. Arthur and I were three months past that crucial marker. I knew that another naked happy hour would lead to me making a large, late lunch. On this particular Saturday, if I succumbed, it would be hard to pry myself away before the president of the co-op board stopped by for Bloody Marys. Arthur had invited him for two o'clock.

I was already more immersed than I cared to be in the cloak-and-dagger tactics of Arthur's real estate caper, though here, too, I admired the man's tenacity. It was clear that fanged Fran despised Arthur, yet he refused to let it deter him. Where the vaunted apartment was concerned, Arthur kept burrowing in deeper, displaying either—my jury was out on this point—his fatal flaw or his fatal charm. I fully recognize that to some Arthur comes across as insufferable. On the other hand, he has stubborn determination—a cousin to loyalty, which in my experience is a virtue in short supply and of crucial importance. Anyone who's met my family need not be Freud to question why.

I suspect that if I truly gave myself to Arthur, he'd be mine forever, someone I could count on years from now when the two of us had migrated to a gated community midway between Boca and Fort Lauderdale. I could see us gazing at the ocean through misty bifocals, he complimenting me on the nice piece of veal I'd roasted for dinner. Still, hanging out with the co-op board president today would be too much. When Arthur mentioned it I said no.

"Jules," he pleaded, "he's bringing the missus. You can't let me down now."

Watch me, I thought. "An audition is work." I'd walked into the bathroom, my silky red robe tied loosely, exposing enviable cleavage. My body mass index might fly above average, but the girls are so high and round that in a ladies' locker room I've caught women gawking, and more than once I've been accosted by an underendowed female wanting the name of my surgeon. "Dr. DNA," I like to boast. My tits are the only good thing my family ever gave me, and I frequently deploy these airbags to prevent accidents from happening.

"Can't you blow it off?" he asked. "Besides, I've never heard of an audition on a Saturday afternoon."

"It's off-Broadway." New Jersey, to be exact. "It could be a good part." *The Taming of the Shrew.* I was shooting for you-know-who.

Arthur rested his hands on my hips and looked at me intensely. Barefoot, I was only inches shorter than he. His eyes, one of his better features, are the color of whiskey, and as I looked into them, I saw need. I like to be needed. But even more, I like to be begged. "Yes?" I said, pitching my voice slightly beyond purr.

"Please," he answered, as he fingered the top of the red rose tattoo two inches above my left nipple. "I'm counting on you. Don't you want me to get this apartment?"

The answer to that question was blocked by a brain blizzard. In an ideal world, my friend Quincy wouldn't have been dumb enough to sing like a canary about this fucktabulous apartment, thus putting me in the position of having to decide whether or not to tell Arthur about it. But with the wheels in motion, careening toward a crash, my heart—beating under the tattoo—told me I needed to support Arthur. He was, at least for the moment, my man, a commodity far scarcer than an apartment.

"If you insist," I said, and leaned forward to kiss my frog, my Ratty, my

Art the Fart, who played a mean game of online Scrabble and loathed punk rock as much as I did. In some ways, we were a team. Besides, I might be able to make the audition if I beat the hell out of his place by three. "But you'll owe me."

"Consider it marked in my ledger," he answered after an exceedingly long, wet smooch.

"Have you shopped for this party you're throwing?"

"I stopped by a deli yesterday."

"Show me." I prayed that he'd sprung for some rich, bloomy cheese— I was salivating for a triple-crème cow's milk Savarin—along with pâté and cornichons. He pointed to a small plastic tub of hummus, some poly-bagged pita, and a half-eaten Gruyère, dry and small as a child's block, along with a few stalks of flaccid celery. This was how he intended to knock the socks off El Presidente. "You're kidding, right?"

"What, not enough?"

I considered this a teachable moment and scribbled a list—milk, butter, flour, eggs, and fully erect celery. "Go immediately to the Koreans on Columbus and get everything here along with three bouquets of roses, whatever color looks freshest."

"Three?"

"For Christ's sake, they cost eight dollars a dozen. Can you say 'investment'?"

An hour later, a circle of pastry was puffing to perfection, and Arthur had returned from the next-door neighbor, who had lent him four Baccarat bar glasses. Lacking an alternative, I let him keep his napkins, which featured a tomato wearing a sombrero. The doorbell buzzed.

"Welcome," Arthur said, ushering in a tall, stooped gent and his gnocchi-shaped wife. I stepped forward and extended a freshly mani-cured hand. Yes, Clambake was a fine shade. I caught the guy staring down at my boobs and praised the Lord for inventing clingy V-necks. "Julia," I said. "Arthur's friend." God only knows how Arthur might introduce me.

"Basil Worthington, and may I present my wife, Maude." He looked around Arthur's living room. "You know, I've never been in this line. We're in the front."

We knew.

"It's not as dark as I thought," he added, noticing a square foot of light filtering in from windows that faced the side street. The glass, I noted, could use a good Windexing.

"But not as sunny as the apartment where I'd love to live," Arthur said, and, for no explicable reason, laughed.

"Ah, a man who gets to the point," Basil Worthington replied. "Let's talk about that."

And so we did.

CHAPTER 13

Talia

Tom's parents' place looked both better and worse than I expected. From a distance, the gabled cottage appeared to be ripped from the cover of a weeper novel. Only when you crossed the home's threshold did the dreamy mood collapse like rotted wood. First there was the color scheme, burnt-toast brown and, for a splash of color, rust. Picture a lawn mower left out all summer in the rain.

Mildew filled my lungs. I was glad that at least, unlike my apartment, none of the windows was sealed shut, perhaps because no one had liberated a paintbrush here for years. I raised each sash and let the evening breeze blow through the rooms, ruffling decades of Wells ephemera. Ancient birthday cards, dog-eared Sears catalogues, and flyers for long-past regattas sat cheek by jowl with *Reader's Digest* condensed books. A cracked leather-bound copy of the *Iliad* peeked out of the cubbyhole of a rolltop desk. If I'd had the time to thoroughly snoop, I'd surely have uncovered a stock certificate or two, perhaps from 1929.

But I didn't have time. The next day's docket was dusting and bed making interrupted by scrubbing, shopping, and pest eradication. These are tasks at which I proudly excel. By late afternoon the house looked at least *haimish*, with the season's last roses cut and opening in jelly jars. To reward myself, I took a swim, and recovered a ten-dollar bill visible on the lake's sandy bottom. Afterward I sat on the dock and popped open a frosty bottle of beer from the premier microbrewery of Portland.

As the sun set, I dried off and walked back to the house. Fortified by a mild buzz, I dialed home. After Tom reminded me, again, why no one fond of hot water should risk taking a shower in his parents' place that lasted longer than three minutes, he read me the first draft of the Jackson Collegiate application essay he was composing about Henry.

"You don't think you should take it down a notch?" Within the allotted 250 words, he'd managed to tout Henry as deft, discerning, and keen. "Because a kid knows how to push a DVD into a slot doesn't mean he's going to invent the next Microsoft."

"I want to do him justice."

Every set of parents would be turning in a required written snapshot of their child. "I know this is war, but Henry isn't a video game for intellectuals," I said. "You're presenting him like a superior brand of toilet paper."

"That's something I thought you'd understand." I replayed Tom's tone to test for sarcasm. I'd heard what I'd heard.

"Could you add some humor, maybe? We aren't gunning for MIT."

"Would you rather write it?"

I would, even with the deadline for June Rittenhouse's project already hitting me between the eyes like a badminton birdie. "How about if you fax it tomorrow and I'll give it a try?" In this house I was lucky I'd found a can opener, but there must be a fax machine somewhere in town. "I'll call you back with a number."

· · ·

Quincy arrived a day before the others. She'd driven up from Boston, where crazy Maizie, rehab grad, was performing. As she walked toward the house, balancing several grocery bags, two skinny baguettes obscured her face. Silhouetted against the sun, they appeared to stick out of her head like antennae—Quincy Blue, extraterrestrial, impossibly beautiful, and I'm not sure she even knows it. Her tanned legs stretched long in cutoffs. This I especially envied, since my skin stays as permanently milky as chowder, another reason I had needed to abandon southern California.

I let myself out through the back porch and practically skipped down the stone path. Now that she'd arrived, the R&R could commence.

"I'd have been here twenty minutes ago, but I had to wait for a turtle to cross the road," she shouted.

"Then you met our closest neighbor," I answered as we hugged and I took the bags. They were promisingly heavy. "You made good time."

"Particularly considering I brake for antiques stores. Remind me to show you my clam basket and the Bakelite I got for nine bucks." She was speaking at full gallop, which Quincy does only when excited. "And my taxidermy. What's a home without its own raccoon?"

"Is this all for your new apartment?" I asked.

The grin on Quincy's face switched off. She put down the bag in her arms and pulled out her cell phone. "That reminds me, I need to make a call."

"Good luck with reception," I said as I left her outside. "It comes and goes here, not unlike the sun."

I carried the bags to the kitchen and began unpacking. Miniature croissants, seven-grain bread, a five-dollar jar of mustard, that expensive sweet cream butter, plums, nectarines, olives, almonds, bottles of pinot grigio, and—appropriately enough—quince jam. I was putting the wine in the refrigerator when Quincy walked into the kitchen and sat at the Formica table, an upgrade from when Abigail and Big Tom pledged their troth to Walmart. I'd put out sugar cookies from the best and only bakery in town and tall glasses of cold lemonade, made the way Abigail had taught me, with plenty of sugar syrup and juice from real lemons. Quincy pressed her glass to her forehead before she dug two pills out of her bag and gulped them. She finished her drink in nonstop swallows and looked around.

"Can I steal that cuckoo clock?" She'd recovered her smile.

"I'd like to smack it. It's come here to die." I loved that Quincy was the first to arrive. I didn't see enough of her alone, and she's a woman who listens and weighs what you say. "After you're settled in, I thought we'd drive to town, pick up donuts for breakfast, then go for lobster." I grabbed her duffel. "Come."

At the top of the landing, Quincy stopped to study a densely hung collection of family pictures: Tom and his sisters and brothers celebrating summer by sailing, canoeing, napping in hammocks, climbing trees, roasting hot dogs on sticks, and holding up fish longer than their arms. In the corner I spotted a new addition, Henry waddling on the beach, his face obscured by a large straw hat, a shovel in one chubby paw and the other grasping Tom's hand. I saw Quincy look at the picture, poised to say *aw.*

"Theoretically, you have your choice of bedrooms," I said, not wanting to linger at this shrine to family fecundity, "but don't get too excited." I led her to the front room on the second floor. "This is where I'd thought you'd stay—it's got a view of what we call a beach." I pointed to a moonscape of black rocks. "I figured, given Chloe's habits, you'd be happiest here." Chloe requires postapocalyptic darkness and a white-noise machine, and even then she often spends hours each night reading. She's no one's idea of a roommate. "You could share with Jules." The room had two frilly canopied double beds, yet Quincy didn't even walk to the window to look at the sea before she said, "Let's see the other bedroom."

It was half the size, with a single bed. She stretched out and slowly sank. "I don't think so," she said.

"There's one more bed, out on the sleeping porch. If it turns cold you'll freeze your tush off, but one thing we're not short of here is blankets."

"Show me." We walked across the landing and I pushed open the screen door.

"I love it," she said, though I wasn't sure what there was to love: the bed and view were far better in the big room. Yet she staked her claim by dumping her duffel on the floor.

Quincy's decision puzzled me for the rest of the afternoon, while we took a swim and planned menus for the next few days. I waited for her to explain. She didn't. I decided to take it to the next level, trying first my version of subtlety. "Hey, maybe I was imagining it, but when we were together a few weeks ago there seemed to be some friction between you and Jules." She ducked it. Later, at the lobster pound, I, Talia the assault weapon, fired point-blank. "What the fuck is going on with you and Jules?"

"I don't know what you're talking about," she said.

I jabbered about Henry, which carried us through dessert. We drove home and changed into our pajamas, but I wasn't tired. The air was too sticky, the crickets too vociferous, and my psyche too worried about when I'd get around to rewriting the essay about Henry along with June Rittenhouse's project. I'd started the pitch five times, but each attempt sounded like dreck. I was getting more agitated at the house, which made me even less capable of finding an edgy tone.

"What do you say I open some wine?" I asked.

"I'd say pour," Quincy answered.

I pulled out a sauvignon blanc. I wouldn't know if it was flinty or fleshy, only that it was ice cold and cost less than ten dollars at Trader Joe's. We sat side by side in the screened porch off the front of the house, the bottle between us on a rickety wicker table next to a flickering citronella candle. I'd poured us each a second glass before I worked up my nerve. "I have to talk to you," I said.

"I thought that's what we were doing."

"I'm feeling guilty about something."

"It'd better be good." Her tone was lilting and mischievous, as if she was expecting to hear that I was running off to London with Eliot, my married boss. I turned to her. Her symmetrical face, with its elegant, narrow nose, was framed by shaggy hair she cuts herself. I've always liked that Quincy doesn't take herself too seriously, nor is she quick to judge. I wouldn't be able to have this conversation with Jules, who would give me advice before I'd even uttered a clause.

The words stuck, suddenly, in my throat. Friends don't steal friends' jobs, especially when the friends are going to start a four-day love fest. I wanted to talk about how I was sandbagging Chloe, but I didn't know this Talia, and couldn't explain her, with or without Mean Maxine translating. Quincy was pinning me down with her cat eyes. I defaulted to the misdemeanor. "Tom wants to pull all sorts of strings to get Henry into private school."

"That's what you're feeling guilty about?" She scrunched up her face. "Yay, Tom. If I had a child..." Here she took a long, audible breath. "I'd want him to go every summer to these obscenely expensive camps they have up here and, of course, the best possible school."

"It's not only that I feel like a phony trying to get my kid into a private school, a school that, by the way, we can't afford." I squirmed. Even this was harder than I thought. "Chloe and Xander want the same school for Dash, and...there aren't many spots. We're competing against them."

She refilled our glasses. "Who says you're competing? Maybe both boys will get in."

Quincy had no reason to be familiar with the evil politics of private schools. "Or not. Let's say Dash gets in and Henry doesn't. I think I'd despise Chloe, or at least Tom might."

Quincy took some time before she spoke. "You think it's Henry who will get in, not Dash, and Chloe will be crushed."

I would never second that out loud, but Henry is older than Dash and Tom and I are fairly certain he might be the world's most brilliant child, even if I'm too superstitious to admit this. I shrugged.

"These things happen all the time, friends going against friends." Quincy smirked—yes, that's what it was—then broke into an unreadable chortle.

"I don't want to go against Chloe," I, the towering hypocrite, proclaimed.

"You two should be able to discuss this."

My chutzpah kicked in. "Like you could chat girl to girl with Jules about whatever it was that made you all twitchy when we had dinner in Westport?"

For the next twenty minutes Quincy spilled out an annotated play-by-play. If I was following her, she'd found an apartment so perfect it sounded airbrushed. "After seeing almost fifty apartments, when I walked into this place it felt absolutely like home." Idiotically, she'd blathered to Jules about it, and Jules blabbed to her boyfriend. "She's betrayed me. No ethics." Now Arthur, whom I'd yet to meet but already despised, was, with Jules' help, scheming to grab the place away from the Blues, though Quincy and Jake had put down a deposit on it. "He's trying to break our contract."

There was considerable detail to take in at one-thirty in the morning, especially for someone not acquainted with the customs of buying apartments, but I got the central plot. When Quincy finished, she sat back in her chair and closed her eyes. I thought she might be trying not to cry.

"I can't believe this," I said stupidly. "It doesn't sound like Jules." Not the Julia de Marco I thought I knew, who usually repaid friends with a high rate of interest.

"I assure you, I am not making any of this up."

I could hear the hurt in Quincy's voice. It was going to be a *long* long weekend.

CHAPTER 14

Chloe

In the morning I headed to Maine. I parked my SUV in Westport, where we switched to Jules' new Mini Cooper, a convertible so compact and golden it was like riding in one of the minaudières I see women casually toss on the tables at charity dinners. Jules and I took turns driving and, as usual, she was prepared, not only with a thermos of strong coffee and shortcuts but with rock mixes—classic, indie, alternative. The two of us were harmonizing with Feist when Arthur's name spontaneously combusted. "That fucking Arthur" were her exact words as she looked at her cell phone.

"Excuse me?" I said.

"The dickhead just texted a list of things I should buy for him up in Maine. Lobster Newburg, cranberry chutney, Maypo, and that revolting canned brown bread. Can't he find his way to a grocery store?"

"Maybe he misses you and it's his way of showing he cares."

"Did I not tell you to cut the crap if we were going to be stuck together for seven hours?" This was said with love.

"Tell me honestly, are you cursing the day I gave him your name?"

"Dollface, you did good," Jules said. "I'm only cursing myself." She paused. A mile later, after I thought the topic was dead, she started up again. "When Arthur pulls something like this I want to shoot back with my own list—of his faults. Except I know that the moment I hit send I'll get all 'Julia Maria, you've been dating for almost thirty years, and who've you found who's better?'" She was mimicking her nonna. "'Don't give up on this one, not yet. In the long run, will you turn out any less happy with Arturo than with George Clooney, who, if you haven't noticed, isn't returning your calls?'"

I had to ask, because we'd had this conversation before. "Why talk yourself into a guy?"

Jules glanced at me with a look close to pity. "I appreciate the sisterly support, but have you checked out my ass lately? Each cheek's the size of a pizza pan. What makes you think Arthur isn't settling for me?"

Behind closed doors, I suspect, Jules has a sensuality men can't get enough of, but I think every bad boyfriend she's ever had, along with her mother and father, is living inside her, rent free. "I'm not buying it. You're going to have to convince me."

Two exits and a long Eric Clapton set passed before she tried. "For the record, I do admire many things about Arthur. Number one, he needs managing, and I am a born manager. Two, at least half the time I laugh with him, not at him. Three, he's smart, which I assume you must know, since he used to be your boss. Four, he isn't a drunk, an actor, or a drunk actor. Five, he's straight, and six, he doesn't need Viagra. Seven, he's not a divorced daddy with nose-ringed teenagers whom I'd hate as much as they'd hate me. Eight, neither is he a politician or athlete, whose job description apparently includes philanderer. Nine, he hears me when I call him on his bullshit, and ten, the most important reason of all, he calls me on mine. I've run out of fingers. Shall I go on?"

"Tell me one thing, do you find any of this romantic?" Jules had overlooked what I consider the most crucial element of any couple.

She howled. "Chloe, my child, do *I* look like a romantic?"

"Seriously, in this century, what constitutes romance?"

"Please tell me the answer is you. I don't want to be completely disillusioned."

I cannot deny I had a wedding as old-fashioned as a petticoat. Jules, Quincy, and Talia used to own the pink seersucker bridesmaid dresses to prove it until Jules sold all three to a cousin. Xander—or at least his secretary—occasionally sends me flowers, but I have to admit what goes on between the two of us now often feels less like a date than a board meeting, where the primary goal of the chairman—that would be Xander—is to make sure we're running at a profit. Talia and Tom? I'm guessing what connects them comes from mutual respect and chemistry—I doubt Talia would anoint herself with a word like *romantic*. Quincy and Jake seem to be content to spend an enormous amount of time alone together, which I count as romantic, but might simply be because they don't have a child: the Blues versus the world.

"I'll say this in Arthur's defense—he recommended me for a job."

"See?" Jules said as she tapped her temple. "Did I not say he was smart? Comes off generous and costs him zilch."

I chose not to add that he'd implied he would receive a finder's fee if I got hired.

"Did I miss something, by the way?" she asked. "I didn't know you even were interested in changing jobs."

"I'd go on an interview if I was called. Change is good, right?" Which I absolutely don't believe. I hate change, which, in my experience, is terrifying. I drove a few more miles before I added, "The job's through a headhunter and I haven't actually gotten called yet."

"*If* the headhunter even exists." Jules laughed. "Arthur's seventy percent hot air."

Soon it was her turn to drive, and apparently I nodded off, because "We're almost here" were the next words I heard, while Jules shook my arm. "Chloe, wake up or you'll miss Mayberry."

I blinked. We were apparently floating in a music video for a patriotic country-and-western song. American flags flapped in front of small clapboard houses. Large, hairy dogs wandered unleashed. Kids were riding bikes and running through sprinklers. A few enterprising girls with braids had set up a stand selling whoopie pies.

"Stop!" I shouted.

"No can do. We're an hour behind schedule." We continued past a post office, a pocket-sized library, a store with a hand-lettered sign advertising worms, and a gas station. "And you have to navigate."

I checked our directions. "Look for the intersection past the church and the grange hall."

"Whatever that is," Jules said.

"Wells Point Road," I called out a minute later. It was unpaved, bordered by pines that stretched to heaven. We'd driven about three-quarters of a mile further when we noticed the T. Wells mailbox and turned in.

What I saw was a pastel illustration from Dash's Beatrix Potter book. I expected Mrs. Tiggy-Winkle herself to toddle across the gravel road, all prickles and freshly starched laundry for Sally Henny Penny. The house was yellow with blue shutters. Morning glories crawled up its front porch, which was tilting to the left and crowded with wicker rocking chairs and settees.

I was enchanted by its hollyhock charm. Jules, not so much. She parked the car, stared, and shook her head. "To think we could have been rolling off a plane now, preparing to eat the world's best risotto," she muttered.

We carried our suitcases and as many bags of groceries as we could manage and made our way up an overgrown stone path, past a birdbath and a swing set. I rapped a brass door knocker shaped like a crab.

"It's open," Talia shouted. She emerged from the shadows, a ringlet escaping from under a kerchief.

"What the hell is that around your waist?" Jules asked.

Talia wiped her hands on a faded cotton apron. She gave Jules a hug, then me.

"Is Quincy here yet?" I asked.

"She's out in the rowboat trying to catch dinner." Talia laughed. "Not to worry. I'm marinating chicken to grill." She peeked in the bags and licked her lips. "Woo-hoo. Put everything down here and I'll take care of it. Just go upstairs and make yourselves comfortable." She pointed toward a door. "The two of you can share the big room. Or pick separate bedrooms. Work it out."

We flipped. Jules won the bedroom with two canopy beds. I settled in toward the back. The room was tiny, but frankly, I'd sleep better there, where it was dim and cozy. Talia had put out a bouquet of sweet peas, and the linens were crisp on a narrow bed with pineapple finials.

I hung some clothes in an armoire and tucked the rest—and a brand-new sachet—into the drawers of a warped dresser, on top of which I placed my perfume, an alarm clock, and a photo of Xander and Dash. I was ready to walk down to the lake with my newly purchased book, *Your Three-Year-Old: Friend or Foe?* I searched my suitcase, my handbag, my canvas tote.

I found Talia adding way too much flour to a pie crust she was trying to roll out in the humid kitchen. Clumps of pastry were sticking to a wooden board. "I'm such a moron," I said. "I forgot my book. Is there anything here I can borrow, please?"

"Lots. When she's not into her dark-and-stormys, Abigail does nothing but weed and read. Go to the bedroom where I'm staying—it's off the living room—and check the shelf."

That's when I saw it. While I was crouched next to a bookshelf, deciding which title had the least dust, I heard the phone ring. After the fourth ring, I thought I'd better answer it. As I reached for the receiver the sound stopped, but a breeze from the opened window rustled a stack of papers and my eye caught a fax cover sheet titled *Jackson Collegiate essay.* I stood still and stared at it, a rattlesnake ready to strike. I tiptoed to the door—no one was near—and shut it. I returned to the desk. The fax wasn't mine to read, but that failed to stop me.

The tribute to Master Henry Thomas Fisher-Wells explained in well-supported detail why this tiny male would be ideal for Jackson Collegiate. I read the essay twice. Based on this document, there was no doubt that Henry was destined for greatness. If he didn't negotiate peace between the Sunnis and the Shiites, at the very least, I couldn't imagine why the woman running the school wouldn't select Henry to chair the admission committee, where he could personally reject Dash, who couldn't yet tell an antelope from an anteater. I wanted to collapse on the faded blue chenille bedspread and erase what I'd read, not only from the page but from my memory.

Even I, though, can find my backbone if put to the test. I quietly returned the essay to its place, grabbed a random novel, and hurried to the kitchen. I thought I sounded remarkably cool as I showed Talia what I'd picked. The book was more than eight hundred pages, with a provocative, unmade bed on its cover.

Talia was slicing tomatoes. "*The Crimson Petal and the White?* 'A gripping tale of Victorian England—from whores to high society—by a twenty-first-century Charles Dickens.' Abigail buried herself in this a few summers ago—you had to faint to get her attention."

At least I'd picked the right book. "May I help?" I asked, feeling guilt along with an emotion I hadn't yet identified. I knew it was one of the bitter flavors—jealousy, shock, fury—tossed with ordinary confusion.

"How about the corn?" Talia suggested.

I stationed myself at the table and began to rip husks from each fat ear, plucking away pale green silk. The calendar said autumn, but this fragrance was the essence of late summer and I inhaled it deeply, as if the scent were desperately needed oxygen. I forced myself to concentrate on the task, counting the rotations of the lazy fan spinning in the center of the ceiling. The room filled with silence that I'm sure Talia thought of as sisterly.

Of course, I told myself, there was no reason that she and Tom shouldn't, couldn't, and wouldn't consider for Henry the same school Xander and I had decided was our top choice for Dash. They had every right. What surprised me was the speed and polish of their effort, when—compared to Xander and me—they presented themselves as the most laid-back couple in Brooklyn. More than that was the secrecy. Not that the bylaws of friendship required full disclosure, but something about the whole effort seemed sneaky and disingenuous.

I gnashed my teeth as I husked. Did Talia and Tom think they concealed their contempt of Xander? They all but heckled him for his frantic ambition. I felt a swell of deep affection on my husband's behalf. This sweetly solid summer house, which Talia liked to mock, was a château compared to the sorry bungalow where Xander had lived until a teacher noticed his potential and worked to win him a scholarship. It was at boarding school where he met Henry Thomas Wells III, legacy student. Xander's parents would still have been in the hovel if their only son hadn't made enough money to buy them a new house, though his parents flat out refused central air-conditioning. They even said no to a dishwasher. Not that Xander would ever mention this to any of our friends. He was too proud to admit the extent of his family's poverty.

I reached for another ear of corn, and realized I'd shucked the whole dozen in five minutes. "What else can I do?" I asked.

"Want to set the table?" Talia's hands were busy measuring olive oil. She nodded toward open shelves stacked with Fiestaware.

Questions began popping like firecrackers. Why had Tom and Talia vetoed public school? What had happened to the idea of a special smarty-pants program? Why the big secret about the application, which seemed like the sort of thing Talia would discuss? But while I'd never call myself shrewd, I realized that I should bury my urge to talk about this, at least for now. I'd take my cue from Talia and see if she raised the topic.

"You'll find the silverware in those drawers. The smaller plates and glasses are there." She pointed toward a hutch.

Grateful for the distraction, I made several trips to the patio to set the table, cut dahlias for a centerpiece, and opened the umbrella to shield us from the setting sun. I stepped back to admire the scene, tranquil and inviting. We had several days ahead of us. I'd have to put a lid on my rage and bury it in an undisclosed location.

Talia was snipping basil and mint from pots next to the back door. "What do you think? This isn't so bad, is it?" she said. Her grin was wide and open. A broad-brimmed hat shielded her eyes.

I am cursed with good manners. "It's lovely, as long as you let us help," I said.

"You know work's what I do best."

"Hey, that reminds me," I said. "Do you remember if a June Rittenhouse called me?"

Talia continued to cut herbs.

"She's a headhunter."

Talia moved on to the thyme, then the parsley.

"Arthur said he'd given out my name for a job she was filling."

She stopped cutting but asked the ground in front of her, "What was that name again?"

"June," I said. "Rittenhouse."

She didn't respond.

"Like the square in Philadelphia."

"Hmmm," Talia said, as if she were deciding whether to order chocolate or vanilla. "Right. Oh, yes, she did call. I passed on that message to you, weeks ago."

"Really?" I said, as evenly as possible. "That's odd. I don't recall."

"Yeah, I'm positive." She still hadn't looked at me. "You probably forgot. You've been pretty busy lately."

I'd have remembered that name and noticed that she was a headhunter, since one had never sought me out. I would have been flattered, curious, and surprised.

"Maybe it just wasn't that important to you," she added.

That was when I realized my best friend was lying.

"Well, if it isn't Huck Finn," Talia said, looking beyond me with an extra helping of enthusiasm. I turned. Quincy was walking toward us, her usual baseball cap on her head. *Saved,* I thought, as Talia shouted, "Catch anything?"

"Not a nibble." Quincy put down her fishing pole and threw her arms around me. "Glad you finally showed."

"Hey, you," I said. "You're here one day and you look like you've been in St. Barts a month." I was genuinely relieved to see Quincy, the friend I've always found hardest to know. More than any of us, she lives inside her own brain, but—unlike Talia—I have no reason to associate her with anything less than fair play.

"The easy life, kid," she said, embracing me with her slender, tanned arms. "I'm going to run inside and put on dry clothes. Then I'll be down to help you two."

Talia stood up, her basket brimming with herbs. "While you're upstairs, poke Jules—I heard her snoring."

"My pleasure," Quincy said, and disappeared into the cottage.

"I hope she doesn't chop off her head," Talia said when Quincy was out of earshot. I looked at Talia blankly as she walked to a metal lawn chair and sat down. "Ah, that means you don't know," she said, and motioned for me to sit next to her, which I did. She proceeded with a convoluted tale of avarice and greed. The villain was Arthur, assisted by an equally culpable Jules.

When she was finished, I wished I hadn't heard the story—and at the same time hoped that *The Crimson Petal and the White* would be equally compelling. "You're telling me Jules tried to steal away the apartment that Quincy found first and wants so much?"

"I'm only repeating what Quincy told me."

I refused to believe it. "What's Jules' side?"

"Does it matter? Jules was wrong, no two ways about it."

Who was Talia to talk? "Am I allowed to know this?" I asked.

"Good question. But I didn't want you to be out of the loop. I felt you should know—everyone else does."

This she felt I should know—and why was I the last to learn it? "What am I supposed to do with the information?" I didn't care that I sounded petulant.

"Don't shoot the messenger," Talia said, and shrugged, peeved at my lack of gratitude. "Either forget I told you, or ask Jules about it, or Quincy. Take your pick." With that she walked inside.

I found my way to the water, kicked off my shoes, and tried to talk myself into relishing the ordinary pleasure of bare feet sinking into the sandy bottom. Lapping against my ankles, the late-day September water felt soothingly tepid. I took my cell phone from my pocket, was relieved to see that I had a signal, and called home. "Everything fine," Jamyang said. "Dash ate two lamb chops."

I put away my phone, then pulled it out again. It was after six—perhaps Xander would answer his line himself. He did, but as soon as he heard my voice he said, "I have to call you back."

"Just a second, I promise."

"Something wrong?"

Yes! "It's only this." I counted to ten. "You know how I said I didn't want you to ask Edgar to write a letter on Dash's behalf?"

"I believe your exact words were, 'I'm shocked. Ask your boss? That's cheating. I want our son to get into school on his own merits, like we did.'" He'd nailed my priggish tone.

"I've decided you were right. In fact, I think we should find as many people as we can to write letters. Can you start to ask around?"

"Well, well, have you been talking to Mrs. McCoy?"

"Not at all—I just realized we'd be fools not to play the game by everyone else's rules." The real rules! "I read that in the last ten years the number of city kids under the age of five has increased more than twenty-five percent." I took this fact straight out of *The New York Times.* "With all the competition, it wouldn't be fair to Dash to put forth anything less than our best effort."

"In that case, I'm getting out my checkbook right now and making a there's-more-where-this-came-from contribution to the school."

"What?" He was getting way ahead of me "You can't do that!"

"Other people do."

"But it's such obvious..." I searched for a civilized term. "Pandering."

"Let's see if the school returns the check. And now, Chloe, I really do have to go."

He clicked off, and I stared at the phone in my hand as if it were a grenade. As long as I had cell service, I decided to make one last call. "May I have the business listing for a June Rittenhouse? In Manhattan, please."

CHAPTER 15

Jules

Despite the fact that Quincy was shadowing me like a CIA operative, for nearly three days I managed to dodge any one-on-one. I knew she wanted more than a modest apology. She wanted blood and guts, marrow and bone. Quincy wouldn't be happy until I'd prostrated myself and denounced Arthur as swine. She particularly wanted me to admit that I'd gone with Arthur to scope out the apartment she thought was already hers.

It wasn't happening. I have my self-respect—as well as another niggling worry that was starting to move front and center. But on Saturday morning at the Wellses' dump, I couldn't avoid her. I hadn't been able to sleep, and at six-thirty in the morning I started rooting out the ingredients for waffles. Talia had gotten up early, too. Out of respect for the ungodly hour, we weren't saying a word. That's when Quincy trotted into the kitchen, a centerfold in orange spandex. She sat down and began lacing her blindingly white sneakers.

"If it isn't Sunny D," I said, amiably enough. She ignored me. "Excuse me, Quincy, but I bid you good morning." Perhaps it was my rolling eyes that pissed her off.

"That's it!" She threw a sneaker across the room. It bounced off the screen door.

"Down, woman."

"Hey, you two." Talia sighed like my nonna. "Shall we talk about it?"

"About what?" Perhaps I was coy.

Quincy leaned back in the chair. I swear she flexed her biceps, simply because she could. "Let's clear the air," she said.

"I'm sorry you're upset." I admit that the sincerity of my statement was to an apology like Target is to Tiffany's.

"That's not the point," Quincy countered.

"Jules apologized," Talia insisted, which is how I realized that Quincy had felt the need to unburden her side of our rift to her.

"No, she didn't." Quincy scrunched her reddening face. Cords stood out in her neck.

Talia eyeballed Quincy, then me. "Quincy has a point. You haven't admitted you're wrong."

"Since when are you so perfect?" I directed the question to our hostess.

"This isn't about me," Talia said, stoked with righteous indignation.

"Which is why you should butt out."

"Bully," she snarled.

"Precisely," Quincy said.

"Make your own goddamn waffles." I marched out of the kitchen and down to the lake for a sulk. Within the hour, Chloe arrived at the beach, sent as an emissary at Talia's behest. In the name of team spirit, she tried to appeal to my better nature, but my better nature was in exile. Chloe went on—and on. I didn't change my mind or my lawn chair, and strongly suggested that she go off with the others to bond on another wholesome bike ride while I managed to pass the day alone without a glimmer of guilt.

In the late afternoon, after the three of them had returned, I migrated to the patio. Talia held the charcoal bag upside down and shook it. Like petrified dung, out plopped two briquettes. "No more? Damn," she said. "I'll have to make another run."

"Allow me." I hopped up from the deck chair, its peeling paint rubbing against my smoothly waxed thigh.

"You're sure?" Talia asked.

I walked seven steps and grabbed my car keys. "My pleasure—this book is boring me silly." Although I'd spent the day with a novel fetchingly titled *Peony in Love,* whether it was about heaving bosoms or fertilizing bulbs, I wouldn't have known. My mind kept slowly looping over every numbing detail of the last few weeks of my life.

"Do we need milk for the morning?" I asked. "Ice cream? Anything?" *New carpeting, perhaps?*

"Nope, we're good," Talia said. "Don't be long, okay? I have to start the fire soon if we want to make the movies."

The plan was to go to a double feature at the art-house theater on a college campus twenty miles away. Yesterday we'd had a heated debate on whether each of us was a Garbo girl or a Dietrich dame. That one was easy. I'd love to be all Garbo, glower to garters, but I'm Dietrich to the core, tough with a heart of gold.

"I'll be fast," I promised. I peeled out of the driveway and drove to the village store, where the canned peas and powdered detergent looked dangerously quaint. I made my way through stacks of lobster pajamas, boxers, and bibs obscuring rows of fishing lures, which I briefly considered purchasing in multiples and turning into earrings. I grabbed a sack of marshmallows, eight chocolate bars, and plenty of graham crackers and perused the rest of the shelves.

"Help you out back there?" croaked the humpbacked whale manning the register.

"I'm fine," I yelled. Next to the Fleet enemas I spotted what I needed and headed for the front. The shopkeeper gave me a knowing sneer while I reached for a bag of charcoal, one of many that sat in the front like ventriloquists' dummies. I threw forty dollars on the counter and left.

It was only after steaks, corn on the cob, *Mata Hari, The Blue Angel,* hot fudge sundaes, a hootenanny, s'mores at midnight, and a few hours of fitful sleep that, finally, I prayed to the Virgin Mother and went to the bathroom. I ripped open the box. Its directions suggested seconds would be sufficient, but to be sure, I tinkled for as long as possible. I flushed and waited, breathing heavily as I watched the minutes tick like the nine-month time bomb they were.

Not soon enough, a line appeared. It was faint, a sign from a God that chose to whisper. I reread the fine print. The product claimed 99 percent accuracy, and "even if the marker is light, the result is positive."

I stared at the knotty pine wall, considering what the future might bring, but the future, that bitch, was mum. I heard a knock at the door. "Be out in a second," I said. I ran water in the sink to mute the sound, tore the box to bits, and dropped it in my bag.

It wasn't early menopause, like I'd hoped. It was me, Jules, pregnant.

CHAPTER 16

Quincy

"Let's go over this again." Horton was reviewing his checklist as we sat in a diner, eating toast and scrambled eggs. "I've got your tax returns from the last three years, Jake's pay stubs, and copies of your royalty and bank statements, but how about your monthly financials—stocks, bonds, mutual funds, other assets?"

I pushed the eggs around on the plate. They looked too runny, too pale. "How far back do we have to go?" Perhaps my mother had saved receipts from my Girl Scout cookie sales.

"Three months. Landlord letters—how you doing on those?"

"You have one from our current landlord, but the woman we sublet from in Brooklyn is missing in action." The e-mail I'd sent to her had bounced back, her phone number reassigned to an Albanian restaurant. "I checked Zabasearch, like you suggested. I found a phone number for Priscilla Presley, but nothing for Pinky LaPook." Maybe she'd changed her name. Who could blame her?

"How do you spell that?" Horton asked, jotting down my response. "I'll get my people on it. And I forgot to ask, do you have any pets?"

"A kitten," I said suspiciously. When I got back from Maine, Jake had surprised me with a Tonkinese. I, a dedicated dog lover, had shocked myself by falling in love with an aqua-eyed comet in a downy mink coat. One minute Fanny would be nuzzling like a puppy, the next flying from lamp to lamp. Watching her was my own private nature show. "Don't tell me pets are forbidden," I said, my voice rising. "I remember seeing a cat in the apartment."

"Please calm down," Horton whispered. "All I need is a picture."

"Is this to determine my pet's race?" Given the spadework for our board interview, I'd decided that my potential neighbors must be hopeless bigots.

"To make sure your cat isn't a coyote. Pets can't weight more than thirty pounds."

"I will enroll Fanny in Weight Watchers immediately."

"I didn't make the rule," Horton said. "The better the building, the more persnickety."

"Sorry." I knew I shouldn't pick on Horton.

"If it's any consolation, every buyer despises this part of the process. Focus on the beautiful home you'll have in the end."

"What if my friend's boyfriend finds a way to block us?" Should the ruling powers ever deem to see Jake and me, I pictured Arthur leaping into the air like a stingray, impaling us with his barb.

Horton waved his hand. "He's a mere annoyance." He'd finished his breakfast and looked down at his notes. "Where are we with letters of recommendation?"

This was the worst, asking for favors. "We have Jake's boss and my editor."

"What about someone in the building? Those are gold."

I shook my head. The only insider we knew was Arthur.

"That Hollywood hotshot whose book you're writing?"

"Maizie is twenty. I doubt any of the board members play her music on their nonexistent iPods."

"Their children would know her. These people have powerful kids."

"Okay, I'm on it." Let Maizie find out I had a life beyond transforming her breakups, cosmetic meltdowns, and white-girl ghetto talk into compelling prose.

"Your minister or doctor?"

I hadn't been in a church for years, not even for my wedding, which took place on a Wisconsin beach. My internist wouldn't know me from the fake ficus in her waiting room. "I'll ask my ob-gyn." With my nonstop pregnancies, miscarriages, and exploratory tests, I had Dr. Frumkes on speed dial.

"We also need one or two from friends." Horton didn't mean any random pal who could catch a dangling participle and knew her way around a thesaurus. "Do you have a buddy or two who heads up a foundation or a nonprofit? Chairs a department at Columbia or NYU? How about a pal who works at a major lending institution or consulting firm?" he suggested. "If the name isn't recognizable, at least the letterhead should be."

Jake's college roommate had been a high roller at an investment bank. Sadly, due to a Wall Street tsunami, he now managed a Tuscaloosa Taco Bell. But I had another idea. "I'll get on that," I said as the waiter delivered the tab, which Horton grabbed.

"Mine," he said gallantly as his BlackBerry beeped. "It's Fran," he stage-whispered.

I thanked him and left the restaurant. I started to call Chloe at the office—it was her first week back—but when her line rang, I clicked off. I needed to consider how to frame the request. As I walked up Broadway, everywhere I turned I was taunted either by babies or by stores selling their parents must-have infant Shakespeare tapes, Diaper Genies, and three-inch-long Converse All-Stars.

While I ruminated on what to say to Chloe, she called back. "What's going on, Quince?" The phone line crackled with curiosity.

We'd spoken only yesterday, parsing Maine at its most benign while failing to mention that Jules and I had successfully avoided ever being alone together. Nor did we speak of the tension that prickled among us like poison ivy none of us dared to scratch—or remark on how of all the vacations the four of us had taken, this was the only one that had terminated early amid sudden eruptions of "deadline," "babysitter hassles," "stomach flu," and "audition."

In yesterday's conversation, Chloe had kept returning to Jules and me. Obviously, when I wasn't around, Talia had explained the apartment situation. Chloe had fished zealously for information. I refused to take the bait, worried that her loyalty would be with Jules. Among the four of us, she and Jules were the most unlikely friends, but I knew Chloe adored Jules, and saw in her a splashy, street-smart older sister through whom she could live vicariously, without fear of being blackballed from the Junior League.

"Actually, I was wondering if you could do me a favor, please," I finally said.

"All you have to do is ask." Chloe was chipper. I wasn't in the mood for chipper.

"I need a letter of reference."

"For what?"

"The co-op board."

"That's a pain, isn't it, getting together the paperwork? It's one reason Xander and I decided to buy a brownstone."

Does Chloe realize how she comes off to those among us who can't drop megamillions on a four-story city house? "You're right. It's a pain. Now we need a few additional letters."

"Of course I'll write one."

This was even more awkward than I'd anticipated. "Actually, I was hoping Xander would write it—that is, if he has the time." I hemmed and hawed. "I'm only following my broker's directions, but...do you think Xander could give us a short—it can be very brief—vote of confidence?" I paused. "On business stationery?"

Why hadn't I waited and let Jake make this request? He and Xander got along well enough, while whenever Xander and I were left alone, I felt unglued, afraid he was going to hit on me as he had a few New Year's Eves ago. He'd followed me into the kitchen and pressed his body against my back while I reached into my refrigerator. "You're hot, Quincy," he'd breathed into my ear. "There's something between us. Can't you feel it?"

In the most literal sense I could—and hadn't been able to escape before Chloe had walked in and seen body language that was its own porn movie. We never discussed the incident, neither Xander and I nor Chloe and I. And it never happened again. I hope Xander was too drunk to even remember the incident, but it's there, soiling my permanent record.

Silence hung between the Upper West Side and Brooklyn Heights. "I'll ask Xander," Chloe said eventually.

Her voice had no discernible affect, while mine went straight to stilted. "Jake and I would be extremely grateful." I wanted to get off the phone, but Chloe kept going. "Talia told me about the Jules and Arthur apartment mess," she said.

"Oh?"

"I'm sure Jules didn't mean to hurt you." She'd upgraded to earnest.

Can you prove that? "Jules had no business blabbing to Arthur. Let her boyfriend find his own apartment."

"But he lives in that building."

"So what? And if Jules didn't mean to hurt me, why doesn't she apologize?"

"She has a hard time admitting she's wrong. But she means well."

"Why are you defending her?" My real question: *Why are you taking her side?*

"I'm not defending. I'm explaining."

"Jules is a big girl. She should explain herself."

"Can't we all just get along?" Chloe sounded exasperated, close to whiny.

"What are we, four?" If we'd been in the same room, my phone would have landed on her empty blond head. "I can't talk about this now. I have to get home and prep for an important appointment. Goodbye." And goodbye reference letter.

The preparation I spoke of was nothing more than changing clothes. If I didn't look like a creature from the black lagoon, crazy Maizie wouldn't take me seriously as a New York writer. I got home and exchanged my sneakers, baggy khakis, and pale blue sweater for a black shirt that I tucked into narrow black jeans. They hung even lower on my hips than the last time I'd worn them. I dabbed on two minutes of makeup, grabbed my leather jacket, switched to witch boots, and hobbled to the street.

The Four Seasons is the only place Maizie May will stay in Manhattan, not that you'd find her nibbling on their lemon-ricotta pancakes in the café or that she'd know the hotel's architect, I. M. Pei, from a bale of hay. I paused in the lobby and paid homage to its marble splendor. A minute later, one of Maizie's security guards stood in front of me like a tank and escorted me by private elevator to her customary nine-room suite, the whole top floor of the hotel.

I'd been here before. My eyes no longer bugged out when faced with the mother-of-pearl-encrusted walls or the floor-to-ceiling bay windows blessing the city. Maizie—née Mary Margaret—was seated at the grand piano. "Quincy! Jesus, you got no ass. How'd ya do it? I could lose a few. Juice fast, right?"

"The stress diet," I said.

She picked out the melody of her latest ballad as she asked, "What do you have to be stressed about?" It was, fortunately, a rhetorical question, followed by "Sure ya don't want nothin'? There's plenty left." Spread across a table were the remains of the hotel's Japanese breakfast menu—toasted seaweed, pickled vegetables, a pot of green tea, and a full glass of milk, most likely lukewarm, organic, and soy.

"I'm good. Thanks."

"Then let's rock," she said as there was a knock at the door. Another security guard let in a uniformed woman carrying a large satchel. "Angel! You got here, honey. Set up over there." Maizie pointed to the dining room, then turned to me. "Angel's gonna do my mani-pedi while you and me talk. You ready?"

I pulled out my tape recorder and tested it. "Maizie May, September sixteenth."

"Where were we?" Maizie asked as she plunged her feet into a tub of gardenia-scented water that had, like an offering, appeared before her. "Ah. I was talkin' 'bout my adorable mother, that porker." Our last session had been three weeks ago, yet she resumed practically midsentence. I pressed on and let Maizie and my tape recorder roll, interrupting only to ask the occasional question. Angel produced a fresh bottle of Paparazzi Pink and started buffing and pumicing. Precisely forty-five minutes later, one of the guards tapped his watch and Maizie began to wind down. "So I said to the bitch, 'Fuck yourself, slut,' cut her off, and moved to my own place in Laurel Canyon."

"How old were you?"

"Seventeen," Maizie said. She stood, turned her back to me, and walked—careful not to smudge her toes—to the balcony twenty feet away.

"How old was your mother?"

"Who cares?" She shrugged, looked out of the window, and shouted, "Come over here." I did. "What's that?" Maizie pointed to the hazy blob of blue due north in Central Park.

"The reservoir." Only yesterday I'd run there, admiring my future apartment from the Fifth Avenue side of the water. The time seemed right. "Maizie, I was wondering if you could please do me a favor. My husband and I are hoping to buy a co-op. You can see it." I pointed to a castlelike building. She squinted her heavily mascaraed eyes. In the distance, it was one-eighth of the size of a Lego block. I felt my face getting warm. "We need reference letters. I was wondering if you'd have the time to write one."

Maizie looked at me as if I'd asked her to spot me fifty thousand dollars. "Even if I did have time, which I fuckin' don't, ya know I can't write. That's what you're for."

"It can be short, to the point." I was begging. I was shameless. I was sweaty.

"Write it yourself," she said. After a dramatic pause, her exquisite heart-shaped face broke into a smile. "Idiot. Of course I'll help you. I love ya, girlfriend. You know that. E-mail your goddamn dream letter and we'll fax it back." She walked out of the room.

For the last two years I have met regularly with Quincy Blue, I began composing in my head when I got into the taxi. *During that time I have been consistently impressed by her intelligence, high professional standards, impeccable integrity, and, above all, inexhaustible ability to tolerate my midnight phone calls and endless, narcissistic rants.*

CHAPTER 17

Talia

When I arrived at work this morning, I found a note from Chloe. *June Rittenhouse,* it said. No number. No date. No details. Almost a scrawl. When Chloe and I had spoken the night before, she'd given me messages, but hadn't mentioned a call from the headhunter.

The bagel I'd eaten turned to acid. What did Chloe know and when did she know it? Nothing, I prayed, not that I deserved to have God listen. My guilt was fueled by a round-the-clock backup generator. It would serve me right if June Rittenhouse had called to say the Tribeca job was filled or that the elaborate spiral-bound pitch I'd turned in—thank you, spontaneously regenerated right-side brain cells—hadn't made it to the final round.

I dialed June's number. I'd gotten in early and at this hour expected to simply leave a message. While hoping for its return, I'd have ample time to flagellate myself. But the next thing I heard was "June Rittenhouse." No slacker, June was answering her own phone at eight twenty-five.

"Good morning. It's Talia Fisher-Wells," I said. My throat felt like a pipe gasping for Drano. I cleared it, twice. "Excuse me, but did you call?"

Did you call finally? Mean Maxine hissed. For the past two weeks I'd phoned June every third day, with no response.

"I did," she said, crisply authoritative. "I've been waiting since yesterday morning to hear from you. You're one of the finalists whom the clients want to meet."

"Excellent," I said, relieved that the nights and weekends I'd put into my pitch had resulted in more than Tom's grousing. "Thanks. What's the next step?"

"The creative director has a shoot in Punta Cana that's going to take him away for two weeks, and he needs to see you tomorrow. The slots left are at ten or two."

Chloe would be manning the office. No problem there. But Tom's parents were coming to town, an occurrence as rare as an eclipse and sometimes as dark. Henry and I were to meet them at the Central Park Zoo, followed by a birthday lunch for Abigail at the Metropolitan Museum, where Tom would be joining us. He'd arranged to leave school early. Still, I said, "Two, please."

The following morning I searched for clothes that could take me from the zoo to the Met to a downtown ad agency: I'd need to illustrate my finely tuned innate flair, if I had any, which would be a particular challenge, since while the calendar pretended it was autumn, the thermometer was stuck at ninety degrees.

I decided the day called for the full Ava Gardner, whom Bubbe—admittedly in need of cataract surgery—insists is my stunt double. While hot rollers turned my frizz to waves, I slipped on a butt-hugging skirt and a boxy, short-sleeved jacket I cinched at the waist. Carefully I painted on two layers of red gloss, blotted, and found my notice-me sunglasses. I faced the mirror and saw a 1950s pinup.

So did Tom, who'd walked out of the shower, wrapped in a towel. "Did I miss the invitation for the Rat Pack ball?" he asked. "There's time for me to dress as Dino."

"The shades?" I asked. "Too much?"

"Too much for what? Trying to give my mother a coronary?"

To my instant regret, Mean Maxine offered Tom an accurate but un-necessary knee-jerk response: "No matter what I wear, your mother hates it." Every year, my Christmas gift from Abigail is—*hint*—a Brooks Broth-ers gift certificate. Hence my drawer full of gently worn madras Ber-mudas.

"My mother doesn't hate the way you look—she can't understand it, that's all," he said, staring at my open-toed black platform pumps. Taking his life in his hands, Tom added, "There are times when I see where she's coming from."

I could feel my face turning the Valentine shimmer of my lips, but it was a dead end to explain that my ensemble pivoted around these shoes, which showed my legs to advantage. "I have an interview in the after-noon. For that job I tried out for."

"Really?" Tom said, oozing distrust. He furrowed his eyebrows so low I could barely see his eyes.

"I'm not meeting my high school boyfriend. It's an appointment with the creative director. At two."

He went to his closet and said nothing while he dressed in the full Connecticut—khakis, pink button-down shirt, navy sport coat, rep tie, and boat shoes.

"In case you're wondering, I didn't forget about your mother's birth-day lunch," I said to his back. "I'll only have to leave a little early." I would peel away from the Met at one-fifteen and splurge on a taxi all the way downtown. Extraordinary times call for extraordinary measures.

"I see. And when were you planning on telling me this?"

"I'm telling you now."

He left the room, gave Henry and Pontoon their usual exuberant good-bye, and shouted its feeble echo to me before the front door slammed.

Since I'd reported my job opportunity, Tom had acted wigged out, my ambition putting his lack of it in bold relief. I should have handled the day's change of plans with more finesse, and could hear my father say, *Talia Rose, those who fail to plan, plan to fail.* But this was no time to ana-lyze whether Tom's ire was reasonable or deserved. In ten minutes I'd packed Henry's bag of books and snacks and helped him dress, and we started to walk to the subway stop for the ride to midtown Manhattan.

Big Tom and Abigail were waiting for us by the monkey house, admiring a newly born offspring in the form of a wizened old man. My father-in-law, a more distinguished, even taller version of my Tom, spotted us, gave me a cheery wave, and picked up Henry in one long swoop—"Good to see you, buddy"—while Mother Monkey and Mother Wells offered matching approach-at-your-own-risk glares. I walked in their direction.

I come from a family of smoochers. My parents, Bubbe, and I exchange kisses all the livelong day. "You got an A, *bubbele*?" Kiss, kiss. "You're having a bath, dahlink?" Kiss, kiss. "You're having an appendectomy?" Kiss, kiss. With Tom's "people"—their way of referring to the extended family, as if they were an indigenous tribe nearing extinction, which they might be—you might get a kiss if you were, say, going off to war. Thus, I never know how to greet Abigail, whom I generally stand in front of until she notices me and starts talking.

Today she looked especially bony and stony. I was late, but only by five minutes, which in New York City practically qualifies as early. I'd stowed my belt in Henry's bag along with the heels, temporarily traded for sneakers. I thought I could pass for a Colonial Dame; Abigail's demeanor couldn't be on account of my appearance, unless it was the 'do. Like Big Tom, she has a head of thick silver hair, though I'd only ever seen it girdled in a bun. I once asked Tom if behind closed doors he thought his mother let loose, because if Abigail wanted to be a vixen, she could. I'd seen her plenty of times in a bathing suit that, baggy as it might be, revealed a nothing-hanging body, and in one of her drawers I'd discovered a well-thumbed *Kama Sutra* when I was, swear to God, simply looking for warm socks. But on the subject of his parents' private life, Tom has never cared to speculate. Around his people Tom turns back into one of them, and the husband I love has a hard time having a hard time: along with his sense of humor, he loses the ability to perform the most basic marital function besides taking out garbage.

"Good morning, Talia," Abigail said, giving my ensemble a thorough review. "If we hurry, we can make the penguin feeding." With that she took a balloon from her hand and handed it to Henry. From his perch in his grandfather's arms he gave a great squeal, and the corners of Abigail's mouth began to approximate an expression much like a smile.

"Say 'Thank you, Grandma Abigail,'" I instructed. One juncture between our two families is, at least, good manners.

"Thank you, Gammagail," Henry repeated, his fingers poking the balloon.

If, in gratitude, I'd been able to plant a tree in Israel then and there, I would have.

"Thank *you*, young man," Abigail said, and turned to Big Tom. "Doesn't he look exactly like Third as a boy?"

I hate that name, so bronze medal. But Abigail is correct, even though despite his big blue eyes and 95th-percentile height, my squat, brown-eyed *mishpacha* think Henry is all Fisher. "Got the *punim* of Uncle Solly, the boxer," my father says. "In the old country they called him the Cossack of Kiev." I have not shared this lore with my in-laws. Producing an heir who looks pressed out by a Christmas cookie cutter in the tradition of Wells menfolk has been my shining achievement, which I wouldn't dream of tarnishing.

The four of us proceeded to the penguins. While Tom and Abigail gave Henry a freshman-year grounding in penguin ethology, I tried to spot Roy and Silo, the real-life inspiration for the heroes of one of Henry's books. They'd refused to socialize with the females and had done a swell job of incubating an extra fertilized egg and raising Tango, its eventual chick. But all the penguins—gay or straight—looked the same, beaked babies dressed as Whiffenpoofs.

From penguins we migrated to the polar bears and from the polar bears to the fruit bats. Only then did we push off for lunch. By the time we'd walked twenty blocks to the Met, trekked through the European sculptures, and arrived at the Trustees Dining Room, Tom had been waiting for ten minutes.

"Happy birthday," he said, raising a glass after we'd gotten settled and ordered. "To Mother!"

"To Mother!" Big Tom said.

"To Mother," I managed, although I've never called her that, not even when she requested that I did.

"No one alive is truer than you!" Tom said. Whatever that means, his family says this to one another on every birthday. I've always wondered if it's a line from an Episcopal hymn.

Tom turned to me. "No one alive is truer than you!" I chimed in, though a court stenographer would have omitted the exclamation point. Tom was seated next to me and touched my foot with his. But my mind kept drifting to this afternoon's interview and, dammit, to Chloe. Did she know?

"Talia?" Tom said. "Are you with us?"

I was puzzled. "Oh, *l'chaim*," I offered. "To life!" This is how Fishers toast.

"Hear, hear," Big Tom said. "La high am."

"High am, Mommy," Henry repeated, raising his cup as if he was going to recite the kiddush.

Abigail managed to join in a group laugh. I began to relax, until Tom touched my foot again. This time I got it, the cue to bring out Abigail's present. Weeks ago, I'd ordered a broad-brimmed straw garden hat with a long gray ribbon to match Abigail's wintry eyes. I could picture the hat now, forgotten next to our front door, good intentions gone to hell.

"Abigail, we have something for you that I—" I started to say, but Tom interrupted.

"That we want to give you when you come back to the apartment later this afternoon. We've planned a special dinner."

We had now.

"You are the most thoughtful young man," Abigail said. I spotted mist in her eyes as our oysters arrived.

"How's the dissertation coming, son?" Big Tom asked.

"It's coming." Tom proceeded to detail his progress to Henry Thomas Wells Jr., Ph.D., Dartmouth's most noted John Milton scholar. The discussion lasted well past the arrival of our main course. I was four bites into my Gruyère soufflé, discreetly checking my watch, when Tom surprised me again. "Talia has good news, too—she's being considered for a new job. I'm so proud of her."

He was? All eyes turned in my direction. "Proud of you, Mommy," Henry said.

Two glasses of sherry had made Abigail curious. "Tell us about it," she requested.

I couldn't. To discuss the job out loud was *farboten*. Who was I to thumb my nose at fate in the most obvious, arrogant way?

"It's the same as what I do now," I said, picking my words with caution, "but at a different agency." Even that explanation, dull and evasive, seemed too elaborate for my ears. Abigail and Big Tom turned away in disappointment. I wished I could shout, *But it pays twice as much—one of us has to make some real money.*

"Talia's too modest. It's a great job," Tom said. I thought I detected an edge of contempt that no one else would notice. "In fact, I'm worried she might be late for the interview. Don't you think you should leave? *Sweetheart?*" Passive-aggressive, all right.

Skip the birthday cake I'd ordered? Have Abigail furious until I could make it up to her five years from now, when she turned seventy? But she said, "Tom's right. Chop-chop. You know what Dickens said: 'I never could have done what I have done without the habits of punctuality, order, and diligence.'"

Did she think *I* wasn't diligent? I separated from my soufflé, hugged Henry and Tom, blew kisses at his parents, grabbed my interview-worthy accessories, and wound my way out of the museum.

Finding a taxi took twice as long as I'd planned. The president was in town, causing gridlock *grande*. I arrived at the agency five minutes late.

CHAPTER 18

Jules

"Jules!"

"Sheila!"

Sheila Frumkes, M.D., is my gynecologist, and thanks to me, Talia, Chloe, and Quincy use her as well. Only I, however, get a free ride. I help Sheila put together her wardrobe whenever she's on TV; she waives the fees for my yearly appointment. Tat for tit, since spot-checking my boobs for suspicious lumps is part of the deal.

"What brings you here, love?" she said, looking at my chart. "We usually see you in January." I couldn't tell if Sheila was worried. Her husband is one of the city's cosmetic dermatology czars, and her face hasn't expressed concern, sadness, or shock in years.

"What brings me here is my fervent hope you'll tell me my pee-on-a-stick tests have been bullshit," I said, feeling as ridiculous as the next woman wearing a blue paper gown, dangling her bare legs off the edge of an examining table. If the definition of insane is repeating the same activity, expecting a different outcome, I was certifiable; I'd done four more pregnancy tests.

"Let's have a look." Sheila bent her head low for a pussy peek, wiggled a speculum, and thumped my belly from the outside. "Your uterus is slightly enlarged."

What part of me wasn't?

"But we can't rely on those drugstore tests—we'll need to do your blood," she announced. "I'll send in my nurse. After she's finished, you and I will talk."

One prick later, we were in Sheila's office, chatting about another. "Are you still dating Ted?" she asked, leaning forward in her chair, girlfriend style. Ted and I had once had a double-date with the Drs. Frumkes.

I realized Ted's handsome, scheming face had become a blur. Were his eyes green or was that just the color I'd turned when I found out he was cheating? "Ted's history. I have a different man in my life now."

"You always do. Would this be the lucky father, assuming positive results?"

"He would. But let's leave lucky out of it."

She cast a taut, perfectly made-up eye in my direction. "Please tell me he's not married."

"He's single, perhaps terminally."

"Hmmm." Sheila's tone said, *Do go on.*

"It wouldn't matter who the father of this mythical baby is," I said in a voice loud enough to be heard out on Park Avenue. "We both know I am completely unqualified to be anyone's mother. I'm too old, too selfish, too bossy, and if I didn't want a child at twenty-three or thirty-three, why would I want one now?"

To my horror, Dr. Sheila Frumkes took my hand. "Allow me to speak as both your friend and physician. Let's wait for the blood works, and in the meantime, I urge you to not jump to conclusions. The far side of forty is when a lot of my patients find that their attitude shifts. I've been practicing a long time"—to celebrate her fiftieth birthday last year she got a two-carat diamond belly-button stud to show off her abs—"and in my experience, many women who never thought they would want children turn out to be beyond delighted at a surprise pregnancy, and even more who predicted failure as a parent become outstanding mothers. It's one of the most mysterious, rewarding aspects of my work."

Yeah, yeah, yeah. Sheila could save the rhetoric for one of the skinny thirty-eight-year-olds crowding her waiting room, women who felt if they didn't reproduce they were as incomplete as a bra with one cup. I'm not one of those females who need kids to give themselves purpose and importance and stretch marks to bitch about—and which, in truth, they wear like medals.

"I'll keep that in mind," I lied. "I respect your opinion"—which was, after all, gratis. "When should I call for the results?"

"Tomorrow or the next day, depending on how asleep at the wheel the lab techs are. Now, you'll have to excuse me—I need to break the word to the couple in the next room that it's triplets. They've had two miscarriages." Discretion is not Sheila's finest attribute. "Don't be surprised if you hear screaming."

Triplets should have put things in perspective. But they didn't. One baby was still like one atom bomb or one sex-change operation. It would mutate everything in my life to a shape I couldn't grasp, and I wasn't even thinking specifically—*quelle horreur*—about my body. To start, I supposed I had to consider Arthur.

My ability to fantasize is well honed, so much so that if I can't envision someone in an imaginary role, it's a sign that I don't want to see them in that capacity. Arthur as a dad. Arthur as a partner. Arthur as a husband. Arthur and me as parents. One by one, I pictured...nothing.

I decided to add to Jules' Rules: *If pregnant, keep the news to yourself until you're sure you care what the father thinks.* The truth was, just as I couldn't conjure up Arthur in any version of commitment, I also couldn't guess his response to having knocked me up. He was fifty. Did he want a child? Did he want me? Would he be appalled or relieved if I decided to...

I couldn't complete the thought. Wasn't today already an all-you-can-eat buffet of surprises? A tear trickled down my cheek. Fucking hormones. I grabbed a tissue out of the box on Sheila's desk and dabbed away mascara. A nurse strolled into the office with a chart in her hands, so I got up and walked to the bathroom to collect my thoughts and properly wash my face. On the way, I heard the shriek of joy or shock Sheila had predicted. Whoop-de-do.

I closed the door and admired the décor. The bathroom was limestone with fresh calla lilies, a basket of linen towels, and a shelf discreetly labeled for urine specimens. There were six in a row, each vial like precious eau de parfum.

I walked closer. In the golden lineup was a small glass of pee plainly labeled *Q. Blue*.

Holy Jesus.

I sat down on the closed toilet seat. Quincy: triplets. This was too huge to absorb alone. I needed to share this with someone. Despite the prohibition against using cell phones, I pulled mine out.

Arthur answered on the first ring.

CHAPTER 19

Chloe

"May I refresh that drink?"

"Please!" I'd gulped down my first frosty mojito as if it were limeade. I didn't dare ask the server if the blonde with the dark roots in the next cabana was Maizie May or some other star famous mostly for being famous. Around her were a group of pedicured people in flip-flops, and my eyes ricocheted between them and the evenly tanned women frolicking in the turquoise water. They, too, were playing spot-a-celebrity, and few of them were discreet about it, or anything else. But the abundant chests and Brazil-nut-sized diamond studs were all part of the grand Beverly Hills Hotel experience. I was loving it! I felt deliciously inconspicuous, even in a fuchsia one-piece, one more tropical blossom in the garden where I waited for the ghosts of Clark Gable and Carole Lombard to drift past, hand in hand.

This was my first time in Los Angeles, my first time accompanying Xander on a business trip, my first time away from Dash, whom Jamyang was looking after, and soon, quite possibly, my first time relaxing, if I dare call it that, with Charlene "Cha-Cha" Denton, the wife of Xander's boss.

Charlene is only six years older than I am, but next to her I feel like a rookie. She's one of those women with such lavish charm that she might have acquired it not through breeding or observation but via a transplant. She speaks vaguely of roots "out west," where she and Edgar own a vast Montana ranch and raise emus and grass-fed bison, but a *Vanity Fair* profile suggested that Edgar had met Charlene when she'd waited on him at a cigar bar after she'd escaped from her parents' pig farm near Turtle Lake, Minnesota, not far from where Quincy grew up.

Xander and I had arrived yesterday evening. He had business in L.A. doing whatever it is that hedge fund managers do—I stopped requesting specifics years ago. His schedule was crammed. Mine wasn't.

Under normal circumstances, I would have liked to have visited Talia's parents in Santa Monica. Talia had alerted her mother that I was coming to town, and I arrived to a message inviting me for a walk on the beach followed by tea, which Talia says her mother serves in glasses, even when it's hot. The prospect sounded lovely. I adore Mira Fisher. Yet this morning I'd lied to the Fishers' answering machine, saying I needed to go to an appointment with Xander. I was too furious at Talia to risk spending even a minute with her mother.

After breakfast at the Polo Lounge, I strolled on Rodeo Drive, a disappointing stretch with the same Gucci, Armani, and Prada I'm too intimidated to enter on Madison Avenue. My window shopping took all of twenty minutes. I bought nothing and returned to the hotel.

At that point an adventuresome woman would have asked the concierge to call her a taxi to go to, say, the Getty Museum. Not me. I bought Jamyang some ridiculously priced caviar eye essence in the hotel's spa, left a message for Charlene inviting her to join me, and headed for the pool, where I'd been sitting for more than an hour, half hoping she wouldn't show up. I would happily wait to see her that night, when Xander and I had a dinner scheduled with the Dentons for eight. But Xander had referred to my private time to be spent with Charlene as "sealing the deal." Edgar had graduated from Jackson Collegiate, and both of the school's new red clay tennis courts were named for him. Xander felt it would be brash to ask directly for his boss's help in getting Dash admitted to Jackson. It had to be "spontaneous," and impressing Mrs. Edgar Denton mattered most. It was she who directed Edgar's personal foundation, she whose approval needed to be wooed and won.

And there she was, suddenly, all six feet one inch of her. *Vanity Fair* had compared Charlene to a crane ready to topple, but today she looked as confidently upright as ever. Her sharply angled face was softened by the shadows from a flying-saucer-sized white hat of the sort I'd seen only in photographs of British ladies attending Ascot. She waved as she swanned in my direction, and even that gesture reminded me of royalty, which in certain East Coast circles Charlene was.

"Chloe, darling," she said in her well-modulated voice, as if there were no other person on earth she'd looked forward to camping out with on a steamy California day. She kissed each of my cheeks. "Your suit is precious."

I knew better than to mistake Charlene's comment for a compliment. When she deftly removed her gauzy white caftan, Charlene herself was wearing a shiny black bikini. Her sandals, with their slender, silvery straps, made mine look like hand-me-downs from Mother Teresa. Next to her I felt like a stump covered by a rashy fungus, but I was determined— thank you, lovely, calming cocktails—not to have one of my paranoia attacks. Today I was in service to my child's future!

"Thanks," I said. "When did you and Edgar arrive?" Charlene and Edgar own a jet.

"We left Mexico a few hours ago," she said. "We blinked and were landing in Burbank."

I blinked, too, and the blonde in the next cabana walked in our direction, lurching into my chaise. She scowled, as if her accident were my fault, then giggled loudly, unself-consciously, drunkenly.

At close range there was no doubt: the woman was Maizie! Did I dare out myself as knowing Quincy? "Excuse me," I said, "but I believe my close friend Quincy Blue is working on a project with you?" My statement came out like a question. The sun was in my eyes, which made it hard to see Maizie's reaction, but I believe she took a slow, dismissive scan of me and turned toward Charlene, who ran away with the conversation. "Why, Miss May," she said, leaning forward. " 'Lonesome Trucker' is at the top of my playlist. I'm a truly devoted fan."

Charlene Denton liked Maizie May? I did know, this time courtesy of *The New Yorker*, that in order to prep for whatever encounter might be required to extend and solidify her power, Charlene reportedly reads every column in every magazine, newspaper, and major online source; apparently her daily feed includes *Billboard*. "You must—you absolutely must—join my dear friend Chloe Keaton and me for lunch," she insisted.

I expected Maizie to blow off Charlene as the lamest sort of perimenopausal groupie. Instead she said, "Costume Institute gala, the mermaid in blue fins and the sequined headdress?"

"Good Lord, you noticed me in that crowd?" Charlene managed to make "good Lord" sound clever and original.

After that event, photos of both Maizie and Charlene had been splashed all over the Sunday *Times* Style section. I'd heard rumors that Edgar was one of Maizie's backers, and Charlene, of course, had been on the steering committee. I imagined that she had to be flattered by Maizie taking note of her latitude and longitude in the social firmament, though she acted cool. Not snotty cool, friendly cool. "Cha-Cha Denton," she said, extending her slim hand with its substantial, but not grossly large, marquise diamond.

She'd never asked me to call her Cha-Cha.

"Maizie," the singer said, giving Charlene's hand a quick shake. "You and your friend have gotta join my group." She glanced at her watch. To my eye, its iridescent face and chunky metal band suggested Chinatown, but it might be platinum. "We'll be at the banquette against the wall. Two sharp." She walked away without ever having looked at me again.

"Don't you think Maizie is bewitching?" Charlene asked.

Bewitching hadn't been an adjective Quincy used in describing Maizie, though I'd heard *narcissistic, unreliable,* and *juvenile*. But Charlene's question didn't need an answer. By barely tilting her head, she prompted several cabana boys to zoom in our direction and furnish us with extra towels; mojitos, easy on the ice; a second umbrella; and an enormous basket of crudités sculpted like flowers. Charlene signed the tab and, with that, reached down into her Chanel tote, pulled out *The Economist*, and turned away to read.

I wished I'd brought reading material other than the 833-page novel I'd started in Maine. *The Crimson Petal and the White* was stuffed with historical details, like how many bundles of holly an English family ordered for Christmas in 1875. Still, its cover, with its rumpled bed behind red draperies, looked like trash, and I guessed that little escaped the scrutiny of Charlene's eyes, which matched the sapphire baguettes of her ring. I'm fairly certain that if she were quizzed, she could accurately report Xander's last bonus and the number of square feet we own back in Brooklyn.

Thinking about Brooklyn made me want to call home. By now it was past four in New York, and Dash might be back from Henry Fisher-Wells' birthday party. I'd dodged a bullet on that one, with the trip giving me an unquestionable excuse to send Dash to the party accompanied by Jamyang and a set of blocks that promised to develop sequential and organizational thinking, math concepts, and structural design skills. I was angry—furious!—at Talia, but I didn't want to take it out on Henry. In the last three weeks I'd not seen Talia once. At work we were communicating strictly by phone, e-mail, and succinct notes. If Talia suspected anything was amiss, she'd kept it to herself. With both of our lives generally hectic, our behavior was, I told myself, within the boundaries of normal.

Feeling woozy, though, was not. Between the mojitos and the temperature, tiny, evil *charros* were stamping on my temples, their partners in my tummy shouting *Olé!* as they picked up the pace. I put down my book, willed myself not to be ill, and closed my eyes, pulling my canvas hat over my forehead and hoping the buzzing I heard was from insects.

The next thing I knew, Charlene was nudging my arm. "Chloe," she said. "It's almost two. Want to have lunch?"

I quickly opened my eyes. A slight trickle of drool had dripped down the side of my face. I prayed that Charlene would think it was perspiration, although she herself looked fresh as dew.

"Of course. Let's eat!" I said in that too-fast way people speak when they're embarrassed at being caught snoozing. In truth, the idea of lunching with Maizie May and her girl group sounded like persecution: *the Beverly Hills Hotel—come for the glamour, stay for the humiliation.* But what I said—thank you, marvelous mojitos—was "It will be fun!"

Charlene precisely folded her copy of the Sunday *Times*, the one from London. She removed her hat without disturbing her brilliantly blond chignon, slipped into her caftan, and replaced her hat at exactly the most flattering angle. We walked back to the horseshoe-shaped banquette where Maizie was already sitting. The sycophant to her right got up and let Charlene slide into the seat of honor. This friend-of-Maizie then sat down to Charlene's left, and several other young women followed her. That left either end seat for me, though if I'd gone across to the other side of the restaurant I doubt anyone would have noticed.

"Tell me how a girl from Ocala gets to the top of the pop charts," Charlene asked, as if she were genuinely interested. For the next ten minutes, Maizie explained how she'd been discovered in a Piggly-Wiggly where she was a cashier known to sing about her customers' purchases and how a record producer was in her line buying Okefenokee BBQ Sauce while he was home visiting his parents. Maizie told the tale with considerable animation, though she was repeating the story not, I guessed, for the first time. Every one of her dedicated followers hooted loudly or yelled "No shit, girl" at regular intervals.

As we nibbled shrimp cocktail and chopped salads, Charlene continued to steer the conversation. The two headliners discovered that both of them owned homes not far from Mazatlán and compared notes about a party given by a gentleman named El Gigante. The more they chatted, the more it became clear that Señor Gigante's nickname was inspired by an appendage that Maizie seemed proud to know intimately. I wanted to break into the conversation but had as much social currency as a beggar at Bergdorf's. My only card to play, I decided after twenty minutes, was to once again bring up Quincy. "How's the book going?" I asked during what I thought was either a lull or Charlene taking a deep, cleansing breath.

Maizie looked at me and laughed—at me, not with me, I guessed. Yet I added, "With my friend Quincy Blue. Your ghostwriter."

"I know who you mean. I'm pissed at that skinny twat, if you want to know the truth."

I could feel my face reddening, and it wasn't because the café's fans had lost their battle against the heat. "Really?" I said, with alcohol-fueled boldness. "What's the problem, if you don't mind my asking?"

"She got knocked up. Just when I've decided I'm really into the book and have some face time to finish, she goes off and disappears because"— Maizie switched to a flat midwestern accent to mimic Quincy's—"her doctor won't let her git on a plane. She was supposed to meet me last week after my show in Seattle."

"Quincy's p-p-pregnant?" I sputtered.

"Not just p-p-pregnant. She's having a litter."

"Quincy's having twins?"

"If only. No, triplets."

My mouth hung open. Hot tears began dribbling down my cheeks. Triplets!

"You seem surprised. I thought she was your best friend, woman," Maizie roared.

Through my mojito haze, I reminded myself that I shouldn't be angry at Quincy for not having told me. Given her medical history, she probably was afraid to say anything until she was further along, and she'd informed Maizie only because she was forced to. But I felt like a fraud all the same, especially when Charlene added, "Yes, that *is* odd that you don't know. Curious indeed."

Where did that come from? I wanted to throw my drink in Charlene's sweat-free face. Cha-Cha Denton was ... disloyal. She cared only about impressing Maizie May. No, that wasn't all. Charlene Denton could pretend all she wanted that she was refined, but the real Cha-Cha was a nasty, overly ambitious, despicable she-devil. This insight occurred with another: the mere thought of calling upon Charlene to help Dash get into school seemed, in a flash, ugly, wrong, and dirty. I didn't care what Xander would say. I couldn't let our innocent child's future be tainted by such a nasty conniver.

I decided she really did look like a crane, not a piece of construction equipment as much as some sort of ghastly bird with a nose that was too long, a neck too scrawny, and knees too knobby. And her hair looked like a polygamist's wife's!

I hated hearing Quincy's news in this way, but my friend was pregnant! Quincy and Jake were going to have an instant, enormous family. I wanted to run back to my room and call her with congratulations. I wanted to ship off dozens of tea roses and the Silver Rain perfumed body lotion I'd seen in the hotel's spa. But, obviously, I could do none of those things. If Quincy had wanted me to know, she'd have told me.

If I couldn't speak to Quincy, though, I had to speak to someone. Certainly not Jules, who barely tolerated children, Dash included.

I rolled the linen napkin between my fingers and realized that left . . . Talia. Yes, I wanted to speak to Talia, who up until a few weeks ago I'd considered to be my dearest friend. *Dammit, Talia,* I thought, only slightly aware that the conversation around me was continuing. *Why did you have to ruin everything by snatching a job meant for me and for being sneaky-strange about the whole school business?*

Talia and Charlene: connivers. How different were they? I grabbed an untouched mojito and, without excusing myself, left.

CHAPTER 20

Quincy

Three babies: one for each we're mourning, plus another chickpea-sized miracle. I wandered through my days with a beatific smile.

Dr. Frumkes assured me I had no restrictions. Perhaps I shouldn't hike the Appalachian Trail, but neither did I have to retire to a hammock. My mind was a Slinky, coiled tightly, unable to land on any topic that wasn't related to the magic in my still-flat belly. I felt like a cocktail shaker, buoyant with excitement, nausea, and disbelief.

Though in theory I could proceed with Maizie's book research—Dr. F. said I could fly to Seattle for meetings—I couldn't concentrate on writing, other than to deconstruct each quiver in my journal. I begged our editor for an extension, to which she and Maizie sullenly agreed.

With the exception of those isolated, uncomfortable conversations, Jake and I hadn't spoken of the pregnancy to anyone without a medical degree. I would have liked to tell Talia, but I knew she'd feel it would be a jinx to discuss my complicated gestation at this vulnerable stage, and if I confided in Chloe, she'd be calling and texting to track every belch; I'd suffocate under the chokehold of her well-intentioned advice. And the gifts—hours after I'd told her, three layettes would be delivered, perhaps accompanied by a trio of wet nurses.

That left Jules. In other words, no one, although I'd considered Horton, whom I'd been calling daily to see if the co-op board had scheduled our interview, since top of mind was our now urgent need for larger living quarters. Today he answered, as he always does, halfway through the first ring. "Nope, zero news on the date," he said.

"What happened to hello?" I asked.

"What happened to patience?"

"Do boards drag their feet simply to psych out prospective owners? It's cruel, the way they're behaving." I was still madly in love with the apartment, but if our hopes for it crashed, I'd scrape myself off the floor and find an alternative, fast. There was no way five Blues could survive amicably for long in a seven-hundred-square-foot one-bedroom.

"Are we that worried about the big, bad, bald boyfriend?" Horton added.

"Should I be?"

Before he answered my question, he put me on hold to take another call. This gave me a chance to consider how sensible it was for a family to make a home anywhere in Manhattan. A saner couple would be putting all their energy into trying to retrieve their down payment while they frantically searched for a house in the suburbs—the most affordable outpost of, say, Anchorage. But I could barely grasp that I was pregnant. That was sufficient change for the moment.

Three minutes passed. I was ready to give up on Horton when he returned. "Stupendous news, Mrs. Blue," he said. "The board can see you and Jake—next Wednesday."

Thank you, God. "Finally," I said, with an audible exhale. "Where should we meet you?"

"Me? I, Horton, your lowly broker, am persona non grata. Not even Fran gets invited. You and Jake handle this meeting solo, not that I don't wish I could be a fly on the wall." At that, he cackled. "When you arrive at the building, the doorman will direct you. The interrogations are usually held in a board member's apartment."

"That's it?"

"Feel free to ask me anything. Go ahead, start."

"What should I wear?"

"Dress as if you're going to a funeral."

"*Will* it be a funeral?"

"You and Jake are attractive and likable. Your financials are solid. You don't have any pets—"

"Excuse me—remember Fanny?" The kitten was sleeping on my keyboard, and I was already worrying that when the babies came along, she'd grow into a velociraptor that would claw out their eyes.

"Right, you have a kitty. No problem there. Nor do you have kleptomania, a tic, or halitosis. The board will like you, trust me. The most crucial thing to remember is that you want to come off as having not a doubt in the world. This means you ask no questions. Zip. You should also absolutely not volunteer that you are going to renovate. Tell them you don't even plan to paint. Co-op boards fear renovations like a pizza fears a fat man."

"But the place is a disaster. Haven't they seen it?" *Or taken a sniff?*

"Dr. Walter hasn't had a visitor in a decade. The thing is," Horton stressed, "you can't let on that you think anything about the building is less than perfecto. Do not—do you hear me?—comment on the fake Oriental in the lobby or those low-rent draperies that are two inches too short." This much I was sure I could handle. "And do not get chatty. You don't want these board members to think you have a personality, none whatsoever. Think white bread. Mashed potatoes. Channel Nicole Kidman."

"I have a sufficient amount of money, impeccable manners, and absolutely no taste," I replied in a robot's voice.

"Quincy, my girl. Not funny. Repeat after me: 'These people are not my friends.'"

As if, even for a second, I'd ever thought they were.

. . .

Five days later, a white-jacketed manservant ushered us into the home of Basil Worthington and offered to take my coat. I handed it over, wondering if this gentleman's gentleman had been trained to report on whether the label was authentic. He hung my bona fide though well-worn Burberry in a space strangely devoid of tennis rackets, snow boots, winter hats, suitcases, shopping carts, or umbrellas—items that tumbled out of our small, dark coat closet every time it was opened. We followed him through a roomy foyer, circumventing a gleaming round table whose focal point was flowers that looked . . . fake.

Someone with turquoise silk roses is going to judge us, I grumbled silently as we were shown into a parlor. Six people waited. Two were women, one thin and elderly, the other chubby and about my age. The men ranged from a well-tailored guy who could win a most-freckles contest to a scholarly type in a cardigan, a silver-haired giant, and one pale dumpling in a red sweater. In each lap sat a dossier, presumably containing records of every penny Jake and I had earned, squandered, donated, invested, or grudgingly given to the government, along with letters attesting to our irreproachable character.

Jake and I had gone over Horton's instructions and role-played the answers for what we felt would be the most predictable questions. Assuming the board would be typically sexist, we agreed that Jake should take most of the hits. I felt ready.

"Why, have a chair," the giant boomed. His half-glasses rested on his veined, bulbous nose. "Basil Worthington, board president," he said and extended his hand, big as a catcher's mitt, first to Jake, then to me. I waited for him to introduce us to the rest of the board. He did not.

The man's eyes suggested that we park ourselves on a low love seat across from a lacquered coffee table on which a pitcher of ice water was placed alongside a stack of posy-sprigged paper cups exactly like those I'd last used to pee into in Dr. Frumkes' office. Next to the cups sat a plate of what appeared to be homemade chocolate chip cookies. Several of the members were already munching. No one invited us to dig in.

I sank into the upholstery, leaned back, and felt three feet tall. Better to pitch myself forward and at least appear to be a grown-up. Jake did the same. We looked like two nervous crows—we'd each worn a black suit—perched on a barbed-wire fence.

"So, you want to live in our building," Mr. Worthington bellowed. The living room was at least twenty feet long, but Basil Worthington had a voice better suited to a stadium.

"We do."

To my ears Jake's response sounded overly abridged, as if he couldn't muster appropriate enthusiasm for our glorious prospective acquisition. I am not a chatty woman, but I am a writer and felt an instinctive urge to expand. "We totally love it here," I added. For a crow, my voice came out in a sparrow's chirp, and for a woman who'd been given simple directions to follow, I'd already fouled.

"What is it, Mrs. Blue, you love?" asked the younger woman. She wore a tight ponytail and a tighter smile. She didn't volunteer her name, which struck me as odd, even rude. Her tone was dry, mocking. I decided she hated me on sight. Was it my God-given metabolism? She'd have a good chuckle, I thought, when I put on seventy-five pounds for the triplets.

"I love the absolutely delightful location, for one," I volunteered.

"By that do you mean the Upper West Side, Central Park, or our actual building?" she asked in a near snicker.

"All three actually." Was I allowed to pick three things or did the bylaws limit me to one? "And the lobby, it's gorgeous. A treasure." Four.

"You mean to say you like that rug?" She stopped just short of sticking fingers down her throat in the universal gesture of making yourself puke.

This reminded me that I'd needed no help in that department twice that morning as well as the night before, but I tried to focus. "The Oriental rug? The big one? It's . . . fine," I lied, surely chalking up more demerits on the judgment category of her scorecard.

"Now, Mr. Blue," said Mr. Worthington, grabbing back the floor. "I see you are an attorney. Tell us about your practice." He rifled through our papers. "Taxation law, is it?"

"Intellectual property. The firm where I'm a partner deals with copyrights, trademarks, patents, anything to do with creations of the mind—literary works, art, the whole murky universe of cyberspace, music—"

"A musician," said the other woman, clearly the oldest committee member. Maybe members get voted in for life.

"No," Jake corrected her. "I'm a lawyer."

"Do the two of you play any musical instruments?" she asked, switching to disappointment.

"I played the sax in my high school's jazz band," Jake offered.

The woman was crocheting what appeared to be a coat for an exceedingly round dog. She looked innocent enough, but was her question a curveball? Did she think we might break out the amps and electric guitars every midnight?

"Jake hasn't played that sax for years," I interrupted to say. "In fact, he gave it to his cousin. Let me assure you"—I realized she, too, had not offered her name—"we play no musical instruments, none whatsoever, not even kazoos. We have no talent." I offered this last tidbit as a joke. No one laughed.

The older woman shrugged and returned to her yarn and hook.

"Okay, then," Basil Worthington said. "Mrs. Blue, let's talk about your contribution to the family coffers. Do you work?"

"Yes. I write . . . nonfiction."

"Articles for scientific journals and fiscal reports—that kind of thing?" asked the paunchy guy. He was wan with thin hair and thick glasses. Like small flies, cookie crumbs covered his sweater.

"Not exactly," I said, eyeing the plate of cookies no one had offered.

"Which publishing house employs you?"

"I used to work at *People* but now I'm a freelancer. I write books."

"Books! Tell us, what sort?"

I could feel Jake's thigh pressing mine. "Biographies," I said.

"A biographer!" The man seemed to be salivating in expectation of an announcement that I was writing the life story of Nelson Mandela.

"Not exactly," I said.

His forehead wrinkled in confusion. "A series of memoirs, then?"

I might be the last woman on earth to think her personal story of sufficient intrigue to warrant a memoir, let alone a series. "I'm a collaborator, a ghostwriter, of celebrity autobiographies."

"Would we know any of the titles?" asked the tweedy, shaggy-haired fellow who'd apparently swallowed an English-professor.

"I'm not sure you'd have heard of any of the books I've written," I admitted. *Malibu Barbie* had paid a decent advance but gone straight to the remainder table along with the other stories of 1980s sitcom stars. "You see, as a ghost my name isn't even always identified as an author. I work behind the scenes and"—I used my fingers to show the size— "usually get only a tiny acknowledgment." Right after the celebrity's psychic, dog walker, and personal trainer, those other VIPs without whose forbearance, generosity, and support she couldn't have written the book.

The professor appeared suspicious, as did everyone but Jake, who was trying to reenter the conversation. Basil Worthington ignored him.

"How curious," Mr. Worthington said. "Could you clarify, please, Mrs. Blue?"

"Well, sometimes I get a *with*."

"A *with*?" He took his glasses in his hands, raised his eyebrows with their springy gray hairs, and looked baffled.

"As in 'so-and-so with Quincy Blue.'" He waved me on. "I might get an *and* on my next book." *And* was infinitely more high-status than *with*. My agent's negotiation with Maizie's people on that point had looked promising until I canceled the Seattle sessions. Now I'd be lucky to get cover credit at all.

"What's your next book?" Mr. Worthington asked.

"A biography of Maizie May," I said to him and six other blank faces. "The singer and actress." No reaction. "Her latest release went platinum."

"I gather that your contribution to the family incomes rises and falls," he correctly surmised. "Do you expect this book about Miss May, is it, to be a bestseller?"

"A bestseller?" I echoed. Jake's eyes were bearing down on me, but I couldn't simultaneously stop to decipher their message and answer the question. "That's impossible to predict—you never know when a book will take off—but maybe, well, yes, I think so. Yes, definitely," I said. "Her fans are legion"—*legion?*—"and they adore Maizie!"

"Okay, then," Basil Worthington said. "Moving on. Tell us more about yourselves. Are there any little Blues?"

Wasn't the question illegal, like inquiring at a job interview if you were a Hare Krishna or simply had a thing for flowing salmon-colored robes? I'd let Jake handle this one.

"Not yet."

"Something you young people want to tell us?" Mr. Worthington asked, twinkling.

"No," I said, although on cue, my babies united in protest. A surge of bile began to rumble somewhere above my crotch and slowly move north.

"If I may, Basil?" asked the bitch with the ponytail, who turned to me. "Opinion's divided regarding our next capital improvement. One proposal is to turn unused basement space into a kids' playroom, another faction wants storage bins for each apartment, and a third group's been working to create a landscaped roof garden—teak furniture, sun umbrellas, geranium pots, that sort of thing. Strictly in theory, Mrs. Blue, how would you vote?"

"Pardon me for asking, but should I assume they all cost the same?"

"Yes." Her expression said, *Obviously, you moron.*

"They all sound...completely and utterly lovely," I said, taking the wimp's road.

"Your preference, Mrs. Blue. This is not a trick question."

So you say. If I brought three toddlers to a roof garden, I'd be afraid one would dive off. A playroom made sense, but did I want to out myself as Mrs. Fertility? Jake and I had decided not to mention the pregnancy on the chance that someone on the committee thought children were good for nothing but disturbing the peace.

"We'd go with the storage space," Jake jumped in to say, sensibly enough.

"Mrs. Blue?" the woman snarled. She definitely hated me. Had I fired her when I ran my department at *People?*

I looked into Jake's eyes, which seemed to be saying, *Answer the god-damn question.* "Okay, well, storage, definitely," I said. Who couldn't use extra storage?

"Mr. and Mrs. Blue," asked the youngest man on the committee. Until now he had been silent—aggressively so, I thought—sitting back, sizing us up. "What do you intend to do with the apartment?"

Open a crack den? "Could you please define *do?*" I heard Jake groan ever so slightly.

"Improve," he said. "I doubt that place has been painted since 1985. Not that the owner isn't an angel." He paused as Proustian contentment seemed to float across his freckles. "I grew up in this building and every Halloween Dr. Walter gave out caramel apples. I can still remember when I bit into one and lost my front tooth."

The idea of biting into a sticky-sweet caramel apple brought on a wave of fierce queasiness that begged for my attention. "You'll have to excuse me," I said, standing abruptly. "Mr. Worthington, where's a bathroom, please?"

He pointed toward a long hall. "The second—no, the third—no, the second door on the right," he said as I bolted. I opened the second door. From a linen closet, the pungent odor of mothballs flew into my nostrils. Sudden cramps tightened as I tried the third door and found—yes!—a toilet. I retched into it three times, flushing twice after each deposit. When I was certain I had nothing left inside me, I rinsed my mouth and weakly mopped my forehead with dampened toilet paper. I looked for a window to open, but it was an interior powder room and the Worthingtons hadn't invested in an air freshener or even set out a dish of shriveled potpourri. I took a moment to gather my strength, then gingerly opened the door and walked back into the living room.

Jake was speaking to Basil Worthington, one-on-one, my coat slung over his arm. The other board members had disappeared.

"Feeling better?" Mr. Worthington asked.

"Much," I answered. I knew I was blushing. "We went out for Indian food before the meeting."

"You get on home now," he said to Jake. "The little lady needs some rest." Again the twinkle.

Riding down in the elevator, Jake asked if I was okay, and nothing more. As we walked across the grand lobby, I took a good look at the rug. "Horton's right. Hideous."

"Just as well," Jake said. "I wouldn't get too attached to anything here."

We walked a few more steps. "That bad, huh?"

"My date wouldn't stop jabbering," he said, "though I kept signaling for her to zip it."

We should have worked out hand signals. "I bungled it, didn't I?"

"Barfing makes a certain statement."

"What went on when I was in the bathroom?"

"A line of questions about how we'd found the apartment listing. The implication seemed to be that someone had given us a sweetheart deal."

"Which one brought that up?"

"The bitch," Jake said as I followed him through the revolving door that led to the street.

"Quincy!" someone squawked, bumping me as I put one foot on the sidewalk. "How'd the meeting go?" Jules stood inches away, her large chest practically pressing against mine. I stared at her incredulously and, I suppose, stupidly. "This woman, Jennifer, who lives next to Arthur is on the committee," she volunteered.

Something told me Jennifer wasn't the woman with the crochet hook, a weapon that wouldn't have been safe with me. A taxi pulled up to the building to dislodge its passengers. I yanked Jake's hand.

"Gotta go," I said, catapulting myself into the cab, followed by Jake. Neither of us spoke.

A few blocks away from our apartment, Horton called. "If you're answering this call, I assume the conquering heroes can talk. Tell me everything."

"On a scale of one to ten, I give it a two." In my analysis, vomit didn't make the cut.

"I assume you at least followed my directions."

We Minnesotans have a hard time telling a lie. "I did dress well."

He whistled. "Don't worry. I've had clients turned down when they were positive everything went hunky-dory but also the reverse. That building is known for its stick-up-its-ass board, but it's inscrutable. They could swing either way. Sometimes they vote right after the meeting. Do you think the committee hung around when you left?"

"Definitely not." I felt even guiltier. If I hadn't been holed up in the bathroom, maybe the board would have voted and we'd be delivered from our misery.

"It could be tomorrow—or two months from now. With these decisions, the only rule is there is no rule."

CHAPTER 21

Talia

I walked to the second floor of a cast-iron building that 120 years ago might have been a sweatshop and pushed open the door for Bespoke Communications. The ceiling soared for thirty feet, but the waiting area was cramped, furnished with a couch draped in a fuzzy white throw, a cowhide rug, and mismatched wooden chairs not unlike those I'd found discarded on the curb and claimed for my dining room. Depending on your point of view, the ad agency's aesthetic was shabby or chic.

Opinions might be mixed as well about the receptionist's appearance, but for one day of my life I'd have loved to know what it was like to have this woman's hair—platinum blond, razor-blade straight, cut in zigzags and spikes. A tight black sleeveless T-shirt showcased a Bugs Bunny tattoo on her slim but well-sculpted biceps. Her spindly heels were at least four inches tall. Next to her, I felt like Marie Osmond.

"I'm here to see Jonas Winters," I said. "Talia Fisher-Wells."

"It's Winters Jonas," she said in the accent of Liverpool.

"Of course," I answered, positive the headhunter had reversed the guy's name as I had.

"If you could fill out these forms?" She handed me a clipboard with a sheaf printed in an elegant, hard-to-read typeface. The paper was creamy and thick. Only question number three threw me: *How did you hear about the position?* I was tempted to says, *I snatched it from a friend, but now that I look around, this doesn't seem like her kind of place, so I'm feeling 10 percent less guilty.*

A few more minutes passed, which gave me time to ruminate, rarely a good thing. I hadn't been on a job interview in years and wasn't at all sure if I could project even a drizzle of confidence. And I was itching to see if my lip gloss needed repair, but didn't want to primp in front of the blonde. Instead, I decided to text Tom to say I'd arrived safely, a subliminal apology for cutting out early from Abigail's birthday celebration. Tom didn't answer, so I texted both Quincy and Jules. I'd been lost in self-absorption and hadn't spoken to either of them for a week, maybe two. As I was reading Jules' response—*Crazy busy, miss you more*—the receptionist looked up from under her shaggy fringe and announced, "Mr. Jonas will see you now." She returned to her newspaper, and added, "In the corner down the hall."

I gathered my portfolio and found his office, three times as large as the reception area. "Winters Jonas," said a man who stood behind an ebony desk almost as bare as his egg-shaped shaved head. His accent was old-time Brooklyn. He, too, wore all black—a tieless shirt, jeans, and boots—though his eyes were the dark blue of my father's prayer book.

"Talia Fisher-Wells, good to meet you. Very impressive submission." He shook my hand. On a table behind his desk I spied the spiral-bound project I'd been asked to complete. It rested on the top of a stack of what I assumed were other candidates' pitches, one in a hot pink box tied with a silk cord, a flourish I admired.

Jonas' voice was friendly, which I appreciated, along with the fact that we weren't wasting time on chitchat. "Thanks," I said. "I enjoyed writing it." This was almost true. If I weren't under enormous time pressure, I'd like crafting campaigns for $3,000 ostrich messenger bags, long-wearing mineral eye shadow in seven shimmering shades, and porcelain dishware with fourteen-karat ducklings, ideal for trust fund toddlers—far more inspiring than my usual stain remover, cream cheese, and frozen diet dinners, even if they were packed with 23 grams of protein and rainbow-hued crisp but tender vegetables.

"Tell me, Talia," he said, rolling my name around in his mouth as if it were a sucking candy, "what is it you love about writing ad copy?"

Besides being easy? Could I honestly say I was proud to use whatever talent had been given me to convince people to buy things they didn't need? What a waste of ability, for which I never felt I should take more credit than for being five foot seven and left-handed. I realized the God of Abraham, Isaac, and Jacob was in my head, rehearsing a sermon, and I tried to chase Him away.

"I love the challenge." I aimed to sound determined yet relaxed as I repeated words I'd rehearsed. "Creating ads requires a deft use of language and psychology. I try to figure out how to leverage both to persuade people. It's like Scrabble: having a decent vocabulary only matters a little. The winners are players who strategize, and that's what I do well." I thought I sounded coherent. Maybe I was in my element after all.

Winters Jonas had shifted positions, and a wide slice of afternoon sun made his chiseled features look almost handsome if you discounted the glints off his bald dome. He was peering at me, and I decided his eyes had brightened. They looked more like the Aegean lapping next to a Greek island. When I walked into the office it hadn't occurred to me that he was even remotely attractive. I was beginning to change my mind. He seemed to be emanating power, the capital-P pheromone.

"Thinking of ads is like being at a fantasy camp for my brain," I decided to add.

"Interesting," he said. "Could you describe your management style?" As he spoke, he fondled a large shell, his desk's only adornment. Had he found it when he scuba-dived in some exotic locale? I pictured him wearing a black wet suit. I had always wanted to try scuba diving, but Tom's idea of a beach vacation involved rickety old rowboats and worms.

This time I answered even more quickly. "I like to roll up my sleeves and lead by example." I felt satisfied with the response, but the man be-hind the desk seemed to expect more. "And I always keep an open door. If someone has a problem, I listen, and I know which buttons to push to motivate my staff."

I said this though I had no right to consider myself a manager, least of all one with a style. I'd managed a move to New York, a pregnancy, and a meager bank account, but never an employee, discounting an intern. Yet my interviewer grinned, as if to say, *Yes, the answer to the question was B, and you nailed it.* His teeth were straight and unusually white, and his smile created crinkles around those blue, blue eyes. My bosses had all been women or males with C-minus looks. Would it be distracting to work for a good-looking guy or simply a terrific perk, like free cappuc-cino?

"Talia," Winters said—we were on a first-name basis now—"there would be travel with this job. When we pitch business or meet with clients, we often do it on their turf. Is this a problem?"

Flying to Europe on someone else's euro, staying at an exquisite hotel with no child panting for apple juice at five-thirty in the morning, sipping a glass of vino when we took a break? I answered him with what I hoped was my own dazzling smile.

"My schedule is extremely flexible," I said, although it wasn't. Tom knew I was going on a job interview, but we had never discussed business trips, which weren't required where I currently worked, not counting the occasional jaunt to a suburban industrial park. Having me gone for days at a time would not be easy without a nanny as backup. It occurred to me that with Jamyang on the payroll this position made far more sense for Chloe, and after she met Winters, she might be able to get over the foyer's décor and the receptionist's wardrobe. I tried to concentrate on the con-versation, but the guilt I'd eradicated had returned in full force.

A black dog bounded in and ran to Winters' side. I watched him pet the animal's sleek fur. No wedding ring. "Meet Axel," he said. "You do like dogs, don't you?"

"He looks like my Pontoon. Any border collie in him?"

"Haven't a clue," he said. "He's a rescue dog."

Not only was Winters an ace ad man with a droll downtown office and high-end clients, he was a humanitarian. "I adore dogs," I said, immediately regretting my toady enthusiasm.

He smiled again. "Talia, do you have any questions?"

Are you married? Straight? And why do I care? "How quickly are you moving on this position?"

"Assuming we land an account we're very close to getting, I'll move fast. I've narrowed our search to you and two others." I wondered which of the pitches I'd noticed hadn't made the cut. I hoped it was the pink one. "What's your availability?"

Married! Taken! Monogamous! "I'd like to give three weeks' notice."

"Fair enough. What compensation are you looking for?"

The forms I'd been asked to complete had a space for my current salary, which I'd left blank. I'd hoped he'd name a figure first, but two could play this game. "Something in line with my ability."

"Okay, then. What are you earning now?"

Cornered, I doubled my salary to make it full-time, inflated it by 30 percent, and quoted a number. He shook his head. Bad shake or good shake, I couldn't tell. "Aha" was all he said, getting up.

"May I show you my portfolio?" I asked, not that it was my strongest selling point. I could hear my own hesitation.

"Of course." He opened it with his strong hands and flipped through it slowly, questioning me on every spread. After a good ten minutes he looked up and smiled.

The interview, I realized, was over. When I'd had a chance, should I have volunteered how much I'd like going on sales calls, bragged about what an asset I'd be? *Too late now, Talia Rose Fisher. Mrs. Fisher-Wells.* "Thank you for your time," I said.

"A pleasure," Winters Jonas said. "You have a lot of energy."

Did I come off like the kind of woman who can't stop dancing in the aisles at a rock concert?

We shook hands. "We'll be in touch," he said. He smiled and turned toward a sleek laptop on the shelf behind him. That's when I remembered one of Jules' Rules: *Always ask for the business.*

"I'd like this job. I think I'd be an asset to Bespoke Communications."

"Really?" he said, regarding me with amusement.

"If you don't hire me, you'll have made a grave error," I added, standing tall, seeing myself with blond, straight hair, sitting in first class, jetting to Barcelona and Berlin, cities I'd yet to visit.

"I'll keep that in mind, Talia," Winters Jonas said, chuckling.

I walked out the door, down the dim hall, past Blondie. When I reached the sidewalk, a circle of people had gathered two abreast. I got closer and saw the attraction, a man wearing a cross and a broad black hat, *shuckling* like a rabbi while he read from the Talmud.

"Is he a Bob Dylan impersonator?" the woman beside me asked.

"A Jew for Jesus," her boyfriend responded.

I walked away as fast as I could and didn't look back. Mean Maxine and I knew the evil eye when it showed up on Broadway and Prince.

CHAPTER 22

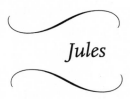

Jules

In that lobby, could Quincy have ditched me any faster? I didn't get a good long look at her, except to notice she was wearing the same raincoat she'd had when we were roommates. I'd have loved to see if someone pregnant with three babies was triple my size. I might have liked to have a real chat, though even under ideal circumstances I'd never ask her opinion about what the fuck I should do next in my life, and not only because, officially, I'm not supposed to know she's pregnant. Neither Talia nor Chloe had mentioned Quincy's delicate condition, so either the little mama hadn't told them yet or—ouch!—those two biddies had been sworn not to talk about the blessed event to the likes of me, the woman robbing Quincy's triplets of a home.

"Good evening, Miss de Marco. Can we help you?"

Oh, that you could. "I'm fine, Esteban, but thanks," I said. All the doormen had learned my name. It's highly civilized to be greeted whenever I enter this lobby, but as I walked across a rug so plug-ugly it would go begging on Craigslist, it occurred to me that the snoots here must think simply that because this was their address, they had style. I'd have bet my ass that was the crew that had picked the rug. I wondered how many owners are like Arthur, who bought here when the neighborhood was a gulag.

As I got off the elevator, I heard the howling. That meant one thing: Arthur had been paid a visit by his neighbor. Her horselaugh rang through the hall.

Jennifer is one of those women aroused by competition. Until I erupted on the scene, I doubt she'd have grunted hello to my Artie when they bumped into each other tossing garbage down the chute. Now, with me across the hall several nights a week, she pops up like spam. I've suggested that he install a firewall—shouting "I have a girlfriend" would be a start—but he loves the pig-in-shit attention.

Turning my key in the lock, I could hear her say, "The wife got so rattled she had to make a bathroom run." When I walked through the door, tears were running down Jennifer's cheeks, streaking gullies in her makeup. *Should I hand her a rag? Offer to hose her down?*

"Holy crap!" Arthur said, apparently unaware of my presence. "What else went on?" He poured wine into his guest's half-empty glass. It was from a bottle I'd brought two days ago.

"The woman could not stop talking. Diarrhea of the mouth and—whatever!" Jennifer whooped again and took a big swallow, which brought on a coughing spell.

"Hello!" I shouted as I put down a bouquet of yellow roses and a bag containing Hostess Twinkies and bacon. I'd been craving both, along with the obscenely expensive red beet sorbet at Rosa Mexicano. I hoped Sheila had been correct when she announced there was a baby inside me, because I'd already gained seven pounds. The buttons on my shirts were popping. "Could you give me a hand here?" I yelled over the hilarity.

"Jules, doll," Arthur said, walking toward me. He gave me a showy tongue kiss and let his hand linger on my ass. I leaned against him and joined my arms around his waist. *Jennifer, eat your jealous little heart out.*

"I was filling Arthur in on tonight," she said with her usual stuck-on-herself air.

"The 'confidential' meeting?" I asked.

Her beady eyes darted to Arthur as if to ask, *Whose team is* she *on, anyway?* "Arthur's a close friend whose interest I support," she sniffed. "I thought he deserved to know." To her credit, she kept her tone light, despite the defensive position.

I'll admit I was curious about the Blues' interview, but my interest was trumped by a far more dominant need to prevent Jennifer from enjoying the luxury of feeling essential. Last I checked, I don't suffer from adult-onset idiocy.

"Cut to the chase," Arthur said. "When's the vote?"

"Basil's call." Jennifer shrugged. "He'll schedule a second meeting to chew up the buyers whenever he feels like it, and we'll vote at the end. Secret ballot."

"It's a democracy?" I asked. These days, so little is.

"Not exactly. Let's just say you don't want Basil on your bad side, not if you'd like to install a washing machine or get your new couch delivered on a Saturday. He's the imperial wizard."

Jennifer's analysis of this ant colony might be mildly intriguing, but no other good would come of having her hang around. When Arthur left the room, I deployed the most basic of Jules' Rules: *To make someone disappear, ignore them.* I turned my back on Jennifer to fill a vase, which I took with casual propriety from a cabinet in the wet bar, and concentrated on cutting the roses' stems under running water, meticulously plucking away thorns and excess foliage. After two minutes of silence, Arthur reemerged from the bathroom, zipping his fly, and Jennifer stood to say goodbye. "I'll call as soon as I hear anything," she promised as she flounced away.

"Why ya leaving, Jen?" She looked at me cross-eyed and walked out. "Now she's probably pissed, and where's that going to get me?" a petulant Arthur asked after the front door closed. He walked toward me and put on a hangdog expression. "Why'd you scare her off?"

Corollary: *Don't feel obligated to answer a question merely because someone poses it.* "Twinkie?" I asked as I stood back to admire the flowers' lush fullness, not, I hoped, unlike my own.

He looked at me as if I'd said, *Industrial-strength sodium stearoyl lactylate, darling?* "How can you eat that crap?" This from a man who considers pork and beans a company meal.

"I offered you a snack cake, not a glass of weed killer," I said as I bit into the spongy confection.

Arthur pulled me toward him, which I allowed, and tried to kiss away my incipient foul mood. He obviously wasn't up for a fight, and neither, frankly, was I. For all his faults, Arthur was not without talent in bed, and that's where I wanted to wind up, as soon as possible. One thing led to another, and then another.

"Doll, is it my imagination, or are you even more voluptuous than the other day?" he asked as he unhooked the oldest, most stretched-out bra in my lingerie drawer. I'd been wearing it on the loosest hook, but it still created cleavage dangerously rivaling Aretha Franklin's and, when removed, left an angry red ring around the softness of my rib cage. I wanted Arthur's question to be another I left unanswered, but he persisted. "Seriously," he said. "You look different."

"You and your imagination." I aimed for nonchalance, but this was like saying, *Omigod, Arthur, your hairline is receding, I never noticed.*

"Getting your period?" He leaned back and looked at me.

We were now in the vicinity of land mines. "Artie," I said, moving my hands to parts of his body that I felt certain would lead us away from the line of fire if serviced, "you're right, maybe I'm late. I've never been regular." Another lie. My periods were as reliable as a utility bill.

He started fondling the tattoo on my breast, but his touch on my swollen flesh felt like sex abuse. I flinched.

"A tad PMS-y, are we?"

A tad retarded, are we? I'm having your goddamn baby, you cretin. One minute I'd be visiting the site for Planned Parenthood and every other earnest resource where I could be counseled on Trying to Decide. The next, Sisters Chastity, Consuelo Lingus, Butch, and Dildo—the bitch quartet that haunts my high school memories—had lined up to hiss, *Julia Maria de Marco, we will not allow you to sin. You are not going to harm your precious unborn child. You are not going to even fucking think about it. Just try.* All the nuns I ever knew then joined them in a line of shrill, frowning sopranos, their rulers keeping time with the message: *You fornicating ho, what did you think would come from banging thirty different guys in almost three decades?*

Perhaps they didn't say *bang.* Maybe the word was *boff* or *hump*, but I got the message. Sisters of Mercy, my fat ass.

I backed away from Arthur. "No!" I shouted.

"What's this about?" he asked.

To my absolute horror, I started to weep. I probably looked worse than Jennifer during one of her spastic laugh attacks.

"Shit, Jules—what's wrong?" Arthur looked genuinely concerned, until I swear I saw him smile. "Is it Jennifer?"

I wanted to strangle him with my bra until his eyes popped out. "That loser?" I said, wiping away my tears.

Arthur leaned back on his sturdy haunches and looked smug. "You're worried she's got me covered on the nights you aren't here."

To think that the innocent lump of cells multiplying inside me had half of this douche's genes was, in itself, a compelling pro-choice argument. "Arthur, I don't give a shit what you do with Jennifer," I said, drawing out her name until it was as long as a plumber's snake. Yet I realized it wasn't entirely true. I suddenly did care. "Except the way the two of you are trying to trash Quincy's chance to get the apartment."

"Julia de Marco, what are you implying?"

"I'm not *implying*, Arthur Weiner." I managed a snarky laugh. "I believe I'm being explicit."

"Fuck, you don't think I deserve that co-op as much as a complete stranger?" He sounded as hurt as he did angry.

"She's not a stranger, not to me," I blurted out. "Quincy is my friend."

"Oh, really?" he said. " 'Quincy is my friend,' " he mimicked. "So what does that make me?"

"I'm going to have to get back to you on that one."

I took a moment, dressed at my leisure, and left the bed, the room, and the apartment.

CHAPTER 23

Chloe

After California, I decided I required a makeover, inside and out. Not the kind involving Infallible Lustrous Never-Fail Lip Color and a haircut that cost double what my first semester of college had. I wanted to become a tough cookie, someone who would never again get scammed by a friend. In my survival-of-the-fittest world, I needed to reconstitute myself as more lean mean protein, less sugar and boggy fiber.

I'd begun to inhale self-help books and motivational tapes, often while I walked on the treadmill. Before bed, TiVo'd *Oprah* episodes became my sound track for a vigorous free-weight workout that balanced the yoga I started practicing five times a week. I'd also dived deeply into Internet chat rooms, but since I wasn't a pedophile, gambler, sex addict, or date rape victim—just your basic wuss for whom a fearless act is wearing a red strapless dress—I found no help there.

This morning, as I stirred fat-free milk into my coffee—if I was going to evolve, my seven pounds of baby weight weren't going to make the trip—I started to list my goals. *Get Dash into Jackson Collegiate* was number one, followed by *Find new job*, despite the fact that I had no more natural ambition than a parakeet. As I composed my third goal, *Start work-ing with a therapist and/or life coach*, Xander walked into the room and kissed me behind the ear. He smelled of mouthwash and lime aftershave. His uncombed dark blond hair, wet from the shower, dangled over his forehead and tickled my neck.

"A life coach?" he asked. "What's that? More to the point, why?" Xander is a man too busy to be introspective. There's the firm, his athletic club, his Harvard B-school alumni organization, golf, his rare-book col-lection, and subscriptions to the *Financial Times* and three other newspa-pers he reads cover to cover. Dash and I factor in there, too. But mostly there's his stability. Xander makes a mountain look like mush.

"I thought I could do with a little improvement," I said after I kissed him on the cheek, walked to the fridge, and removed a pint of rasp-berries. I washed a handful, blotting each jewel gently with a paper towel before I used them to adorn my organic Greek yogurt mixed with health-food-store granola. I stood back and admired my virtuous breakfast.

"If this is a pointless quest for perfection," Xander said as he poured his coffee, "that's..." About the time people abandoned carbs, he'd cut out cursing. Déclassé! "Nonsense," he said finally.

"It's not nonsense," I said carefully. "I need to clarify and achieve goals." *Like you do instinctively.* Xander won't admit he's in constant re-finement, a process so embedded into his character he wouldn't recog-nize the effort.

"You sound like those programs you watch," he said, and gulped cof-fee, then stared at the mug. "What is this?"

"Decaf."

He poured his coffee in the sink and reached for his briefcase. "The problem's not with you and me, is it?"

"I never said I have a problem. I simply want to talk things through with someone who's..." Smarter? More analytical? "Objective."

"Talk to Jules," Xander suggested. "That woman's got the answer for everything." My husband hasn't forgiven her for telling him all the reasons not to buy a Jaguar, this after he'd just bought one. That his alter-ego car has logged only slightly less time in a mechanic's garage than in our own has merely made Xander resent Jules more. "Or Talia. What's that term, BFFs? Isn't that what you two are?"

"Who are you?"

"What? A guy's not allowed to read in the john?"

I made a show of looking at the clock. "Didn't you say you had an early meeting?"

"That I did, you endlessly fascinating creature." Xander kissed me and began to walk toward the door. "To be continued," he said. "I should be home early tonight. Eight-fifteen at the latest."

I returned to my notepad. To my knowledge, not one branch of my family tree, not even a distant, twittering leaf, had ever been treated by a shrink. McKenzies have a hard enough time talking to one another. Yet seeing a professional seems like the right step when you can't change on your own. Quincy saw a grief counselor after she lost her baby; Jake made her go after she'd worn only pajamas for a solid month. Talia has dropped in and out of every stripe of therapy—psychoanalytic, cognitive, Gestalt, short-term, long-term, and possibly occupational. Maybe it was a shrink who'd encouraged her to think only of herself!

I decided a psychiatrist wasn't the answer. Wouldn't a brain-probing pro judge me and declare that I was squandering my husband's money and would be better served by tutoring children less privileged than Dash or pulling weeds in Prospect Park?

I went to call Quincy. It was seven forty-five, and eight until two was her sacred writing zone, which she claimed to blast through with only bathroom breaks, because later in the day, she said, her brain was a turnip. Or was it a rutabaga? Whatever the root vegetable in her metaphor, respect for Quincy's schedule was precisely why I tried her then, not later. That and the fact that I was curious to know if what Maizie May had blabbed could possibly be true. Once my mojitos had worn off I mistrusted everything that girl had said.

Quincy answered after several rings, her voice thick as paste.

"I'm so sorry," I said. "Are you sick?" I was ready for her announcement.

"I had one of those nights . . . I guess I finally nodded off again. What time is it?"

I told her.

"No!" she yelped. "Maizie and I have a meeting this morning."

"You okay?" She sounded not only sleepy but skittish, as if I'd caught her with a man who wasn't Jake.

"Forget about me," Quincy said. "Tell me quick. Everything copacetic?"

"Couldn't be better," I lied. "We should plan a lunch." We hadn't been face-to-face since . . . could it really be Maine? "How did that co-op interview go?" I remembered it had happened while I was away. I hoped she wasn't angry that I hadn't asked about it sooner.

"Excruciating—and the vote's still not in," she answered, yet quickly added, "Listen, I can't talk—got to get downtown to see the diva. I'll e-mail you later and we'll figure out lunch in a week or two?"

"Sure." I clicked off, deflated. I could have used some solid, grade-A Quincy just then, regardless of whether or not she made her announcement. Exposure to Quincy made me feel more grounded, as if I, too, had read Keats.

I did my goodbye routine with Dash and Jamyang, who were off to the park, then I washed my bowl, refilled my mug, read the Style section, sorted junk mail, rapped my knuckles on the marble counter in frustration, and finally called Jules. "Forget it, Arthur!" she snapped halfway through the fifth ring.

"I'm not Arthur."

"How fortunate," she said. Jules breathed heavily, a dragon flaring her nostrils.

"Want to talk about it?" Not that I felt even a tickle of certainty in having answers for whatever "it" was.

"I wouldn't know where to begin. Let's leave it at saying you wouldn't want to be me today." She groaned. "Or any day."

"See, that's where you're wrong," I said. "I need your advice."

"What room are we redecorating now?" she asked with dramatic

weariness. We have a deal. I run my decorator's suggestions past Jules—
a good thing, or my living room walls would look like fried eggs, not
lemon mousse.

"This time it's personal. I need a makeover."

"I wouldn't say this to just anyone, but in your case, Chloekins, you
can't go wrong with blonder," she said after the briefest of pauses. "You've
gotten too ashy. With those blue eyes, go one down from Happy Honey,
but definitely not all the way to Innocent Ivory. Want to use my colorist?
He's—"

Normally I take pride in not interrupting, but this time I did. "It's the
inside me I want to work on." I sounded more strident than the woman
I hoped to become.

"But you've got it all—Brooklyn's best address, the cute kid, the hunky
hubby. Whatever would you want to change?" This was Jules being face-
tious; she's no more a fan of Xander than he is of her.

"What do you say I buy you lunch and explain?"

I expected her to work me in next month, but she named a bistro
tucked away in Soho and said she could meet in three hours. If that alone
didn't tell me something was off, her appearance did. Jules-the-hand-
model's nails looked as if she'd recently raked an arboretum's worth of
leaves, and instead of the usual chocolate-brown waves that swirled over
her shoulders like frosting, her hair hung in a limp ponytail. She was
wearing large red glasses and a baggy black shift topped by a cardigan in
a color that looked like a swamp. Yet I found my way to a compliment.
"Those glasses," I said. "People will think you run an art gallery."

"Liar. I'm a living mug shot."

I began to study the menu as if it were notes for a driving test I'd
flunked five times. Jules choked on water she'd gulped. I tried to overlook
the behavior of this Jules impostor. "Red or white?" I said. We were, after
all, in a café known for its wine cellar.

"Nothing for me, thanks." She ripped into the bread basket, soaked a
hunk in olive oil, took a bite, and hailed a waiter, announcing, "I'm starving." At least her usual appetite and command with waitstaff were intact.

Within twenty seconds a young man who might have walked off a run-way stood next to our table.

"*Bonjour*," he said in an accent that sounded like French crossed with Italian. "My name eees Michel. Care to hear de specialties doo jo-o-r?"

"We're good, Michel," Jules answered, though I'd never known her not to deliberate over daily specials as if they were stocks she was thinking about buying.

"Mademoiselle?" the waiter asked, turning toward me.

"Ah, well, I'll have the salade niçoise. Dressing on the side, please."

"*Grazie*, mademoiselle." He swiveled his narrow hips toward Jules. "Madame?"

Jules let the insult slide. "The five-napkin hamburger," she said, "charred on the outside, rare in the middle but not too bloody, and on a separate plate, please, the fries, very crisp, with vinegar, not ketchup." When our waiter had walked away, she turned to me. "What's with this 'on the side' nonsense?"

I am a teaspoon to Jules' ladle, who seemed to have put on a few pounds. "Trying to improve my eating habits," I admitted.

"Ooh, fun." She liberated another chunk of bread. "Tell me, what's the crisis that brings us to this table?"

"It's less a crisis than a quandary."

"Chloe?" Her look said, *I've got places to go and people to see.*

"The time has come for a confidence upgrade," I announced. "I was hoping for a pep talk. At least some sort of rule you could quote."

"Like *Never announce you're on a diet when your friend has polished off the bread?*"

"Exactly."

Jules leaned forward, resting her chin on her hand, and peered directly into my eyes. "Forgive me for busting your chops. I've got my own stuff going on, that's all. As a matter of fact, I do have a thought. I've always believed you get confident by finding the voice inside you that's had the answer all along. Go with your gut."

I played back the words. My mother's diction, patrician and silvery, came through, but mine was lost in a din. "What if you can't hear that voice?" *And are afraid of what the voice is saying?*

"Give yourself time. Listen harder and ignore your fear."

I'm sure my face was as blank as a vanilla wafer. "But how?"

Jules starting roaring. "This is rich. You actually think *I* have answers. Can't you tell I'm bullshitting you?" Only when she'd finished gobbling her burger did she speak again. "You have all the clear thinking and force of personality any woman requires. You just need to activate it, and I'm going to give you a test to get you started." Jules took a deep breath. "I want you to listen and say exactly what's on your mind, but not until I ask you to." She emphasized her point by wagging a fry. "Ready?"

I always failed pop quizzes. "Okay," I said, with serious reluctance.

"Think about a close friend, the first who comes to mind. She's got her good qualities, but in your heart of hearts you've never thought being cut out to be a mother is one of them."

Since Talia had wronged me, she'd become my mental home page. I imagined her with Henry—reading together, taking him by the hand as they crossed a street, comforting him when he cried, and beaming as he climbed a slide. Did I secretly believe she was a rotten mother?

Nope. Talia was an excellent mother and, until lately, my source for practical information. Who else had known exactly how to toilet-train? Get a child to stop sucking his thumb?

"This friend becomes pregnant," Jules added.

I wasn't connecting the dots. Three times I tried to stab a leaf of limp lettuce. I realized that Jules must be referring to Quincy. Had Quincy talked to her about being pregnant and not me? That hurt, especially because last I'd heard, the two of them were squabbling over Arthur trying to hijack an apartment with Jules' help. I'd tried to avoid getting in the middle—if ever there was a woman not born to be an umpire, I'm it.

"The friend doesn't know if she wants the baby."

I was starting to feel alarmed. Could Quincy be so traumatized by her miscarriage she was afraid to be pregnant again? Was that why she'd sounded strange this morning? Were she and Jake having couple trouble?

I stopped chewing and placed my silverware in the all-finished position. This conversation had put me on edge, and whether I passed or failed this test, I wanted it to be over. Yet Jules kept it up.

"There is an added complication," she announced. "The pregnant friend doesn't know if she ever wants to be married, at least to the father of the baby."

I played back the sentence in my mind. Without warning, my skin felt clammy, though on Jules' forehead I could see a drop of perspiration. She had fixated on my eyes as if they were beach balls in the ocean.

"The pregnant friend is up shit's creek." She asked, paused, then asked too quietly, "What should she do?" Somewhere in the restaurant a cell phone rang. A door slammed. A waiter dropped a tray of dishes. "Chloe, your time is up," she whispered. "The answer, please?" With that she crossed her arms on the table and closed her eyes.

I looked at my friend as if I were seeing her for the first time. Julia Maria de Marco was drowning. She'd turned to me. She needed me.

Synchronized with the voice inside my head—my own firm, confident, and, I hoped, kind voice—I said, "Oh, Jules. Why didn't you tell me sooner? What can I do to help?"

CHAPTER 24

Quincy

Every night, illuminated by heartburn, my anxiety did flip turns. Yet I couldn't deny that my fear was being trumped by glee. I, Quincy Peterson Blue, was bringing three lives into the world. Jake and I had even, gingerly, started referring to the embryos by name—Peanut, Speck, and Jubilee. I'd read about a woman who against 1-in-200-million odds had given birth to identical triplets, and I pictured three mini Jakes, minus his chest hair, watching ESPN.

I was feeling sufficiently elated so that at least once a day I considered forgiving Jules, and twice got as far as lifting the receiver to call. But I wasn't that big a person, and since I couldn't face down Jules, I felt forced to dodge Chloe and Talia as well. If Talia knew about my pregnancy, she'd be horrified that I'd hexed it by having already bought cribs, one by one, on eBay. But, practical midwesterner that I am, I had, and this was the day to start refinishing them.

I removed the carefully chosen nontoxic materials from their wrappings, and in minutes our small living room floor was blanketed by a drop cloth on top of which lay an obstacle course of eco-friendly stripper, plastic scrapers, brushes, sandpaper, steel wool, soapy water in a bucket, and glossy white paint. I opened the window to let the air ventilate the room, closed off Fanny in the bedroom, turned to a jazz station, and slipped on a protective mask and my slick black neoprene gloves. Within minutes, I began to get lost in the civilized drudgery of furniture rehab.

I imagined the cribs in a row, my babies snoozing in morning light that streamed from the sun hanging high above the East River. The image was a reminder, as regular as the buses that *vvvroom*ed below on Broadway, that Horton had delivered no news about whether the apartment was indeed ours. It had been three weeks since the inquisition.

"Not yet," he'd said when I'd called last week to ask if we'd passed muster. "Absolutely normal. Boards don't give a flying fig that you want to get on with your life."

Jake added his harrumph to the conference call. "This is why people buy condos."

"And why condos tank first if the economy takes a dive," Horton sniggered. "Co-op boards—especially this one—are hairsplittingly discriminating about financials. You'll sleep better knowing you jointly own a building with other fine, upstanding citizens like yourselves."

"Spare us the lecture, Horton," Jake said.

"I hear you," he said. "In that case, I wish you well in finding a condo."

We both knew he was mentally adding, *In your price range*, since condos tend to be pricier than co-ops.

I brushed on a generous swipe of stripper and stood back to watch purple paint begin to bubble off. For the last two weeks, Jake had been suggesting "as insurance" that we look at other apartments. I told him it felt disloyal to Horton, who'd worked hard on our behalf, but that was, I had to admit, minor. I always thought Talia was the superstitious one, but I had a thoroughly irrational premonition that the minute I considered another place—the very second I crossed its threshold—a cosmic cyclone would suck away the home I already thought of as ours.

I needed to stay monogamous. If I was patient, glad tidings would arrive. Hadn't the same voodoo worked with getting pregnant?

I had finished stroking paint remover on the first crib and moved to the second when the doorman buzzed to announce a visitor. By the time I slipped off my gear and clambered through my land mines, the intercom's ear-piercing screech had stopped. I called downstairs.

"Delivery for you," the doorman said, "but I thought you were out. I'll send it up."

I wandered out the door and down the hall to wait for the elevator. When it arrived, a massive bouquet of pinkish orange helium balloons floated toward my face. I checked—no card. I walked the tribute to my apartment and tied it to one of the two chairs by the small glass table where we ate our meals. Then I dialed Jake.

"Everything okay?" he said, sounding as if he expected to hear I was headed for the ER. We had an unspoken agreement never to discuss my earlier pregnancies, but I knew he thought about them as often as I did.

"What's with the balloons?" I asked. "Why are we celebrating?"

"Q, I wouldn't even know how to send balloons. Whatever you got isn't from me. Should I be jealous?"

"You should always be jealous. Sorry to bother you."

Sorry to be ridiculous. Pregnancy was pureeing my brain. Could the balloons be from Maizie? No, she received balloons—she didn't send them. They were most likely a sales ploy from the dry cleaner opening across the street; every resident in the building must have received a bunch. To corroborate my theory, I pulled off my bandanna and rode down to the lobby, positive it would be festooned as if a parade were about to kick off from our building's front door. But the lobby looked perfectly normal, if you considered polka-dot upholstery normal for anything other than a child's room. I retrieved the mail and returned to my work, starting in once again on the second crib.

Five minutes later I stopped midstroke. A peace offering—that's what the balloons were. From Jules. Deeply bereft about her behavior. So embarrassed she couldn't bring herself to speak to me directly. The only way she knew to make amends was with a showy gesture, her MO from the moment we'd met, right around the corner, when this neighborhood was filled with junkies and OTB patrons, not cafés and Pilates studios. Years ago she'd arrived with roses, a lavish lavender bouquet.

My mind quickly wove a plot. Belatedly, Jules felt like a jackass for telling Arthur about the apartment. She recognized she was wrong and wanted to make amends for her grievous slip in judgment, brought on by a pathetic need to impress her boyfriend.

Holy smokes: Jules missed me as much as I missed her. She wanted to say, *Sorry, Quincy—please forgive me.*

As I worked on the cribs, I chewed through my analysis. Did Jules think she could buy me so easily? Why couldn't she apologize out loud, with grace and humility? I stared at the balloons and was tempted to open the window even wider to let the insipid gesture float to the heavens.

Yet what did it say about me that I couldn't accept an apology? Had I made high treason out of a midget misdemeanor, blown a clumsy faux pas into Apartmentgate? Jules had been disloyal, no argument there. She'd thought only of her own good fortune or at least Arthur Weiner's, not mine. Then again, she hadn't tried to seduce Jake after giving a raunchy toast written on a napkin, like my first cousin Mary Ann from Mankato had at our rehearsal dinner.

I put down my brush. At the time I'd programmed my phone, Jules obviously ranked as Best Supporting Someone. I pressed 2 on my speed dial.

"Jules de Marco," she answered, all business.

"It's me," I croaked, as if I hadn't spoken in a year.

"Shit, really?" she asked. "Mrs. Jacob Blue." She whistled. "Word sure gets around."

"Excuse me?" She sounded derisive, defensive, not the least apologetic.

"I know, I know. Chloe made you call."

What was she yammering about? "This has nothing to do with Chloe."

"After two months of being pissed and avoiding me, you randomly decide to reach out. Why now?"

"It was about the b—" I started to blubber, but cut myself off. *Why, indeed?*

"Ah, about the baby?" she said.

Make that *babies*. How did Jules know? Had Dr. Frumkes told her? Wasn't that a breach of medical ethics? But those two were, as Mom would say, as thick as thieves.

"Excuse me?" I said.

"Pretty un-fucking-believable, right?" Jules asked, full with sarcasm.

That's one way to put it, a way so coarse I had no idea how to respond, and was grateful when my phone bleeped with a second call. "Got to take this," I said as I clicked through to Horton.

"Where *are* you?" he asked, all salesman bravado.

"In my living room," I said, dumbfounded, sweating, ready to literally kick a bucket. "You?"

"I stopped by and left a little something to cheer you up. Did you get them? I wish they'd been diamonds," he said, all in a whoosh. "For my favorite-favorite."

Now I understood. "The balloons are right here. Very cheery. Thanks a lot."

"Quincy, love, the balloons come with news. The board made its decision."

CHAPTER 25

Chloe

I'd gone from good to great to *grande*. In the last weeks, I'd had four job interviews, all of which went—fingers crossed—stupendously, and I owed my mojo to Autumn Rutherford, Mojo Maker, Ltd. When I dropped *mojo* into a conversation last night, Xander glanced at me as if he'd wandered into a stranger's bed.

While most people get referrals for mental health professions from friends, Quincy seemed to be dodging my calls, Jules was—understandably—taking a hiatus from pro bono work, and Talia was the last person I'd ask. I was too embarrassed to check with my doctor. Jules refers to her as the Pussy Queen—to see me squirm, I'm sure—but Dr. F. and I have never become pals, since I'm always stuck for small talk while spread-eagled. So I began to look for a therapist in cyberspace and surfed right into an ad. "Olympic athletes have coaches," it pointed out, on the chance that this was news to anyone. "CEOs use executive coaches. Coaching is a prerequisite for success. How much more productive could you be if you had your own life coach? You owe it to yourself to find out!"

I was sucked in like a Cheerio to a Dustbuster. For days, I pored over websites of life coaches. There was Harriet, with her "feel the energy" tattoo, as well as a pretzel-limbed brunette wearing a serene expression—Suki Moonbeam, née Suzy Metzenbaum. But it was Autumn who won my heart. She promised not only to locate the "secret key to success" but to teach clients to "clean out their mental closets." Nothing satisfies me like getting rid of junk, be it in a handbag, an attic, or, to Xander's horror, an old camp trunk. (In all fairness, that bug collection smelled a bit off.) I see cleaning as a shortcut to a better mood. Who needs drugs when there's Fantastik?

Within minutes, I'd signed up for the Jump-start Your Life introductory program, which would be conducted by phone, since Autumn's HQ was in Arkansas. At only $500, these sessions would go a lot farther to help me "walk the walk to complete fulfillment" than my last visit to a shoe department.

Autumn's method was built on a foundation of quizzes, the first designed to throw a spotlight on "using color to light my life." She lobbed out questions, and I felt as if I were back on the Miss Porter's School tennis courts, where I'd rarely failed to return a ball. Favorite food: ripe strawberries dipped in dark chocolate. Movie: *Love Actually*. Wine: chardonnay. Music: Harry Connick Jr. Art: Renoir. Holiday: obviously, Valentine's Day. Flowers: my mom's slipper orchids, on which she'd lavished more attention than on me. Bird: male peacock. Fast food: Dunkin' Donuts. Book: *Jane Eyre*.

We zipped through a hundred questions. I hung up feeling enormously pleased that Autumn Rutherford, wholly accredited by the International Life Coach Institute, was getting to know me at a level that not even Xander could match. That evening I began to complete an online career test she'd e-mailed. Was I decisive? Was I? Probably not. Did I like working with animals? No! Charismatic? No again. Had I garnered the respect of my peers? I doubted it. Was I fair? Yes! I gave myself a pass on that one as Xander walked into my study. "What are you doing?" he asked. "You've barely pulled yourself away from that computer in days."

"Job hunting," I said, as matter-of-factly as if I'd said I was checking the weather. I'd scheduled my Autumn appointments during hours when Xander would be away. Who needs a buzzkill? I had just started using that word, too: buzzkill, buzzkill.

"Good for you—it's about time," Xander said. "Remember Joe Thrombosis? His wife wants to start some sort of diet website for women. I told her to call you."

"Why?" I was wearing a sleeveless T-shirt and lifted my arms to check for flab.

"Back down, fighter," he said. "It sounded interesting, that's all, and how hard could it be?"

After he left the room, I'd make a note to bring up his tone with Autumn. But Xander seemed in no hurry to depart. He sat in my reading chair and put his feet up on the ottoman. "When's Dash's appointment at Jackson Collegiate?"

"Wednesday." I'd reminded him of this every night at dinner.

"Do you think he's up to it? Have you been working with him?"

Couldn't Xander see I was busy? "Yes and yes." I returned to my screen. "If he doesn't go on strike." That afternoon, when I took Dash's vegetable puzzle off the shelf, he'd whined, "No peas, Mommy, please!" as if I were going to force him to eat a bowlful the size of his head.

I continued on with my career test well after the time Xander finally took the hint and left the room.

• • •

When my session with Autumn started the next day, she kicked it off by revealing, at a quick clip, that "pink is your missing link." She advised me to "embrace your traditional femininity and use it to advance goals, equally balanced between home and the workplace." A blink of pink would be a private sign to remind myself "to be bold without sacrificing your essential self." The pinker I could make my life, the more uplifted and motivated she said I'd become. I loved this approach, like a fashion magazine reminding lawyers to wear push-up bras in case they forgot they were women.

The next morning, I put aside the green tweed pants suit that I'd selected for Dash's school meeting in favor of a pale pink skirt and matching sweater I hadn't taken out of my closet in two years. For good luck, I ate half a pink grapefruit for breakfast, which I finished as Jamyang walked Dash down the stairs.

"Aren't you the little gentleman?" I said.

"Like Daddy," Dash said, adjusting his bow tie and grinning. In the gesture, I saw Xander's face and pulled Dash into my arms.

"Excited?" I asked. His freshly shampooed hair smelled like tangerines. "It's going to be an adventure," I said as we clasped hands.

Dash and I walked to the car, long as a hearse, waiting for us. Having a driver was easier than driving myself. We arrived with time to spare. A young man dutifully lettered our name tags and we strolled down the hall, stopping to admire bulletin boards covered with finger paintings and haiku. *Night passes my eyes / Jogged by a staccato beat. / Can light make me see?* This young poet had read my mind.

The regular students were getting settled into their homerooms, the girls in navy pleated skirts, anklets, and white blouses, the Peter Pan collars edged with lace, and the boys in a uniform much like what I'd selected for Dash—white shirt, khaki pants, and neat oxfords, though their ties were long with rep stripes. The school felt orderly yet warm. I liked it even more than at our first visit.

In the classroom, Dash immediately started zooming a fire truck across the floor. I chose a prime seat on the other side of the room. Around me were an agreeable cluster of well-scrubbed strangers and their offspring, the adults trying to hide under fake camaraderie, pretending they didn't feel their child's entire academic success hinged on the next hour. Every person looked recently barbered or blow-dried, dry cleaner's fumes all but wafting off their freshly pressed clothing.

Dash was starting to dig through the costume bin when I heard a fuss. A loud child had backed into the room. The boy was a good bit taller than

Dash and wore an old, oversized jacket. Dash took one look and ran to his side, shrieking, "Henry, Henry. Henry," and proceeded to tug at his sleeve, dragging him toward the blocks. The Messiah had arrived. Dash worshipped Henry Fisher-Wells.

I looked for Tom Wells, who always could keep his son in line, and started to scoot over to make room for him. I like Tom—he's as solid as a guy comes—and the regrettable by-product of the cold war between Talia and me was that it meant I'd stopped having conversations with him if he answered the phone when I called their apartment. But it was Talia who walked through the door, wearing one of her more regrettable ensembles. I recognized the tiger scarf because I'd given it to her, though I'd never pictured it accessorizing a droopy gray skirt and a shirt that any self-respecting Goodwill shopper would pass by. She came toward me immediately.

"What are you doing here?" I asked, shifting back ever so slightly. "Weren't you supposed to be in the office?" If our mutual desk was empty, it was Talia's problem.

"No. You were," she said, accusation in her voice, and hissed something about our having arranged a switch. I had to admit, though only to myself, that it sounded . . . familiar. I had agreed to the change before I realized it conflicted with the school appointment. But I'd e-mailed Talia again and made it clear that I wanted to stick with our original plan. I was 90 percent sure I'd sent that e-mail, which I'd redrafted several times so it didn't sound overly apologetic, my customary position.

I took a moment and tried to capture an aura of pink calm as I fondled my long strand of pearls. There must be something to Autumn's approach. To my surprise, I felt in complete control!

"But it's my regular day off," I said evenly. Talia wrinkled her forehead and turned away. I'm sure she was furious, as the new Chloe would be. The old Chloe would have assumed the snafu was her fault. I adored the new Chloe!

The teacher clapped her hands. Dash obediently followed her direction and took a chair at one of two tiny tables. Henry stood in the corner, piling block atop block. The teacher stepped away from the tables and stood over Henry, trying to cajole him into joining the group. He ignored her. I glanced at Talia, who looked smugly amused. "That big kid over there is ruining it for everyone," the mother next to me said, none too quietly.

"Henry," the teacher said. "This isn't how Jackson Collegiate boys and girls behave."

Mother Hen gave Henry a stern look, and then—point, Henry Fisher-Wells—the arrogant little rooster said "Fuck" repeatedly as he came at his own building like an enemy bombardier. The minute the curse flew out and his building crashed the whole barnyard went rogue, kids leaping out of chairs, scattering in every direction.

"Does that child have Tourette's?" the man on the other side of me asked. "This isn't a special-needs school." Half of the kids were staring openmouthed, and the others, Dash among them, had joined the party. I wanted to pounce on him and pull him back, but he'd already hurried toward his hero, singing something that I prayed everyone thought was "cluck, cluck, cluck, cluck a duck."

CHAPTER 26

Talia

"We need to hurry, *boychik*." Whenever I used my father's nickname for Henry, he gave me a dimpled grin.

"I'm not *boychik* today," he said as he tried without success to tie his blue cape around his chicken-wing shoulders. "I'm Superman."

Another generation, another fleet of flying heroes. Maybe this one would live up to the honorific, but now wasn't the moment to test the theory. We needed to be at Jackson Collegiate in forty-five minutes. Mean Maxine had insisted that for Henry's cattle call, I give serious consideration to attire. After I hit the mother lode at a consignment store, Maxine and I settled on a red Fair Isle sweater and cords.

"Superman has superpowers. He doesn't need a sweater," Henry said, folding his arms in a stance that resembled Tom's as much as you-know-who's.

"It's November. Superman might catch a sniffle if he isn't warm enough." And I still needed to dress myself. Hoping my son and I would appear as if we'd sprouted from the same bog of DNA, I'd laid out a gray pleated skirt, a cardigan whose moth hole could be deftly covered by the starched cuff of a white shirt, old but newly polished flat brown boots, and a Hermès scarf given to me by Chloe for my last birthday. I'd blown my hair as straight as my abilities allowed.

"That sweater's for girls," Henry sneered as he walked to his drawer and pulled out an orange sweatshirt, nearly fluorescent, the top half of his Halloween costume. "Superman changed his mind."

"Henry, no," I said. "Today's like a really important play date."

He wrinkled his brow. "Okay, Mommy. Then close your eyes till I say when." I heard the hoofing of small feet, a door closing, and "when."

I opened my eyes to a grinning Henry, the orange sweatshirt covered by a scuffed black leather jacket that hung past his hands by inches. He looked like a pubescent Keith Richards. "Please take it off." I looked at the clock.

He switched to the whining channel. "You said today was special."

Perhaps the Jackson Collegiate evaluators were softhearted child advocates, not fashion fascists, and would admire my son's moxie. "At least put on the pants," I sighed, holding out the tan cords. I helped him into them and zipped them up. He did the snap. I handed him sneakers and then unsuccessfully searched the room for his brush, not that it made much difference. Henry had been blessed with my hair—it sprang from his scalp like rotini. In monkey mother mode, I worked my fingers through his curls, stood back, and admired my WASP impostor, not unlike Mr. Lifschitz himself.

"Handsome," I said, kissing his forehead. "Now sit down, please, and play while I get dressed." It took three tries to tie my scarf so I didn't look like Annie Oakley—and then we were out the door. To my eyes, I looked air-dropped from Greenwich.

Several of our neighbors hadn't yet taken down their Halloween decorations, and as we raced along the long brownstone blocks to the subway, Henry pointed to make sure I didn't miss each ghoul, ghost, and wisp of polyester spiderweb.

"I love our street," he said. I did, too. I felt lucky to live here, crowded as we might be. On the surface Park Slope might look like the Upper West Side of Manhattan, but this is a true community. Kids trick-or-treat not up and down elevator banks but at doors where people know their names, and nearly every Saturday, except in the dead of winter, you can count on a stoop sale from which you might buy, say, a five-dollar broken-in black leather jacket sized for a third grader.

Two weeks ago Tom had informed me of today's visit. It fell on one of my workdays, and he wanted me to rearrange my schedule—which I did—to escort Henry. "The director already knows me," he pointed out. "Betsy has to see that you're on board, too, and that Henry lives up to my brags." Sexism played no small role. Tom didn't want Henry's mother to come off as Executive Mom. The subliminal crawl I'd read during the general meeting I'd attended was that the complete Fisher-Wells family would be under scrutiny. I intended to scrutinize back to see if this school deserved my son, if it was educational heaven or a hill of bricks tottering on a threadbare reputation.

There were seats on the subway, an auspicious sign. At our destination a few stops away, an older man—any male under the age of forty would be more likely to trip you as he bolted up the steps two at a time—helped me lift boy and stroller to the street. I pushed Henry at a quick trot along the block and a half to the school, arrived breathless and damp, parked the stroller, and asked to be directed to the classroom for nursery school interviews.

"And you are?" the young redheaded gatekeeper asked.

"Fisher-Wells—Henry and Talia."

At the pace of a gentleman, he located our names, then hand-lettered stickers for both of us to wear. "It starts in five minutes," he announced. "Down the hall—second door on the left," he added.

As I walked in that direction, tightly holding Henry's warm, chubby hand, I inhaled the aroma of lemon oil emanating from the rich mahogany paneling, and noticed that on the bulletin boards there was poetry. I stopped to read some haiku. *Leaves that have lost life / are crinkly tissues of gold. / Man dies and is dust.* And by the same Olivia Samson, *A sea of eyes and / Ear and minds. / But why do / I play solitaire?* Had anyone, I wondered, rushed this budding Emily Dickinson to a psychiatrist?

From the classroom where I was headed, I heard high-pitched voices. I opened the door, and while I searched for an authority in charge, a small boy ran over to Henry and tugged his jacket.

"Henry!" he said. "Blocks!" It was Dashiel Keaton. Each time I saw that child he had become more impossibly appealing, even if that day he'd been dressed as an accountant. I searched the room for Xander or Jamyang. But the parent I saw was Chloe, a vision in pink, fingering her pearls and sitting against the far wall, riveted to *Clifford the Big Red Dog* as if she were reading the surprise ending of her own biography. Only when I was standing over her did she look up.

"Weren't you supposed to be in the office?" she asked.

"No," I answered. "You were." Last week we'd confirmed the switch by e-mail. On that I'd have bet Henry's life.

"But it's my regular day off," she said with reproach. "I'd never miss this."

There had been—I tried to be charitable—a miscommunication. It was now a good thirty minutes past the time when Eliot, our boss, would have expected one of us to sail through the office door. It was I who'd take the heat for the unexplained absence; he didn't care if Chloe and I traded days, as long as her tush or mine was warming the desk chair. Any minute now he'd be bellowing like a lost moose—and who could blame him?—that he had no copywriter to brainstorm with in that morning's meeting. It would probably be at least eleven by the time I rushed Henry to his sitter, and then I still needed to take the train to the office. Half the day, shot.

There was only one immediate response to this problem—turning off my phone. I'd do some fast talking later. I shrugged and sat down.

"Like the scarf," Chloe said as a jumper-clad teacher clapped her hands.

"Children, children," she shouted, "I want each of you to take a chair at one of the tables. Now." Every potential student except one scurried into place. Henry remained engrossed in constructing a tower of blocks. The teacher walked to him, bent to his level, and spoke gently. "Now, Henry," she said, "wouldn't you like to join the others?" He added two stories to his high-rise. "And wouldn't you like to take off your jacket?"

"No," he explained. *I'm busy* was his implication. He took another large block and created what I clearly saw as a bell tower. I imagined him in it, gun in hand, surveying the terrain.

"We all have our jobs, and yours is to join the other children." The teacher sounded aggressively patient, aware that every parent in the room was curious about how she'd persuade this recalcitrant participant to play by her rules.

My son narrowed his eyes and sized up the woman with a look of deep disdain I hoped he'd never show me. "No, *thanks*," he said, and returned to his blocks. Could he, I hoped, at least get points for manners?

"Henry." The woman sucked in her breath and peered down through heavy glasses as if her reputation was at stake, which it was. "This isn't how Jackson Collegiate boys and girls behave."

"Okay, fuck it," Henry said as he crashed the blocks in one furious swoop. "Fuck, fuck, fuck."

All the children and adults turned, impressed by what I have tried to stress to Henry is vocabulary reserved exclusively for automobiles. Tom and I did use that word, but only on the rare occasion when we rented a car and tried to negotiate the civil unrest that is city traffic. Circles of perspiration soaked my scratchy white shirt as sweat collected at my hairline. The room went silent—except for Dash, always in awe of Henry, singing, "Fuck, fuck, fuck, fuck, fuck a duck." Chloe gasped before she glowered in my direction. I shrugged back to her and mouthed, "I'm sorry."

But I wasn't. I was positive she'd agreed to work today.

As Henry threw up his hands, he looked toward the worshipful faces of the other kids. Giggles, some of them coming from the parents, rippled toward my superhero. If a three-year-old can have dignity, Henry did as he followed the teacher. She seated him across from Dash as I noticed another teacher scribble on a clipboard—*Henry Fisher-Wells revealed his first sociopathic tendencies at age three,* perhaps.

"Now, children," the head teacher said, "we thought you'd like some snacks." The scribe walked to a shelf holding trays and transformed herself into a waitress offering graham crackers, grapes, and cubes of cheddar cheese. Most children daintily grabbed one or two of each. Dash wrinkled his nose, looked at Chloe, and took nothing. Henry, whose breakfast had been half a peanut butter sandwich and a juice pack that he drank on the subway, filled two handfuls, dumped them on his plate, and returned for seconds.

The teachers brought glass pitchers of apple juice to each table. "Who'd like to start?" one of them asked. Tom and I had never let Henry try to fill his own glass at home. The teacher, that sadist, turned toward him and asked, "How about you, Henry?"

"Yes, ma'am," he said, using a four-letter word he definitely hadn't learned from me.

"In that case," she said, "go ahead." *Be my guest, sucker.* "Class, Henry is going to show you how pouring from a pitcher is done. Let's...all... watch."

He lifted the pitcher, which might as well have been a barbell, tilted its spout, and poured perfectly. He looked in my direction. I blew him a kiss, sorry I couldn't swoop him up in my arms and shout, *Mazel tov.* One mother nearby patted me on the shoulder and another gave me a thumbs-up. Neither was Chloe.

"When you finish your treats, everyone may play." The moment the teacher uttered the sentence, Henry bolted, knocking several cubes of cheese onto the floor, and returned to the block corner, the bigger boys trailing him. For the next ten minutes he was architect, foreman, and head engineer, barking orders as he supervised the construction of yet another colossus. I hoped it was as clear to the teachers as it was to me that my son was a natural leader, perhaps the next Frank Lloyd Wright.

I was percolating with motherly pride and ambition as I turned toward Chloe to make an effort to talk, but she was chatting up the assistant teacher. Clearly, we each had our own agendas today, and she didn't know the half of it. Just as I'd temporarily shut down thinking about the story I'd cook up later for Eliot, I'd managed for a whole hour not to brood about whether I'd be offered the Bespoke spot—the one Mean Maxine and I both referred to as *Chloe's job*. That's when I heard a small voice call my name. "Mrs. Fisher-Wells!" it said. "Look!" Dash was wearing a plastic pince-nez on his tiny, upturned nose and carrying a doctor's bag. "Are you ready for your checkup?"

When Chloe heard his voice, she turned and beamed. I squatted down to Dash's level. He thumped my chest with a stethoscope, peeped up at me with his dimpled smile, and thumped again. "Just fine," he announced, and grinned.

"Why, thank you, Dr. Keaton," I said. He'd missed the lump in my throat and, as I looked at Chloe, the pain in my gut.

CHAPTER 27

Chloe

Jamyang was waiting outside Jackson Collegiate when our nightmare ended. The car dropped her and Dash at home and continued into Manhattan for my own two o'clock interview. I threw on a black wool jacket that I'd had Jamyang bring and decided I looked creative enough for an ad agency.

With ninety minutes to kill, I had the driver park a few blocks away from the agency, bought him coffee and a ham sandwich, and went into a bistro to grab a cup of green tea and review my notes. I was ready to order when I noticed four women at the next table toasting one another. Their drinks were pink, which matched their cheeks. It seemed like one of Autumn's signs. "What are they drinking?" I asked the waitress.

"House specialty, something retro, kind of like lemonade. Pink Ladies," she said. "Very popular."

"I'll try one," I said. A real drink would relax me. I was studying the printout I'd made of the agency's account history when the server brought me a darling beverage topped with a maraschino cherry. It tasted like no other lemonade I'd ever had—though far sweeter than the mojitos in California.

As I sipped, I tried to prime myself for the interview. The headhunter who was Arthur Weiner's friend had seemed strangely surprised to hear from me when I tracked her down. We'd had a short, halting conversation, but after I faxed a résumé with a polite note, a few days later she set up an appointment at an agency. "The owner was ready to make an offer," she'd said. "I had to convince him to see you, and he only agreed because your background is exceptionally strong."

Exceptionally strong. I felt as if I were listening to chamber music!

I reviewed my notes, again, and checked my watch. Still too early to leave. I ordered a salad and, feeling more mellow than I had in months— thank you, Pink Lady!—decided to go for a second drink. I sipped and nibbled, sipped and nibbled. There was definitely something in that cocktail, something wonderful. I decided to make it my signature drink. I'd never had a signature drink, and the thought made me warm and happy.

I looked over my notes one last time and got up to leave. The room swayed.

I was drunk—let's call it tipsy—and this was not good, not at all. Ever since an unfortunate pre-Xander frat party, when I woke up in the bed of a guy I'd never seen before in my life, I have judiciously monitored my alcohol intake. Marijuana? Forget it. When anyone passed a joint, I only faked taking a puff. But I heard Autumn's melodious voice in my head reminding me that everything was going to be fine. By the time the interview started, the effects of the drink surely would have worn off. I shouldn't get my knickers in a twist! Today Autumn was speaking with a British accent. I bought a box of mints at the drugstore next door and then told the driver to take off.

At Bespoke Communications, I was welcomed by a platinum-haired receptionist. She was arranging a bouquet of carnations. Pink!

"Hi," I giggled and introduced myself. "Those flowers are gorgeous." They were ordinary enough, but a compliment never hurts.

"Mr. Jonas is expecting you," she said. I giggled again. The receptionist walked me down a narrow hallway and led me into a long, dark room.

"Chloe Keaton?"

"Mr. Jonas?" A man spun around in his chair and stood to shake my
hand. Winters Jonas was utterly bald! I pictured him in his bathroom, trying to get a smooth shave. It couldn't be easy, especially on the back of his
skull, but I hadn't noticed any scabs or Band-Aids. "We have on the same
jacket!" I said. His was black, too.

"Ah, yes," he said. "True."

Was the floor crooked? Probably. This building was the kind of firetrap
that in downtown Manhattan passes for charming. I looked up and
smiled at Winters Jonas, who smiled back. I felt better than I ever had in
my life. Apparently I was getting adept at this job-hunting business!

"So, Chloe, tell me about yourself," he said.

I knew my lines. "I'm a skilled leader," I began, trying to embrace my
traditional femininity while I advanced my goals. This meant crossing
my legs at the ankles and keeping the smiles coming. "I enjoy the respect
of my peers. My skills are unsurpassed, but the talent of which I am most
proud is my ability to build and mentor a team."

Did it matter that the only team I'd ever led was for tennis at Miss
Porter's? Mr. Jonas seemed to buy it. "What's your MO to achieve this?"

"My mojo!" He pinned me with his dark blue eyes, but I wasn't going
to let that throw me. "I roll up my sleeves and lead through my own example of passion, high energy, creativity, and hard work."

"Chloe, let's have a look at your portfolio," he said. We did, chatting at
every page, augmented by laughter, a lot of laughter. The interview lasted
an hour!

That evening, when I woke from a nap, Xander asked me to report on
the appointment. I couldn't recall a thing. I wasn't even sure how I'd gotten home.

CHAPTER 28

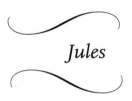

Jules

Arthur didn't know it, but—cue the theme from *Law and Order*—Mr. Cheap was on trial. Every hour, I changed my mind about the poor knucklehead. I woke up believing I had emotional leprosy ever to have allowed myself to get in the family way by him, but as soon as I had my tea—coffee was on hiatus for Mama Jules—I softened. Honestly, who's a ten? My Artie Fartie worshipped at my bunioned feet. The guy thought even my most brain-dead prattle deserved to be nominated for an Emmy. Goddess status worked for me, and as Calvin Coolidge said—or was it Mark Twain?—I could live for two months on a good compliment.

While Arthur was in Texas on business, perhaps he'd read up on how to be a better boyfriend. He'd slipped way out of character and made a reservation at as snooty a French restaurant as a West Side zip code would allow, although I happened to know that Carmine, the maître d', was Italian.

My pop once told me you can always trust a guy named Carmine, the only time the weasel spoke the truth. His theory has been ratified. Carmine of Picholine will murmur in my ear to tell me to steer clear of the wild Scottish grouse because it's loaded with birdshot, and that the olive-oil-poached cod is bland as paper but, ah, the sheep's milk ricotta gnocchi with parsley pistou—ecstasy. When I'm wearing my personal shopper hat, Picholine is the venue where I fête clients to thank them for dropping thousands on clothes I've selected for their lumpy carcasses. And evidently Arthur had taken note. Tonight we were meeting at eight-thirty, which gave me ample time for preening.

I decided it behooved me to spend the rest of my afternoon being ministered to at the good–as–Madison Avenue salon I've never told a soul about. I asked Sophia, the shop's sainted owner, for resuscitation—deep conditioning, haircut, blow dry, hydrating facial, deep-tissue massage, and when I came clean to her about my maternal state as well as my evening plans, she insisted on throwing in makeup gratis, clearly her version of a mercy fuck. I departed feeling lusciously transformed in the way that a woman can feel only after having dropped hundreds of bucks on female necessities, and I'm not talking Kotex Overnight Maxi Pads, especially not now.

I'd hurried home and dressed strategically, choosing a sensual swish of red silk, second cousin to a caftan. It featured a plunging neckline, which I garnished with a long toss of amethysts that nestled in my bosom: as I tell clients, a décolletage without jewels is like a museum wall without a Caravaggio. I anointed myself with the Joy eau de parfum I reserve for first nights at the opera, grabbed my velvet shawl, hopped in the car, and at precisely eight twenty-five pulled into a garage. The restaurant's door was framed by a Thanksgiving still life of corn stalks and squash. Time was marching on, along with my little bugger. I'd best march, too.

I pushed open the door and was met by the twinkle of chandeliers wide as Scarlett's hoop skirts. I took in the excruciatingly tasteful tamped-down shades of gray and taupe. They aren't my colors—oyster tones depress me more than Chihuahuas in turtlenecks—but the décor was the visual equivalent of an antianxiety drug, which I needed badly. I didn't know what Arthur had going on, but I knew what I did, and I promised myself I wouldn't leave that night without speaking what was in my heart, most likely why my necklace was set to vibrate.

Carmine led me to an intimate corner table. A guy whom it took me a second to recognize as Arthur was already seated. There must have been a sale at a trading post. He was wearing a fitted black suit, an embroidered black shirt, a shiny black tie, a belt with an embossed silver buckle featuring a long-nosed animal I couldn't quite make out, and a black Western hat. Had Willie Nelson died or was Arthur merely fed up with country music hunks getting all the sartorial breaks?

He stood and leaned in my direction. We were eye to eye, even with me in four-inch heels. I glanced downward. Boy howdy, Arthur was wearing cowboy boots. Had he packed a lasso? My mind traveled to a dirty place that wasn't El Paso. I looked into his eyes, grinned, and kissed him back. Bitch and moan as I may, my Arthur isn't a slave to fashion, or many other conventions. You've got to like that about a guy.

"Evening, Sheriff," I said.

"You gorgeous thing, I am one lucky dude," he said. "I could eat you up."

I suppose the sociable response was "Right back at you," but I had to know. "Arthur, what's tonight about?"

He grinned. "Don't jump the gun." While I looked for a holster, he added, "I missed you, that's all. You miss me?" I answered by stroking the back of his hand with its short, pudgy fingers. "I know you think when I'm away all I do is pay for porn, but the truth is, this time my mind was mostly on you."

Like the dandruff-sized diamond in the middle of Arthur's black onyx pinky ring, buried in that remark was something special. "What exactly were you thinking, partner?" I asked. Arthur appeared ready to answer, but then the waiter showed up.

"Champagne for both of us," Arthur boomed.

"Will that be a bottle, sir?" the waiter asked.

"Two glasses will be fine." He pointed to the most modest choice on the menu, and turned again in my direction. "You haven't commented on my duds."

"You look good, actually," I said, which was almost true. "But you've got to lose the hat."

He shot me a pout, yet tenderly parked the Stetson on the banquette. Our drinks arrived. "To us," he said, raising his glass. As our flutes touched, he winked. "I've got something for you."

Arthur ducked his head under the table, which allowed me to gulp some champagne and spit it into my water glass. As his pate's shiny top reappeared, I spied a box whose size alone is known to inspire female palpitations. Despite that fact, what I felt was a sudden flurry in my belly followed by a small twister that spiraled quickly upward until I felt an urge to gag, which I tried to suppress.

This brought about a facial expression Arthur apparently read as glee. "Now that's what I call a reaction." He grinned.

My insides did a samba. Arthur centered the ring box, a flip-top job, in front of me as I pushed myself up from the table and managed to whisper, "Excuse me—bathroom run."

I broke out first in a sweat, then the chills, and regretted that I'd left my shawl on the back of the chair. I would have liked to have swaddled myself and taken a nap, perhaps for the next eight months. I was in no shape to make the kind of decision that an engagement ring demands. I sat in the stall with my head in my lap for as many minutes as I felt I could remain without Arthur sending in a posse, then got up and wiped away most of Sophia's mascara, gone sadly awry. I tried to return to the table holding my head high, but my legs had turned to Play-Doh. Perhaps my wobble set off seismic waves, because Carmine ran to my side and extended his wiry arm. "You look pale, Miss de Marco. Is the food not to your liking this evening?"

"Carm, I'm sure the food will be superb," I said. "We haven't even ordered yet."

"In that case, stay away from the sea scallops," he murmured without moving his lips as he escorted me to the table and pulled out my chair. A ring box still waited.

"Doll, you okay?" Arthur asked, genuine concern creasing his high forehead.

"Fine," I lied. "All better now. Sorry."

He patted my arm in a fatherly way, not that I'd had any personal experience with how that actually felt. We picked up our menus and studied them in silence. The waiter appeared to take our order.

"What'll it be?" Arthur asked.

"I'll go with the pear and endive salad, and . . ." Each choice sounded more richly revolting than the next. "I'll pass on an entrée, thanks." Relief blossomed on Arthur's face: I would not be ordering the $145 five-course game tasting menu. My queasiness had subsided. My misgivings had not. "I'm going to try the sweetbreads to start," he said, "and . . . the sea scallops."

I shook my head.

"I meant the lamb," he told the waiter, checking for my approval, which I granted. "Now, where were we?" Arthur pushed the box in front of me. "Open it."

For a proposal, I doubt I would have scripted "Julia Maria, I adore you, the most divine creature who's ever lived, and I want you to be my wife for all our days on earth and life eternal. I will, forever, be your devoted slave and protector." But I also wouldn't have gone with "Let it rip," as Arthur suggested.

I reached for the box as his sturdy thigh rubbed against mine. I undid the white ribbon while I fantasized about a princelier paramour sliding his hands under a virginal negligee and slipping it off my creamy shoulders, revealing my breasts in their standard, highly enviable pre-pregnancy condition. Discreetly, I scanned the restaurant to try to memorize the surroundings. Roses, check. Candles, check. Classical music, check.

"Jules, doll," Arthur said as I was about to the flip the lid, "you should know I decided this was you. Well, you and me."

Just as I've never contemplated my fantasy will-you-marry-me speech, I'm also not a girl who's conjured a mythical engagement ring. I haven't, in fact, been a girl for a long time. Even at eleven, I felt ancient and wise. Chloe has a round two-carat stone, tasteful, unimaginative, and vastly overpriced, she and Xander being the only people I know who stroll into Harry Winston and buy a ring retail. Talia and Tom wear plain matching bands that Talia's dental technician uncle, Seymour, made from purloined gold fillings. Quincy—if I can still count her as a friend—wears a Victorian antique, a sapphire that matches her eyes.

What kind of ring said Jules? Perhaps, befitting my age, several carats of rock in an emerald cut. That, however, definitely didn't say Arthur.

A rule I've chosen not to abide by is that sometimes a woman has to compromise. Yet I knew I'd settle for a chunk of cocktail bling in any color of the rainbow as long as it wasn't brown or beige, and providing it was at least the size of an olive. I lifted the lid.

Inside the box was a bigger, heavier twin to the pinky ring on Arthur's hand. The diamond chip was larger, just. If Arthur's diamond was a no-see-um, this was a gnat.

"Put it on," he urged. "Let me help you." He removed the ring from the box. It didn't fit my fourth finger. He pushed it onto my pinky, sat back, and waited for my gratitude, or at least a snappy comeback. "We're a real pair, don't you think?" Arthur was on his own joy ride.

"Ya think?"

Rule number fourteen: *Nature abhors a vacuum.* Create a pause and someone will fill it. Arthur squirmed and turned his eyes toward his empty champagne glass. This didn't bring me closer to understanding if my brand-new trinket was only that or a proposal. I needed to know: I felt foolish enough being me right now without making a presumption of grand proportions. I continued to gently glare.

"Jules, okay, here goes," Arthur said, after a throat clearing that sounded like a garbage truck doing its business. "The way I see us, we're the perfect combo, like, hmmm, a hot dog and mustard." He waited for me to approve his simile. I was able to control myself. "Think about it.

We have great sex. We both love to eat and laugh and watch basketball and Turner Classics. Neither one of us is getting any younger, and as my mother always said, two can live as cheaply as one. So, I was thinking..."

He sucked in air—and his stomach—dramatically. "Should we take the next step?"

I employed my well-honed echo technique. "The next step?"

"You know, living together." He shifted in his seat, which allowed me to get a better look at his buckle. *Armadillo.* Nasty, plug-ugly critter. I was afraid it would jump off his belt and bite off my hand.

"Where, exactly, would we live?" He didn't respond. "Did you see yourself moving in with me?" He didn't have a driver's license and wouldn't know mulch from corned beef hash. Arthur Weiner was as hard to picture in Westport as litter.

"Okay, I'm being theoretical now," he said, as if an idea had occurred to him that very minute. "What if you were to sell your house and we pooled our...funds...and bought a place together and I'd invest my profits...for the future?" I waited for more. "Maybe we could get that apartment we saw in my building."

You don't say. "The one Quincy and Jake are dreaming about?"

"Forget about that—it's not going to happen," he said with a sweep of his hand. "I have it on good authority that the board decided the Blues were in collusion with the brokers and the old lady's business manager. They got rejected. The pittance they want to pay was way below market value. Bad for the building to give the joint away. Depresses the value of everyone else's property. Though if anyone gets a deal, it should be an insider." With each statement, his face got redder.

"Can you prove this collusion?" I asked.

Arthur waved away the question. "Listen up. I've got it all worked out—we could buy the apartment, flip it, and move into something far bigger and better. Like I said, we're a pair. Sonny and Cher, Liz Taylor and Richard Burton, Bonnie and Clyde."

Perspiration gathered in my cleavage. "Didn't those people all wind up divorced or dead?"

"Jules, what do you want me to do, get down on bended knee?" Arthur looked exasperated, and frankly, who could blame him, the way I was yanking his chain? "The point is, we're a twosome."

It had been years since a man had given me even bad jewelry. This ring was hideous and insignificant, but it was an invitation. I sat back and stared at my almost-full glass of champagne. Who did I think I was?

"The thing is, Artie, we're more than a twosome," I said softly, staring into his dark brown eyes. "We're a threesome."

He looked puzzled, then unaccountably pleased. "You want a three-some?"

"Do I have to spell it out? I'm pregnant."

"You're *what?*"

"You heard me."

"Not funny, Jules."

"No, it isn't."

Shock and confusion contorted his face as he leaned away from the table, away from me. "You can still get pregnant?"

"Yes, you fuckwit, and it's yours."

Carmine was there to revive Arthur when he passed out.

CHAPTER 29

Quincy

I opened one eye and watched Jake survey the corpses of four dozen balloons. It looked as if a school of salmon had washed up into our apartment to die. "Q, was there a terrorist attack?"

I pulled my grandmother's afghan, yellow faded to beige, over my head and stroked Fanny's back. "There was," I mumbled, "I'm the terrorist."

He walked to the couch and curled next to me. Jake is a furnace, and I could feel his warmth through the nubby wool. "I wish I could have been here to see you murder the balloons."

"You don't," I said. After I hung up with Horton, after I screamed and cursed and cried, I attacked each balloon until it surrendered. As I poked and stabbed, I imagined them as members of the committee that had rebuffed us without explanation. But the last two balloons weren't members of that jury. They were Jules and Arthur, who got it with a razor blade. I sliced my thumb in the process.

"Want to talk about plan B?" Jake asked when a few minutes had passed. He smoothed my hair.

"No." The word slipped out as a groan. I had no energy to snap.

"Would that be no as in later or no as in not ever?" I didn't respond. I needed a good, long sulk before I decided the answer, and Jake knew better than to cajole. "Got it," he said as he pulled away. I heard him go into the bedroom, but soon he emerged and gently closed the front door behind him. My arms were wrapped around my midsection, my mind trying to wish away disappointment, my eyes pressed shut.

When I opened my eyes, the room was dark. I'd fallen into a black hole of a nap. I lay in the stillness, chilled, yet devoid of desire to rouse myself. Regardless, my bladder had a clearer idea. I pushed up slowly on one elbow. That's when I felt it.

The sensation was neither sharp nor throbbing, clouded by déjà vu. As I shifted position, a warm stickiness dampened my thighs. I didn't even glance downward. I didn't want to bear witness. A woman who couldn't have been me walked to the bathroom, pausing efficiently to grab her cell phone. After she dialed, she pulled down her jeans and pale yellow cotton briefs and squatted on the toilet.

"It's Quincy Blue," she said. "For the doctor." The nurse-receptionist put her on hold and the ghost-woman didn't protest. She was frozen, with all the time in the world. When the nurse-receptionist returned the woman found the words. "I might be having a miscarriage," she said with utter calm; *again*, with even higher stakes.

"Dr. Frumkes will call you back," the nurse said, her voice now buttered with concern. "Please try to stay calm, Mrs. Blue."

I knew that whether Dr. Frumkes called in five minutes or five hours, what was meant to happen could not be stopped. I hung up and looped between the couch and the bathroom, all the while trying to reconnect with the memory of my mom in the hope that she'd offer consolation and sapient wisdom. "The days are long, but the years are short," she used to say—that is, before she lost the ability to speak at all—whenever I complained of restlessness. The phrase refused to calm me. "Don't assume you always know what will happen next," Mom said, as she often had. But that insight felt tired. I was certain I did.

What would Alice Peterson do? I leaned back on the couch and saw her across from me in the easy chair, her bare feet crossed at her slender ankles. She was about the age I am now, with long blond hair streaming down her back. My mother put down a Dorothy Sayers mystery, marking her place with a grosgrain ribbon, walked to the kitchen, and put water up for tea. When she returned to the living room, she bent low to flip through her albums and pulled one out. Sweet baby James filled the room. Even as a young girl, I instinctively knew that James Taylor reminded her of my father, another James I'd never met but whom I'm told I resemble, the same craggy cheekbones and rangy limbs. Certainly I didn't inherit my mother's curvy but slender softness.

I, little orphan Quincy, wanted my mother. I wanted a child—children—so I could become my mother, raising her from the dead with every caress, every loving gesture, and every firm but tender reprimand. When I was pregnant the first time, I'd decided that if one of my daughters was a girl, she'd be Alice Jane, after Mom. I hadn't changed my mind.

Mud Slide Slim and the Blue Horizon was playing when Jake returned. "Missing Mommy, huh?" he said.

I nodded, though Mom was never Mother or Ma, Mama or Mommy.

"Takeout okay?" he asked, a large plastic bag swinging in his left hand. Let other people keep their lumpy mashed potatoes, their chicken soup. I have lived in New York a long time. Comfort food means shrimp pad thai turbocharged with tamarind and chili pepper. "Feeling better?" he asked.

Before I could answer, my phone rang. "Quincy, what is it?" Dr. Frumkes asked.

I gave her my report, ending with, "I'm pretty sure, well, not entirely, but worried I'm losing these babies, though nothing much has happened in the last hour." Bitter experience had taught me this wasn't necessarily good news.

Jake was waving his arms for attention, his face disconsolate.

"I need to see you," she said.

"But everything's quieted down. Honestly. What difference is it going to make?"

There was a long pause. "Then you absolutely must check in with me every hour and, if it comes to that, anytime during the night—if it's eventful—and of course, first thing in the morning," she clucked. I love my ob-gyn despite this tic. "You have my cell and home number, correct?"

I told her I did. Both were committed to memory. Jake's hands flapped with the time-out sign as I spoke. "Shouldn't we go to the ER?" he mouthed.

"Jake's wondering if I should go to the emergency room," I, the obedient wife, asked. "You don't think it's necessary, yet?" I repeated for his benefit. "Yes, I can be patient." Jake looked anything but. "Of course I'll lie low."

"When did this start, Q?" he asked as I hung up.

What did it matter? "Maybe an hour ago, or a little before."

"Are you sure we shouldn't go right now to see the doctor?"

"I know the drill. I'll see her the instant I really have to, I promise."

There was nothing more to say. I settled back on the couch. Jake brought me dinner on a tray. We ate in silence. I made another short but dramatic trip to the bathroom, and then the action stopped. I read, choosing *The Murder at the Vicarage*, and eventually Miss Marple and I went to bed, fingering the delicate necklace—three tiny diamonds on a thread of gold chain—that Jake had given me the week before. One stone for each baby, Peanut, Speck, and Jubilee.

To my surprise, I slept through the night and woke to the whir of a coffee grinder. Towels beneath me were dry. I moved at a glacial pace, sitting, standing. Jake heard me and rushed to my side, clasping my elbow as if I were ninety-five.

"Honey," I said. I tried to smile but failed. His solicitude, well-intentioned as it might be, rankled. "I'm not going to break," I said, perhaps because I already had in every way that counted. Jake left the room.

I washed my face and stared in the mirror. Dark circles, a pallor. I ran a comb through my hair, brushed my teeth, and wrapped myself in a ratty navy velour robe. When I came out, the table had been set. Raspberry jam glistened in a small white crock. Jake had scrambled eggs. Tucked into a linen napkin, monogrammed *AP*, were pieces of golden toast nestled like babies in a bunting.

He poured my coffee. Decaf, of course, but surprisingly good. "Do you want to call the doctor before you eat?" he asked.

It was not quite seven. "I'll wait a few minutes," I said, and we ate leisurely, exchanging sections of *The New York Times* and *Wall Street Journal*. Jake looked up twice as if to say, *Now—call now.*

I dragged out the meal so long that Dr. Frumkes called me. "What's happening?" she asked.

I described my unexceptional night, listened, and hung up the phone. "She wants to see me before her regular patients," I said. Jake started to speak, but I interrupted. "You don't have to come along," I said. "I know you have depositions today."

"An associate can handle it." He sagged with disappointment. "I want to be with you."

Having Jake by my side would make it harder. Without him, I'd be more able to impersonate a woman possessing the brute force of courage. "I won't disintegrate. I can do it alone."

Jake is a proud man, a strong man, a tender man. "Those are my babies, too," he almost whispered.

"You're not going to change my mind." I tried to speak with love. I believe I succeeded.

"I want to come."

"Not this time."

A half hour later I was sitting, alone, in one of my doctor's examination rooms. As soon as she walked into the room, my determination washed away. "Why does this keep happening to me?" I asked in a gush of tears. "It's not as if I'm sniffing formaldehyde."

She put her hand on my shoulder. "Let's have a look. Feet in the stirrups." The internal exam was brief, followed by the usual.

"Pain?"

"No."

"Bleeding?"

"Off and on. But it stopped."

"Dizziness?"

"No."

"Fever?"

I shrugged. "I didn't take my temperature." I should have.

"Weakness?" Dr. Frumkes asked. I nodded. "I feel all wobbly."

"Excuse me," she said. She walked out of the room, leaving me to flip through a two-month-old copy of a magazine featuring shots of unbearably adorable infants and toddlers of every race held by their diverse and frequently famous parents. Every family had a dog as photogenic as they were. I was debating checking out the "Picky Eater Tool Kit" when Dr. Frumkes returned.

She stuck an instant-read thermometer into my mouth. "Normal," she said. "That's good. Now here's the deal." She clucked as she placed her hand on my shoulder. I took stock of her gel nail tips and tried not to hold them against her. "I'll be straight. I don't like what I'm seeing here, Quincy." I held my breath. "But until we do a sono, I won't have a definitive answer."

She'd strayed off script. Past speeches had always pivoted around *miscarriage*. Her face was calm as a cake. Then again, it had been aided and abetted by every wrinkle filler that's known a hypodermic needle. I thought about how Jules and I used to laugh about this at Dr. Frumkes' expense, and it infuriated me that even now, Jules had barged into the examining room, though it was I who'd invited her. Damn Jules—why had she given me reason to despise her? Jules is made of tough stuff. If she'd been here, it might have been better. I shut down that thought in one blink.

"I know this is very worrisome and painful," Dr. F. went on to say, "but it is what it is. I've arranged for your test." She handed me a piece of paper with the address. "Right away."

When I reached the reception room, there was Jake.

CHAPTER 30

Talia

"Sure you don't want to take the car, *bubbele?*" my mother said as I left her house. I was raised in that green clapboard bungalow and half my heart still lives here. It's not in the arm of Santa Monica that looks amputated from some ritzy suburb, on the Brentwood side, near Montana Avenue's requisite Waterworks and Williams-Sonoma. My parents' house is closer to Venice, to scruffiness, to residents who'd sooner pry off a fingernail than vote Republican. I adore its shelves sagging with Great Books and *National Geographics*, though the gnarly sycamores out front tilt the sidewalks like a giant's hands. I especially love that I can walk to the Pacific, blocks away. I love that I can walk, period, and pretend Santa Monica isn't Los Angeles. This may explain why I was able to fit easily into Brooklyn, which I refuse to see as New York City.

"Mommy, it takes twenty minutes to walk to the farmers' market— why drive?" I'd announced that I would cook dinner and was off to buy peppers for vegetarian chili, the only recipe I have committed to memory, since Tom prepares most of our meals. He is the more accomplished cook, with time free in the afternoon, and in our unspoken contract, this helps keep things even. But I didn't care to expose this infrastructure to my mother, who, despite her liberal leanings, can rarely be found at home without an apron.

"Suit yourself, Talia sweetie," she said. Each s jingled like a charm. "Henry and Bubbe and I have a lot of catching up to do."

Tom had sat out this trip, never his favorite destination, no matter how much he adores my parents. Henry and I were here for an escape that conveniently coincided with my father's seventy-first birthday, which was the next day. I'd booked a flight at the last minute, eager to flee as much as to celebrate. I felt sticky with guilt, so much so I hesitated to ask Chloe to take on two more days in the office. But e-mail is a beautiful thing, allowing the writer to fake an attitude as well as an expensive call girl. I'd made the request, doubting that Chloe would refuse—she should have felt guilty herself. She had to know she belonged in the office the day of the school interview.

Self-reproach must have been emanating from me like the scent of garlic, and my mother read me as if I were a billboard. "What's wrong?" she'd asked twice. When Henry and Bubbe both went down for their nap, my mother brought us glasses of tea and a plate of her almond mandelbrot and sat across from me on the screened porch, waiting for the big spill. "Trouble with your marriage, my darlink?" she asked, stroking the top of my hand.

"Everything's fine," I said as evenly as possible. To criticize Tom would diminish my father, who, as a chemistry teacher, never produced a major income. Worthy men, worthy occupations. I was trapped in a saga of consequences I could discuss with no one, especially since I'd stopped seeing a therapist. Even certified social workers cost plenty. So I chased my own tail. If Tom earned more, I wouldn't have tried to filch a job meant for a friend, wouldn't be sweating the cost of private school tuition, which, despite the generous stipend Tom seemed convinced Henry would receive, wasn't going to cover uniforms, trips, and the tennis and guitar lessons Henry would inevitably want in order to be like every other boy. I wouldn't have been sweating, period, racking up a ticker tape of grievances against myself. Did I mention that I was feeling guilty?

"Problems at work?" my mother asked.

"Only that we've lost a major account," I answered. This was not untrue. Gas prices were crazy high over the summer and people shopped less, hence a downward spiral in advertising. My boss, Eliot, droned on about it so much I'd stopped listening.

"Are you worried that you'll lose your job?" ▲

I wasn't until my mother said it.

"Don't look so shocked. You read the papers." I don't, much. I'm one of those traitors who skims online, less often than I should. "The economy isn't what it was."

I was even less in the mood for political discourse than maternal dissection. Hence, the stroll to southern California's souk, the farmers' market, bursting with Persian lemons and scolding signs. No preservatives! No pesticides! No smoking! No bikes! No kidding!

I was fondling a handful of watermelon radishes when a voice said, "If it isn't Talia Fisher-Wells." Standing in front of the Santa Rosa plums was a tall man in sunglasses and a black baseball cap worn backward. I squinted at his face, obscured by the sun, and when I didn't greet him, he said, "You have no idea who I am, do you?" He could have been my debate partner from tenth grade, a boy from Hebrew school, my senior prom date. "Admit it, Talia Fisher-Wells," he said, stretching out my last name. He chuckled again, and I was certain it was at my expense. "You don't have a clue."

The voice, tinged with New York, echoed in my memory. I delivered my most luminous smile. "Great to see you. What are you up to these days?"

"Isn't it obvious?" With one hand he hoisted a bag of apricots. With the other, he removed his sunglasses.

"Oh my God, Jonas!" The man for whom I'd been leaving daily messages. I'd gotten the feeling that he would make a fast decision—unless he'd made it and didn't have the chutzpah or manners to tell me.

"Actually, I prefer my first name," he said, extending his hand as if we'd never met. "Winters." His tone was warmer than I'd expected. "Don't tell me you came all this way to ask about the job."

"My parents. They live on Ashland."

"You? A California girl?" The Beach Boys never sang ballads about frizzy brunette bookworms who crocheted yarmulkes for their high school boyfriends. "Did they move recently?"

"You'd think, to listen to them, but it was thirty-eight years ago." *The job—that's what I want to talk about. Is he going to make me ask?* "What brings you here?"

"A visit to my brother," he said, "and to take a meeting and dodge your calls."

"Well?" I smiled again. *You schmuck. Spit it out. I'm a big girl.*

"I'll be honest," he said. How refreshing. "We lost a few accounts." Anxiety and deception, wasted. "But yesterday I signed a client, so the job's definitely on again."

I brightened, picturing myself taking free business trips that included visits to my parents.

"I owe you an apology," he had the grace to say, "for keeping you waiting. You and one other candidate are finalists. I promised myself I'd make up my mind when I got back next week."

I turned to make sure none of my mother's friends was crouching between the dates and the tomatoes and moved a little closer to Winters. "For what it's worth," I jumped in, "I'm very interested."

"I gathered that." He grinned back, and I felt his shoulder brush mine, barely. "Want to talk about it over coffee?"

Henry would be waking up soon, but I didn't see this as a choice. "Why not?" I said, and let him steer us toward a small table beneath a white market umbrella. He placed his hand on my arm and I felt an extra stab of guilt as Mean Maxine registered, again, that while he was not handsome, Winters had an appeal that was in his eyes and his arrogance. He'd swaggered into this century from the 1950s. Winters was bald, where Tom had a thick head of hair, and why was I comparing?

I regretted that I was wearing a skimpy halter unearthed from the back of the closet, jeans that failed to meet any definition of fashionable, and old sandals exposing toenails I hadn't polished in months. The highest praise I could offer myself was that my hair was clean.

Since this was Santa Monica, a posse of dogs was tied to the legs of several tables. Winters crouched to meet an especially eager specimen. "Goldendoodle?" I asked. There had to be a law. Every dog was some version of doodle.

"Labradoodle." He turned in my direction and said, "Talk to me," three of the most seductive words in the English language. I tried to take a stab at answering the question on one level while avoiding what was going on sub rosa, but that got harder when Winters Jonas added, "Why should I hire you for this job, besides that you're gorgeous?"

"I doubt you can find a better copywriter," I started, not believing or acknowledging the compliment, though I was glad that in the shade of an umbrella, this man might not have been able to see the color rising in my face. "I'm fast, I'm sharp, I'm—"

"Tell me about Talia," he said as he slowly stroked the dog. Obediently, she rolled over for a belly rub, spreading her legs. "The woman."

I tried not to stare at the triangle of dark curly black hair where Winters Jonas' shirt was open at his neck, but I didn't know where to look. "I grew up here."

"I got that." He let go of the dog and rested his chin on both hands. They were crossed in a steeple. The gesture said, *I have all the time in the world.*

"I transferred east for college," I added, and reeled off a few résumé items—editor of the literary magazine, resident adviser—while a server, flame-haired, slender, finely featured, took our orders for iced chai latte.

Winters didn't give this female a second look. He concentrated on me, drilling through my defenses. "What makes you passionate?" He asked the question as casually as if he'd said, *Can you pass the salt?* Our lattes arrived with biodegradable wood spoons.

This was no longer plain conversation. I couldn't say I didn't like it. "Results, words, ideas," I answered. "People who love their life."

"Are you one of those easygoing, life-loving people?" His tone mocked.

"Exactly." Any cool I'd ever had obviously hadn't made the trip to this coast. I looked away, searching for the artificial sweetener. There was none.

"I doubt that," he said. He stirred two spoonfuls of brown sugar—I assumed it was the expensive sort from Belize—into his latte and leaned back; I wondered why I felt as if he had taken a step forward. "Oh, you love parts of your life. But I can see something's missing, something major."

What was missing in my life was candor and honesty. That's all I cared to concede, but only to myself. "Winters," I said deliberately. I wasn't going to be baited, and it occurred to me that this was a test. For what exactly, I couldn't say. "I obviously want a new job. Your job. I mean, the job you are trying to fill. Everything else in my life is fine." *Not that it's any business of yours.*

"Don't go all defensive on me," he said as he raised his hands in the genuflection of *whoa.* "It's simply that in my experience, it's the hungry person, the not-exactly-thrilled-with-his-life guy, who gets ahead, who has that spark. That's the person I want on my team."

His laugh was a low ripple in a sea lapping against a beach the color of cashews. He said *team.* I heard *bed.*

"Everyone else is a little fat and lazy," he added. "I can see you're not fat, but..."

Mean Maxine demanded my attention. *Wax poetic all you want about beaches and laughter,* she said, *but what sane woman would even want this job, or be up to the sparring if she got it?* Mean Maxine was dead-on. And yet.

"Listen, I'm sorry for fucking with you. I hope I haven't offended you in some way."

"Let me count the ways," I said, reaching for a smile, but I don't do innuendo well. I was out of my league, or at least out of practice.

"Say," he asked as he downed half his latte, "I keep meaning to ask—do you know a Chloe Keaton? I believe you two are at the same agency."

I knocked my glass into his lap. The server appeared with a pile of napkins. As she mopped the icy spill, my mind sputtered. Winters placed his warm hand on my arm as if to steady me while I spat out apologies. "Chloe? Of course..." I was trying to think of what to say, pretending I didn't enjoy the touch on my skin, when inexplicably I turned around. Walking toward me was a man with a loping gate exactly like Tom's. Next to him, running to keep up, was a small boy, the image of Henry.

I blinked. Tom shouted, "Surprise," which Henry repeated.

Try wriggling out of this one, Mrs. Fisher-Wells, Mean Maxine said. *You are so getting what you deserve.*

Chapter 31

Jules

Another of Jules' Rules: *Doing nothing has a way of turning into something.*

I'd broken one of my own commandments. For weeks I'd toyed with calling Sheila to schedule a procedure, but when I started to punch in her number, my hand froze. This had nothing to do with a reversal in personal politics. I, a pro-choice militant since I understood the concept, had put my money where my mouth is only the day before, when I sent off a chunky donation to NARAL. But I was in suspended animation and didn't know if hormonal voodoo had caused my paralysis, much as it had heartburn, constipation, and my dearest friend, perpetual hunger. I was charging the refrigerator like a rhino.

Was something deeper and darker reeling in my psyche? I suspect that people say I'm not introspective. I can handle that. It's not the worst thing to be, a woman who has never chewed her cud. Except now.

Arthur had to be revived by Carmine's second-best brandy, after which I rushed home. For most of the ride I was twenty miles over the limit, powered by mortification, which gas stations should offer as a premium alternative. I asked myself throughout the drive and all night long, *why* had I told him? Now, days later, Arthur felt we were splitting the mental rent on the snake pit where I was trapped. I told him he had to stop with the texts, the e-mails, the calls, the cards, and especially the flowers. Correction: the cheap cretin didn't think to send flowers.

When I was ready to talk to him, I would. In the meantime, I wanted to speak to an individual with mental ballast who happened to care about me. I've been known to go to confession, but this wasn't a problem to take to church. Much as I like a whiff of incense and feel immensely proud that my people built Rome, the Pope and I do not see eye to eye on most issues, starting with every pesky detail associated with not having babies. Nor did I have the time to find a shrink, not that I'd trust one. Some women would turn to their mothers. Mine, of course, is out, in every sense of the word, as is my sister, though like Liza Minnelli, she stages regular comebacks. Last we heard—from Hefty Harry, who owns the other half of Ma's house—Maria was a croupier in Atlantic City. She'd changed her name to Margaux and her boobs to 38DD. When HH spotted her working a craps table, she pretended she didn't recognize him, despite his Niagara Falls comb-over, but that was definitely my sister's tramp stamp sagging down her butt cheek, captured on his iPhone.

For a chat, I was left with friends. Obviously, Quincy wasn't an option. I'd gotten the feeling that Chloe wanted to step up to the big leagues and start giving me advice, but as sincere as she might be, I didn't need an amateur trying to deal with my emotional dyslexia. So, folks, the dial landed on the last one standing. I waited to call until seven-thirty on a weeknight, and I was picturing Talia in Brooklyn watching Tom slave over a hot pot thick with sustainable vegetables.

It was St. Thomas who answered. "Hey," I said. I like him fine. Tom Wells is bighearted and smart without a Mr. Hedge Fund stick up his butt. Yet he spoke my name as if he was trying to break it.

"Love you, too," I said.

"Hang on," he grumbled. I heard Talia shrieking, "Let me talk," and Tom shouting, "Say you'll call her back. It's just Jules."

You selfish prick. For one moment, Just Jules wanted to be the center of the universe. I was about to hang up when Talia came on the line. "Sorry, it's not a good time," she panted. "How late can I get back to you?"

"Anytime from midnight to five a.m.," I said.

"That bad, huh?" she answered. "You sound like dreck. We're having a little marital turbulence here, but I promise I'll call. I'm so sorry."

Not, I'd have bet, as sorry as I was.

As the night progressed, I worked through tasks and treats I'd selected with distraction in mind. I ironed napkins, printed out invoices, deep-conditioned my hair while rereading a chapter of an Anne Rice novel, ate a pistachio Nutella sundae, and at eleven o'clock switched on HBO. After twenty minutes, I'd liquefied into a swamp of tears and perspiration. Had I still been in high school I'd have done what this movie's cutely dimpled baby mama did—give away her infant, turn the page, and get on with her life. Except... I didn't want to witness my body turn into a Buick only to deliver my little cannoli to a woman who thought she'd be a better mother than I.

Holy epiphany. Had I just thought of myself as a mother? The world had stopped spinning.

If I couldn't have this child, I didn't want anyone else to, either. Was I a selfish, horrible, burn-in-hell bitch? Probably. I was a cockroach in a baby food factory, mold on cheese, a bathtub ring. I had worked myself right down to Nazi sympathizer when I heard the phone. I checked caller ID. Not Arthur.

"Sorry," Talia said. "I wanted to call back sooner, but..."

"But you're ready to blow Tom's brains out, and here I've always cast you as Ozzie and Harriet's unflappable grandchildren. What happened?"

"Oh, nothing," she said, but I could tell she wanted me to ask about her giant problem.

"Don't keep me in suspense."

"He surprised me when I was in California," she explained. "Flew out on a whim in time for my dad's birthday, which was an incredibly kind gesture and—long story short—he found me having coffee with a guy. It was a work thing, but Tom didn't like what he saw."

This was a problem? But attention had to be paid. "Just asking, but were you two professionals fondling naked, let's say, while you were drinking whatever people drink now in L.A.?" I stared at my toes and wondered if I should switch polish colors. Clambake looked too festive for my mental state. I needed to pick from the vampire palette.

"Tom thought so. He harped all weekend on the body language he claimed to see. Usually he's a sweetheart—you know that—but he has this insecure streak."

We'd taken a curious detour. I'd always assumed Tom Wells' rarified lineage rendered him as solid as Plymouth Rock. "I'm no Tom expert," I said, "but I know your husband well enough to say he isn't the sort to pick fights over nothing. Tell me straight, dollface. What's with this other guy? Someone special? A man you want in your life? Already in your life?" I escalated to taunting and didn't care. I felt wickedly happy, simply because there was trouble in someone else's paradise. *This* was a distraction.

"No, no, and no, I've told you." Talia's voice was exactly how you'd speak if you were afraid that your husband might be lurking ten feet away. "The person with whom I was having an innocent latte was simply a guy with a good job opening."

When Talia does *whom*, I know she's pissed. "You already have a good job," I pointed out. Every mother would kill for a deal as sweet as the one she and Chloe split. The company even paid for vacation, health, and dental, though neither of them worked full-time.

"I have a good half job." She paused dramatically. "While I have the expenses of a whole life." I heard exasperation. "This would be full-time and I think it would pay well." She paused again. "He hasn't offered a thing yet and maybe won't, at least to me. He's taking his time. I think he enjoys the torture."

Burn-in-Hell Bitch identified a spasm of sympathy. Is anything more humiliating than sucking up to the Man? Exactly why I'm my own boss. "Who's this mogul dangling a job in front of you?"

After a seven-second delay she answered, "I'd rather not say."

Intriguing. This was what I needed, all right, not chores and beauty maintenance. All of a sudden I was in Tom's camp. "What's going on?"

"Absolutely nothing. I've told you everything." Which I doubted. "It's your turn," she said, working hard to keep from sounding angry. She was failing. "What's going on with you?"

"Oh, nothing, really. I have an audition tomorrow. I'm picking new wallpaper. I booked a hand-modeling job for a jewelry company with a line of cocktail rings. I'm pregnant." I tossed it out, light as confetti, a flurry of snowflakes blowing off a spruce.

"And I'm a natural blond *shiksa* with a trust fund. Jules, it's getting late."

One Mississippi, two Mississippi.

"Ah, Twenty Questions," Talia said. "You're breaking up with Arthur?"

I pounced. "Are you suggesting I should?"

"That's not what I'm suggesting, and you know it." She groaned. "You're always on his case. I thought maybe . . . Any friend might think . . ."

"You thought wrong," I said, at risk of defending Arthur. Did Talia and the others have nothing better to do than gang-bang my flawed relationship?

"Work-related?"

"Colder."

"Is Arthur an alcoholic? Is he seeing that Jennifer you told me about? Did he give you herpes?"

"Colder, colder, colder." For someone who calls herself "a creative type," Talia has zero imagination.

"It's late. I give up. What's on your mind?"

My fingers stroked the fuzzy purple throw on my lap. In the large gilt mirror across from the couch, I looked rather like an empress, but that's not how I felt. "Like I said at the start, I'm knocked up, my friend. In the family way. Big with child. Preggers. Didn't Chloe tell you?" Apparently not. What was going on with those two that I wasn't even conversational filler?

Now the dead air was at Talia's end. "Seriously? Shall I be congratulating you?" she asked, quietly, cautiously. Her voice sounded almost fearful.

"The jury's out."

"How far along?" She was whispering.

"Far," I whispered back.

"My God, why did you let me blather about my stuff? This is huge."

"You don't know the half of it."

"Have you told Chloe?"

"Oh, yeah," I said. "I thought my news would be front page, column right, but I guess not."

"Where will you be tomorrow around eleven?" Talia said after what seemed like a pause long enough for me to have read a page in the Constitution. "I'm renting a car to see a client in Stamford first thing in the morning, and afterward I could swing by. We could talk this through."

"That would be...lovely. I'd like that," I said, more formally than I'd intended. "Now go find your husband and jump his bones. Do penance whether you're right or wrong. Tell him the last thing you want to do is fight. Tom's a great guy. Don't fuck it up."

Why is it that the way other women should solve their problems is always blatantly obvious? It's easier, at least for me, to shovel out kindness than accept it.

I got off the phone, put on my heavy-duty rubber gloves, and washed my dishes. Finally I took myself to my own empty bed. After one last, long hiccupy cry, I slept.

• • •

Talia showed up bearing brownies and a crisp paper bag brimming with froths of lavender tissue paper. "Oh, Jules," she said as we embraced. Neither of us seemed willing to let go. "Open it," she said as she mopped her eyes and nodded toward the gift. I whipped out a bed jacket trimmed with marabou, its peachy satin suiting a buxom forties movie star. "I bought it for Christmas," she said, "but why wait?"

I slipped the jacket over my daytime home uniform, a black sweater and velvety pants that I pretend aren't sweats, and gushed gratitude, all while I hoped that Talia wasn't scrutinizing my body and wondering if I'd been using pregnancy as an excuse to go on the ice cream diet. We walked into my kitchen, the steam from my caffeine-free herbal tea flushing my face. I brewed Talia espresso. The milk was already waiting in a crystal pitcher, the sugar cubes next to dainty tongs in a silver bowl. Like a lazy cat, I craved a spot warmed by the sun and settled myself in the chair next to the window, but with Talia there, there was no calm in the room. I'm used to being a conductor, not a jittery first violin.

At least she got right to it. "I was pregnant in college." Talia twirled one of her curls, a gesture activated whenever she was waiting for a bomb to detonate. "I was nineteen, a junior. I can barely remember the guy's name. Jason someone. I just knew that I wasn't ready to have a baby—it wouldn't have been fair to ... to anyone. I never even considered going through with it and ..." She spoke at length of talking things over with a campus minister because she was too embarrassed to see the rabbi, of the kind souls at Planned Parenthood, of keeping a secret from her parents and the teenage father. She described her morning sickness, as if to prove that she wasn't making the whole thing up.

But I am not twenty. I am a grown woman with three bedrooms and a financial portfolio heavy on steady-Eddie blue chips and bonds. I have started to save for retirement, took out disability insurance last year, and have calculated that I should be able to hold off on collecting social security until I'm close to seventy. I pay my taxes each year by February 15. I, not Tom Wells, am fucking Plymouth Rock.

"Do you ever think about that child?" I interrupted to ask. Did she see it in each passing stroller, in every YouTube video with break-dancing babies? I knew that would happen to me. The nuns would get me in the end.

"I'm Henry's mom now," Talia said, too quickly, as if that explained anything.

"Obviously, ending the pregnancy is an option," I said, not wanting to torture Talia just for the hell of it. "I've made an appointment." This was a lie. "I'm about seventy percent sure I want to go through with it." I wasn't sure of a thing.

"I have to ask—where does Arthur fit into this picture? Have you told him?" She seemed eager.

"In a moment of insanity I said something," I admitted. "But this is my decision." I was fairly sure Talia's look spoke disapproval—that I made Arthur's opinion matter because he couldn't unknow what I'd told him. But I needed to steer away from the shipwreck that was my life. "Tell me more about the job thing and the business with Tom."

"You want to talk about that?"

I nodded.

"It's at a boutique agency, Bespoke Communications. Know it?"

"Don't think so. It's Latte Man I want to hear about."

"His name is Winters Jonas."

"Really? He and Arthur may have worked together once." Who could forget a name like that? I was also fairly certain that not long ago Arthur had mentioned some job in this guy's office that he thought would be ideal for Chloe.

"Arthur knows him? Really?" Talia said as she found another ringlet to twirl and looked at her watch. "Eleven?" she said, as if she'd just mastered telling time. "I'm going to need to get back. Sorry I'm in a rush, but..." She grabbed my hand, which I wanted to toss off. Too much soul baring before noon; I wished I hadn't heard her confession. "I'm here for you, no matter what," she added earnestly. I despise earnestness. "I hope you know that. We all are."

I snorted. Not Quincy!

"If you go through with this, I'm with you a hundred percent. I'll go along with you if you..."

Even women who believe passionately in the right to choose will waltz around the actual word *abortion*, especially when they have given birth to a child they love.

"Thanks," I said as I stared out the window at my tidy lawn, every fallen leaf bagged and carted away. "Promise you won't disappear over the next few days, okay? And good luck in getting this job, if that's what you want."

The phone rang. I was grateful for a reason to stop posturing. "Arthur," I mouthed as I answered. "Fine, thanks," I said politely. I didn't care to be observed in battle-ax mode. "Really?" I said. This was interesting. This was new. "I'll call you back—Talia stopped by and can't stay."

We bid our goodbyes, Arthur and I, Talia and I. More hugging, more sniffles. I finished my blueberry-apricot muffin and half of Talia's, hung up my new bed jacket, plucked dead leaves off my houseplants, and stared out the window. I called a few clients, then finally dialed Sheila's number.

I cleared my throat and explained what I had in mind. The receptionist switched me to a nurse who explained the drill. An ultrasound I'd expected. But counseling? What had I ever done to deserve that?

"When's her earliest opening?" I asked. "Tomorrow at four? I'll take it. Great." But there was nothing great about it.

CHAPTER 32

Quincy

"Quincy and Jake," Dr. Frumkes said as we sat in her office, "I have good news and less-good news." *Which first?* her face asked. I squeezed Jake's hand. "I'm sorry, but two of the embryos did not survive."

"How do you know?" Jake asked.

"We can no longer find them on the sonogram." There were other words as well, sounds that got sucked into a vortex of medical gibberish that meant nothing beyond *dead*.

My heart revolted. These were not embryos. They were Speck and Peanut, or maybe Jubilee and Speck, imagined, loved, gone. In the time it took to draw a breath, my red sweater turned black, my soul shriveled. Dr. Frumkes' mouth kept moving, but I couldn't listen. I needed to insulate, to stuff cotton batting into my ears, to crawl inside myself. Jake's grip became fierce, trying to ensure that I didn't drift away. He cupped my chin in his other hand and turned my face toward his. "Quincy, did you hear what the doctor said?"

I stared at him. *Pick on someone else, God.* "Doctor, can you please repeat what you told us?" It was Jake, struggling for normal.

Dr. Frumkes leaned forward and took my hands. "Quincy, we've had some unfortunate luck here, and I'm profoundly sorry, but—please hear me—one of the embryos is absolutely fine. Healthy. Viable. We've got a fighter." She stopped for a moment. "This happens."

I would rather have had all my news bad than false hope. I was able to say nothing. Breathing became coal miner hard.

"Are you hearing me?" the doctor asked.

"Define reasonable," I said finally, inflectionless.

"There's no medical reason to believe this embryo won't develop," she said, precisely and a bit too loud, as if she were afraid we would lawyer up and sue for malpractice. "This is still good news."

I nodded to indicate that I had heard. She advised modified bed rest—I would be allowed to walk a block if necessary—mentioned the term *grief counselor*, and gave me a name and number. We were instructed to be in close touch, to return in one week without fail. We were dismissed.

Your family dies in a plane crash but you survive. Are you happy or sad? You win the lottery the day your parents split up. Happy or sad? Everyone gets laid off but you. Happy or sad? Life is a bully, trying to make philosophers of us, seeing how much we can take.

Not that much, not that day. I was inept, a dishrag of an expectant mother, a failure. How could I protect my remaining baby?

Like used-up prizefighters, Jake and I shuffled out of the doctor's office. "We should eat," he said. I mutely followed him around the corner to Madison Avenue, where we fell into a diner buzzing with customers, since there is no hour of the day when New Yorkers don't scarf down eggs, home fries, and toast. The hostess showed us to a booth and we slid in. Without checking the menu, Jake ordered lunch; I, tea. We stared at each other, too fearful to be happy for what remains, too overcome to say a thing.

The food arrived and ten minutes passed. Jake picked at his cheese omelet, refused a coffee refill. My tea grew cold. "I've got to get out of here," I said.

He paid the bill and held me tight. "I'll ride with you," he said as we waited by the curb and he tried to flag a cab. "I'll take the day off."

"No, I'll be fine." I prefer to mope solo. "I'm going to go home and sleep." Perhaps for a week.

"You sure, Q, honey?" As if I was made of papier-mâché, he helped me into the taxi.

"I'm sure. I just want to get in bed." We kissed before he shut the door.

Once I arrived home I immediately threw a quilt over the three cribs in the living room.

CHAPTER 33

Chloe

With some couple, opposites attract. Not Xander and me. Some people say we look alike, but it's more than that. Both of us crave organization, and one of our rituals is a quarterly meeting where we order in pizza and look at our life as if it were the Federal Reserve. Thanks to these summits, we have an up-to-date will (which I need to amend so that Talia doesn't inherit the aquamarine earrings she has nearly bitten off my earlobes), a safe-deposit box inventory, and files of folders subdivided by genus and species—mortgage, stock and bond portfolio, charitable donations, tax returns, paint colors, captioned personal photographs, and DVD and book lists, as well as appliance warranties with their manuals. Xander is Keaton Inc.'s president, I its secretary-treasurer.

When people behold our bountiful possessions, they must think we take them for granted, like a tall man does his height. But I believe one reason we've been blessed is that we're willing to pay attention to the small stuff. We dot the *i*'s.

The previous day had been the first of the month, when I looked over my calendar to sign and address cards from the dozens I bought at the beginning of the year and intended to mail four days before each occasion. That was when I realized five months had elapsed since our most recent economic caucus. Xander had had me cancel the last huddle because he was working late—he'd been doing that even more than usual—and I'd neglected to reschedule. At dinner, I reminded him that we were due for a powwow.

"I don't have the time for that right now, hon," he said, not even looking up from his black cod, orzo, and roasted asparagus with Asiago cheese, a cooking class menu I'd reproduced with A-minus results, though Xander had made no comment. "Maybe next month."

"But it's been a while."

"I've got a lot going on," he said with what felt like a rebuke. I must have pouted, because he frowned and added, "Could you back off? I need a little space right now."

Since when did my husband, so fussy about language that he looked wounded if I blurted out "irregardless," use "space" that way? His sentences were always heavy with op-ed words. Cohort! Context! Cogent! Cognizant! Coalesce! Cohabitant!

"Space for whom?"

"Excuse me?" he said.

"I feel as if you've checked out around here." I didn't even know why this flew out of my mouth. It wasn't as if we'd been overlooking, say, sex. We had a date every Tuesday and Thursday at ten-thirty and Saturdays at eleven-thirty, and at our last quarterly meeting we'd decided to wait at least nine more months before trying to conceive a second child.

"Checked out?" he said, his face reddening. Then, in slow motion, he cocked his head, as if to survey our dining room. For that evening, I'd found pink tulips for the table, lit candles, tried hard. I'd dimmed the chandelier, and on the sideboard was a glistening bowl of blackberries I planned to serve with biscotti I'd baked myself while Jamyang was feeding Dash his dinner. "Who do you think makes all this possible?"

I threw down my napkin, ran up to the bedroom, slammed the door, and threw myself on the bed. I didn't even fold back our white velvet duvet, as smooth as a skating rink, though I tossed away the pillows so my makeup wouldn't streak the shams. They landed on the thick carpeting with a soft thud, scattering a pile of fabric samples across the floor. I glanced at them with annoyance; I'd asked my decorator for pale pink toile, not the historically accurate rose Marie Antoinette might have used to upholster a minor château!

I waited to see if Xander had followed me upstairs, but I didn't hear his footsteps. I forced myself to take deep breaths and tried to recall Autumn Rutherford's tape from that morning, which was rattling in my brain. *You can do no wrong at this juncture,* she'd sung into my ear as I walked the treadmill. *Take risks. Even what turns out wrong will right itself. Adopt a what-will-be-will-be attitude and what will be will be very good indeed. The potential for your life has no limits. Look at every opportunity.*

Autumn's prognostications had seemed sensible when I'd heard them earlier. I wanted to believe her. I blew my nose, dabbed my tears, and tried to remember the gist of the rest. *You may have been hurt in the past and so find it hard to trust people, but don't let suspicions get out of hand* had been intermingled in her wisdom. I had a long and winding road ahead of me if I wanted to reach the apex of self-improvement.

I decided to listen to the next day's tape right then. I pulled my iPod from the bedside table and stuck the buds in my ears. *Look in the mirror,* Autumn trilled. I got up and walked to the full-length mirror. *Who is that? A star in the making! Lady Luck is shining on you.* I'd have to take her word on that, since I looked like I'd gone through a half marathon, not a short crying jag.

I realized I was being a brat. Xander provided for us luxuriously, yet had little time to enjoy anything himself. Before I saw him again, I'd best reapply my eye makeup, but I wanted to soak up a bit more psychological rehab first.

Think of your life as a beach book so juicy you can't wait to turn the page and see what thrilling escapades will occur next in the heroine's life. Become that heroine. Write your own story. Make it anything you want.

I closed my eyes and tried to take myself on a more daring path, but I couldn't see beyond my own front door, which I'd recently repainted in cerulean blue and had refitted with a shiny brass knob. Maybe I wasn't thinking big-picture enough, but except for my subzero confidence, my life already felt close to ideal—Dash, our Keaton Inc. prosperity, and certainly Xander, though I'd like to have him be, as Autumn would say, more present in our lives. My beach book was going to hit the remainder pile the week it was published. It surely wasn't going to warrant reviews, even in someone's sloppy blog. Certainly it wouldn't be optioned for a movie!

I opened my eyes and noticed, as I got up to walk to the bathroom, that the light on my phone was blinking. The first message was about a job that had struck me as respectable but dull. It was at a large agency and my assignment would be on floor accounts, the challenge being that people in the Swiffer Generation, as the interviewer referred to people I assumed were my age, didn't place a high priority on the state of the wood beneath their feet. The recording was from someone in human resources. "Great news!" she warbled. "Mrs. Keaton, we are delighted to make you an offer. Please return my call at your convenience, any time after eight in the morning." I was even less enthusiastic about the job knowing the hour at which the busy bees there would hit the desk. The second message was from my decorator, who'd found a collection of antique maps she wanted to hang in Dash's room; some weeks ago, Xander had vetoed the idea of re-creating a log cabin. The last message was from Winters Jonas, from Bespoke Communications. "Chloe, let's talk once more," he said, and left his cell number. His voice was a low growl. "It's down to you and another candidate."

I'd hoped to complete my twenty-four-tape crash course in ego repair before I needed to make major decisions. How should I react to antique maps in a young child's room? Xander would probably find them brilliantly educational, but what if Dash started jabbering about, say, the country of Yugoslavia and his friends thought he'd made it up? He'd come home furious for having been led astray, and demand to know the truth about the Tooth Fairy, too. If I was dithering about antique maps, I certainly wasn't up to accepting a job or possibly choosing between offers. A smarter job hunter would enjoy playing one position against another, but I understood this game even less well than football or bridge.

I redid my makeup and changed into a flowing white robe Xander had given me last Christmas. I walked first to his library, my rustling satin the only sound except the big clock ticking in the hall. His library door was closed, no lamps lit or richly scented pipe smoke wafting into the hallway. I continued down to the living room and dining room. Empty. "Xander," I called out, quietly, for fear of waking Dash. I got to the garden floor and saw that his jacket was missing from the hook in the hall. I heard noise in the kitchen and opened the door, hoping he'd be there and that our mutual apologies would outdo one another.

But it wasn't Xander. It was Jamyang, who had her back to me, brewing mint tea. She turned and looked up, pushing a wave of black hair away from her face, portrait perfect, with eyes darker than charcoal. She smiled ever so slightly. "I'll be finished in a minute," she said, spooning dainty drops of honey into the green glazed stoneware cup that she kept in her room. Did she think that to place it in our cupboard would violate boundaries, or was she afraid that our decadence might contaminate her purity?

"No need to hurry," I said, hoping she wouldn't. I wished Jamyang and I might talk, perhaps not exactly as friends, but I wanted, at least, her respect. I worried that she thought I was spoiled and pesky. In the months since she'd joined our household, I'd never succeeded in sparking conversation, light or otherwise, though Jamyang's vocabulary had expanded right along with Dash's. Our exchanges ventured only as far as practicalities.

"Yes, ma'am," she answered, although once we'd gotten past "Missy Chloe," time and again I'd suggested that she call me by my first name.

I looked at Jamyang's tea and realized I craved some hug-in-a-mug hot chocolate. My cooking instructor always spouted off about how it was a crime to use anything less than the darkest imported chocolate, the more bitter the better, with pours of heavy cream and organic milk to which he added vanilla beans, cinnamon, and slivers of candied ginger. His production would take me thirty minutes. But our teacher was across the river in the Village, most likely dreaming of wild rabbit stuffed with foie gras and truffles. I dumped a packet of Swiss Miss into a saucepan, poured in whatever skim milk remained in the carton, and waited for my concoction to simmer while I scavenged for mini marshmallows and pictured my cooking instructor having a stroke.

As I went through the steps, I felt Jamyang's watchful eyes. Could I, who had a good ten years on Jamyang, move to the other side of the globe, unfamiliar with the language and customs, the money and transportation system, and manage even a fraction as well? I knew the answer to every question. Did I honestly want to know what she thought of Xander and me? Perhaps her silence was a gift.

"Dash ate an avocado today," she said. "And two clementines." She had the kind of round, full lips Hollywood celebrities used artificial fillers to fake. Had Xander noticed? "And he could use some harder puzzles. Smart."

"Thanks," I said, thinking that she knew Dash's brains came from Xander, not me. "I'll pick some up tomorrow."

"And new pajamas."

Usually Jamyang wore baggy jumpers over long-sleeved T-shirts and leggings, her hair tightly braided. But that night she was in a sleeveless T-shirt, which showed slender arms toned by repeatedly picking up a growing boy. Her feet were bare—pale and as exquisitely formed as a marble statue's. To my surprise, her toenails were painted a trendy shade of bloody red. Why had she gone to the trouble? Perhaps the real question was, for whom?

Did Xander notice Jamyang, an orchid flowering within his own home? Did she want him to notice her? I told myself I was a crackpot to think this, but couldn't stop.

"I'll see you in the morning," she said. "Good evening, ma'am."

"Good evening, Jamyang, sweet dreams." She turned away and padded noiselessly into the hallway that led to her room.

My hot chocolate was ready. I poured it into a gaily striped red mug and sipped it while I read trashy magazines in bed, waiting for Xander. Usually I relished photos of celebrities shoving toilet paper into their trunks or conveniently falling in love with their costar right before their movie release. But before I got to Fashion Police, I'd closed my eyes. I'm fairly sure sometime later, Xander kissed me goodnight.

When I woke in the morning, he was already in the shower. "Good morning, sunshine," he said a few minutes later as he strolled toward his walk-in closet with its still life of suits—navy or charcoal—neatly hung on wooden hangers. He selected a charcoal pinstripe and turned toward his ties—stripes, dots, and small geometric patterns, arranged by color. "Which cravat does the lady prefer?" He held up two, blue and pink.

"Pink, definitely." Was he going to pretend our words the night before hadn't been ugly? Did he think I'd acted like a child, and was going to magnanimously overlook my behavior?

He started dressing. Crisp white shirt, light on the starch. Discreetly engraved matte gold cuff links. Black lizard belt. Well-cobbled, perfectly shined Lobb shoes, heels always in repair.

"Xander, about last night," I said.

He took his thin gold watch from the velvet-lined box where it rested every night. "Honey, I can't be late." He kissed me on the cheek. The faint citrus scent of his hundred-dollar-an-ounce cologne lingered after he left the room.

It was eight-ten. I called the Swiffer lady to get the details on her offer. The salary was more than twice as much as what I earned now, although of course it was for a full-time job, not a part-time one. She wanted my answer within a week. I thanked her, told her I'd be back in touch soon, and put a note on my calendar. I knew I was going to say no, but it seemed rude to reject her on the spot.

My next order of business was my Autumn Rutherford tape. *If partners and loved ones try to clip your wings, do whatever it takes to protect your autonomy. If you lose it, it won't be easy to recover,* she advised.

At nine o'clock I dialed Bespoke Communications. "Chloe Keaton for Winters Jonas, please," I told the receptionist.

CHAPTER 34

Talia

"Good to see you again," Winters Jonas said. Apparently he was not going to apologize for keeping me waiting. I'd been sinking into a burgundy love seat in a dive so poorly lit I couldn't even pass the time by proofing the copy I'd written that day for Eliot. I could hear my mother saying, *Talia Rose, who has a job interview in such a dump?* But this was where the blond receptionist had told me to meet him. My skirt had ridden up, and as Winters sat beside me I pulled it over my knees.

I'd ordered sparkling water. "Can't I talk you into a glass of wine?" He waved over the server. "The syrah, please," he said after he perused the short list.

I was too vain to take out my glasses to read the menu. "Make that two," I said.

He leaned back and at an angle, his face slightly in shadow. Once again, he was wearing black, a turtleneck, subtly expensive. On his wrist was a Patek Philippe, the model with a perpetual calendar and diamonds twinkling on the bezel. Its face and band were black. The only reason I could identify the watch was that Xander owned its twin, an engagement present from Chloe, who'd taken me along on a giddy shopping trip.

"Talia," he said, "this hasn't been an easy decision." Was this putz going to tell me I was the loser? Couldn't he have e-mailed? "I hope you don't think I've been jerking you around." I did, I did. "You've been on my mind a lot since California."

The wine arrived. He lifted his glass and slowly swirled its contents. A bossa nova beat was playing on the sound track, inspiring the couple next to us to sway in their seats.

"I won't pretend I don't have some hesitation—your background isn't a custom fit," Winters said. I hoped he couldn't hear me gulp. "But my instincts tell me I'd be making a mistake not to hire you," he added, "and I always respect my gut." His smile looked nothing less than genuine. But then he bent forward to remove an eyelash from my eye.

"Just a minute," he said, his breath cool on my face. Was this *schmuck* going to kiss me? But he sat back in his chair and repeated the words I'd been hoping to hear: "I'd like you to take the job."

Not praise to make a woman break into song. Still. "Great news," I said. "Thank you."

He reviewed the salary—almost as much as I'd asked for—and the accounts, each more interesting than my current assignments. "I'd like you to start in two weeks," he said, "and meet me in Napa, where I'm pitching a major winery." From a slim leather satchel he withdrew a folder, both black. "You could start working on it now."

"I'm flattered," I said, and was equally flummoxed. "When do you need my answer?"

He moved the folder toward me like a gift, and his body moved ever so slightly in the same direction. "Now would be good."

"How about after the weekend?" It was Wednesday.

"Friday."

"Friday."

"But I'm willing to toast your decision now. Another round," he said to the server. "Please." When it arrived, he raised his glass. "To a brilliant association with Talia Fisher-Wells."

After we clinked our crystal, we moved on to discuss restaurants in Santa Monica, and I was aware that Winters' glance returned more than once to my legs. Then again, I was the woman who for this occasion had shortened this skirt, finishing the hem last night. I looked at my men's Timex, a distant cousin many times removed of Winters' timepiece. I was late. I downed the remaining wine in two swallows. After an awkward moment—was he going to reach to embrace me?—I took the folder. We shook hands.

I'd been offered a job, a great job. I should be giddy, trying to decide whom to call first—Tom or my parents, then Jules or Quincy. Why was Mean Maxine cackling so loudly I couldn't think?

CHAPTER 35

Quincy

For the past forty-eight hours I'd wept with such ferocity you'd have thought I'd been peeling sacks of onions. As the light faded and the apartment became increasingly chilly—the landlord stinted on the heat—I burrowed under a blanket, Fanny by my side. In the late afternoon I lit a candle and found myself wishing I knew how to pray. I wanted to be thankful, to see the clichéd glass as half full, but I was in no condition for happiness. Not yet. I had learned to expect the worst.

When Jake came home, he wanted to talk. I placed my finger on his lips to quiet him. "Later," I said. "Maybe tomorrow." What was there to say?

Between dreamless naps my only solace had been reading. The day before, I'd been a mistress to a horny, hirsute British king. That day I was in Mumbai, immersed in Parsi culture, steady in escape, when Maizie penetrated my sanctuary via the curdled tone of her assistant. "Hold for Ms. May," the woman commanded when I picked up the phone.

I'd finished writing *Crazy Maizie* a week earlier. I'd begun her life story when the public met her, a frilly JonBenét whose mother's taste in kids' clothes led to leopard, sad on any little girl, truly unfortunate on one so freckled. We frothed through puberty. Seemingly overnight, Maizie had been blessed by DNA deities—hetero males, evidently—who'd transmogrified her into a babe. Then we rocked on to the present, when Maizie counted Grammys the way others do eggs in the fridge. I had the three-hundred-page manuscript bound so loose sheets wouldn't fly into the sea at whatever beachfront resort Maizie was secreting herself in while recovering from liposuction. After I dispatched the oeuvre, I'd managed to suppress the memory that I'd ever written it.

I told Maizie's assistant I would hold. Since I was already floating in an existential haze, I wouldn't have noticed if I'd been left hanging there for one minute or thirty. But soon enough, Maizie shrieked, "Hey, you really nailed me in this book, Q." She was not a young woman known for her Zen-like restraint, though our professional arrangement precluded me from asking her to use her inside voice, and it offended me that she had co-opted the name only Jake uses, but I'd had to let that go. "The scenes with my old lady? Genius."

Mama May was a viper. The scenes had written themselves, especially when April May chugged the Hatorade and ranted about Maizie on *The View*. All I'd had to do was take notes.

"But the parts about my men?" That would include a trifecta of managers who had cheerfully exploited her since she was thirteen. "You've left out the best stuff."

"I had to. We've gone over Libel 101, remember?"

"I don't care how you fix it. Just heat it up."

The remaining half of my fee was due upon Maizie's acceptance of the manuscript. We needed this money, which Jake had been asking about just the other night. To scrape together a down payment for the apartment, we'd lost interest that would have accrued on the large sum we'd withdrawn from our mutual fund, plus there was money down the drain for the lawyers and various applications. Every time I thought about the dollar tally of our rejection topping off its psychic cost, I wanted to strangle Jules and Arthur all over again.

"Let's go over what you have in mind." I was ready to activate the tap-ing mechanism in my phone.

"I'm out of here in ten minutes—how's Friday morning at eleven?" It would need to be okay. She owned me.

"Sure. Call you. Bye."

"Don't hang up so fast," she said, and laughed. "Sometimes I think you hate me."

The truth was that Maizie was a guileless creature. It's me I often de-spise, for getting a master's in nineteenth-century English literature and sweating out a thesis on *Middlemarch* only to allow myself to land at the bottom of the literary food chain, rubbing up against online "content" providers.

"My friend gave me tickets for his show tonight, but I can't use them—I thought you and the hubby could."

"Thanks, but I'm sorry. I can't use the tickets...the hubby is travel-ing." He wasn't—Jake was in his office, calling me six times a day. But I didn't see us going to any concerts in the near future.

"Take someone else. Don't you have girlfriends?"

Interesting question. We used to hang out together—Talia, Chloe, Jules, me. That had gotten harder after three of us married and all of us scattered, yet there'd been a time when I could persuade Jules, at least, to drop everything and go anywhere. She was unflinchingly faithful, con-sistently amusing. I missed her laughter and company, not for the first time.

Talia also used to be an excellent companion, though I'd stopped ask-ing her to join me when, time after time, she'd say she needed to be with Henry. Tom did the early shift, she'd explain, and their deal was that in the evenings, he got to swim or bike or shoot hoops at the Y.

That left Chloe. For her, child care has never been an issue, it's—this is a direct quote—the "big life." Her evenings are a glut of catered parties she both gives and attends, charity benefits, culture vulture venues—the theater, the ballet, the opera—and casual dinners at restaurants Jake and

I reserve for milestone celebrations. I suspect that she equates last-minute with last-ditch and that she looks down on my infinitely smaller existence.

"Are you there?" It was Maizie, wailing again.

"Sorry, the connection faded out there for a minute," I lied, sort of.

"Whatever," she said. "I won't take no for an answer. I'll have my assistant call with the details." She hung up.

I replaced the phone and walked to my closet. Under the beach towels, behind the heating pad and sewing kit, I'd stashed a decade-old picture of me with Jules, Chloe, and Talia, our faces plump with anticipation. The image was from one of our Sunday dinners, taken by a rare guest, because we liked reserving those evenings for ourselves, Jules treating us to four-cheese lasagna or a pot of her nonna's meatballs and gravy, Talia trying to bake like her mother. We were gathered around the long oak table in the rambling apartment blocks from here that I wished I'd never given up and could live in now, filled with kids.

All of us own a copy of this photograph, enlarged and framed in ornate silver, a Christmas gift from Chloe. Until recently I'd displayed mine on my dresser. I wondered if the others had also tucked theirs away.

Were these women still my friends? Asking the question made me feel crusty with spite, stiff with the rigor mortis of resentment.

On the Discovery Channel, I once saw monkeys perfectly content to do tricks for cucumber slices until the day one lucky primate started being rewarded with sweet green grapes, the simian equivalent of Godiva. The rest of the sorority—I'm positive these monkeys were female—came down with an epic case of rivalry. They wouldn't perform their tricks until they, too, got grapes.

Had I, Quincy Blue, become a grapeless monkey, envy eating my life from the inside out? When I considered each of the women to whom I'd once felt close, the creeping distress was almost nauseating.

Most of the seven deadlies come with an up side. Lust? Orgasm! Go for gluttony—you've enjoyed stuffing your face. Sloth? Your dishes pile up as you sniff through a movie marathon, sustained by candy bars whose wrappers litter your floor. Wrath feels euphoric while you're telling your boss to fuck himself. Pride is a state Americans go out of their way to cultivate, and greed may mean you have a pile of money, at least on paper. But with envy you simply feel slimy, each pang shrinking you smaller.

I stared at the photo and realized that an ugly part of me begrudged Chloe and Talia their uneventful pregnancies. I coveted their healthy sons and the fully rounded sense of family each had come by as if it were a government entitlement, and while I didn't wish Talia and Chloe ill, I couldn't be in their presence right now, forced to fake happiness. Maybe it would be different if this pregnancy stuck. *If.* I wanted my baby. I missed the babies who would never be.

With Jules, it's different. I've never envied her. I've admired her. Yet as long as I'm looking at myself with full frontal honestly, I have to admit that arrogance—and married-lady hubris tossed in her single direction—has salted the stew. Perhaps Jules has sensed my contempt. She is nothing if not perceptive. Had she hornswoggled Jake and me out of that apartment because she sensed my condescension? Because she envied us?

No excuse, I told myself. If Jules' life hit a few speed bumps—let's say she lost her winning Mega-Millions lottery ticket when she brought a coat to the dry cleaner—I would take pleasure, a minor compensation I have surely earned.

I returned the photograph to its cave and myself to my novel about Mumbai, but I'd lost the thread of the story. I tried to nap, but sleep defied me, knowing I pitied myself more than I pitied Jules. I had to be in some way responsible for not allowing two of my babies to live. That was the place to which I kept returning. *I've failed.* I reached for the phone and dialed Jake, the only human to whom I dared reveal myself.

"What is it? What's wrong?" he said. Too often now, this was his greeting. "You've got to phone your doctor," he said after I'd told him. "Maybe she can give you something to calm you down."

I knew she wouldn't, though she'd remind me about the grief counselor I'd never called. "Am I a horrible person?" I asked, wiping tears from my face. "Is this why—"

Jake cut me off. "Nothing's your fault. Don't do this to yourself. It just happened. Miscarriage is Mother Nature's way of correcting a mistake."

One more woman with whom I had a bone to pick.

CHAPTER 36

Talia

One moment I was peeling a carrot and the next Tom was insisting, "You're not telling me everything."

I kept reminding myself that when I was observed in Santa Monica, sharing laughter with Winters Jonas, if I'd been the least bit provocative, it had been on behalf of the Fisher-Wells Fund. "Stop *hocking* me. You're being a jerk," I said, as witless and childish as I felt. Squabbling did not become either of us. But Tom was right. The day before, I hadn't been, as I'd claimed, at a free introductory belly dance class. I'd been getting the best job offer of my life.

He threw the dish towel onto the counter and walked out of the kitchen. Before he picked up his gym bag, he announced, "You've changed, but I am exactly who you signed up to marry." With that, he was out the door.

One day you have a well-muscled marriage and the next it's as flabby as your abs after childbirth. So sayeth Mean Maxine. You start to see your husband through a cataract of doubt, 20 percent less amusing, 40 percent more annoying. Even the color of his hair looks dulled, and you wonder if he's seeing you the same way. You're cornered where disappointment meets frustration, robbed of energy, because you are a mother, a breadwinner, a woman who has to carry on, and, dammit, not the sort to shirk.

Yet things could be worse. You could, for example, be Jules, whose out-size problem had been on my mind all day.

"Mommy," Henry bellowed from the living room, snapping me back to attention, "can I have my applesauce?"

"Henry," I shout back, "remember, bath first." I'd popped in his fa-vorite *Cars* DVD, handed him a cut-up toaster waffle, and called it a proper dinner. Henry didn't answer, so I marched into the living room, snapped off the TV, and scooped up my sticky boy. "To the bathtub, you," I said.

He proudly undressed himself and peed in the toilet while I drew the water. "Bubbles, Mommy," he said. "Don't forget the bubbles."

We'd used the last of the bubble bath two nights before. All a-flutter about meeting Winters, I'd never gotten to the drugstore or, for that mat-ter, the library. The books would be overdue, the late fees mounting, the child disappointed. "No bubbles tonight, boychik. Tomorrow, I promise." This one I hoped I could keep.

"You promised last night," Henry, my conscience, reminded me.

"I'm sorry, sweetheart. Mommy forgot." Had I really become a mother who spoke of herself in the third person? Mean Maxine snickered. "But here are your people." Henry was fond of tiny action figures, and I could count on him to play with them until the water grew cold. I handed over Lightning McQueen, Chick Hicks, Batman, Robin, random pirates, di-nosaurs, and astronauts, and sat on the edge of the tub, impressed by my son's lengthy attention span but, I could not deny, bored. Which made me feel guilty. What kind of mother is bored? Henry activated his reper-toire of voices—squeaky, whispery, creepy, automotive—looking up at me every minute or two. I chirped approval punctuated by obligatory *vroom-vroom*s, but my mind kept volleying between the offer from Win-ters, with its invisible strings attached, and the conversation with Jules.

When I'd made my emergency landing at her house the day before, I'd expected to see the real Jules, not a tearful impostor. This had put me as much in shock as the fact that she was pregnant and couldn't decide what to do next.

I'd always depended on Jules for stability. She's the one who's kept us together—Quincy, Chloe, and me—the whalebone in our corset. I realized that she and Quincy were on the outs, for reasons that seemed obtuse on Jules' end, and which I hoped would be temporary, yet I hadn't counted on Julia de Marco herself being unhinged. As we sat in her kitchen, her anxiety had been contagious. I'd hoped to rise to the occasion and offer comfort, yet I'd been relieved when my allotted time was up.

I'd walked out of Jules' kitchen dumb with amazement. I'd known her for years and never once detected the faintest pining for motherhood. For an actress, she'd done an appalling job of concealing her disinterest in Henry and Dash. Nor did she seem to be burdened by the proverbial biological clock most childless women hear clanging even in their sleep. I'd have taken Jules for a woman who, on discovering she was pregnant, would have slipped in an abortion between the dry cleaner and the tailor.

Was she frozen because she'd mixed up her decision about the baby with whether she should raise the child with Arthur, which would mean having him in her life forever? To that I said if anyone was up to the job of being a single mom, it'd be Jules. Why hadn't I told her that? I'd already called her twice and she hadn't called me back. If her hesitation was because she needed a friend to hold her hand while she took the next steps, I would be that person. I hoped I'd gotten that message across.

"Mommy, Mommy, I'm cold," Henry said. He shivered dramatically and stretched tall, having grown, I swear, since the previous day.

I wrapped him in his hooded towel that looked like a bear and breathed in his fresh, buttery smell. "Let's get dry and put on pajamas, then we'll do dessert and a book."

"Can I wear my Superman PJs?"

If Daddy has washed them, you can. "We'll see." I followed Henry into his bedroom nook. The pajamas were freshly laundered, neatly folded in his drawer, smirking in my direction. I handed them to Henry, who started to dress himself.

"Meet you in two minutes, mister," I said. "You pick the book." I returned to the kitchen, poured applesauce into Henry's chipped but beloved blue bowl, and placed it and a spoon next to a small glass of milk and two oatmeal raisin cookies—one for Henry, one for me. Tom had baked the day before, ratcheting up the fiber by substituting whole-wheat flour for white. The result was less revolting than I'd expected. Super-Mensch won the bonus round.

Henry trotted into the room in his fuzzy slippers, hoisted himself onto the chair, and handed me *Guess How Much I Love You?* "You start, okay?" he said. He shoveled in applesauce while I read. When we got to our favorite part, he lip-synched, "Little Nutbrown Hare and Big Nutbrown Hare discover that love is not an easy thing to measure." This was where we improvised. "I love you a hundred hugs," he said, and grinned, his widely spaced pearly teeth on display.

"I love you two hundred hugs and a ginormous smooch," I said, planting one on his belly. Mean Maxine stuck her fingers down her throat; she could go to hell for thinking less of me because I was drippy sweet with my son. We finished the book and progressed to tooth brushing, and then Henry's bed, a cot he would soon outgrow. As we cuddled, I heard the front door open, and in twenty seconds Tom stepped to the bed to kiss Henry goodnight. He walked away without acknowledging me. I began to tell Henry an installment of *Talia by the Sea,* the spellbinding rip-off of *The Little Mermaid.* Today our three-year-old heroine and her sidekick, Sammy the Seahorse, befriended Stewart the Starfish. They all lived in a *shtetl* under the Santa Monica pier.

"Tell me again the name of my school for when I'm big," Henry said when my storytelling ended.

He was stalling. I said, "Jackson Collegiate—maybe," and nothing more, except goodnight. The minute the school's name popped out, I regretted it, and wished the public school was known by more than a number. It sounded like a place where imaginations went to die.

I didn't want all of us to be disappointed if Jackson didn't select Henry for a jumbo scholarship, but that wasn't all. As the weeks passed, I'd begun to think of this school as a *dybbuk* in a navy blue blazer. The tension between Tom and me had begun to go off the charts when we set out on the path to that school. A place where I was convinced that we'd never feel comfortable with its Chloes and Xanders, parents who wouldn't wince when their Dashes and Dylans hit them up for a two-thousand-dollar cello on top of ice skates, tennis rackets, and new sneakers every other month. That night, I decided, we would chew this through and spit it out.

"Hey," I said. Henry was tucked in and I finally was able to sit on the couch and open *The New Yorker*. In an austerity move, we'd canceled our other subscriptions and bought the *Times* only on Sunday.

"Hey," Tom said, looking up from our computer. It occurred to me that I should stand behind him and massage his neck. We hadn't touched in two weeks. Like a crippled woman throwing off her crutches to hobble to the faith healer, I slowly propelled myself across the room and placed my hands on the knotted muscles of Tom's broad back. He flinched. I stopped. *You've got to do better than that*, Mean Maxine said. Gently I started to knead.

"Your hands are cold," he said.

"They'll warm up," I said, and continued. I hoped he would speak first. He said nothing, and then words sputtered from both of us.

"I'm sorry," I said, although I hadn't decided exactly what the apology covered.

"It's the secrets that get me," Tom said.

His admission trumped mine. I am a klutz of a liar, even when I haven't been drinking wine, which puts my brain on seven-second delay. When I came home the night before, I might have predicted that Tom would ask for a belly dance demonstration. A more cunning wife would have hummed an Arabic tune, grabbed a scarf, and shimmied across the room. Instead, I stood as stiffly as a camel in the desert sun and outed myself as a person with something to hide. One bad lie begot another. I should have told Tom two days earlier that I'd scheduled an interview with the man I'd hoped would be offering me a job. If my parents had known how I'd acted, they'd have started by calling me foolish, and I'm sure I wouldn't have wanted to hear the rest.

"Sorry to disappoint you," I said. "But I'm not really all that mysterious." I was aiming for self-deprecating; I landed on sarcastic.

He swiveled toward me. We were no longer touching. "I'm sorry to disappoint you," he said, "in so many ways."

This was when I should have murmured, "You're wrong—I'm not disappointed at all." But since I was, I gracelessly continued with the small speech I'd rehearsed. "I was thinking that we should forget about the private school, the extra costs, no matter what. Henry should go straight into public pre-K. It would be a load off."

"Always worrying about money," he snarled.

The Tom I knew never snarled. Perhaps his behavior was because I said things like, "I worry about it because you don't."

This made him glare. "I doubt the answer to anything is to deprive Henry of the best possible education."

"I hardly think public school in this neighborhood is deprivation."

Tom stood. "I'm not trying to be a hardass about this," he said. "I'll think about what you say, but I'd rather not talk now." That was something. "Anything else?"

I felt as though I were in a conference with an academic adviser. I probably shouldn't have leaped to item number two on my agenda, but I couldn't help myself. "That guy I was having coffee with in California?"

"Oh, yes," Tom said with his own scum of sarcasm. "I do vaguely recall."

"He offered me a job."

"Good for you. I suppose it pays exceedingly well?"

"It would." I reported the salary, more than twice what he earned.

"Congratulations," Tom said, and scrunched his face. "But I'm confused. If you have this offer, why do you want to can the idea of Jackson Collegiate, or not at least play it out and see if Henry gets a scholarship?"

"Because I'm thinking of turning down the job."

"Why in fuck's name would you do that? The two of you got along so famously."

All those weeks I'd been waiting to hear from Winters, and now that I had his offer, it felt coated in *schmutz*. I couldn't tell Tom, *I don't trust myself around him,* because that was the smaller piece of it. Mean Maxine woke the dead with the bigger half of the answer. "Because it's really Chloe's job. I went on the interview under false pretenses."

When I finished, all Tom said was, "How could you?" He shook his head. I crashed into his disappointment and disgust as if it were an iceberg. Again, he slept on the couch. I didn't sleep at all.

Chapter 37

Jules

When Arthur got out of the taxi carrying flowers, I thought I'd have an acute myocardial infarction. I tried to overlook that they were gaudy red carnations and gold mums pumped up with baby's breath, my least favorite floral filler even under normal circumstances. They appeared to have been coordinated with his jacket, which was as plaid as a bagpiper player's.

"For you," he said as I opened the front door. He handed me the bouquet. In his other hand he clutched a drugstore shopping bag. As he bent for an embrace, I looked down. Arthur was still devoted to his cowboy boots. He seemed to be breathing heavily, the evidence hanging in the frosty air. Perhaps he was as nervous as I was.

"You must be freezing," I said. He stepped inside and handed his coat to me, revealing a fine-gauge cashmere V-neck in a flattering shade almost exactly like Benjamin Moore Purple Rain. I'd given it to him after I'd noticed that every sweater in his wardrobe was acrylic.

"You're looking well, Jules," he said. His voice lacked his usual glee. I liked regular Artie better than this dour stand-in.

"I'm a little pregnant, not stricken with TB," I said, eyeing the bag he'd set down on the floor. "What's all this?"

"For you." Cereal on sale? Mouthwash? I pulled out a large Whitman's Sampler in the familiar yellow cross-stitched box. "The two-pounder," he added.

Nonna's favorite. "You shouldn't have." He seemed glad he had; the corners of his mouth twitched into a smile. "We'll crack it open later. Thanks—I'll put these in water, and then lunch."

I'd thrown together tuna salad and deviled eggs and defrosted a ciabatta from my favorite Italian bakery. I couldn't predict the conversation, but I knew my life had expanded beyond the sunny lane of small talk. I seated Arthur across from me, to be on the lookout for signs of lying—excessive blinking or absent eye contact, perhaps. "What's on your mind?" I asked, hoping we could get right to it. I had, after all, an appointment this afternoon that I did not want to miss.

Arthur filled his plate and sampled the tuna and eggs. "I've been doing some thinking," he said, holding his fork aloft. He wasn't wearing the pinky ring whose twin I'd left on the table at Picholine. I delicately salted an egg and brought it to my mouth, willing him to continue. "I want to be a stand-up guy here. What is it you'd like me to do?"

Jules' Rule: *Let your opposition make the first offer, to state their terms, financial or otherwise.* "What is it you'd like to do?"

"Clear the air."

"Clear away," I said. "Ask me anything."

"The first thing... I've been wondering..." He rotated his shoulders like a novice prosecutor warming up before a judge. "Let me rephrase. I really hope you'll tell me... is, well... whether this pregnancy is something you'd been hoping for and, ah, planning, all these years."

I wanted to cut his head off with the machete of truth. Did Arthur M. Weiner, with his inclination for stinginess and love handles, see himself as a stud service I'd utilized under false pretenses to conceive a child? Did he think I was the kind of woman who'd been longing for said child since her first period? I stood up and started wagging my finger in his face.

"If I'd wanted to become pregnant—which, I assure you, I did not—I would have tried to have a baby years ago with ... Never mind. Or I'd have conceived a designer specimen with the services of a turkey baster and a painstakingly selected sperm bank deposit," I shouted. Why dog-paddle in the shoals of the gene pool? I'd have chosen a donor who was green-eyed, multilingual, an Olympic swimmer, a Nobel Prize winner, a chess champ, and an excellent salsa dancer, endowed not only with a fine set of the masculine basics but an elegant nose and sensuous lips, deeply in love with opera, poetry, and contemporary photography. "I assure you, I would have done this when I was twenty-nine, not thirty-nine." I caught the double take. "Okay, forty-three. This event isn't a feathery little tremor. It's a nine-point-five disaster. Who the fuck planted this idea in your head? That flabby-assed neighbor? What's her name?"

"Jennifer."

"*Puttana.*" I was speaking so quickly I'd started to cough. To Arthur's credit, he offered to Heimlich me, which I declined in favor of a back wallop.

"Sorry, sorry, sorry," he said. He cast his eyes toward the heavens. "Jesus, I certainly didn't come all the way up here to upset you. Can we please have a do-over?" I drained my water glass, gobbled a hunk of ciabatta, and waited. "As I tried to express in the restaurant the last time we saw each other," he said, "you're like nobody else. You're the only woman I want next to me in bed—or anywhere. The way you cook and kiss and do it. Even the way you make tuna ... "

My secret ingredient is dill, and I add mayo spoonful by spoonful, judiciously monitoring the ratio of tuna to mayo. Plus it's got to be Hellmann's. With a shudder, I briefly recalled the case of the Miracle Whip, an unsolved mystery for these past ten years. Some call it salad dressing; I call it spackle. Talia wouldn't have snuck the economy-size jar into our apartment, and Chloe bought only what I put on our list. My money has always been on Quincy, daughter of Minnesota. I believe Miracle Whip is the state condiment.

"Go on," I said. I wasn't surprised that my mind had wandered— Arthur and I had covered this ground before.

"As far as the two of us go, well, we're a pair," he said. "It's like we were raised in the same playpen." I rested my chin on my hands and waited for him to continue. "But now, because of the...baby...there's more to think about. In fact, all I've been doing is thinking...." He trailed off, and I'd be damned if I'd help him. "Anyway," he concluded as he tapped his foot madly, "where I'm going with this is, you would make an incredible mother."

I was fairly incredible at executing any number of tasks, but this was a compliment I had a hard time believing. "I guess I should thank you," I said nonetheless.

"You're welcome," Arthur said, "but I'm not done. One of the things I like—I mean, love—about you is that you've never busted my chops about wanting to have a kid. Every other woman has started in with the baby talk by the fourth date."

"I knew I was perfect."

"But the thing is, I'm not," he responded, somber and sedate. "I'd make a rotten father."

You do crosswords in ink, compute baseball averages in your head, and know the lyrics to every Roy Orbison song. You have a fine baritone—I hear it in the shower. You're gainfully employed. You don't have a time share at the track. You'd be ten times the pop my old man was. Maybe I am motherly after all, I thought, *the way my instincts jumped to Arthur's defense.*

"I've never even let myself get a dog, no matter how much I love them," he lamented. Wherever we stroll, Arthur stops to scratch the head of every passing canine. If the creature is a puppy, he practically sticks his tongue in its mouth while he rubs the ecstatic animal's belly. Quite the show. "A child is such a commitment." *Oh, really?* "I'd like to spend my life with you—I don't want to lose you—but I don't know about the fatherhood part." He sighed and put his head down on his forearms.

Feeling no obligation to offer consolation, I grabbed the plates and headed into the kitchen.

Arthur got up wearily. Without talking, I started loading the dishwasher as he brought in the glasses and empty serving dishes. The tuna bowl was scraped clean. The kid inside me would have to go straight from the hospital to the Duke Weight Loss Center.

"Do you want me to make you coffee?" I asked. In my fury I'd already wiped down the counters and sterilized the sponge for four minutes via the microwave's highest power setting.

"That would be swell," he said as he came up behind me and circled my waist with his arms, pressing against me. His hands moved up to my tender breasts and lingered until I winced. They traveled to my neck. Softly he held aside my hair and murmured, "Jules, Jules, Jules, you always smell so damn good."

I removed myself from the embrace and stomped to the freezer, where I kept the coffee beans. How many cups to brew? Who'd ever thought the answer to that question could reveal my position on a moral dilemma? I decided to go with one and a half. As I prepared the beans, the kitchen filled with the seductive aroma of Costa Rican dark roast. I started the coffee and turned around. Arthur had left the kitchen.

When I walked into the other room, carrying one mug of coffee, he was sitting on the couch. The Whitman's Sampler was on the coffee table, its wrapping removed. Only Arthur, I thought, would have started in on it himself. "Want some?" he asked.

I'd never been a woman to say no to a bon-bon. I walked to the table, hoping that if he'd eaten a piece or two, it was the peanut clusters that make you wish you had a dental hygienist on retainer. I lifted the top of the box. One piece of candy was missing. In its place, dead center, south of a dark chocolate buttercream, north of a truffle, west of a nougat dipped in milk chocolate, and east of a white chocolate patty adorned with a pink doodad, sat an honest-to-God piece of jewelry. I was eyeball to eyeball with an oval amethyst the size of my thumbnail set horizontally in matte gold, cabochon style. It was a ring, perfectly purple.

"Chloe helped me pick it out," Arthur said, galvanized with glee. I gave him a skeptical look, which encouraged him to continue. "She took me to this hole-in-the-wall on Forty-seventh Street."

"But she never shops in places where she doesn't pay at least retail." I've never grasped the concept or the math, but being overcharged apparently makes Chloe feel as if she's getting more for her money.

"The jeweler is Morty Rabinowitz. His wife is my friend June—she goes by Rittenhouse professionally. She's the one who sent Chloe on a job interview, thanks to me." Arthur was beaming. "Here, Mommy, put it on," he said, lifting the bauble from its frilly paper wrapping.

He got down on one knee. "This ring says I'll be there for you."

CHAPTER 38

Chloe

"We're going to the liberry," Dash said, stretching his arms toward me with a book in each hand. Jamyang had incorporated a reading hour into Dash's routine.

"Library," I repeated. "That's wonderful, sweet prince. Bring back some good stories."

"Then the playground," he said. "With Asher and Jack."

"Who are Asher and Jack?" I directed my question to Jamyang.

"Nice boys," she said. "They go liberry, too."

"Why don't you invite them back here to play one day?" I suggested. She nodded. Did that mean yes or no? I no more felt I could press her on this than correct her grammar and pronunciation.

"Ready, Dash?" she asked. For my son, she put on a smile. "Don't forget your mittens."

He giggled as he plopped himself into his stroller, put the books in his lap, and shot up his right hand for a high five. Who taught him that? I kissed Dash goodbye and waved them off, reminded yet again that any control I thought I had was melting away faster than jam on toast. I looked out the window and waited until they'd turned the corner. I couldn't start until they were safely out of view.

For the last week Xander had continued to be edgy, switching on his standard hail-fellow humor only when someone who wasn't me was around. For her part, Jamyang was as inscrutable in my presence as always, but my suspicion was mounting by the day. I had to know what was going on.

Feeling like the intruder I was, I tiptoed down the short flight and stepped first into the bathroom directly outside Jamyang's bedroom. The towels, embroidered with daisies, were folded in thirds and neatly hung. Next to the toilet were copies of *People* and *Glamour,* both from months ago. I snooped behind the shower curtain: Suave shampoo and hair conditioner, and a razor. Nothing special or incriminating. I opened the medicine chest. Most of the jars were foreign brands, presumably brought from her homeland, though I spotted Crest toothpaste, a bottle of nail polish in the vampy shade I'd seen on her toes, a rosy lip gloss, black mascara, and an eyelash curler. The only surprise was the stealth with which I was invading our nanny's privacy. I could hear Autumn Rutherford telling me to stop before I'd completely debased myself, but I moved to the bedroom.

At first glance the cozy space looked exactly as I remembered. The double bed was tidily made with yellow chintz linens, which I'd selected to complement the apple green walls, although an aqua corduroy reading pillow now squatted on the bed like Buddha. The framed poster from the New York City Ballet that had hung in my first apartment remained on the wall, but the photograph of Prospect Park had been swapped for a calendar featuring tranquil mountains, its words in an exotic alphabet.

I walked to the dresser and, hands shaking, slid open every drawer, taking pains not to disrupt Jamyang's precision. Bras and panties, plain as paper, were neatly folded next to socks and leggings. Her sweaters and T-shirts were arranged by color, all muted shades of blue, gray, and green, not a stripe or a print breaking the monotony. I looked into the closet. A black dress in a silky synthetic hung limply next to black pants and a down coat, its modest price tag still attached. The shelf above was empty except for a small bag from Sephora.

I stepped back into the hall. The drone of the furnace was the only sound I heard. I told myself to get a grip, to stop. I couldn't. A demon Chloe inhaled deeply and returned for a second look.

I gasped. Inside the shopping bag, wrapped in red tissue that I scrupulously unfolded, was an unopened bottle of a scent—*my scent*, the only one I ever wore, Xander's favorite, Romance. Every morning I allowed myself two spritzes, with one more before bed.

Could Jamyang have bought the eau de toilette for herself? Not at sixty dollars a tiny bottle. Had Xander bought it for her? Why not give her my underwear? I wanted to rip the tissue paper to shreds, but I forced myself to replace it exactly as it had been, and turned back to the bedroom.

Stop! I heard Autumn order. I ignored her. On the bedside table was a snapshot of Dash, Xander, and me. The picture had been taken last month. I'd printed out images to send to my parents but discarded this one, since on closer examination I realized my eyes were closed. I resembled a corpse. Xander, however, looked especially handsome, as did Dash. Jamyang must have fished the photo out of the garbage. She'd placed it in a small silvery frame, next to a stack of three books. An English dictionary was on top of a paperback I could recognize from four feet away, a preachy self-help tract about raising three-year-olds. The book beneath it was brown leather and well-worn. A Bible, most likely. I'd assumed Jamyang was a Buddhist. I walked to the table for a closer look.

It was my childhood favorite, and not just any library copy, but one of the few volumes in Xander's literary tabernacle that belonged to me: *Jane Eyre*, its pages dry and cover worn, yet worth thousands, a present from Xander for our second anniversary. It was the most thoughtful gift I'd ever received.

I stood still and pictured Jamyang struggling with the English, but nonetheless identifying—as I once had—with the wisp of a governess whose unadorned beauty, hard work, and blunt nature had beguiled the Byronic hero. I wondered if the Byronic hero of Thornfield Manor, Brooklyn Heights branch, knew the book was here. More to the point, I wondered if the Byronic hero had recommended the book to the impoverished waif who was yet another skeleton in one of his many closets. I wondered if he had delivered it personally, to this room. I wondered if he had tarried, trifled with her affection. If her heart had heaved. I felt as if I'd swallowed a cat and its tail was sticking out of my throat, choking me. I collapsed on the bed and flipped rapidly through the book to look for clues—a love note or a revealing bookmark, perhaps—but *Jane*, that mouse, yielded no secrets.

With guilt matched by my anger, I returned *Jane* to her hiding place beneath the other books and opened the table's drawer. I didn't know what I was looking for—birth control pills, a letter in Xander's handwriting, tickets to Venice? The drawer was empty except for a black leather diary. The entries were, to me, unreadable.

With a deep sense of shame, I saw myself as the madwoman in my own attic, dumber than those teenagers who gain fourteen pounds, get a bellyache, go to the bathroom expecting to poop, and walk out with an infant, never once suspecting they're pregnant. In my effort to reinvent a better Chloe, had I missed the Big One?

I thought I'd made progress. Recently I'd been proud of myself, ripping pages from magazines when I liked the way the clothes were put together, each morning cobbling together the looks from garments hanging in my closet, often with excellent results. I had never once bought myself jewelry, but when I took Arthur shopping for Jules' ring, I spotted a brooch—a lizard!—and not only bought it but haggled down the price. On the bulletin board above my desk, I'd copied a list I'd found of ways to become happier and had adopted them as my sixfold mantra.

1. *Act the way you want to feel.*
2. *Play fair.*

3. *Stop keeping score.*
4. *Identify the problem.*
5. *Remember there is only love.*
6. *Do what ought to be done.*

Do what ought to be done! I would. As Jane herself said, laws and principles are not for the times when there is no temptation. I smoothed the wrinkles on the bed and darted out of the room and up two flights of stairs. Jamyang might be a silent wren to my ditzy canary, but at least canaries can sing. Panting, I pushed open the French doors to Mr. Rochester's inner sanctum and inhaled the woodsy scent of tobacco smoke, his library the only place where the master smoked a pipe. On the shelves, the books stood still as toy soldiers, defying me to snoop. But I did. I did!

Aside from the gap in the Brontë section, nothing seemed amiss. The brass-studded green leather wing chair sat as thronelike as ever, the tapestry ottoman a disciple at its foot. On the table was Xander's silver magnifying glass, crystal paperweights, and a book of matches from a restaurant we'd eaten at the previous winter.

I turned on the lamp, sat down at the desk, and surveyed the objects on its surface: a closed laptop, a letter opener engraved with the name of his firm, a cherry box holding sheaves of monogrammed stationery, and a pewter mug—a gift from Tom Wells in thanks for being his best man. That no work seemed to have been done here in months didn't surprise me, given the hours my husband—*my* husband—was keeping at his office.

The large file drawers, where Xander kept our financial records, were locked, darn it, but the desk's pencil drawer slid open, only to reveal mundane supplies—a stapler, tape, and stamps that were now two cents short for a standard letter. It would serve Xander right if his mail got returned! I checked the wire wastebasket. Empty.

Beneath the desk was the printer. I crouched down for a look. Sitting in its tray was a piece of printed paper. I pulled it out and read it once, twice, then a third time. The words were in English, though at first they made no sense. I read it once more.

I returned the paper to the printer. Who was this man I was married to? I didn't know him at all.

CHAPTER 39

Quincy

Mom and I were driving to Montana like we did every August, our station wagon cutting through fields that God had colored to match my goldenrod crayon. I was thinking about how my grandparents would kick off my days on the farm with the smell of sizzling bacon, and move on to chicken feeding, pony rides, and pineapple upside-down cake. We'd end up every evening on the front porch, Gramps pointing out the Milky Way in a black satin sky, Grammy knitting in the dark.

My eyes were shut tight, drifting in the sepia of memory, when Fanny started to lick my face. I realized it was time to shake off my dream and attend to my new ritual. Every morning I'd been gluing a star on my calendar to celebrate that Jubilee and I had gotten through another night. I was reaching for the stars when Horton called.

"Good morning, sunshine," he said. "You get my fax?" Apartment listings, which he'd started sending again a week ago, had been piling up unread.

"Haven't had a chance yet."

"Too busy, are we?"

I'd used Dr. Frumkes' required rest as an excuse to retire from life. Jake and I had been getting by on takeout and had cycled through every cuisine twice—Chinese, Thai, Japanese, Mexican, Vietnamese, Turkish, and Italian—and were debating Ethiopian. But now that Maizie had signed off on her manuscript, I was restless. I supposed this was a positive sign. I'd seen the doctor, and she'd given me a green light to go out for up to two hours each day as long as I was "sensible." Is there a day in my life when I haven't been?

"I promise I'll read the fax and call you back."

"The listings from a few days ago already have bids," he said. "It's still a hot market. Today's apartment should not be missed. It's in an outstanding family-friendly building."

"You do realize the familyless may sue if they hear you talking that way?" I'd read that a listing advertised as "walking distance" from anywhere offended people in wheelchairs and "near churches and synagogues" caused atheists to initiate a class-action suit.

"Excuse me, but we're talking a classic six on Riverside Drive, with a recently renovated kitchen, a bike room, and a locked storage bin."

This was a reason to cheer. We city folk have been known to arm-wrestle over the highly coveted basement space required to warehouse sleds, camp trunks, and leaves for the dining room table. "Tell me more," I said, feeling a squeak of curiosity.

"Motivated owners—the husband lost his job," Horton added, a bounce in his voice.

Poor guy. Not only had his income and identity evaporated, he'd become a reason for a broker to dance a jig.

"This one won't last," Horton added.

"Isn't that slogan engraved on your business card?"

"Go ahead, blow me off. Raise your baby in a shoebox—see if I care. Better yet, move after the tot's born. You can pack between the two a.m. and four a.m. feedings."

"Fine," I said, clutching the fax in my hand. "I'll look at it." I had no reason not to humor Horton, who other than Jake was the person I'd been speaking to most often. Talia had visited—twice—and while Chloe called every few days, she preferred to talk on Facebook, where she'd "joined the cultural conversation." Jules and I weren't speaking at all.

The building was only two blocks away. I swaddled myself in winter wool, knowing that the closer I got to the river, the chillier it would be. I spotted Horton, dressed in dark green, planted by the entrance like a to-piary. When he saw me, he tipped his fedora and proclaimed, "You're going to love it."

As I shambled through the marble hallway, I hoped that I would. I was feeling just optimistic enough to imagine I might get excited about a new home for the Blues.

The elevator took us to the tenth floor. Horton rang the bell and, hear-ing no reply, turned a key. A narrow foyer opened to a sparsely filled liv-ing room whose copies of *Architectural Digest*, cowhide rugs, and rattan sticks diffusing a potent grapefruit scent all screamed "staged." Through French doors I took in a Stickley dining set that matched the one my mom had inherited from her parents. It was hibernating in her house in Minneapolis, which I'd rented out fully furnished. I hoped the tenants were taking care of the table as I caught a fleeting image of Jake feeding a baby in a high chair pulled up to its side. As quickly as it came, I blinked away the fantasy, turned, and saw Horton pointing to a limestone mantel. "Check the fireplace," he gloated. "It works."

I bent down to evaluate three birch logs on the grate. I got up and asked, "Where's the kitchen?"

"Follow me." I obeyed as Horton pushed open a swinging door. He hadn't lied. Everything was spanking new—granite, stainless steel, or startlingly white. I'd have felt comfortable having surgery there. "Uh-huh," I said as he pointed out one state-of-the-art appliance after the next. *Remind me why I need a warming drawer*, I said to myself.

"Come see the maid's room," he said. We squeezed into a space slightly larger than a Honda. "It could work for a child."

If you give it growth-stunting drugs. "Where are the real bedrooms?" I asked, my enthusiasm wilting.

"Other side of the living room. Wait till you see the view from the master." Horton led the way to a large suite. To the west, the Hudson rolled along on proud display. This I liked. He opened two doors to show off deep walk-in closets and a third to a bathroom whose phantom stylist had forgotten to remove price tags from the thick white towels. "His-and-hers sinks," he crowed. "And the shower has steam."

"Jake would like that," I said, feeling obligated to shore up Horton. "Where's the other bedroom?"

"Down the hall." We made two sharp turns. "I know it's not huge..."

From the room's sole window I saw the sooty bricks of another building, six feet away. I couldn't imagine raising a philodendron here, let alone a child. We returned to the living room and Horton reached into his briefcase. "Here's the pro forma," he said. My eyes raced to the bottom line. This apartment was no bargain. Even if a low bid might be accepted here, Jake and I would be strapped trying to handle the charges, especially since with a baby I could no longer take on as large a project as Maizie's. I felt a thud of familiar disappointment, along with a distinctly sour feeling I couldn't categorize. As I tucked the information in my pocket without speaking, we retraced our steps to the building's entrance.

"You're not excited," Horton said.

"Honestly, I wish I were."

"I'm not gaming you, Quincy. This building's solid—well financed, down-to-earth neighbors, low monthly charges, and a fair price for this amount of space." He ticked off each attribute on his finely gloved fingers but saw I was unconvinced. "You're comparing this place to Central Park West, aren't you?"

"If we're going to be mortgage-poor, I'd at least like to be in love."

He sent me a look that was not unkind. "Get that place out of your head. It was a gift from the gods."

The gods giveth. The gods taketh away. I couldn't help noticing a pattern. "Speaking of that," I said as we walked—quickly, since it had started to drizzle—"did it ever sell?"

"Off the market. Talk on the street is it's in contract to an insider, but there hasn't been a closing yet."

I put one foot in front of the other and gritted my teeth as Arthur and Jules dive-bombed into my mind. They were hand in hand, admiring the pink, yellow, and white flowers that bedecked the park in April like party decorations. The happy couple were leaning out of the fourteenth-floor window of their living room, straining to get a better view of the forsythia, callery pear, and cherry tree blossoms. Suddenly there was a bloodcurdling scream as a body tumbled through the air, arms and legs spinning like a pinwheel, ending with a noise as loud as an explosion.

Whoops. The strangest things happen when people overreach, I thought as I put names to my other feelings—envy, jealousy, and the lingering taste of anger.

CHAPTER 40

Talia

"Mommy, do I have a play date today?" This was the first question Henry, who'd become heavily invested in his social calendar, lobbed at me.

"Not today," I said, still blurry.

"Mommy? Mommy?"

Who else does he think is in this bed? Tom hadn't been here for almost a week. Fully awake now, I said, "Yes, *boychik*."

That made Henry smile. "Is today the day we're visiting Aunt Jules?"

I glanced at the clock. "We're leaving when the big hand gets to the twelve and the small hand to the eight. Did you color her a picture?"

"Oh, crap—"

"Henry Thomas, what did you say?"

"I mean, uh-oh. I forgot." He scurried out of the room, leaving me to wonder how well Tom was disguising his rage when I wasn't around. If Henry was near us, Tom sprang into what I used to think of as his normal self, but when we were alone, he throbbed with politeness, even his posture stiff.

I needed a break from the permafrost. For that day, Henry and I had planned an adventure, to take the subway to Grand Central and the train to Westport, where Jules would pick us up and we'd stay overnight. She'd promised surprises. Henry was hoping for a Thomas the Tank engine; he considered it the height of social injustice that Dash Keaton owned one and he didn't, when it was his middle name. As for me, if I rolled off the 10:09 to a rosebud-strewn path and was thrown to the mat as Jules' matron of honor during a quickie marriage ceremony, I'd be no more shocked than if she announced that we were guests at her bon voyage party before she emigrated to New Zealand to raise goats.

I knew four things: Jules had been ducking every question I asked. Tom had been speaking to me only when we were with Henry. I had never been more miserable. And I should have seen all this coming. *Only a fool is her own informer,* Mean Maxine reminded me every day, I never should have told Tom I'd gone after a job that might have been Chloe's *beshert.*

I dragged myself out of bed and into the bathroom. While I was showering, Henry ran into the bathroom and screeched, "Mommy, Mommy, it's buzzing."

"Put it down on the sink, please," I screeched back. "And don't drop it. Be gentle." My bet was that Jules had called with a request for some delicacy she couldn't find in her local market—the apple and rosemary jam she slathered on scones, perhaps; I'd insisted she give me a shout-out with a list of any last-minute items she needed. Only after I washed away the goo in my hair and moisturized every inch of my thirsty skin did I check to see who'd texted. *Need u today after all.* At least my boss, Eliot the Oracle, had added, *Sorry.*

I wanted to hurl the BlackBerry against the mirror. How dare Chloe be MIA—again—and let me discover the information through Eliot, the paycheck-writing side of our triangle? Once upon a time she'd have called, lubricated with embarrassment and regret, and slobber on about an emergency. I wouldn't be hearing of this disruption in my life—and Henry's—from the Oracle, whom I phoned immediately, though it was only minutes past seven. "Really?" I said. "I was set to go out of town."

He offered a tepid apology before taking off on Chloe. "Asleep at the wheel" crescendoed to "This job-share thing will work only if you two make it work, and I get the feeling you aren't even talking." Before I defended my answer, he spat out, with more anxiety than annoyance, "Do you think Chloe's looking for another job?"

Of course I did. "No, never," I answered. "Something major must have come up. Don't worry. I'll be in as soon as I can." I hoped he'd been keeping track of my superlative attendance record. "I—I have to ask you a favor, though," I stammered. "Would it be all right if I brought Henry to work?"

There was an unnerving pause. "Why?" he asked. "What happened to your backup child care?"

Miss Poppins on retainer? "Our backup nanny came down with . . ." I stood buck naked and clammy. "Legionnaire's disease."

He responded with the kind of wheeze that arrives with a shrug. "Sure, bring the little guy. Maybe he can help with the vacuum cleaner campaign."

I didn't know who'd be most disappointed—Henry, Jules, or me—and had started rehearsing a lie to tell my son and my friend when Tom entered the bedroom, dressed for school. "Why not the clap?" he asked. "You know that nanny of ours is the biggest slut north of Brighton Beach." As he sauntered through the bedroom en route to the bathroom he swatted my butt.

I've never been a skilled marital ninja. Fights agitate me, their tension like binding shoes I can never wait to kick off, and I wasn't going to risk mangling this opportunity for détente. I forced my face into a pleasant expression and tried to disguise my suspicion of Tom's sudden buoyant behavior. "You heard?" I replied. "Sucks, doesn't it?"

"Why do you suppose Chloe's done this?" I'd miscalculated. Tom's condescension was like a splash of dirty water, returning me to simmering skepticism. Why didn't he simply ask if Chloe knew I'd tried to steal the job, the one I hadn't bothered to tell him I'd turned down, a decision I now regretted almost as much as going after the job in the first place?

Since I'd told Winters Jonas I was declining his offer, on at least four occasions I'd picked up the phone to call and try to reverse my decree, before I reminded myself that someone else undoubtedly had been thrilled to accept the position and might have started working at Bespoke already.

"Don't be a dick," I said, and turned my back on Tom.

"You're right." His tone didn't indicate whether I should expect another barrage. "The dick apologizes."

"Apology accepted," I said after a moment, although I didn't know if it was a comprehensive apology or a minor footnote.

"My class has a field trip to the Museum of Natural History today. Henry can come along and be their mascot."

How could I refuse when the alternative was for Henry to suffer through copywriters debating how to sell OCD-inclined consumers on the merits of hypoallergenic filtration systems, comfort handles, and advanced sound-dampening technology?

"I accept, thanks." But I couldn't work myself up to even a hug.

I found Henry in the kitchen, chomping on cinnamon toast Tom had made for him. "Pumpkin, there's been a change of plans," I said. "Instead of going to Aunt Jules' today, Daddy's going to take you to the museum with the dinosaurs." I was prepared to embellish with details about an ice cream cone and a plastic brontosaurus, but Henry flung his toast in the air like a mortarboard and shot out of his chair, shouting, "Daddy, Daddy? Are you really, really taking me?"

I was near the front door when Tom stopped me. "I've been thinking about what you said about public school," he said. "The one in our neighborhood is pretty good."

One arm in my coat, the other arm out, I looked up at him. *Tell me something I don't know.* "I get that," I said, wearier than a woman my age had a right to feel after eight hours of sleep. "It's no Jackson Collegiate, but it's free, and if we become involved parents—"

"Will you let me finish?" His tone stung. "I've been talking to people at the playground." Female people, I assumed. "Some of them are very high on P.S. 282 over on Sixth. Strong gifted program, chess, excellent student/teacher ratio. But most people think P.S. 107 on Eighth is the up-and-comer. The thing is, last year, there were two hundred sixty-three applications for only eighteen spots—the odds are harder than getting into Harvard."

I appreciated that Tom had done due diligence, but why did we need to discuss this now? I heard only a blizzard of numbers. "Okay, I was wrong. We'll wait it out, and if he doesn't get a scholarship at Jackson, we'll send him to one of those schools."

"Hold on. There's more. I have it on good authority that if we're willing to write a letter to 107's principal, declaring sincere interest in her school and promising we won't flip-flop should Henry get a scholarship from Jackson later, there's an excellent chance—but no guarantee—he'll be accepted." He paused. "You'd think the system for public school would be democratic, but it isn't."

I inhaled the information. "But you've already mailed off the Jackson Collegiate application?" Tom had worked on it for weeks. "Let's say this Princeton of pre-Ks turns us down. Henry could still possibly go to Jackson, assuming he's accepted? So this might—just might—be a win-win, unless, of course, we get rejected everywhere?"

"Talia, you're not reading the subtext." *You never do,* his face said. "If we go for 107, we go for it alone. We'd need to pull the application at Jackson, because we might hear from them first. To proceed any other way would be dishonorable."

God forbid anyone in this family is dishonorable. Oh, I forgot. I was. "Our son's education is one big crap shoot?"

"That about sums it up," he said. "Your call."

CHAPTER 41

Chloe

I ran up the stairs, clutching the creamy sheet of paper I'd discovered in Xander's library. Sweat soaked the starched shirt I'd put on a few hours earlier. I ran to the bathroom to splash water on my face, then stuck my iPod buds in my ears. Maybe Autumn Rutherford's morning podcast would take down my heart rate.

Repeat after me, she said, low and sonorous. *Do one thing a day that scares you.* I'd knocked off that one, and it was only early afternoon. *Living in the moment could be the meaning of life.* Was it or wasn't it? *The bad news: time flies. The good news: you're the pilot.* Her voice was really low. Was Autumn a transvestite? *The conscious brain can hold only one thought at a time—make it positive.* I should be thinking about something loftier than Autumn's gender. *Success is determined by how you handle setbacks.* We'd see about that. *Listen hard, then ask strategic questions.*

I had the questions and I wanted answers, five minutes ago. I ripped off my clothes and earpiece and stepped into the armor of a black suit Jules had insisted I buy after she ruled my wardrobe entirely too floppy. Within ten minutes, looking like Morticia Barbie, I was in a taxi; within thirty, at the door to the familiar bronze tower known as the Seagram Building.

Usually I met Xander downstairs at the Four Seasons, where we'd start our evenings with a perfect Manhattan for him, Lillet for me. In better weather I'd twist up my hair, channel Holly Golightly, and wait by the fountain in the broad piazza of concrete out front. But that day I was a woman with a mission a lot more *Apocalypse Now* than *Breakfast at Tiffany's*. I charged through the stony lobby, ignoring flocks of uniformed employees, and stepped into the elevator.

Denton Capital Advisers, where Xander labored in the killing fields of financial service, trying to put the fun in hedge fund, occupied an entire upper floor. The elevator door opened to a long foyer, where a pale blond receptionist offered up a wan smile. I didn't recognize her from the previous year's Christmas party, which made me wonder when that year's gala would be. Shouldn't we have gotten the invitation, always an extravagance of parchment and gold engraving?

"May I help you?" the receptionist asked when I'd steadied myself in front of her desk—an excellent Sheridan reproduction adorned by an eye-popping orchid. The last time I'd been there, everything had been the color of newly minted dollar bills. Charlene had put her mark on Denton.

"I'm here to see Alexander Keaton, please," I said, barely controlling my hyperventilation.

The young woman tapped on her keyboard. "I'm sorry," she said, returning her face in my direction. "We don't have a listing for anyone with that name."

"It's Keaton," I said. "With a *K.* K-E-A-T-O-N."

She repeated the process and smiled, her teeth white enough to glow. "Madam, are you sure you have the right company?"

Madam? Did I look like her mother? "Keaton, Alexander?" I repeated.

"Perhaps you got off on the wrong floor? This is Denton Capital Advisers." Her tone was neutral, yet I wanted to strangle her with the rope of pearls that dangled over her beige dress.

"I realize that." My voice cracked as my heart raced. "Edgar Denton is a close personal friend." I hesitated. "Could you please see if he's in? Tell him that Chloe Keaton would like to say hello, please."

"Do you have an appointment, Mrs. Keaton?" the receptionist asked, hardening like ice.

"No, I don't." I strained for civility. "Please, it's important!" *God forgive me!* "Someone is seriously ill."

"I see." She picked up the phone. "Francesca," she asked in a voice 10 percent louder than necessary, "a Chloe Keaton wishes to speak with Mr. Denton. Could you please convey that message?" She listened while she made contact with the mirror behind me. "You may take a chair if you wish." She returned to her computer, perhaps to order a personality.

I perched myself on a taupe suede sofa and considered calling Xander, but I didn't want to talk in front of *her*. Ten minutes passed, and I stood to leave. That's when the receptionist answered the phone and looked toward me. "Mr. Denton would be pleased to meet with you, if you care to wait a little longer."

"A little longer" was thirty-five minutes, which I passed by trying to re-call a mantra from Autumn. I fixed on *The conscious brain can hold only one thought at a time—make it positive."* Perhaps Denton was a CIA front, not a hedge fund.

"Mrs. Keaton?" I opened my eyes, which I hadn't realized I'd closed, to see the hawkish face of Mrs. Branzino, she of the sleek black chignon, red talons, and hooded gray eyes, Edgar Denton's personal assistant— some said more—since before Xander had worked at the firm. She took my hand, which I found odd, since whenever I'd been in her presence she'd directed all her conversation to Xander, not me. "How *are* you?" she asked. I silently followed her into Edgar's office.

I like Edgar. He belonged to the same fraternity as my father, who'd made the original connection for Xander. Edgar got up from behind his desk, kissed me on the cheek—one cheek only, unlike Charlene—and es-corted me to a straight-backed chair. On the lacquered table, two tum-blers were filled with ice, placed next to small bottles of Evian. He sat in a matching chair to the left. "Water, Chloe dear?" he asked.

As he said my name, I failed to stanch my tears. When I blinked, Edgar handed me a linen handkerchief, gently saying, as if talking to a child, "How are you doing with all this?"

And then I knew.

"It must come as quite a shock to learn that Xander has parted ways with Denton."

As if this explained anything. "Why?" I sputtered. "And when?" We could skip how.

"It's best if your husband explains that to you."

I hadn't realized Mrs. Branzino was standing behind me like a chaperone. She appeared at my side, and I understood that my audience had ended. Edgar patted me on the back and said, "Everything's going to be fine."

Can you promise that? I thought as Mrs. Branzino escorted me out, past Xander's office, his former office. Its door was closed. Did she think I was going to make a run for it, to make sure he wasn't hiding in his private bathroom? She took me all the way to the elevator and stood before it until the door opened and closed in front of me.

When I got to the lobby I pulled out my phone and dialed.

"Alexander Keaton," my husband answered.

"Where are you?"

"Chloe, is that you?"

"Of course it's me. Where *are* you?"

"As it happens, I'm having an espresso now," he replied, light as champagne.

"I'm in the city unexpectedly. I was hoping I could meet you in your office." I prayed that he'd give me the address of another company. It could be in the grittiest alley of the South Bronx, next to a toxic waste dump in New Jersey! I didn't care, as long as it had a phone and a desk.

"I'm at Trump Tower," he said. "I can meet you downstairs." He clicked off before I had the chance to ask more questions.

CHAPTER 42

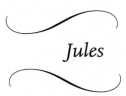

Jules

I sat on the paper runway leading to the stirrups at the foot of the examining table, trying to concentrate on whether there might be a fortune in marketing gowns to replace the sad blue kimonos common to the Western world. Outside the door, I heard the Morse code of Sheila's heels as she tapped her way in and out of other rooms. I was considering getting dressed and making a run for it, hoping the good doctor might forget I was there, but that was not to be.

"Jules," Sheila said as she stepped inside and studied my chart. "What's the problem?" In that question was every central issue of my life.

My voice turned on like a faucet that had been closed for months. As if Sheila were a shrink, not on pussy patrol, I stammered, "I came here today to...do it...but I can't. I'm frozen. I feel guilty going ahead—and guilty not going ahead with this. What the fuck should I do? I'm running out of time."

"What do you want to do?" she asked. The shattering kindness in her question reminded me why I'd appointed Sheila as my gyno in the first place. Just when you thought she was all silicone and Gucci, she'd connect on a deep molecular level. This had happened before, when I'd felt a lump that—thank you, Jesus—vanished on its own.

"I don't know what to do." I hit on *don't know* as if I were slamming golf balls.

"Then, dear Jules, doing nothing is its own decision, and"—Sheila's exquisitely outlined dark eyes, pools of brown glinting with amber, softened as she turned to knock her countertop—"will be its own reward, both for you and your beautiful baby."

She'd said it. Not the embryo, the fetus, the intruder, the mistake: the *baby*. Not just anyone's baby, *your* baby, *my* baby.

I took in the enormousness of those two small words and began to tremble while the room swayed. I grabbed my chest as a sharp pain sliced through it. "Shit," I moaned. "Now I'm having a heart attack." As the room went dark, I felt as if a ceiling fixture were falling on me, ripping me in half. *At least I'm in a doctor's office,* I thought as I squeezed my eyes closed against a burst of light.

"Water?" Sheila said sometime later, a worried nurse standing by her side. I tried to lift my hand to accept this offering but couldn't move my arm. Sheila brought the cup to my lips.

"What was that?" I croaked.

"Panic attack," Sheila said. "Textbook case. We see it all the time, only usually from the daddies."

"Are you going to send me to a hospital?" I hated hospitals, places where daughters like me were required to visit whiny, helpless, attention-seeking, chain-smoking mothers.

"No, I'm going to send you home," she said. "After you've rested." She looked at her watch. "We're here for another hour and you're welcome to stay."

"I have a Xanax in my bag." My new client was a psychopharmacologist.

Sheila managed to give me a look of reprimand. "Absolutely not."

I thought it best not to inquire about Ativan or Klonopin. It would be hard enough being somebody's mother without producing a child with two heads. *Somebody's mother.* I worried that I'd surrender to another wave of panic, but if anything, I felt numb.

"Do you meditate?"

"I've been your patient for twelve years. We've gone out socially. What do you think?"

"Right." Sheila began to stroke my hair. Fighting every instinct, I didn't pull away. "As your doctor, I want you to at least enroll in a yoga class. I can recommend several excellent prenatal programs."

Was she going to start in on breast pumps? Hemorrhoids? Peanut allergies? Preschool applications, Chloe's most tedious obsession of late? Sheila caught my flinch.

"Actually, we can discuss that on your next visit." She looked at a calendar. "For the foreseeable future, please stick to the basics we went over before—no caffeine, which includes Coke and chocolate. But not to worry. Sex is okay."

Hot sex, cuddly sex, oral sex, anal sex, morning sex, insomnia sex, reconciliation sex, public-place sex, shower sex, back-seat-of-a-taxi sex, airplane sex, phone sex. None of it was a temptation. Sex was what had put me in this condition.

"I'll remember that."

"Now, is there someone you can call to take you home? The father, perhaps?"

I'd seen enough of Arthur for one day, and what good would he do anyway, carless as he was? Chloe answered before her phone finished its first ring. "Hi there," I said. "I'm pregnant."

"Not exactly a news flash."

"I'm going to stay pregnant," I added. "For about six and a half more months."

She responded with surprising quickness. "I never expected anything else."

"Then why didn't you speak up?"

"Not my place," Chloe said, though had she been in my situation, I couldn't imagine that I wouldn't have run my mouth. "What do you think of the ring? Do you love it? I've been waiting all afternoon for you to—"

I interrupted her blathering. "I know this is asking a lot, but is there any chance you could pick me up at Sheila's and drive me home?" Requesting favors is a practice with which I have had limited experience. "Please?"

Chloe showed up in a half hour. I spent the first five minutes in the car trying to listen to suggestions for baby names—did I actually look like the kind of woman who'd name her son Marco de Marco?—and the remaining forty with my jaw dropped while I listened to a tale about a man I found hard to believe could be Xander Keaton.

CHAPTER 43

Quincy

It had been two years since I'd set foot in Minneapolis. On the last visit, for my mother's funeral, it was lilac season. Now, as I stood outside the airport, a northern wind slapped me in the face, a wake-up call asking why I'd made the trip. But after last week's phone conversation, I didn't feel I had a choice. I'd bought my tickets with Dr. Frumkes' blessing: I approached normal life cautiously, more fatalist than optimist, allowing myself the most modest sprinkling of hope.

"Quincy, dear," a voice had croaked when I'd picked up our phone. "Do you remember me?" Of course I remembered my childhood next-door neighbor, the saint who for the final year of my mom's life had checked on her almost hourly, delivering mysteries, walnut fudge, and eventually sympathy.

"Sylvia, how great to hear from you," I said. "Merry Christmas." The holiday was ten days away.

"Same to you and that handsome husband," she said. "Please forgive the early morning interruption."

"It's not so early," I said. "It's already past nine in New York."

"Of course," she answered. "I'm such a goose."

There was a pause, which I restrained myself from filling. Sylvia Swenson was the kind of woman whose health you learned not to inquire about unless you had twenty minutes free to put your feet up for a soliloquy about heartburn and hearing aids. Nonetheless, my heritage prompted good manners. "How is everyone? Janelle and Dwight? Susan and Hap? The grandkids?" My brain surprised me by delivering the names of my earliest babysitters and their graying, interchangeable spouses, who now lived in trim ranch houses on modestly landscaped quarter-acre lots fringing the city.

"Very well, thank you. But dear, I'm not phoning about them," she said.

That's when I realized something must be wrong, because second to ill health, Sylvia never missed an opportunity to ramble about her children's latest minivans and diets and their offspring's hamsters and hockey leagues. "It's your tenants, Quincy dear. Those people you rented your mother's lovely house to." She enunciated "those people" as if she were biting into one of her lemon drops.

Rarely a month passed without a grievance shouted on letterhead from Mrs. Crybaby, Esq.'s firm, return receipt requested. *What about the mice?* We'd never had vermin before, discounting squirrels that ran relays around the backyard. *Would you pay for a gardener?* Esq. and her husband couldn't mow the lawn and pull a few dandelions? *Would you lower our rent, considering that we've repainted the house ourselves?* They hadn't asked for my permission to paint the walls the blackish green of a Bavarian forest, and after looking at the photographic evidence, I decided my renters had managed to turn an interior already heavy with oak wainscoting into something as gloomy as a grave.

Besides, as Jake pointed out, the Crybabies were getting a bargain. After Mom had died, the woman I'd met with from Gopher Homes Realty set the price, which I was too grief-stricken to question. The next day she'd presented me with a three-year lease to sign and happily pocketed her commission. But this broker was no Horton; whenever I wanted her to run interference, she was invariably AWOL, leaving to close on a property that she made clear was far more important than mine. The problem this time was noise, Sylvia reported—loud parties every night. "They could wake the dead," she said, and instantly apologized, for fear that I'd think she was referring to Mom.

After the Gopher Homes broker failed to return several calls, Jake offered to travel to the Twin Cities for a showdown. This made no sense. He was starting a major trial, while my days—even my months—stared back at me like unfilled parentheses. I was feeling, if not mellow, at least fueled by appreciation for my stable pregnancy. Even the betrayal inflicted by Jules had begun to feel remote. Which was how I came to return to my childhood home, having succeeded in making an appointment with my tenant, a Dr. Miller, on the pretext that I was in town for business and wanted simply to say hello. The meeting was scheduled for Tuesday morning.

When the taxi pulled up, I was sucked into a cyclone of nostalgia: pedaling my bike on the elm-shaded street, drawing a hopscotch grid on the sidewalk, reading *Betsy-Tacy and Tib* while curled on the window seat. I was prepared for the house to look shrunken, smaller in reality than in my memory, as homes and old boyfriends generally do. But 4924 Oliver Avenue towered above the other houses on the block, its two stories crowned by a smaller third floor that sat on the brown shingled roof like a top hat. The house was too sturdy to be called graceful—standard-issue Arts and Crafts, without a swirl of whimsy—but the fortress beckoned me as if she were a stout grandmother, all but giving off the scent of baking bread.

I rang the bell, expecting to be greeted by a member of a Rolling Stones cover band. A man in a Mr. Rogers cardigan answered. He was silver-haired yet unlined, half-glasses dangling from a cord around his neck, in slippers, resembling a rocker no more than I did Dolly Parton.

"Good morning," he said. "Peter Miller." He extended his hand, which was large and warm. "Welcome to the Twin Cities." He chuckled. "What am I saying? I'm welcoming you back to your own home."

Welcome. The word kissed my soul. This supposed giver of ear-piercing parties chuckled as he motioned me into the vestibule. The red tiled floor gleamed, and on all but one birch bark hook—we'd bought them on a trip to Itasca State Park, to see the headwaters of the Missis-sippi—were the knit caps and tartan scarves common to an upper Mid-west winter. He added my coat to the empty hook. "The coffee's ready, and I hope you don't mind that it's decaf," he said as he directed me toward the dining room, where two places had been set with striped plates and large orange mugs. "Corn muffin?"

I'd eaten pancakes in the hotel coffee shop but didn't say no. The man smiled as he poured the coffee and steamed milk. "Delicious," I said, not knowing how to start the conversation I'd come here to have. From a far-away room, classical music played.

"I apologize for being hard to reach," Peter Miller said. "I've just re-turned from Panama."

"Vacation?"

"Working on the canal. I'm a geologist at the U, with a grant from the Smithsonian."

"How interesting," I said as I buttered my muffin. "I guess that means you've been out of town recently?"

"For six months. My son was staying here with my wife, until..." He turned his head, seemingly transfixed by a beam of morning light pierc-ing the leaded glass window. "My ex," he added as he faced me again. "We're separated. She's moved to Oklahoma."

I stumbled for words. "I'm so sorry"—and not only for this stranger's altered marital status, which he seemed to regret, as well as for invading his privacy, but for what seemed like the complete absurdity of my mis-sion. I was sorry for everything but the coffee and especially the muffin. I could have eaten two.

He waved away the awkwardness. "What brings you to town, Mrs. Blue?"

"Quincy," I said. "An interview." I started yammering, and the polite emptiness on this geologist's face told me Maizie May had never made it onto any of his mental maps.

"I gather from your message this was the house you grew up in," he said after I stopped talking a Sylvia Swenson streak. "Did you want a look-see?"

More than anything. "I don't mean to trouble you."

My tenant smiled and got up from the table. "Come on." He began to lead me through the downstairs rooms, every one immaculate.

I could see my mom in the pale blue kitchen making soup from the vegetables she'd grown in our garden; carrying pop bottles to a basket next to the back door—Alice Peterson recycled ahead of her time; reading in the sunroom, whose faded cushions she'd sewn years before; looking for a volume from the encyclopedia—it was still there—in the living room, whose many shelves were now half empty. I saw Peter Miller focus on a large gap; his wife must have taken her books. He looked toward the wide stairs underneath a stained-glass window patterned with grapes. "Want to see your girlhood room?"

I made a show of looking at my watch. "Darn," I said. *Darn?* "I arranged for the taxi to pick me up in fifteen minutes."

"But you've come all this way." Now he was a father gently lecturing a daughter home from college. "Go up there—I'll be here."

I walked the stairs, pausing on the landing to look out the window at the crabapple tree, which, come late May, would be in full pink flower. Then I tiptoed up to the second floor and opened the first door. We'd used this bedroom for my grandparents every Thanksgiving, Christmas, and Easter. Now it was a study, with rows of bookshelves. *Geology Essentials* by Peter Miller, Ph.D., sandwiched between sports biographies and Civil War histories.

The second door had led to my mother's sewing room, with jars full of buttons and baskets of remnants she would turn into doll clothes. In the Miller household, this was an athlete's shrine—rows of shiny trophies spoke of a young man's accomplishments.

The third bedroom had been mine. Where twin beds with cherry head-boards once stood was a frilly canopy bed, exactly the sort I'd prayed for years that Mom would buy. I walked inside and circled the perimeter. The white milk glass ceiling fixture was unchanged, two popcorn balls dangling from my ceiling. This room, too, had books—*Anne of Green Gables*, *Little Women*, Judy Blumes. But they weren't my books, and much as I wanted to settle into a red corduroy armchair tucked into a corner, I forced myself to continue to the third bedroom. Here I found, quietly abandoned, an elaborate set of drums, amplifiers, and two electric guitars: guilty as charged.

Called by Mozart, I ventured on, across the square center hall. Behind the next door was the far larger bedroom where Mom had been a prisoner of the Alzheimer's that had taken her life far too soon. I peeked inside to find her grand sleigh bed, its heavy cherry sides and headboard as much throne as bed. It was made up with lacy white linens not unlike those she'd used herself. I could picture her sleeping, her breath whispering in time with *Eine Kleine Nachtmusik*. She looked content, her silvery blond hair spread across the shoulders of her pale blue nightgown. Her eyes were closed. I imagined that she was peaceful, dreaming, maybe even of me.

That's when I felt it. The sensation was, at first, like a guppy doing laps in my belly. Not until the twitch repeated—twice—did I understand it for what it was. My baby's first kicks. From the window, a crisp winter sun spotlit a circle on the braided rug. I stepped into it and could feel not only my unborn child but surely my mom, who was blessing this visit and this new life, wishing for me all the comforts of home.

I lingered for a minute, maybe two. "You okay up there?" I heard Peter Miller call.

"On my way down," I shouted, though I wanted to stay rooted within the golden halo of what I was sure was an angel, not that I would mention her to Jake. I walked downstairs.

"Got a moment for a refill?" my tenant asked. "I'm hoping you might give me a chance to explain some things."

Ah, he knew about the parties. "Only a few minutes," I said, checking the grandfather clock. We sat again at the table.

"I want to apologize for those reams of hostile letters my wife kept sending your way," Dr. Miller began as he refilled my mug. "I suspect you're here partly to see if I'm as unhinged as they suggest, and I can't say I blame you."

"Oh, no," I said. "Not at all."

"You'd have every right to think my wife and I were a bit off. The truth is, she—my ex—was—is—unwell—manic-depressive—and when she's in her frantic phase, there's no stopping her. And, you see, she's an attorney. Was an attorney."

"I never took those letters seriously." I hoped he wouldn't notice that I squirmed.

"That's a relief. Thank you. In any event, I'm glad you're here, because with my change in circumstances . . ." Now it was he who was stumbling. "I have the opportunity to return to the canal in a month's time, and the truth is, this house is far too big for me now that I'm alone, with my wife gone and my kids away at school. I'm lost in this much space. I know I have one more year on our lease, and I certainly will honor my obligation, but Mrs. Blue"—here he looked truly forlorn—"should you want to break the contract and seek another renter, the truth is, you could command a far higher rent. With Lake Harriet only blocks away and all the running and biking paths in the park . . . did you know that you can run for miles, all the way to the river?"

"Excuse me," I said, and walked to the living room to look out front. My taxi waited. "I hate to be rude, but I really do need to go. I'm sorry for being abrupt, and I want to thank you for this chance to stop by. I'll definitely think about what you said, Dr. Miller—or is it Professor?"

"It's Pete."

"Pete. I'll talk it over with my husband, and we'll see what we can do." I couldn't resist a smile, and not just because my guppy was doing another flip turn. "I promise."

He helped me on with my coat, and we shook hands. I stepped quickly down the walkway to the curb, hoping Sylvia Swenson hadn't spotted me, and had the driver take me to my hotel. I'd planned to spend the late morning and early afternoon at the Walker, visiting with sculptures I thought of as old friends, but instead I collected the small bag I'd stored at the hotel and went straight to the airport.

"I got a seat on an earlier flight," I reported to Jake before I boarded.

"Great," he said. "Did you give that bastard what for?"

"Not exactly," I confessed. "There was a misunderstanding."

"That's a relief. Hope the trip wasn't a waste of time. Did you at least stroll down memory lane?"

Over a loudspeaker, my flight was called. I'd thought about waiting to ask until I arrived in New York, but I'd lost my impulse control, along with, suddenly, any desire to raise my child in an apartment house, where—no matter how fancy—the downstairs neighbors would complain about small feet running on a floor or little fingers pressing all twenty elevator buttons.

I felt my face break into a smile, like ice splitting on a lake. "Jake," I blurted out, "how do you feel about moving to Minneapolis? I know just the house."

The decision felt less like escape than a sweet return. If I didn't need to board my plane, I even might have called my friends. Including Jules.

CHAPTER 44

Chloe

I've always felt that Fifth Avenue, come late November, is one long, irresistible *bûche de Noël*. Wearing my cheeriest coat, my ritual is to start at Rockefeller Center for the lighting of the tree. I stake a claim near the ice skating rink and wait for hours, letting myself melt into the city's most polite crowd. Once the switch is flicked, I drift north toward Central Park with the happy herd of parents and children—feeling nine years old myself—to gawk at windows bedecked for the holidays.

It's only when I pass Trump Tower that I avert my eyes, trying to ignore the shouting monument to glitz, to overkill, to everything charmless that this city can also be. The building spoils the avenue like a belch at a baby shower. Yet this was where Xander had asked to meet. I walked into a lobby so brassy it could be a set for a movie titled *1984: The Real Story*. If I blinked, I could imagine that the women I saw weighted with shopping bags and dogs the size of Cornish hens were wearing linebackers' shoulder pads, reeking of Opium perfume.

Twenty feet from the entrance, I stopped. I wanted the man in pinstripes to be an impostor, the living proof that the last few hours had been imagined. But there was Xander, his arms crossed in a stance both defiant and defensive. I found it hard to focus. The features in his face slid around like pieces in one of Dash's puzzles; his skin looked pale as a French mime's. When he came close to kiss me hello, I withdrew.

"Where are we going?" I shouted over the din of running water. A waterfall! In this humid atrium I wondered if a cockatoo might dart out of the shadows and peck at my head or if I'd be chased by an oversexed orangutan.

"Follow me," Xander said, leading us up an escalator and into a Starbucks. As if it were a first date, he pulled out a chair for me at the largest table, where his laptop was opened next to a pile of papers. "Excuse me for a second," he added. "I need to thank Sophie for keeping an eye on my stuff."

I glanced in the direction of a brunette barista who gave me a wave. I had the feeling she knew exactly who I was. In a minute Xander returned with two coffees, as if it were nothing but normal to be meeting like girlfriends. He set down the cups and spread out packets of sugar. "French roast okay with you?" he asked.

"Xander!" I snapped. "I want answers, not caffeine."

His voice was a whisper, higher than usual. "People are staring. Can you calm down, please?"

I looked around. Faces at other tables blurred as if they'd been painted by Matisse, a Matisse who liked mink, the occasional shearling, and overpriced denim. I searched for self-control and compassion, but could get reception on neither channel. I felt duped, humiliated, scared. It was a killer combo, and I fought every instinct to cry, trying to act as Jules would, perhaps not the Jules of today, but the real Jules.

"Xander," I said, as evenly as I could, "please explain why you're no longer at Denton. I showed up there and felt like a horse's ass." He winced. "The receptionist hadn't even heard of you!" He looked in my direction, mute. "Did you suddenly get tired of hedge funds?" The pressure had to be daunting, though I always suspected that without it, my Master of the Universe wouldn't have a pulse.

"I loved my work," he said. "You know that."

"Do you have something else lined up?" I took out the sheet of water-marked paper I'd found in the printer hours ago, when life as I knew it hadn't yet imploded, and shoved the résumé in his face. "Why didn't you discuss this?"

"Strictly speaking, I didn't really do anything wrong."

"*Wrong?* What are you talking about?" I felt a rising level of dread that was making me shiver as it turned my skin clammy. "I need answers!" My voice was raspy. "I deserve to know."

"Can we take a walk?"

"Stop stalling! Tell me now. Here. Do you have any idea of how pissed I am?" *Pissed off enough to use that word.* "How worried? How mortified I felt at Denton?"

Xander loosened his tie, one I'd chosen for a Father's Day gift. The pattern of tiny black triangles hopped in front of my eyes like fleas, and the tie had a spot, which in itself was disturbing. The Xander I thought I knew was meticulous.

"I was always one of the fund's top five earners," he began after a noisy sigh. "About four years ago a guy I trusted, a money manager type, offered to compensate me every time I'd steer customers his way."

I noticed that the tail on Xander's fine Egyptian cotton shirt had bunched at the waist.

"It was a slam dunk for my clients. His company was one of the first to go green—they made solar panels and that kind of stuff, for Christ's sake. It was easy to get people to invest, made them feel like do-gooders while they racked up obscene profits."

As I started to catch the general drift, I felt my stomach cramp.

"Believe me, no one complained when they saw their statements. My customers thought I was God."

God was sweating and cracking his knuckles. Near his nose, he had a pimple.

"This went on without a hitch for a few years, with everyone all back-slappin' happy, until an exposé appeared in the *Journal*. Internal problems at this company, rumors of the CEO resigning, then a market correction. Not a major dip, but noticeable. Around this time, it got back to me that the . . . person . . . I'd been dealing with had started shooting off his mouth on the golf course, saying he had me on his payroll. That's when Edgar heard."

Xander rubbed his wrist. He wasn't wearing a watch. Had the Patek Philippe, with its eighteen-karat white-gold case—which the average person, like me, might take for stainless steel—landed in a pawn shop?

"Actually, it was Charlene who heard." He called Cha-Cha Denton a name I thought only other people's husbands used. "Edgar took me to his club. He was smiling over our martinis—you know that pit bull look he gets?"

I was glad I didn't.

"I was such a fool that day. I thought I was going to get promoted, at least see a bump in my bonus. I made a boatload of money for the firm," he continued, as if he were talking only to himself. "My numbers were double digits. But Edgar knew the history of every client I'd talked into the deal, had each one detailed in a dossier with the letterhead of the law firm he keeps on retainer."

As the magnitude of Xander's wrongdoing unfolded, I wondered if he felt the way I did, wanting to be anywhere but here.

"I didn't lie or deny." His eyes darted around the room, never connecting with mine. "For Christ's sake, I wasn't the first or the only guy to do this! It's an open secret that Edgar was a pretty smooth operator himself—that's how he was able to start Denton. I was just the moron who got caught."

Xander made a sound like a bitter gurgle. This alerted the rubberneckers at the next table, who'd been drinking in our whole conversation along with their Tazo tea.

"Edgar pontificated about how he was disappointed, that I'd been like his son, the son who'd let the old man down. How I'd tarnish the firm if word got out, and he wasn't going to let that happen." My husband ridiculously gesticulated with air quotes and looked straight at me, talking faster now. "I thought it was a warning, until he said I should let him know the day I'd be leaving. Offered me a settlement, all spelled out. Thought he was being generous. He gave me forty-eight hours to sign." He mentioned the name of a Dartmouth friend, a criminal lawyer. "Sam said I didn't really have a choice. I left Denton the next day."

"When was this?" I croaked.

"Two months ago."

"You never said a thing!" The buzz around us deadened. Though a good wife might have laid her hand on the arm of her unhinged husband, I realized my only consolation, small as it might be, was that I was enjoying Xander's discomfort. "The thing I don't understand is, *why?*" I said, quietly and with immense control. "Why did you do something you knew was unethical? Corrupt. Taking kickbacks?" I choked on the word.

"Gratuities. It's common industry practice."

"Common was the last thing I thought you were. You broke the law. How could you have been so stupid? You'll probably wind up in jail. Did you go to Harvard Business School to make license plates?"

"Chloe, you're getting hysterical. That's not going to happen."

"Maybe not. But at the very least I can't imagine you'll ever get another decent job again, at least not in finance. And you've done something horrible—to Dash, to me. You've ruined your own name." I didn't care that my voice was shriller with each accusation.

"You're wrong. Sam negotiated a rider so that the details of what I did—"

"Your crime?"

"My *behavior* would stay confidential."

"Everyone at Denton and all their friends must know about this. And it doesn't mean you aren't guilty. It doesn't mean you weren't..." What word to choose? "Sleazy. And let's say no one's aware of this but us and a bunch of lawyers and Edgar and Charlene." I pictured her face, smug, and wondered what she had known when we were together in Beverly Hills. "I still have to know why you took such a risk."

I heard a laugh crossed with a grunt. "*Why?* You are such a child. Do you have any idea what our monthly nut is?"

We both understood that the question was rhetorical. "You're telling me this went on for years," I said. "It must have started around the time Dash was born, when we bought the brownstone." Xander nodded in agreement. "But we never had to buy that house, the antiques, all those rare books, the cars—we never needed any of it. When I think of what you spent on cigars alone..." I wagged my finger near Xander's nose. "It was you who wanted it all, more than I did."

I didn't expect him to say, "That's BS—you wanted everything as much as I did. Maybe more. Cut the crap and stop being so dammed sanctimonious. I did it all for you."

I wasn't going to ratify this comment. I felt ancient, haggard, ill, and—to be honest—guilty myself, of gullibility, of empty-headedness, of my own greed. I pictured Xander's integrity whooshing down a toilet, along with my innocence, as I considered the questions I should have been asking every day for years. After close to five minutes I wiped away the snot that had dripped on my chin and took my husband's hand.

"Okay," I said. "What now?" Xander, the captain of the good ship *Keaton*, failed to respond. I knew the plan would be up to me.

CHAPTER 45

Talia

I have always loved the first day of school, the electricity of expectation crackling even when the weather is soupy hot. Today the calendar announced September, but the temperature was stuck at ninety, as it had been for five soggy days. The classroom was clean and orderly, so colorful it looked animated. It had, however, no air-conditioning. The head teacher was a large young woman with arms that looked as comforting as pillows. Her sleeveless dress, too neon green for her floury complexion, revealed darkening stains. She was deep in conversation, trying to make herself understood by a mother who apparently spoke no English.

Henry had been magnetized by a tall, leggy girl, the bossy type who at four possessed the authority that frequently accompanies silky hair and impossibly long eyelashes. Behind her, my son was a wagging tail. The girl's name tag said Ella. By the time Ella turned ten, she'd probably have more finely honed instincts about handling men than I ever would.

I let my eyes survey the room and was drawn to a circle of mothers, strangers to me, jabbering. "Don't look now, but that's her," one whispered, loud enough for me to overhear.

"Who?" another mother asked, raising an eyebrow toward the doorway.

"You know, that blonde whose husband swindled his clients? It was all over the *Post* for weeks."

"Mrs. Kickback Keaton? I think you're right. Look who's slumming."

That's when I saw Chloe, here, after all those months. She was trying to detach herself from Dash, whose eyes were narrow with suspicion, his pinchworthy cheeks angled into planes and valleys that resembled his father's. Dash had shot up over the summer and was no longer a full head shorter than Henry, nor was he dressed in anything remotely adorable. No suspenders, bow tie, or sweater featuring an animal. I could fast-forward and imagine that, year by year, Dashiel Keaton would become increasingly handsome. I missed that bashful boy.

When the "Greed, Graft, and Glory" profile of Xander had appeared in *New York*, I'd called Chloe. My message went unanswered. The following week, after the bloggers latched on to Xander's story, wearing it out with their self-satisfied puns and strained analogies, I'd sent her a string of e-mails. Each bounced back, undeliverable. Finally I snail-mailed a note I'd rewritten several times. *This must be rough. Thinking of you. I'm here. Call me if you feel like it.* I'd hoped for a response. Nothing.

Seeing Chloe, Mean Maxine was urging me to avoid eye contact, to hide my face in my newspaper. *You're the last person she wants to talk to* crawled along the bottom of my consciousness like a warning for a tropical storm. But there are times I need to tell Mean Maxine to take a hike. My heart was ready for a risk, no matter how bumbling.

I gathered my tote and Henry's brand-new backpack and sidestepped through the parents, students, and school supplies—you'd think these kids were off to war, not pre-K—and got within a foot of Chloe, facing her back. I willed her to turn, but my telepathic entreaty was no more effective than my earlier communication. I lost my nerve and turned to slink back to the other side of the room. That was when she swiveled.

We'd last seen each other nine months ago, for her office going-away party. I'd wished her well and got no warmer a response than did the receptionist and the IT guys. Chloe's face looked thinner now, and where there'd been fullness, newly revealed cheekbones created a sharper architecture. As if she were trying to recognize me, she squinted, and faint crow's feet fanned her eyes. These signs of life took pretty to something more.

"Hello," I said, louder than necessary. "Isn't it great that the boys will be together?" After smiling, barely, Chloe paused long enough for me to be certain she'd hoped Henry would have ended up anywhere but this school, this class. "Hello, Talia," she answered, all business, and then she turned her attention to Dash. "What do we say when we meet someone?"

He extended a small hand with newly clipped fingernails. "Good morning." His face was stern.

"Good morning, Mrs. Fisher-Wells," she corrected him. He repeated her words.

"Good morning, Dash." I shook his hand. "Are you excited about starting school?" He burrowed into Chloe's thigh. "You remember Henry, don't you?" I wondered if he did. "Do you see him over there?" I pointed to the playhouse. Henry appeared to be serving Ella tea. "I bet he'd love to see you."

"Go over and say hello," Chloe said. When Chloe put a hand on his back, he walked toward the children.

I'd gotten as far as putting myself near Chloe—what came next I hadn't worked out. There was everything to say, but all I could grunt was, "How's it going at Bespoke?"

"Well enough," she answered, composed, her gaze neither friendly nor unfriendly. "The hours are long. I'm fairly exhausted. There's a lot of travel. You? How's the full-time schedule?"

When Chloe left, I'd taken over her half of our shared job. My salary had doubled, but so had my frustration; I felt bored and underpaid. Tom and I figured it would take until we were fifty to accumulate a down payment for an apartment. "The hours are long," I said. *And dull.* "I'm fairly exhausted." Boredom will do that to you. "But there's no travel, unless you count New Jersey." If I were sent to San Francisco—or Milwaukee— I wouldn't complain.

I considered the stampede of questions I couldn't ask. *Did you suspect Xander was up to something before it happened?* I had not. *What's going on with him now?* A while ago Jules had implied that he'd checked into a psychiatric facility, but out of loyalty to Chloe, she revealed nothing more. *What does it feel like to have reporters on your stoop?* I'd combust, along with my marriage. *How do you like being a breadwinner?* Proud but resentful, like I do? *Are you upset that Dash didn't wind up at Jackson Collegiate?* Betsy O'Neal had told Tom that the Keatons had turned down a spot offered to Dash. *Where are you living?* I'd done my share of online stalking and spotted a listing for their house. After a few weeks, the ad had vanished. Had they found a buyer? Rented it? Left the house unoccupied? If Dash was in this school, had they moved to our district or had they applied from a different part of Brooklyn?

What I most wanted to ask was, *Will you forgive me?* On anyone's ethical seismograph I'd admit that what I'd done was wrong, small-minded, hurtful. How wrong could be settled by Talmudic tribunal, though I was holding fast to the notion that chasing a job earmarked for Chloe was a misdemeanor, not a felony.

Tell it to the judge, Mean Maxine sniped. *You tried to steal a friend's opportunity, intellectual property meant for her. You acted under false pretenses.*

No matter how I or any philosopher looked at it, my behavior diminished me, and apparently it had put a full stop to my friendship when, as it turned out, I was certain that Chloe needed me most. Whom did she have in her corner? Quincy had folded into herself, had moved on. Jules was as overwhelmed as anyone I'd ever known. That left Xander, whom Chloe most likely wanted to kill. I knew I wanted to kill him on her behalf.

"Can you go out for coffee after we leave?" Eliot was expecting me, but what the fuck.

This time Chloe responded quickly. "Sorry—can't."

Not *Let's do it another time.* Not *I wish I could; let me look at my calendar.* Not *I'll call you.*

I wondered what I could say next that wouldn't send me shooting through a trapdoor to Chloe's hell, bad friend division. I wanted to tell her that with me, she didn't need to pretend to be brave, and that if she wanted to play a game of darts aimed at my head, we'd give it a go, as long as afterward there was the promise of laughter. I wanted to give her a hug, to say I was sorry. But I simply stood with my arms hugging my body to steady myself, certainly looking as foolish as I felt.

"Mommy, Mommy." Every mother turned toward the voice, but the call was for me. "Can Dash and I have a play date?" Henry had abandoned the lovely Ella, perhaps for the next decade, and he and Dash were perched atop a tower of large blocks, king-of-the-world style.

"Children," the teacher called out before I could answer. "It's time for you to each find a place at the table. Our school day is going to begin. Moms and dads," she added, doing a 180 across the room, "remember, today pickup is at noon."

"Tom's coming later," I said to Chloe, not that she'd asked.

"He'll see Xander then." Her most revealing comment of the day.

We gave our sons a goodbye kiss and walked out the door. "Shall I call you, to arrange a play date for the boys?" I asked when we reached the corner.

"Let me think about that," she said with a cryptic half smile, after a lengthy pause.

Chloe headed to one subway, I to another, walking away from each other, step by step. Halfway down the block, I stopped, turned, and shouted her name. I was ready to run after her and tell her that we couldn't leave things this way.

She had vanished.

CHAPTER 46

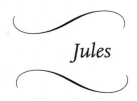

Jules

As I became big, then bigger, with child, Arthur and I went—his words—
"on hiatus," though hiatus was put on hiatus seven times for sex. Still, by
month nine the sight of a penis made me gag. One night, my dress already off, he started to unbuckle and I batted him away. "I just can't," I
said. "Don't take it personally."

He did. "Okay, okay, I'll keep Mr. Weiner in my pants. But don't
leave—we have things to discuss."

"We do?"

"That's my kid in there!" He pointed to my belly, which stuck out like
an awning that matched my behind. I was one of those women "carrying
all around," a polite way of saying I wasn't merely pregnant, I was fat and
pregnant. "I've been thinking about this a lot. I want in on his life. I'm an
only child. You might be carrying the last Weiner."

Again with the pleading. It was true that Arthur had given me a ring,
which I wore when we were together, but neither of us had initiated discussion about whether this piece of jewelry came with a promise. I con-

sidered the bauble strictly a token of kindness, because in his way, Arthur has that quality.

"What do you have in mind?" I said as I let him zip my pup tent.

He placed his hands gently on my shoulders and turned me toward him, his face as serious as I had ever seen it. "Julia Maria de Marco," he said, "marry me."

The following week I'd be having a birthday that would hurtle me solidly into a slot Ma's generation called middle-aged. In my long time on earth, this was my first proposal. Arthur's offer was, theoretically, tempting. Okay, it was a goddamn concerto, but it came with him attached. Pregnancy might have changed my body, but my brain was pretty much intact. Kindness notwithstanding, Arthur was Arthur.

"Let's sit down," I said. As we walked to his living room I hobbled a bit—a varicose vein snaked toward my knee like a gnarly root. I pushed aside a pile of magazines, settled my bulk on the couch, and hoisted my leg onto the coffee table. Arthur sat next to me and put his hand on my thigh. I removed it. "Marry? You, me, man, wife?"

"That's the usual definition." He was back to a grin, gaining confidence.

"Usual" is not how I prefer to think of myself. "Why follow convention? First of all, we didn't plan this pregnancy."

"The baby is a gift from God."

"Are you suddenly tight with God? You've always said you were an agnostic. Would you want a wedding at St. Theresa's and the Infant Jesus on Victory Boulevard?"

"I just know I want us to be together, to have you two in my life."

"That's charming, but where would we live? Not here, for Christ's sake—it's much too cramped." And the thought of his moving into my home had all the romance of head lice. I liked my spices alphabetized, my bathroom to myself.

"I might still get that apartment. The old lady died, but Basil said when her estate's settled I'm first on the list."

Never! Obviously, that co-op carried a curse. Maybe it was because of pregnancy and my new no-woman-is-an-island philosophy, but I'd finally admitted to myself that it hadn't been my finest hour when I told Arthur about that apartment in the first place, and by going to see it with him, I'd dirtied my hands all the more. Twice in the last month I'd actually walked into a church and considered going to confession to make good on that particular sin. The last place I wanted to raise my child was at the scene of the crime.

But there was a bigger question at hand. "What you're talking about, Arthur, isn't you, me, man, wife. It's you, me, Mom, Dad. Am I right?"

He stood up, but rather than answer, he disappeared into the kitchen and returned with a beer for him and apricot nectar—my new obsession—for me. "You, me, Mom, Dad—that's a start, if you promise it's forever."

I thought of my deadbeat pop, Surfer Ted, and every other fucker who'd broken my heart. "How can I promise forever?" How can any woman?

Through my support hose, Arthur started to massage my leg; his caress was tender, his fingers touched with witchcraft. "Jules, Jules, Jules," he murmured. "Plenty of women make that promise, every day, in long white dresses."

He tilted his head like a beagle, and my heart bent, too. "Okay, Artie. No to marriage, but," I said, very, very slowly, "yes to your being the baby daddy."

Beads of perspiration broke out on Arthur's forehead. I was fairly certain they were from relief, although he asked, "Is that no to marriage now or no to marriage ever?"

"It's don't bring it up—if I want to, I will."

"If you're saying yes to me as Daddy, can I be in the delivery room?"

This time I didn't hesitate. "No fucking way." It would be bad enough to endure labor on my own surrounded by a team of trained professionals. I had refused to talk, listen to a lecture, or look at a film about it. Why women felt otherwise was inexplicable.

"Okay," Arthur said. "I can live with that. Daddy. I like the sound of it."

When the day came, it was Talia who met me at Lenox Hill Hospital, just as it was she who'd been my partner at half a Lamaze class. Panting like a tired old collie? No, thanks. Natural childbirth sounded like unadulterated hell, and I'd gotten over hoping to become canonized after Sister Dildo's cavalcade-of-saints class. Dildo had had me at St. Lucy, whose eyes were gouged out. A bad copy of a Renaissance painting hung in our classroom, featuring a girl carrying eyeballs in a dish as if she were serving dim sum. No sainthood for me. I wanted as many drugs as Sheila would be willing to inject. I would gladly pay extra.

Talia didn't stay at my side long. In the end, I had a C-section. The baby was breech, standing straight up. Leave it to me to produce a kid too lazy to turn around, though at least her posture was excellent. She weighed less than seven pounds, and since I'd gained more than sixty, my first thought was that I'd be eating sashimi for years.

After recovery, I was wheeled into a private room. A few minutes later, a tightly swaddled bundle the size of a Perdue Oven Stuffer was placed in my arms. I brought the sleeping baby to my lips and softly baptized her with a kiss. "We de Marcos don't have a great track record, my darling," I told her, "but I'm going to try to change that." I'd picked Sienna's name months earlier, choosing it for the city of my great-grandmother's birth, a city I'd always hoped to travel to with my friends. I stroked my baby's tiny scalp, with its wisps of dark hair, and wondered if that would ever happen. Well, if it didn't, I could go there with my daughter.

"We are going to be best friends, Sienna Julia, I know it," I said. "Mama has a lot to teach you. You see, my precious, I have these rules...."

CHAPTER 47

Chloe

"Chloe?" It was Winters on the intercom. "All set?"

"Ready!" We were pitching a new client. I'd have liked to say it was Chanel or even Talbot's, but it was Wax Maxx, a day spa that specialized in Brazilian landscaping. Winters had suggested that to prepare, I should sample and expense some of the competitors, which—after I blushed a shade of pink never seen before in nature—I appreciated because since the fall of the Keaton empire, I'd been waxing myself, one of many economies of which I was proud. Not that Xander had gotten a peek at my landing strip. We hadn't seen each other naked since our world caved in.

"Don't worry about me," Xander had announced when I left for work that morning. That was like saying, *Don't look at the cold sore on my lip.* Worrying about my husband had become my second job. Who wouldn't perseverate about a husband who guzzled Coronas every afternoon while dozing through reruns of golf tournaments from before he was born? Who twice forgot to pick up his son from a play date? Who'd made Ben and Jerry's Chocolate Therapy his only friend, because he couldn't bring himself to talk to his wife?

This was fine, because I wasn't sure what I'd say to him. I expected I'd get over his deception in a year or five. But fortunately, from Autumn Rutherford I'd learned the gentle art of compartmentalizing, a skill for which I'd discovered a talent. When I triple-locked the door of our sublet apartment—no doorman, sunlight, laundry room, dishwasher, or linen closet—and waited for the subway, I morphed into Chloe the conqueror, a woman who percolated with self-respect.

I liked this Chloe, just as I liked how Jade, Bespoke's receptionist, absorbed my advice on where to buy her mother a gift (a lovely robe would never disappoint), how to keep clothes wrinkle-free when packing (tissue paper), and what the curious utensil was to the right of her plate the previous night at Per Se, where her hedge fund boyfriend (run, Jade, run) had taken her (fish fork). I liked how Winters praised 75 percent of my copy on the first go, and I liked even more that I was being paid well and supporting my family. Every other week when my salary showed up direct-deposited into my account, I smiled. But only to myself.

In Compartment Chloe, I might have been alone, but I wasn't lonely. Jules continued to be steadfast, and Quincy and I chitchatted between New York and Minneapolis. Every time we spoke, I sensed her growing affection for her new community, which in its own reserved way must have been speaking to her, literally. The other day she shrieked, "Oh, jeez," when she stepped on dog poo after their puppy, Tallulah, had an accident.

That left Talia.

We'd seen each other at the first day of school. I'd looked up, and she was skulking away like a shy spy. I sensed that she wanted to pick up where we'd left off, and in light of the solar eclipse inflicted by Xander's deception, the events between Talia and me felt blazingly trivial. I should have put them behind me, the way I had when I once walked into a kitchen and found Xander wrapped around Quincy like yarn on a knitting needle.

I'd have liked—make that loved—to reconnect with Talia, especially since my life had taken a ninety-degree turn in her direction. Surely she'd have handed over some coupons she'd clipped or explain how to reserve books at the library. And I could have used the hug. But could we simply hit delete and pretend as if nothing had happened? Perhaps getting back on track was only one e-mail and cup of coffee away. It should have been easy, reconnecting, but just then it felt like trying to rewhip cream. I needed more time.

My intercom buzzed. "The client's five minutes late," Jade said. Before I had a chance to thank her, my cell phone played its tune, which I'd changed to "Anticipation."

"When a recipe calls for a clove, is that the whole garlic?"

"What are you cooking?" I asked after explaining garlic anatomy.

"Pasta puttanesca," Xander replied. My favorite. Progress! "Caesar salad, too. Is it okay to buy dressing?"

"Better to make it yourself. Use that yellow cookbook."

"Okay, boss," he said. I heard his affection, almost like the innocent college boy who'd won my heart ten years earlier. "Also, the UPS guy just rang the bell with a package." We no longer got many of those anymore, since I'd switched to the cheap dry cleaner who didn't deliver and broken up with Zappo's. "It's from Talia."

"Small box or large?" I asked.

"It's a lumpy envelope, one of those padded jobs, fairly small."

"Open it."

I heard the ripping of paper. "I can't believe this," Xander said.

"What is it?" I whispered into the phone.

"A picture," he answered as he laughed. "The two of you are dancing together—I think it's from Talia's wedding. You're wearing that strange black dress."

"Who wears black to a wedding?" Mother had said, but I'd had no choice—I was the maid of honor. Talia had picked it.

"You don't look all that sober," Xander added.

If it had been taken at the reception, I wasn't. "Is there a note?"

"I don't see anything."

"Strange."

"No, I'm wrong. I turned it over. She's written on the back, 'Were we ever this young? See you at Jules' in two weeks. Love, Talia.'" He paused. "What's going on at Jules'?"

"A party," I said. "But I've already told her I'm not going." I wasn't ready to turn back the clock. I wasn't sure I'd ever be ready.

Then Again

Jules stood back to admire her platters and bowls destined for eggs, for roasted asparagus, for scones, and for a cartload of berries. Champagne was icing and a sour cream coffee cake rising, the mother-love aroma of cinnamon wafting upstairs to fill the tiny nostrils of Sienna Julia de Marco. As Jules straightened her smiling sunflowers, Arthur walked through the front door. "Want one?" he asked, hoisting a Dunkin' Donuts bag, a grease spot catching the morning light. Jules bit into a doughnut, and raspberry glop oozed onto her lip. Arthur kissed it away. "Where's my doll?"

"Jamyang is getting her dressed," Jules said.

When Chloe had to let Jamyang go, she'd beseeched Jules to hire her. Since one of Jules' Rules was to know when to throw money at a problem and whistle for help, she did, though she'd pictured a different sort of nanny, half Auntie Mame, half *matryoshka* doll. Jamyang was living now in a bedroom next to Sienna's, and when she crept out of hiding, she went about her business for a remarkable number of uncomplaining hours. Like that day. Jamyang had been up since six, helping prepare brunch in honor of Quincy's visit.

Jules and Quincy had called a truce. When Talia had told Jules that Quincy was moving, Jules thought Quincy had eaten one too many corn dogs at the fair. Minnesota might have ten thousand lakes, but what about the leeches on their slimy bottoms, the mosquitoes the size of nickels, the way folks—folks!—rhyme *roof* with *woof*? If you wanted to live where the sun set at four on a winter afternoon, why not move to Sweden and get universal health care? But Jules pulled a Chloe and sent Quincy a peace offering, knee-high moccasins with five layers of fringe, plus a tiny pair for the papoose. She was rewarded with an instant text from Quincy, who suggested that they have coffee.

The conversation was nothing baroque.

Jules said, "Quincy, I fucked up. I was wrong. I had no business telling Arthur about that apartment, or seeing it myself. I'm sorry. Can you forgive me?"

"I can," Quincy answered. "I do. Let's move on."

It was enough for both of them. Jules didn't see herself as magnanimous. She saw herself as sincere and happy, because there was no one in the universe as deliriously content as a forty-four-year-old who became the accidental mother of a daughter with eyes as dark as chocolate truffles, gazing at her with love. Sienna had brown hair curling around her scalp like miniature potato vines and chubby fingers that Arthur insisted were exactly like his. *Don't all babies have short, pudgy fingers?* Jules wondered. *They will grow.*

She was about to order Arthur to sweep the front steps when she looked out the window and saw the Blues tumbling out of a rented minivan. A small warehouse's worth of equipment was in Jake's hands and Quincy's held J.J. When she brought him inside, Jules could see he had large blue eyes that searched the room like headlights and a head as bald as an egg. Before the greetings were over, the doorbell rang again. Talia and Tom entered with Henry in tow, hurling himself toward J.J. like a bowling ball.

Ready or not, the party had started. Arthur hung coats, Jamyang put Sienna in her high chair, and Jules invited everyone to sit. She swept her arm above the table, the gesture one of benediction. "*Benvenuto*. It's been way too long," she said. She looked at each of them, one by one, but reserved her most admiring glance for Sienna, plump and trussed, a small Jules who banged tiny starfish hands to the music of her mother's voice, then squealed with delight. Either that, Jules thought, or the kid had gas.

"Hear, hear—I second that." Not unlike his daughter, Arthur knocked the bare wood table with his knuckles. Talia and Quincy returned his smile. Being obnoxious, each privately concluded, wasn't a crime after all.

Each of the women had grown in ways they couldn't have imagined when they shared their walled paradise near the Hudson. Jules was basking in contentment delivered by accident. While she doubted that she deserved the richness of her life, she was grateful, almost ready to speak of her happiness out loud.

Quincy had unpacked her life, blue cradle and all (which Jake had refused to leave on the curb, along with hope), halfway across the country to fashion a family from fresh air and fresh starts—Quincy, Jacob, and James J. Blue, with Tallulah barking for attention. Whenever Quincy turned a corner, she could feel her mom's spirit watching over her.

Talia was restless. She had begun to conjure her own gauzy fantasy of escape and longed for the salty air of Santa Monica, though for all its crumbling bungalows it was as out of her financial grasp as Fifth Avenue. Talia did not speak of this to anyone, especially not Tom, yet he knew his wife's disappointment as well as he knew that he loved her and couldn't fix what had gone wrong.

Proudly and privately, Chloe had learned to wear her resilience like a scarlet coat. But for that day's brunch, she had sent regrets.

Regrets, there were plenty of those; the guilt in the room imperiled the oxygen. *If only I hadn't,* Jules thought. From Talia: *What a fool I was to think that a friend, close and loyal, was as easy to find as a penny on the street.* And from Quincy, a realization: *Sometimes you need to blink and move on.* That morning the women recognized that being together was like rediscovering a pair of lost slippers. Their friendship still provided comfort that improved with time. They knew one another like a new friend never could, with a shorthand that understood when to react and when to over-look, when to boost and when to protect.

"Henry has such lovely manners—and he's gotten so tall."

"J.J. is your little clone."

"All I see is Jake."

"Sienna's got your eyes. Those lashes!"

They lavished honeyed words on one another's children, determined to brush away histories as tangled as the roots of stubborn weeds: *Why did you do that to me? Did I mean so little? How could you be so careless with my feelings, my future? Will she forgive me, ever? What was I thinking?*

"The house—show us those pictures again."

"Three stories! It's a mansion!"

"It's not."

"How far below zero does it get?"

"What's the second *J* for?"

"Jubilee."

How could she?

All of them instinctively made sure that everyone got equal airtime.

"I love what you've done with the dining room walls."

"Matching paint to a Japanese eggplant? Who'd have thought?"

"How are your parents?"

Certain questions they would never raise. Why had Quincy abandoned them? Her move six months earlier had seemed impetuous, which their Quincy was not. Would Jake, Yankees fan, be able to root for a team called the Twins? What next, ice fishing? Had Talia started looking for another job? Would Tom ever finish his Ph.D.? Or Jules and Arthur surprise them with a wedding? Was there true love between them, or had Jules given up on that?

They knew better than to ask each other why Chloe hadn't joined them. She was a greater presence in her absence than she might have been in the flesh. Jules thought that she could explain why Chloe had stayed away—she was still absorbing and adjusting to the shock of re-duced circumstances, of deception, of disgrace. But Talia thought their quarrel was to blame. Quincy, however, didn't care about explanations. Having come all this way, she was trying not to take Chloe's behavior as a rebuff. And so the three women splashed in the shallow end.

"Please tell me you didn't bake this yourself."

"I can't even bake a potato."

"What are we drinking? I love it."

"Refill?"

"Sienna needs a change. Artie?"

"Listen up, folks. Henry is going to count backward from one hundred."

"Did you read why Chinese kids are so much better in math—something to do with the way the numbers sound in their language?"

"Then tell me why Chinese Americans still do better in math when they're taught in English."

No one could.

"Your new business, Jules—genius."

"No, buddy, you can't go outside alone. Go play with your cars in the living room."

"Seconds? If you don't eat this, I will, and I have ten pounds left to go."

That day they weren't thinking, *She's getting fat. She's getting gray. She's getting crow's feet. She's getting pissed.* Conversation swirled like milk in coffee, keeping their moods light while they sized each other up—kindly. *She's already lost her baby weight. She's wearing Arthur's ring. She looks good with long hair.*

They were careful not to speak of newer friends claiming loyalties—the other mother and son Talia would be meeting at the park, the linguistics professor Quincy had started to run with along shady lakeside paths, the woman Jules had met for cappuccino after Little Maestros. Jules didn't know what had made her feel the bigger fool, that at Little Maestros she was paying as much as the price of an opera ticket for Sienna to shake her diapered booty to Stevie Wonder CDs or that the other woman was the grandmother of the infant she accompanied, and had taken her for the same. At forty-four!

Mostly, they thought, *I've missed her, and her, and her. I'm homesick for what was, because try as you might, you can't outsource love.* They regretted their cavalier actions and assumptions, these women who'd been casually arrogant enough to assume that friendship could blast—and last—through anything.

When they thought about the future, they were overcome with what might not be—the books and movies they might never discuss; the vacation photos they might not see; the shopping trips not taken to choose a dress for a milestone, one celebrated without them; the whoop of glee the other might not hear about promotions or a child's college acceptances and first love. It was entirely possible that they might not know the woman next to them as she turned fifty, sixty, more, became a grandmother or a widow or a glittering success, when she lost her mother or found her passion; that they would not wind up, as they'd once imagined, as little old ladies sharing a house, making sure the next woman took her meds and didn't break a hip. They wouldn't be holding hands at the end, in a hospital.

Or maybe they would.

They were fragments, starting to forget how it felt to be young and whole, a vase balanced in its symmetry, ready for flowers in bloom. To play it safe, they paged through the old times, finding memories that felt more vivid than the morning's headlines.

"Remember that first New Year's Eve at our apartment, when we rolled out homemade fettuccini and hung it to dry on the shower curtain rod?"

"That pesto—I've never eaten any half as good again."

"My God, we were insufferable. That's when pesto was our definition of sophistication."

"When we didn't know pine nuts from a pair of balls."

I liked us then, they all thought. *I liked us better. Does every woman get a little harder with each year, her true self slicked by strokes of enamel dried to a diamond finish?*

"What happened to the mix tape that boyfriend of yours made?"

"Dumped it along with him."

"His name? It's on the tip of my tongue."

"The guitarist whose hair was longer than mine? Clive."

"No, the tech guy."

"Him! I can't remember what he even looked like."

"Daryl?"

"Darren?"

"Devin! He made it up. You would, too, if your parents named you Milton."

"Hey, Milton's my middle name."

"Arthur Milton Weiner, open that last bottle, will you?"

"The chairs you found on Ninety-second Street—why did we leave them behind? I'm pretty sure they were Knoll."

"Serves me right. I just thought they were ugly."

"How about when we tried to form our own book club? Quincy, were you the one who insisted on *The Witching Hour*?"

"No, that would be me," Jules said as she got up to clear the table. Talia and Quincy followed with armfuls of platters, but when they deposited them on the kitchen counter, Jules said, "You have to see Sienna's room. C'mon upstairs."

When they entered the baby's bedroom, Quincy and Talia wondered whether, should they ever have daughters, they too would be taken hostage by the sugary rush that makes mothers of girls think they are raising a princess. The walls were covered in lilac-sprigged paper, the floor plushly carpeted. Obedient pastel bunnies and Steiff teddies lined pristine white shelves. Over the lace-swathed crib a mobile of iridescent purple butterflies dangled in the air. Quincy oohed and ahhed while Talia walked to Sienna's library, which was tucked under the eaves, near the front window. Yes, there was her gift, a first-edition *Babar*.

Hearing a car, she pulled open the starched white curtains to peer outside. A taxi was pulling away. Then the doorbell chimed "Give My Regards to Broadway."

"Arthur installed it for my birthday." Jules shrugged. "Who knew he was handy?" She laughed, but Quincy detected pride, and when Jules' back was turned, she offered Talia a conspiratorial wink.

"Expecting something?" Talia asked.

"Nope, nothing," Jules said, and walked to the stair landing. "I've got everything I want." Before either of her friends had a chance to consider whether this was an expression of thanksgiving or conspicuous consumption, she shrieked, "Artie, get that, will you?" and returned to Sienna's room. That was where they were, marveling at a rainbow of dresses, when Chloe shouted, "Anybody home?"

Quincy let out a whoop and bolted down the stairs, skipping the bottom step. The women embraced like loving sisters, and as Talia watched, she yearned to do the same. She wondered if she would ever hug Chloe—or be hugged by her—again. She waved from the top of the stairs. Chloe returned the gesture in her direction, but it was Jules, behind Talia, who asked, "How'd we get so lucky, Mrs. Keaton?"

Talia wondered, for the hundredth time, why she'd let small things get in the way of a big friendship. When she'd finally shared the story with her mother, who'd asked again and again why she'd stopped mentioning Chloe, Mira Fisher raised her voice. "Feh! You let that *tzimmes* with the job and school come between you and a friend? Why?"

"I don't know, Mommy" was all she could say. "It seemed important at the time." Defensible, which was not the same as legal and on a separate continent from right.

Chloe hung her coat in the closet next to the Blues' parkas, which were red, and put down a large shopping bag. Peeking from the top was the trunk of a stuffed elephant. "An hour ago I realized that if Quincy went back to Minneapolis without my seeing J.J., I could never live with myself." In the early afternoon light, with her hair pulled into a ponytail, Chloe looked as young as when they'd all first met. But they blinked, and suddenly she was like the rest of them, possibly wiser, definitely older.

"I was wondering when you'd show up," Jules said as she walked toward Chloe, leaving Talia behind, wondering what Chloe truly thought of the photograph of the two of them, both pregnant, that she'd recently sent. The thank-you note had been gracious. Talia saw it as headway. There was no other way to see it, unless she wanted to be a cynic.

"I'm glad you did," Quincy said, draping her arm around Chloe's shoulder.

"Hey, that's what friends do," Chloe said, pulling out the elephant for James Jubilee Blue, a kitten for Sienna Julia de Marco, and a shark for Henry Thomas Wells IV. The other mothers gushed thanks and thought: *Yes, friends give and friends receive. Friends love and friends accept love. Friends find the good in one another. Friends keep secrets, especially when they're not asked, because no one needs to ask them.*

"Friends crash their friend's party because the hostess has always cooked way too much," Jules said.

"Is that one of Jules' Rules?"

"Of course. You must be starving. I'll heat something up."

Chloe turned to look at Talia while Quincy gazed at Jules. *Friends get over things.*

"You're right, Jules, that's what friends do," Talia said. Although she knew that was not all friends do for one another, all four of them felt, at that moment, as if they could sing their histories like the lyrics to a favorite show, one that was sold out, enjoying a well-deserved revival.

"Wait, let's take a picture," Talia said. "I want to remember this." She reached into her bag and handed a camera to Tom.

They smiled for the camera, children in their arms. Talia did remember that day, and so did Quincy and Jules and Chloe. They remembered with love, forever.

Acknowledgments

It's my hope that no friends have been harmed, infuriated, or stood up as I have allowed myself to become ego central in the writing of *With Friends Like These*. I could never have completed this novel without friends like these: Betsy, Dale, Rochelle, and Vicki, my four sister-friends, as well as the Barbaras, the Carols, the Ellens, the Janets, the Judiths, the Lindas, the Lisas, the Nancys, the Patricias, the other Betsy, and the other Sally plus Anita, Betty, Cathy, Charles, Chaya, Craig, Emily, Evelyn, Ina, Janey, Kristine, Leslie, Marilyn, Margaret, Margie, Marlena, Michele, Ovie, Paul, Ruth, Sharon, Shelley, Sheri, and Sherry and last but in no way least Vivian, queen of nitpicks. Thank you all for your warmth, humor, and good common sense.

Caitlin Alexander, you are a talented editor. I am in your debt for your patience and encouragement, along with many others on Ballantine's superb team: Libby McGuire, sharp-eyed publisher; Kim Hovey, associate publisher; Steve Messina, a production editor of great patience; Sue Warga, copy editor; Robbin Schiff, art director; Diane Hobbing, who created the graceful interior design of this novel, as well as Cara Petrus, who crafted its frisky illustration and cover design; Kristin Fassler and Quinne Rogers, whose capable hands have handled marketing; and, of course, Jynne Martin, an outstanding publicist.

Christy Fletcher, thanks for your flawless judgment and consistent enthusiasm. Gratitude, too, to Melissa Chinchilla for your energy in selling foreign rights to this book as well its older sisters, and to Swanna Mac-Nair for your spot-on comments and continued help.

Laura Ford, you've caused me to wonder, what editor isn't, at heart, a social worker? I appreciate your support and friendship.

Robert, Jed and Rory, you are my team, forever in my heart. *Thank you* never stops.

ABOUT THE AUTHOR

SALLY KOSLOW is the author of *The Late, Lamented Molly Marx* and *Little Pink Slips*. Her essays have been published in *More, O: The Oprah Magazine,* and *The New York Observer,* among other publications. She was the editor in chief of both *McCall's* and *Lifetime,* was an editor at *Mademoiselle* and *Woman's Day,* and teaches creative writing at the Writing Institute of Sarah Lawrence College. The mother of two sons, she lives in New York City with her husband.

www.sallykoslow.com

ABOUT THE TYPE

This book was set in Scala, a typeface designed by Martin Majoor in 1991. It was originally designed for a music company in the Netherlands and then was published by the international type house FSI FontShop. Its distinctive extended serifs add to the articulation of the letterforms to make it a very readable typeface.